THE TROLL HUNTER

Also by Keith C. Blackmore

Mountain Man
Mountain Man
Safari
Hellifax
Well Fed
Make Me King
Mindless
Skull Road
Mountain Man Prequel
Mountain Man 2nd Prequel: Them Early Days
The Hospital: A Mountain Man Story
Mountain Man Omnibus: Books 1–3

131 Days
131 Days
House of Pain
Spikes and Edges
About the Blood
To Thunderous Applause
131 Days Omnibus: Books 1–3

Breeds
Breeds
Breeds 2
Breeds 3
Breeds: The Complete Trilogy

Isosceles Moon
Isosceles Moon
Isosceles Moon 2

The Bear That Fell from the Stars
Bones and Needles
Cauldron Gristle
Flight of the Cookie Dough Mansion
The Majestic 311
The Missing Boatman
Private Property
The Troll Hunter
White Sands, Red Steel

THE TROLL HUNTER

KEITH C. BLACKMORE

*For Gail Crouse (who read it first)
and Kate Ann Jack (who read it last).*

All rights reserved. No part of this publication may be reproduced, stored in a retrieval system, or transmitted in any form or by any means electronic, mechanical, photocopying, recording, or otherwise without prior written permission from Podium Publishing.

This is a work of fiction. Names, characters, places, and incidents are either products of the author's imagination or used fictitiously. Any resemblance to actual events, locales, or persons, living, dead, or undead, is entirely coincidental.

Copyright © 2010 by Keith C. Blackmore

Cover design by James T. Egan

ISBN: 978-1-0394-8357-6

Published in 2024 by Podium Publishing
www.podiumaudio.com

THE TROLL HUNTER

1

The worn kingdom of Sunja, perched high upon a flat plateau and surrounded by an ocean of prairie, faced the morning sun. The sky had ripened to a vast, empty blue, and the heat of the day had not yet begun.

Within the high city walls, in a great open courtyard laid out in front of long rows of black-roofed barracks, men spilled out onto the sand like dark specks against a white sheet. A collection of soldiers, dispatched only days earlier from the infirmary, moved onto the parade ground. Some men moved stiffly, struggling with the weeks of inactivity needed to recover from the wounds that had removed them from the war's front. They were the Sujins of Sunja, the killers of the land, the anvils upon which sparks flew when struck, and the first into any Sunjan armed conflict. They knew not why they were being roused so early in the morning. Some were miserably hung over. Some were curious, blinking at their commanders. Some simply snarled as if they were about to be whipped, like wild dogs ready to turn on their masters.

They fell into place, instinctively knowing their formations and carrying weapons and armor. Their chain-mail vests, mended, scrubbed, and cared for like old silver, gleamed in the sun. Dented and scratched belly and back plates hung from their shoulders and were lashed together with strips of leather. Large, rectangular shields decorated the left arm of each Sujin, while the right side was free to grab for the adder-like shortsword each man carried, in addition to any other weapon he chose to bring along. The morning sun warmed them all easily enough, but by afternoon it vowed to cook their mead-aching heads inside their open-faced helmets.

Slash-mouthed officers called Koors inspected the Sujins' armored frames, stalking up and down the formed lines as if they were the tamers of tigers. Here and there, Sujins had their ears scoured red with hateful reprimands, their heads pummeled with inventive threats and promises of hell being a better place. Some of the Sujins still had the scent of alcohol on their breath, and it infuriated the officers catching a whiff of sour breath and reeking pores, as Rusk the Two Knife decided to demonstrate.

"You stinking pisspots! You piles of maggot pus! *Who* on Seddon's bright, given earth decided to take a stinking shite in your mouths during the night? Seddon's bare, bright and sunny ass, you stink to low hell! *Stink!* You'd think you washed with vomit, you stink so much! And which of you sunny maggots decided to actually put some spit grease into your armor last night? None that I can see! Or perhaps you think my damn eyes see about as much as a dog's pink blossom? *Eh?* Where in Saimon's blue balls are my anvils? *Eh?* And who the hell are you? *Dog balls!* Do you lot ever make a poor topper want to drop his drawers and shite on the spot! Just to freshen up the air! Stink! You make the pigs smell of daisies! *Daisies!* You gits do know what flowers are? Any that do, I'll fishhook dead on the spot! If any of you flesh-eaters can even *point* at a flower, I'll personally ram a spear up your dog blossom *just to see your damn eyes pop out!* By Saimon's *pisshole*, that sounds like an idea to me! I'll jigger your boy-loving hide with whatever rust-crusted fly shite-sickle I can find and *that'll* wipe the piss grin off your faces! *Flowers!* You cut down flowers as much as any stupid Nord bastard in your way! Wake up, you asslickers! And if *any* of you *tits* don't like me yelling this morning just step up and tell me!"

No one did.

"Thought so, maggot shite," the officer hissed. The Sujin Koors were the hardest of the hard, and none of the Sujins wanted to draw their attention, especially not Rusk the Two Knife, the Right Koor of Koors, and not this early in the morning. The man was slightly shorter than most, but he had a set of thick shoulders on him. Muscular, tight leather bands armored his chest instead of a chain-mail vest. Metal braces covered his forearms. He wore no helmet and his blond hair was shorn close to the scalp. Blue ice flicks for eyes raked them all, and his face was chiseled into a deep scowl.

Suddenly bored with the soldiers before him, Rusk the Two Knife strutted further down the lines of Sujins, three ranks deep and four hundred plus strong. Taking up his cries, other lower Koors began hollering. The Sujin officers stomped up and down the lines of warriors, ready to smash any man unaware of the world. Orders were given, and heavy packs full of rations were handed out.

"Never thought," Balto paused, eyeing where the officers were, "Right Koors would swear so much."

"Two Knife was only just promoted," Gatesin muttered next to him, his eyes half-covered by the lip of his helmet, giving him a sly look. "Old habits."

Balto nodded. Old habits, indeed. He returned to studying his gear, all ready to go. He scratched at his ear. He shifted the weight of his chain-mail vest on his formidable chest, and rubbed at a nose that had once been crushed by a mace. His nose always ached nowadays, and in the spring it was hard to breathe through. "What did he call us, again?" Balto asked.

"Maggot shite," Gatesin answered, stoically.

Gatesin met the grey eyes of Balto. There was a smile in them, and he, again, thought of how much Balto reminded him of his long-dead uncle. Balto's prematurely-graying hair played a great part in that resemblance. Although the man refused to give his exact age, Gatesin believed him to be only in his early thirties. He also suspected Balto enjoyed being the "old man" amongst the gathered Sujins; age did have some advantages.

"Maggot shite," Gatesin breathed, squinting at the morning sun. He did not like Two Knife. That one was a killer, if there ever was one. Rabid, he was, and Gatesin would not trust the man to protect his back in a fight. In fact, if there ever was a man better off dead, it was Rusk. He briefly thought about doing the deed himself. Maybe bash the man's head in, perhaps when he was sleeping. That would be the safest thing to do.

Then again, Gatesin wondered if the man ever slept. He sighed. His head hurt too much to be plotting the death of a butcher. He was one of those who drank more than his share of mead last night, and the dull knife twisting in his head reminded him of it with every spoken word. Somewhere in the night, he forgot to stop drinking, and kept on until his body simply refused to take any more mead and began to send everything back; however, he did not think he smelled so bad.

Balto saw the pained expression on Gatesin's face. He was a young man with few scars, but aged and worn by war. Balto saw it in the man's blue eyes. The older Sujin also recognized the echoes of mead in Gatesin's face. Foul stuff. He never drank it.

"What did we do to win this favor?" growled Tungang from where he squatted behind Gatesin. "Seddon above, I should be *sleeping* right now. Dog balls! And then to have that punce scream at us. I wouldn't drop a tear if that topper died on the spot."

"Tungang," Gatesin turned, catching the man's glare. "Shut up."

A smile crept across Balto's features. He liked that about Gatesin. The man was not afraid to speak his mind.

However, then Tungang stood up, glaring in the other man's direction. He towered a full two heads over the men around him, including Gatesin, and Gatesin was not a small man. Tungang's black eyes fixed on the Sujin from under a worn battle helmet edged with pale hair. An axe the length of a long sword swung from a fist the size of a melon. Tungang came from a Sunjan tribe of north men, and many believed he was actually three of them disguised as one. His chain-mail was specially fitted for his barrel of a chest, and his arms were sleeveless, as their muscular bulk could not be properly fitted for protection. In fact, the sight of his mighty arms was fearsome enough to take the fight out of most men, and Tungang knew that.

Not Gatesin. Amused, Balto believed that Tungang actually liked Gatesin for speaking out against him when he did.

"You're not helping the knife still in my head," Gatesin said without looking behind him.

"Is it my fault you drank enough to piss like ten horses?" Tungang demanded.

Gatesin grimaced almost comically under the big man's voice. Tungang saw the man's head dip ever so slightly. It was enough to placate the big Tun, and he surprised them all by laughing. "My apologies then," Tungang said. He clamped one of his huge fists down on Gatesin's shoulder. "When it's time for you to sleep, you just let me know. You won't feel a thing." He tapped his temple with one thick finger. "I'll even drag you along by the feet so you won't fall behind the march."

"Noisy Tun," Gatesin grumbled.

"I'm not noisy. I talk like this all the time," Tungang released him. "Especially when I'm in the company of hung-over dogs. Which makes me think…"

"Think quietly, then," Gatesin begged him.

"I was quiet enough when I was a boy. I never said a word."

"You're making up for lost time now," Gatesin replied.

Balto shook his head in admiration. The Tun wiped the floor up with most men for such jabs. However, here was Gatesin, doing the impossible. He was actually bantering with Tungang, outwitting him, and making the man grin all at the same time.

"Which makes me think," Tungang said, intentionally louder, and smiling at the other's discomfort. "Why *are* we out here so early? Does anyone know?"

"We're going to Marrn." Balto said. "I heard Primo talking to Rusk."

"Marrn?" Tungang mulled. "Why Marrn?"

"Probably for the exercise," Balto replied. "No doubt we'll turn around and march back once we get there."

"Good, then," Tungang said. "There'll be Nordun Jackals about. What better way to start a morning than killing a few Nords? Damnation. Just like breaking hen's eggs."

"I imagine if we meet any Nords, there'll be plenty enough to kill," Balto said.

"Never enough," Tungang growled and lapped at the edge of his axe with his tongue. When he bared his teeth, they were red.

Gatesin shook his head reproachfully. He knew better than to show any fear around Tungang. The Northman could smell fear, like a famished wolf around bacon.

"So, they call upon the Sujins. As always," Tungang went on. "The Cavaliers must all be dead by now."

"Perhaps," Balto said, finishing his own preparations. "I hear the war with Nordun is not going well for us."

"Really?" Tungang's mouth was red. He spat blood onto the ground.

Balto spoke again, his voice low, "I like hearing news from the front, even as far back from it as we are. It's been a month since I've been there. We should be there now, fighting. Then we would know the truth. The Nords are a fierce lot, not one gutless one amongst them. I wouldn't be surprised to learn that the king wants an ally in Marrn."

"We don't need their help," Tungang said loudly, ignoring Balto's attempt at keeping things quiet.

"Just my thoughts," Balto said, wondering if there could be another reason.

"I believe you," Gatesin threw in, though it hurt his head to do so. He would put his money on Balto's hunches anytime. Balto thought things through where it hurt most other men to even think.

"Yes," Balto looked contented with himself, "that's what I think, anyway. Marrn doesn't like the Nords warring on their borders. If they received an envoy and a kind word from Sunja, we could very well have an ally. If the Nords did kill us all off, I don't think they would be long in beating their war drums in Marrn's direction."

"What's an envoy?" a man named Hatch asked, squinting at the sun. He stood to the right of Tungang, in the big man's shadow.

"That's us." Balto informed him. "Nordun could be crushed between us and Marrn's armies."

"We don't need their help," Tungang said.

"We're not all like you, Tungang," Balto said.

"Too bad," Tungang replied. "You should be. This war would be over if you were."

A Koor walked up and stood directly before the talking Sujins. Like hushed children, the lot of them immediately quieted. Gatesin wanted to thank the officer.

The officers withdrew, gathering at the front of a storeroom, across from the barracks. There were a dozen men, standing in a circle, listening to this morning's tale from a Cavalier. The sun shone down on the man's silver plate mail. Gatesin sometimes wished he could be a Cavalier. These days, only the Sujins of nobles and wealthy merchants were selected and trained in the ways of warfare from a horse's back, unlike years ago when any who proved themselves a head above in martial arts received Cavalier training. Two or three of the regular Lancers had been invited into the ranks of the elite Cavaliers, but never the Sujins. Though looked down upon as an uneducated lot, the Sujins, admittedly, were the hardest.

They were the toughest in the field, and unfortunately, the first to die. Gatesin rubbed his forehead. Behind him, Tungang was muttering about something. *Seddon above, but the man could talk!* He tried to ignore the man, and turned his head towards the main gates of the Sujin compound, squinting in the bright sunlight. The great reinforced gates were shut. Standing just before them were a group of men that Gatesin recognized as scouts. The need to bring in hired hands who knew certain lands was becoming increasingly necessary as the war continued. Mercenaries, while not as nail-hard as the Sujins, were more than able to fight when pressed or paid. Most wore their own armor and carried their own equipment in some semblance of cleanliness. The Sujins used to have standards for whom they brought on, but it seemed to Gatesin that it was slipping as he surveyed the scouts gathered around the gate. Some of them talked to each other, while others stood off, watching the Sujins just as they were being watched.

One in particular caught Gatesin's attention. He was as tall as Tungang, perhaps, but not as muscular. The man wore a leather vest with long strips that covered his upper thighs. He wore non-standard boots and carried no shield. A necklace of some sort hung low on his chest. Gatesin believed that it was made of bones, long bones, or even claws. Shoulder-length dark hair hung about the man's face, hiding it in shadow. As Gatesin's eyes ran over him, he was aware of being watched, in turn.

Gatesin studied him for only a moment longer, before looking away, thinking with disgust how long his hair was. The scout was definitely not military-trained. Hair like that would have been cropped to his skull long ago. Most of the scouts stood out like boils on a bare white arse.

"Those men are new to me," Gatesin whispered, not wanting to draw the attention of the officers across the way.

"Aye," Balto added quietly. "They look good enough."

"Looks are nothing," Gatesin put in. "Just look at Tungang." The big man heard his name and his frowning face flicked up in Gatesin's direction.

The men's attention was then stolen by a shining figure riding a warhorse. The Cavalier rode down the line of Sujins, inspecting the lot of them. The morning sunlight sparkled off the warrior's plate armor. Balto and Gatesin glanced up at the same time. Gatesin saw the man, saw the face, and his mouth puckered up in distaste and he lowered his gaze. The morning was about to get worse.

Balto stared on, watching the horseman ride along the line, taking his time as if he had it by the throat. The Cavalier scrutinized them all with black eyes. He was a big man, held up by an even bigger warhorse. A wall of dread encapsulated the warrior and it smothered all sound, save for the scuffing of his horse's hooves.

"Is it him?" Gatesin muttered near Balto, giving his boots even more attention.

"I believe so," Balto whispered, trying hard not to move his lips.

"Has he seen me?"

"Not yet. Hmm…perhaps he has."

"Who is he?" Tungang found himself whispering.

"Do you remember the Field of Skulls?" Hatch asked in a barely audible voice. "I wasn't there."

"But, you know of it?"

"Aye, I do."

This impressed Hatch. "It was the second army to fall to the Nordun Jackals."

The Cavalier stopped advancing. He faced a Sujin and began speaking to him. Lines of helmets glittered in the morning sun.

Tungang spat blood into the dirt from his still-bleeding tongue. He believed he had cut it deeper than he wanted. He kept his voice low. "So who is he? A survivor from the field?"

"Yes," Balto answered for Hatch.

"How do you know?" Tungang's voice rose.

"*I'm* a survivor of the field."

"You were on the Field of Skulls?" Tungang regarded the veteran through eyes slitted in disbelief.

Balto answered with a slight tilt of his head. "There weren't many of us. Perhaps no more than twenty or twenty-one, but he was with us. He led us out of that hell, and got us away from the Jackals before they could find us. He saved us, no doubt."

"Tell us," Tungang said, too loud this time.

The Cavalier's helmet came up and turned in their direction. It was obvious to him that someone wanted to be noticed; someone would get their wish.

The Cavalier flicked the reins of his horse and trotted towards them. Gatesin set his jaw. He knew something like this would happen, and with a spear of a headache in his brain, as well.

2

The Sujin ranks became that much stiffer as the Cavalier moved down the length of them as if he were hot iron crushing cotton. The horse came on in no particular hurry, its hooves kicking up plumes of loose dirt. It reined in directly in front of Balto. The man atop the beast appeared even larger at close range, but the Cavalier did not look at Balto. He adjusted himself in the saddle and leaned forward ever so slightly, leather creaking, peering hard at the man with his head down *beside* Balto.

"Gatesin," the warrior accused from atop his war horse.

Gatesin gnawed briefly on his lip before tucking his teeth in. His head came up. "My Lord?"

"Gatesin," the man called Bloor repeated in a dreary voice, as if he had just discovered something priceless was broken. With the sun at his back, his features were swathed in shadow, yet fixed on the Sujin's head.

The pain behind Gatesin's eyes intensified. However, he would not dare move now. Not with this one watching.

"I figured you dead long ago," Bloor stated coldly. "Heard you were strung up by some Nords after a skirmish. Somewhere near the northern bastion just before it fell."

"I heard that one myself, Lord," Gatesin reported. "But untrue."

"Pity."

Gatesin sighed inwardly; he did not need this.

"But you escaped the Jackals?" Bloor sounded puzzled.

"I was never there, Lord Bloor. My commander at the time—Tighkuss—saw the attack on the bastion and managed to pull us all back before they struck. He failed in convincing the other commander there. They were at odds, Lord."

"Ah yes," Bloor raised his head as if smelling something. "Heard of that man. There was a story there, wasn't there? One captain deserting another in the face of a Jackal attack. Tighkuss was arrested, was he not?"

Gatesin nodded. "For a different reason, Lord."

"Different?"

"He was found guilty of adultery first. He liked packing the wenches. Unfortunately, one wench was the other commander's wife. The affair was going on well before the attack on the bastion."

Bloor nodded slowly, as if remembering a joke. "Yes, so he was. Gone now, isn't he?"

"Aye, Lord," Gatesin reported.

"And you remain."

Gatesin kept silent, studying the Cavalier's stallion before him. Even the horse glared at him with evil eyes. It snorted hot breath into his face. Bloor made no move to turn the beast's head away.

"You have a talent for surviving, Gatesin. I'll give you that. And it's a talent I would sooner you did not have." Bloor leaned forward in the saddle, leather creaking. His shaven face came into view. Dark eyes the color of the deepest stone scoured Gatesin's face as if they could rake the flesh from his skull. A short mouth was drawn tight, like a garrote ready to strangle. At any other time, Bloor might have been a handsome man to look upon, but presently, his dour face was frightening.

Gatesin peered directly ahead, in hopes that the hellion paying attention to him would just go away.

Bloor did not. "How is it that you march with us? Who in his right mind would march with you?"

"Permission to speak, Lord."

The Cavalier swung the crushing weight of his stare over to Balto. The veteran Sujin's eyes remained front.

"What is it, dog?"

"I would march beside the man."

Bloor swallowed this. "How long have you served together, dog?"

"Two campaigns, Lord Bloor."

"And you still breathe?"

"To this moment, Lord."

Bloor idly stoked the neck of his massive warhorse and gave it a comforting pat. "I remember you now," he eventually said. "Perhaps the curse has been lifted then, hmm? I suppose we'll know soon enough. I hope you survive this campaign as well then, Sujin. We'll need all the luck we can suck up. Especially now that the plague marches amongst us."

With that, Bloor gave his mount's flanks a kick and the great animal started forward. He gave Gatesin one last withering look before carrying on his inspection.

The horse left behind a steaming gift.

The Sujins waited until the Cavalier was safely out of earshot, then Tungang cut loose in a hard whisper. "Filthy animals. Shitting all over the place. I'd plug its hole if I didn't think it would start shitting from its mouth."

"Best not let the Cavaliers hear you talk like that," Balto warned him in a low voice.

"Yes. No one needs to be reminded that they are riding shite fountains." Gatesin said. Balto grinned.

"What about this talk of curses, then?" Tungang pressed Gatesin.

"You. You're the curse. The moment I met your lacking arse," Gatesin told him, without humor.

"You can tell me," Tungang urged him.

"I have your permission, do I?" Gatesin turned his head to watch the shining back of Bloor being carried down the length of the column. It made his headache pound even harder.

"Bah," Tungang scoffed. "Do as you like. I'll get it out of Balto when you are not around."

"I'm always around him, you ripe bastard," Balto growled. Balto then looked to Gatesin and followed his gaze. The resplendent Cavalier trotted further on down the line, stopping here and there. An armored koch pulled by six horses came into sight.

"What's this, then?" Balto muttered to himself. The koch slowed to a stop alongside the ranks of Sujins. Men appeared and began mulling over the vehicle and the horses, adjusting the harnesses and the bits in the beasts' mouths. The wagon itself was large enough to fit a family comfortably, but the exterior looked harsh and able to withstand falling boulders. Metal plates had been nailed over its heavy wooden frame as well as the shuttered windows, which could only be opened from the inside. Places where a man could jump onto the rig had been spiked with short blades. Even the wheels of the things were plated and spiked. Two drivers sat high in the perch, watching the others swarm over the koch with their final checks. A third man was perched in the rear, sitting in a small armored cradle. He held a crossbow at the ready and scoured the Sujins with an evil eye, as if wondering if he could spare a bolt for one of them.

Gatesin became quiet then as a Sujin Koor approached. He let his breath go in a slow hiss.

First Bloor, now Rusk the Two Knife.

3

"What are you looking at, maggot?" Two Knife demanded of a Sujin. Balto disliked the way the man talked. He always spoke in a tone of challenge, except to his superiors, of course. With them, he kept his mouth shut, and sucked up all instructions given to him. Balto did not trust him. Seeing him here, this day, on this march, darkened his feelings about the entire trip. Throughout the five Klaws, Rusk had gathered a pack of Sujins, infamous in their brutality on the battlefield, and though Balto had never served with any of them, he had heard plenty of tales from those who had. Rusk was a man no one wanted to be around for too long.

Rusk the Two Knife strutted past the lines, pausing suddenly to meet the dirty eye of Tungang. Rusk stabbed back with his own glare and Tungang looked away.

"That's right, you Tun of pig shite," Rusk warned. He stepped directly to where the big man stood and faced the Northman with both fists on the hilts of the twin shortswords hanging off his hips. Both pommels had ringlets so that Rusk could yank them from their scabbards and flip them into his hands in a flash. "You look away. Don't ever look at me again. You don't impress me in the damn least. Why don't you go on over to the Jackals' side and help them die? You'd certainly make me fight all the harder, knowing you were over there. Saimon below, I'd pay good coin to carve you up. Get rid of that stink in the line. Did your mother stink like that, or was it one of your fathers? I've heard how bloody bad you are on the front. I'll see to it you're next to me, then— you and whoever else you think can help you. I'll tell you something else. Before I die, the exact moment before I cross over, I wish to be a Tun. Yes I do. There'd be one less Tun in the world, then."

Tungang said nothing, and kept his face blank. The Right Koor leaned in close, his mouth a spiteful line. Eventually, Rusk slowly nodded. This Tun knew his place. Losing interest, Two Knife strutted along the other Sujins, glaring at them all. He had better things to do than to pay attention to this assorted pile of pig scum. The sooner he got out of the service of Sunja, the better. Two Knife didn't feel he was destined for great things, but he felt he could do better than this rabble. Marching by his subordinates, his hands resting on the two blades from which he received his preferred name, he snarled and grimaced and barked insults at the Sujins. He despised these dogs, despised them for their blind devotion to a king who cared more about the hair on his toes than their lives.

Rusk stopped and surveyed the long line of them. What had the king done to deserve such loyalty? As far as Rusk understood, the man was an aloof idiot who inherited the throne from his father. There were rumors that he had never stepped foot on a battlefield. If true, and Rusk believed it was, it galled him to think that he pledged his life to a man who never knew combat. By Saimon's blue pisspot, he hoped that was not true. Rusk stopped again, hoarked as if summoning up lung curds from the depths of hell, and spat into the ground. That was what he thought of kings.

He felt the reassuring pommels of his blades, his two best personal friends. He did well with them, understating the reality that he was a terror on the battlefield when the swords were in his grips. Rusk smirked. Taxmen were good at what they did. Farmers did what they could with what they had and hoped for the best growing conditions. However, what he accomplished with his swords was legendary, modesty be damned.

He had entered the ranks of the Sujins two years ago and by his twin swords he carved his way to the position of Right Koor, just short of a captain's rank. He remembered the day the quartermaster had issued him a shield—a monstrous rectangular wall to be hung off his left arm. There was no way that Rusk was going to use that. He threw it back at the man, who cursed him for being a git. By his marked words, Rusk would be dead in the first encounter with the Nords, nailed to the ground in the first storm of arrows.

Truth be known, the idea sobered Rusk, and he took the shield back. Not to use as a shield, but more of a roof against archers. He hated them more than Cavaliers. Warriors could not be warriors with those bastards waiting half a field away and plucking on their bowstrings as if they were jilted harps. In any case, he took the shield, and in the first encounter with Jackals outside the town of Ushik, Rusk took the lives of thirteen Nords. The number was enough to be recognized by the Koor commanding the Sujins at the time, though Rusk considered the Nords to be nothing more than little girls with knives. He knew of the stories of the Jackals and their reputation for being fearless. Rusk could not believe them. It made him sick to think of them. The only reason the Nords were doing so well in their war with Sunja was because of the sheer mass of them. They were like a plague of black flies, easily swatted. However, he earned his name that day when he flung aside his shield and brought forth his butcher's blades and tore into the Jackals as if they were standing still.

Rusk eyed the Cavalier at the head of the line. Cavaliers, Lancers, horsemen in general were another breed altogether. Where archers could not stomach the sight of their own work, Lancers and the like were useless if you took away their meat. That was Rusk's opinion of them all. Four-legged skewers of meat, they were. Take them out from under a Lancer and you had another piece of meat, tender for the cutting, soft and unwilling like a virgin's breast. Cavaliers, now they actually could stand on their own feet and mesh it out when necessary. The only trouble about them was their damn pious attitude. The bastards' noses were so turned up that if you smashed one, the elation could, perhaps, be compared to being kissed on the forehead by Seddon above. In the beginning, Rusk took it as a personal insult that he was not invited to train with the Cavaliers. He felt he was Cavalier material, perhaps with the potential to be the best there was. However, ultimately they were a womanly lot, and much too concerned with keeping up the appearances of armor and their horses. They gladly passed on the dirty chores on to the Sujins. Rusk had no qualms about getting bloody in war, but he despised being used in such a way and then being deprived of credit. Seeing them now as they actually were, he would turn down any invitation to train with them. He hated them, a hate born from rejection, from knowing he was better than any of them, or so he told himself.

Rusk was more than pleased with his rise to Right Koor. Now, he had someone else to carry his shield into battle. On the whole, the Sujins were no longer the war-mongers of yesterday. Yet, there were some that retained that fearless killer instinct, possessing the ferocity that Two Knife himself prized. He personally saw to it that these dangerous Sujins who shared his way of thinking made their way into his command, men who would cut the throats of their own babes if he told them to. He kept these Sujins close to him. Dogs such as they had to be fed with an iron gauntlet, and they had to know who was feeding them.

Two Knife looked away from the Cavalier. Four hundred Sujins were here this day, along with forty Lancers and two Cavaliers. All were charged with protecting the contents of the war wagon. He turned back to see Bloor trot over to the vehicle. The Cavalier studied something on the side of the transport. A man in the driver's seat began talking to him. *Bloor!* Now there was a drop of his father's seed that should have perished with the thousands of others. Bloor was master and commander of this foray, right arm and ear of Lord Winter, High Commander. In truth, Lord Winter's decision to place Bloor as commander surprised Two Knife. He and a good many others thought Tarco would have been placed in charge. With Tarco's connections, he could get almost anything he wanted. Rusk supposed Tarco was livid with the decision of Lord Winter, who still had the ear of the king. Lord Winter gave Tarco the chore of selecting the Lancers from the ranks of those released from the infirmaries, men fresh from their healing and waiting for word to head back to the front. Bloor passed off the duty to Rusk to choose the Sujins, and Two Knife arranged it so that *all* of his lads were in the ranks.

Two Knife wondered how Bloor would fare up against his twin blades. He would have to kill the horse first, but that wasn't a great concern. It was a pastime with him, pondering how a particular warrior would fight him. He had precious few other amusements beyond that and wenching. Again, he mulled over the imaginary contest. Without his beast, how would Bloor do? Perhaps Two Knife would find out soon enough.

Bloor inspected the wheels on the right side of the koch for a third time.

"Checked them myself, Lord," the burly driver said from his perch. He looked down at the Cavalier, but not by much. The man's horse was enormous. Probably not much on speed, but Torham suspected the thing could run for days. The fires of Saimon's abyss would probably burn out before that monster.

The side portals of the koch were closed and sheets of iron gleamed meat-red in the morning light.

"Check them again," Bloor rumbled. "And the harnesses of all the horses. Make certain of everything."

The driver paused for the briefest of moments. "Yes, Lord. Right away."

"And Torham?"

"Yes, Lord?"

"I'll be checking again before we leave."

"Yes, Lord." Torham said, head bobbing. Nobody needed to be disciplined by a Cavalier.

Bloor scowled at the wheels and the nailed plating of the outer rim. He scowled at the shuttered windows and the iron bracing of the door itself. Solid enough, but safe? It would have to do. In truth, the entire koch would have to be constructed of iron to be safe enough for Bloor, and there would have to be a Klaw of fighting men instead of the mere four hundred gathered here this day, but a Klaw was both impossible and unrealistic.

Torham was talking to him and Bloor nodded, though he heard nothing the driver had said. He found himself trying to see past the plating of the shutters. What was it like in there? Shut away from all the madness outside? Bloor swore softly and looked to the front of the column. Standing apart from the Sujins was one that caught his eye. Tall and hunched over like a cane, the man dressed in a vest of black leather armor was one of the five scouts for the escort. At this distance, his features were as dark as a stain of wine in the morning sun. He stood still, like a wild thing suddenly aware that eyes were upon him. Bloor also believed he was being studied, in turn. He had heard from Primo that one of the scouts had a second profession of hunting. Primo did not say what. There was a predatory look about the fellow, and Bloor suspected the hunter was a skilled one. Unfortunate, however, and the thought set the Cavalier's head rocking gently to and fro.

Two Knife watched Bloor, not bothering to hide his grimace. The Sujin Koor abruptly turned then, his senses detecting movement behind him. Under the glare of the sun, he squinted at the brute of a Sujin possessing steely eyes. The man nodded in greeting. An assortment of blades hung from his person, but Rusk knew that the man preferred the battle axe lashed to his back. He liked to smash in skulls with it, especially when the victims were already half unconscious.

Desso, a Koor, was the first to see things Two Knife's way.

"What is it?" Two Knife asked him stiffly.

"Lads are ready," Desso reported, his voice a growl. His mouth appeared to barely move underneath a black moss of beard. It always amazed Desso that Two Knife seemed to know when someone was behind him. That sixth sense made him an incredibly deadly adversary, especially in the dark. In broad daylight, Rusk would be a handful for three men.

Two Knife said nothing. He glared again in the direction of the Cavalier. The bastard was again talking to Torham. That made Two Knife nervous. Torham was a punce. The thought occurred to him that he should kill Bloor at the first opportunity—at night. A quick stabbing while the man slept in his blanket. The thought was a tempting one, yet he dismissed it after only a moment. Bloor would die on his feet and not in his sleep.

"What's he doing?"

Desso craned his neck to see, pushing back his helmet.

"What is he doing?" Two Knife repeated, wishing he knew.

Desso wasn't certain if he should answer or not. He decided not to, figuring silence to be best. He had learned, long ago, that at certain times it was best to feign ignorance. Then, a new sound came to their ears: a steady tattoo of boots upon the ground. Both of them turned at the heavy beat and Two Knife's grimace deepened. A group of huge men marched into their midst and took up position around the koch. The plate armor of the men clattered as they marched, and their conical helms threw long shadows to the side. All of them held the legendary pole axes of Sunja: weapons as long as spears and topped with a single axe blade. The force from one, especially when swung by one of those monsters, was enough to split an armored man down the middle.

"What are they doing here?" Two Knife hissed, as his eyes widened. Desso had heard the man talk like this before and certainly wasn't going to say a word now. Two Knife had struck down Sujins in the field when they gave an answer that wasn't wanted.

Sunja's Royal Axemen were marching with them. Desso knew that Two Knife had not been able to talk to any of them.

"What are *they* doing here?" Two Knife whispered again, gaining control of his surprise. He half-turned to Desso, realized who it was he spoke to, and rolled his eyes. There would be no answers from Desso. Two Knife did not have him for his conversation ability. He had Toffer to bounce ideas off.

"Go to the head of the column," Two Knife commanded, and left him, heading in the direction of the Axemen. He took a quick count as he went. *Twenty*. Out of a force of a hundred or so, the king had lent a fifth of his legendary bodyguards to this escort. If any merit could be given to the reputations of these walking hellions, Two Knife would have more than his hands full with just one.

His head reeled with the unfairness of the Axemen's appearance. He managed to strut in his unhurried way towards Bloor and the koch, but his mind was trying to fathom why the Axemen were here. Each step made the group of bodyguards seem even larger. They were as big as that goat-head of a Tun—even bigger perhaps. Certainly, there were none smaller. The king selected all of his Axemen on the basis of size, strength, and skill with weapons. Size was a powerful dissuader in any confrontation. The reputation of the Axemen as unholy terrors in close quarters was equally powerful, and here were twenty of them! Why hadn't that silver-plated teat on a horse mentioned them to him? Wasn't Rusk a Right Koor and privy to that sort of information?

Bloor ignored the approach of Rusk, even when his officer stopped directly beside his horse. Bloor greeted the Axemen formally and began giving them explicit instructions on guarding the koch. From his perch, Torham's eyes were fearful. Two Knife's answering glare forced the driver to compose himself. He listened to Bloor drone on about the importance of the Koch, and while Two Knife waited for his chance, his mind posed a question: a Cavalier up against an Axeman? What would be the outcome of that contest? Torham shot him another questioning glance and Two Knife's jaw clenched. *Idiot!*

Bloor finally turned in his saddle and regarded Rusk the Two Knife. "Yes?"

Two Knife cleared his throat. He wanted to sound untroubled. "The Axemen. We're becoming quite the force."

Bloor said nothing.

"Only twenty?" Two Knife asked, his voice level. Bloor again said nothing, staring down at the Sujin.

"Is there anything I should know about? To inform my officers?" Two Knife asked, trying to scratch out any information from the Cavalier.

Bloor cast him a dour stare. "Your officers?" he inquired, sardonically.

Rusk's face froze. "My apologies, Lord. I meant *your* officers."

"Now you think," Bloor went on with a deadly quiet air, "that your apologies will make it all right again?" That caused Rusk to blink. Uncertainty filled his mind.

That expression of indecision pleased Bloor, but nothing on his face suggested that. Outwardly, he appeared to be contemplating having the man before him hewed in two by the nearby pole axes. "Say it again," he commanded.

"My apologies, Lord," Rusk said immediately. He did not want to appear insolent to the commander. There would be time enough to collect payment for all slights against him in the near future.

"And remember it," Bloor said, dismissing Rusk with his eyes.

"But, Lord," Rusk went on in a careful voice. He would never live it down if any of his henchmen heard him speak to this pig in such a way. "Is there anything I should tell *your* officers?"

"No," Bloor said and gave the reins of his horse a flick. The great beast snorted. "Are the Sujins ready?" Bloor steered his horse around the man and did not see the way the Koor's face twisted up in resentment, vanishing before anyone could notice.

"All are ready, Lord."

"Good. When I reach the head of the column, have all other officers there. And check the Sujins again for readiness. See to it all are ready to move when I give the command."

"I already…"

"See to it again. And report directly to me. Don't make me call out for you."

"Understood, Lord," Rusk the Two Knife replied, loathing this Cavalier but realizing now he had to rethink things. Twenty Axemen! This was not supposed to happen. How was he going to get through *twenty* Axemen? Fuming as much as he dared, he stalked off to carry out Bloor's instructions.

Bloor trotted his horse to the head of the column, taking his time and stopping at the troop of Lancers standing across from the Sujins. The cavalry men sat at attention on their horses. They dared not say anything to this man before them. To them, Bloor was an enigma, a legend. The orphan adopted by the taskmasters, hammered into a Cavalier, who tore holes of death through hordes of Nordish Jackals, and the only Cavalier to survive the Field of Skulls. If just one of them got so much as a nod from the man, he would be envied by the rest. Bloor inspected them long enough for Rusk to carry out his instructions.

When the Cavalier finished with the horsemen, he turned to the column's head. A handful of officers there saluted him with bows. Bloor remained astride his horse and studied them all with an intent look. He knew them all by reputation only. Most of them were bad, at that, with the exception of two. There was Primo, a solid Sujin and a survivor of several Nordish campaigns. Bloor hoped the man lived for a long time. Near him was the Right Koor Lancer called Quent. He was man who looked uncomfortable, dismounted as he was, even though he held his horse by its reins.

There was also Bloor's unofficial rival, his second in command during this journey, and his second greatest pain in the arse, Tarco.

The Cavalier stood by his own horse, holding its reins in his hand. On this mission, he stood in Bloor's shadow and he knew it. The High Cavalier Commander, Lord Maullus ordered him to acknowledge it. The two Cavaliers locked gazes. An unfriendly smile spread over Tarco's face and Bloor thought of how a pedophile must look when he stumbles onto a helpless child.

"I want to know something, Bloor," he said.

The commander looked in his direction, silently granting him permission to speak. Though second in command, the position his father had as the minister of defense for Sunja granted him certain privileges. Tarco got the choice of almost any duty, even if he was away. If he was out in the field on some duty, he had aides delay missions he favored until he returned. He usually possessed full command, but if he didn't, his advice as second in command was greatly considered. He was a burden to endure, and most officers despised having to listen to the man's voice. However, listen they did, else word might get back to his father on how he was ill-treated or ignored. No one wanted to find themselves reassigned next to a Jackal breeding ground. Jackals liked to weapons-train on living prisoners if they had them.

It wasn't that Tarco was a bad Cavalier. Bloor simply had no time for the man or the man's quest for blood. Tarco had decided early on in his military career that carving his name in the dead flesh of his adversaries was the best way to earn a reputation. Bloor understood that, but the way that Tarco sought danger to heap fame on his name was enough to make Bloor sick. However, Tarco stood before him. Damn his father.

"I want to know," Tarco demanded, making himself sound entitled, and that in reality, Bloor was second to *him*. Inwardly, the Cavalier commander sighed; it was starting already. "I want to know where Alwan is? I usually see that hellion riding somewhere in your shadow. But this day I don't. Where is he? I would have liked to have seen him before we left."

Bloor scowled. "No, you would not, Tarco. That man hates your guts as much as I do, and he would need little excuse to show them to the light of day."

Tarco reddened. "How dare…"

"Shut up. Or I'll have you hauled away for causing dissention in the ranks before we even get started, makes not a lick of difference to me. And you'll address me as my rank commands. That is your first and last warning."

The man's eyes near bulged from their sockets, but he kept his tongue. He glared at the mounted Cavalier, and Bloor stared back every bit as hard. The others dared not to move. The way Bloor put the nobleman in his place impressed even Rusk, and he relished it when Tarco averted his gaze to the ground. Rusk straightened his back, causing the Sujin Koors who stood directly behind him, Desso and Toffer, to do the same. The commander continued to give Tarco the hardest of eyes, almost as if he wanted the man provoked, but Tarco did not meet them. There was something in Bloor's tone that always unsettled and angered him. There was the absolute sureness in the way he talked. It always made Tarco doubt his own words, and for that, in addition to their past, he hated the man.

"That goes for the rest of you," Bloor warned them all, "except I'll likely just take your head and answer to Lord

Maullus or Lord Winter later. I'm sure I'll have their approval. If you doubt this, feel free to try me."

Primo stood stiffly, looking straight ahead. He needed no threats. On this day, on this march, Bloor was commander. The Lancer Quent nodded his understanding. Tarco's unprofessionalism surprised him. He thought the Cavaliers were better trained.

"Now, then," Bloor went on after a slight pause. "I'll tell you what has been charged to us…"

The words that came made even Tarco's head rise. He thought he knew what they were transporting, but in truth, the real nature of the koch momentarily stunned him and the surrounding officers—with the exception of Two Knife and the Koors near him.

4

They marched north within the second hour of dawn's light, the long column slipping out of the city like a steel snake taking to sand. The armored figured of Bloor rode up and down the line as the force moved along. A sour-looking Tarco rode his horse at the head of the procession and Two Knife marched beside him. Following them were the first two hundred battled-hardened Sujins. They wore fearsome scowls, some pensive, some mindless, but all ready for the command to kill something.

The Axemen made up the middle of the march, their fearsome pole arms raised high. They surrounded the slow-moving koch like a barbed-wire fence around tree trunks. Following them were the remaining two hundred Sujins, as grey and hard as the deepest bedrock and every bit as formidable looking. It would take an army of Nordish Jackals to seize the koch and its contents.

The procession left the shimmering city of Sunja, and by afternoon, they had crossed the fortified bridge of Maston, and rumbled into the Plains of Evun. Farmers, up before the dawn themselves, straightened from where they toiled and wiped the sweat from their eyes. With scythes in their hands, they watched the Sujins march by. Some raised hands to shield their eyes from the glare of the sun, while others simply squinted with screwed-up mouths. They all wondered what was afoot. A war was being fought and the farmers had been instructed that, in the event of invasion, the first act of defense would be setting fire to the great plains. It was best to burn an invader from the land and then deal with a mindless fire. As the farmers watched them go by, more than a few of them wondered if that terrible blaze would finally be birthed.

The force marched on, and by early evening, the distant dark plumes of an immense forest just barely could be discerned. Scouts urged their horses to designated points on the horizon, wary of threats, but they did not expect any real action. The war with Nordun was more than a three weeks' march away. The only possible threat this close to Sunja was brigands, and if they were foolish enough to mount an assault, then the more the better. They would be fresh meat for the butchers and a welcomed diversion. It would also save Sunja days and coinage trying to root out their ilk from the timberlands.

At the end of the first day, they camped on the open plains, just outside of the Hrand Forest. Bloor did not intend to risk an ambush in a wooded area at night. The orders to erect field fortifications came at early evening, and just as the sun disappeared below the horizon, they had thrown up two thick, earthwork walls, tightly packed and some three feet high. They parked the koch in the corner where the two walls met in an "L," and the grim royal Axemen split their force of twenty into two watches.

"Who are they expecting, I wonder?" the man named Hatch muttered aloud, watching the Axemen form a protective ring around the koch. "There is no one here. No one. No Nord or brigand would be this close to Sunja. Would they? So, who are we expecting trouble from? The walls and ditches should be protection enough. And why did we have to carry our own food this time? Where are the supply wagons?"

He and a group of Sujins lounged around a small fire pit and digested the evening's meal of tough rabbit stew. The remainder of the meal was in a pot, hanging from a spit laid across the fire, the smell of broth lingering in the air.

"Maybe they don't like the looks of you?" Gatesin spoke nearby, lying flat on his back and staring up at the clear night. "And maybe we got too fat in the infirmaries?"

"There is Marrn," Balto spoke in a low voice, lying down near Gatesin. He laced his fingers together and sighed as he took the weight off his feet. The night was pleasant, and if one was lucky enough, perhaps they could spot a falling star. Balto believed that a star falling from the sky was a good omen.

"Bah," Hatch remarked, scratching vigorously at his crotch and drawing a disturbed look from Gatesin. "I'm not worried about those dog lovers. They're just fine to sit behind their own walls and watch us and the Nords smash each other. Maybe even make short work of whoever wins."

"What in Saimon's hell are you scratching at?" Gatesin grated.

"The pair you don't have," Hatch threw back.

"Hard to believe you'll have a topper left if you keep that up. You'll be a damn fine farmer if you can scratch the land like that."

"Must've been that last wench I was with," Hatch remarked with a contented smile. Gatesin did not want to pursue the conversation any further. Hatch was prone to fleshing out details one would rather not hear.

The conversation lulled for a moment. "Good country, this," Balto observed and stretched his feet out to the campfire, enjoying the warmth at his soles.

"Aye," Hatch said after a while. "I plan to retire out here sometime, Seddon willing."

"Become a farmer?" Gatesin asked, a crook of a smile on his face. If a Sujin actually lived long enough, he could live his last days fighting a field and die hunched over with farmer's rot. It was an old joke amongst the more senior of them.

"Horse shite on that," Hatch growled. "Open up a tavern—a big one. With an upstairs and clean rooms and bedding instead of the lice holes you see along the road."

"With all the brigands about? You're a brave man!" Gatesin commented.

"It'll be a brave man to come and take a dart at my livelihood. I figure a nice tavern should draw the rabble to me. I want them to come. Easier to clean up the countryside that way. I'll make a killing on selling their weapons and armor."

Gatesin and Balto chuckled. Hatch was a practical sort. There was always a side thought to his way of thinking. They watched the man smell the same fingers he used to scratch himself.

"I thought of starting a brothel myself," Balto said. He dreamed of it often.

"You're joking," Gatesin said.

"A whorehouse?" Hatch exclaimed softly, his eyes shining at new prospects.

"A brothel," Balto corrected him. "And just that. It's the ideal business for me. I can give free women to the ones guarding the ladies. Clean rooms for the women themselves. Allow them to keep three-quarters of their price and the rest goes to me. I will make up for it on food and sauce. Maybe even marry the oldest after a while…" A sigh left him. He had thought long and hard on his future and this appealed to him the most. "A nice ending."

"Count me in, then," Gatesin said. "Be a fool to work at a place like Hatch's, anyway." He liked listening to Balto's voice in the evening. There was a gravelly sureness to his every word. The old man of the group would utter a sentence and pause, collect his thoughts, and start again. It was a comforting rumble, and not one man would dare interrupt him while he was mid-ramble. It would be like interrupting a bard in song.

"Hmm. Does sound better," Hatch agreed, only after he decided Balto wasn't about to continue. He began thinking of partnering up with the man. They were old companions. "But a whorehouse?"

"Brothel," Balto clarified.

"A *brothel* will be a bigger target for hard cases, don't you figure?"

Balto gazed up at the twinkling night sky. "Then I'll make a killing on the weapons and armor."

"That's my idea," Hatch said

"A good one," Balto granted him. "Maybe we could become partners? We could take on Gatesin over there. If he's still alive when we get around to it."

"I'll live," Gatesin promised him. "I can guarantee that."

Tungang and a group of other Sujins returned from first watch and plopped down amongst them with a beast's yawn. "What are you punces talking about?" He produced a wooden bowl and reached for the hanging pot. He made a face at what he dredged up, before making way for the next Sujin with a bowl. "And to think I got the best of the muck. Any bread about?"

Hatch tossed him a small loaf.

"Sweet Seddon! You toppers were hungry enough to eat this slop?"

"Here's a man, now," Balto said, drawing Tungang's suspicious attention. "What will you do when the Sujins are done with you? Will you really go back to your father?"

"Let a man have his bite first," Tungang said, digging into his food. He smacked his lips loudly, causing Gatesin to frown. He disliked noisy eaters.

The Tun barbarian bit into the bread, chewed for a moment, and said, "Maybe. Or maybe I'll stay about and make women out of any bitches you call daughters."

Laughter broke out amongst the campfire, and even Tungang smiled at this unexpected success. Balto chuckled, but then he realized the man just might do exactly what he said. Tungang continued eating nosily.

"What about farming?" Tungang shook his head.

"Only be more farms for me to burn, anyway," Gatesin commented.

Tungang regarded them all. "If I see any of you around my father's smithy, I'll cut you in half and make a gate of you," he threatened, his mouth full.

"Seen that before." Hatch remembered a time. "Damnedest thing! A Tun hewing a man in half with a pole axe. Biggest horse-shagger you've ever laid eyes on."

"Bigger than I?" Tungang said through another mouthful.

"He said horse-shagger," Gatesin told him. "Not sheep."

"I thought you had quit sheep," Hatch commented, with a wintry grin.

Tungang continued eating. "Funny gits, aren't ye? Why don't you just all go to sleep then? I'll protect you."

"What sleep?" a man named Tavan asked ruefully, before anyone could counter the Tun. "The watches have been tripled tonight. I heard from Tarco."

"And Bloor allowed it?" Hatch asked, his face doubtful.

"He did at that. He leads this rabble. I guess he should have some say in things."

"Sly one, aren't ye?" Hatch retorted, not appreciating the Sujin's sarcastic reply. "Never thought I'd hear the day when those two would be put on the same ship together. I heard they hate each other's guts."

"Where you'd hear that?" Balto asked. He felt sleep tugging at his eyelids, and shifted to get a little more comfortable.

"Around," Hatch assured his companion. "Word doesn't have to travel down this line, I tell you. Seems they have a long-standing feud with each other, as well. Over a woman, it seems. One that Tarco had a fancy for."

"Tarco had a fancy?" Balto rumbled softly.

"*Bloor* had a fancy?" Gatesin asked, drawn into the conversation now.

"I heard that Bloor insisted on Tarco coming along on this outing," Balto added.

Gatesin turned on his sword brother. "You *knew* he was leading us? And you didn't say a word?"

Balto shrugged. "I forgot," he said simply, earning himself a scowl from the other man.

"A bad omen, this," Gatesin muttered.

"You," Balto yawned, "are one to be talking about omens."

Tungang abruptly stopped eating. "What of omens then? And what about Bloor and Gatesin? What was Bloor going on about earlier? How does he know you?"

"Eat your bloody grub, Tun," Gatesin growled, in a low voice.

The Northman's face cracked in amusement. "Why should I?"

"Aye, why should he?" Tavan asked, even though he barely knew Gatesin. Gatesin gave the man a mild look of resentment.

"Go to sleep all of you. There are triple watches on this night and Primo will be about soon enough, I wager," Gatesin said, trying to shift the attention off himself. He then slapped at the ground, sending both dirt and a message flying in Balto's direction. It was all Gatesin needed, having Tungang and the others sniffing about what he would rather have kept silent, but the warning was lost on Balto.

The man was already asleep.

5

"Rusk!" Tarco roared at dawn's light. He pointed a huge, accusing finger at a nearby Sujin. "Find that bastard. He has a lot to answer for this day."

The soldier saluted and departed, leaving the Cavalier to curse Rusk again, not worrying in the least about who overheard him. Sujins! There were reasons to have them in the Klaws of Sunja. However, in Tarco's mind, none of them were of any worth. A rabble of ineffective cutthroats to the last man. Nothing compared to the Cavaliers, and this morning's farce was proof enough for him. To think that an entire shift of Sujins failed to take their turn at night watch. It was beyond him. How did Rusk manage that trick? The notion made Tarco's stomach sour and placed him in no mood for inspection. He might just throttle one over the barest detail. He gazed out at the encampment's defensive perimeter. Everywhere, the Sujins were breaking down camp.

Rusk appeared moments later, looking like a sleepy rat. He saluted. The action only infuriated the Cavalier.

"What's this I hear about a missed shift?" Tarco demanded.

"Aye, Lord. Missed. I've already looked into it and I know the officer responsible. It seems he felt some the men were sloppy in the day's work and took in it upon himself to reward them with the extra hours. The other ones got to sleep."

"Weren't you in charge of the watch?"

"I'm sorry, Lord...I was sleeping."

This was too much for Tarco. He placed a hand on his sword. "So, you like to sleep, do you?" he asked, with a deadly air.

"What's going on here?"

Tarco's hand dropped. There was only one man in camp that possessed that barrel-deep voice. He turned about to see Bloor, unarmored and wearing the traditional greens and whites of the order. Bloor glared at Tarco. In fact, it was rare *not* to see Bloor glaring at something. However, this time Tarco found himself to be the object under that thunderous gaze. He shriveled backwards a step before finding his courage.

"What's going on is that this stupid topper let a Koor decide who slept last night and who didn't. You're in time to see punishment meted out."

"You're not going to string up anyone," Bloor said in a low voice, darkly amused that Tarco thought he actually could.

"What?"

"Rusk," the Sujin straightened when Bloor addressed him. "Get the men fed and ready to move within the hour. Go."

"Lord Bloor," Two Knife saluted and left, barely suppressing the urge to flash the smuggest of looks in Tarco's direction. There would be another time.

Tarco faced Bloor with his fists on his hips, his blood rising high and hot enough to make his cheeks flush and his right eye twitch, "You have a reason to let this go?"

Bloor nodded once, slowly.

"Then what is it?" Tarco chewed on the words, rather than spoke them.

"Killing an officer won't help morale."

"You're concerned about morale?" Tarco's voice rose along with the color in his face. "What happens if we are attacked today? Most of these damn Sujins will be half-asleep!"

"That won't happen."

"That..." Tarco managed before his voice left him. Had the man been drinking? "How in Saimon's hell do you know we won't be attacked today? Where is this magical ball of yours?"

"Killing an officer—one of their officers—won't impress the Sujins or bend them to us. And they're Sujins. They've fought when they were tired before. They're trained to go on until they drop. They can do a day's work, I wager."

"You *wager?*" Tarco gaped at Bloor as if his head were suddenly missing. "You're so damned certain we won't be attacked this morning, and the mighty Bloor is willing to *wager* on it? Who are you? I demand to know who it is I'm talking to! Since when is a Cavalier commander content to let things lie on chance! Sweet Seddon, Bloor! They're supposed to die on our *word!* Why are you so concerned about what the Sujins think?"

The shouting made more than a few nearby heads turn in the Cavaliers' direction, but when the shouters were recognized, the curious onlookers quickly found something else to look upon.

"Do you know why I finally conceded to allowing you on this expedition, Tarco?" Bloor shifted tactics. "It was that, despite my particular dislike for you, I consider you to be a more-than-capable Cavalier. Show some wisdom in this case. Let the man live."

Tarco was amazed. "You are lecturing *me* on how to discipline *Sujins?* You? Didn't you once lop off a hand that had touched your goblet by mistake? Or have you forgotten that incident? A good many have not, and I'm one of them."

"I'll remind you, Tarco," Bloor stepped in close to the man, intruding upon his personal space. "I am the King's chosen officer here. And your father is nowhere in sight. You take your orders from me. Question my decisions, and I'll see to it you won't ever do so again."

"You're threatening *me*?" the veins in Tarco's neck were clearly visible.

"You will issue orders this day as if last night did not happen."

Tarco blinked in spite of himself.

"Is that clear?" No reply. It drew a weary glare from Bloor.

"Clear, *Lord*."

Bloor nodded. That was better. "I'll see to any punishment being met out. Me. Now, send out the scouts and that will be that. Understood?"

"As you wish, *Lord*."

Bloor almost smiled his disgust at the antics of this child. At times like these, it would be a pleasure to rock his hand across the other's conceited features. With effort, he kept his face blank. "Good. See to it then." Bloor turned halfway around to look at the encampment. "I'll be about." *Watching*, he left unsaid.

Tarco was certain that the pompous ass would be about somewhere. It was all he needed, to be challenged by a man who undermined authority whenever it suited him in the field. Fuming, Tarco made to leave, and Bloor, once again, noticed the veins in the man's neck. If the commander could incite his subordination just a fraction farther, those royal blue branches would surely rupture. However, he held his peace and merely stared down the other man.

Tarco snarled and spun about. He would tell his father about this day. Bloor let the man leave. He watched as Sujins deftly moved out of the storming Cavalier's path. No one would be blamed for staying out of his sight for the next day or two. Tarco had a reputation for being hard and taking out frustrations on whoever was handy, not unlike Bloor.

However, Bloor did what he did to maintain order. Besides, he had been feverish, half-drunk on mead, and suffering with a hacking cold during the goblet incident. It was something he would sooner forget. It had become an unwelcome tale around the campfires, though it did serve him well in keeping his troops in line.

Tarco would be dealt with, in time, and that time was approaching.

Bright sunlight spilled over the land, and in another section of the collapsing encampment, Rusk the Two Knife marched up to a single man standing alone, considering a suit of mail lying on the ground before him. "Morgat!" Two Knife shouted, drawing the attention of all nearby. The man came to attention immediately.

Rusk came up close to the man and peered into his eyes. "Did you get a good night's sleep last night? You sack of sheep guts! You worthless topper! Did you? I hope so, because you'll need everything you got to get through this day. By Saimon's blue *balls*, have I got a day for the wide-eyed likes of *you*! You won't even have the time to piss. And if you think I'm joking, we'll both have a laugh when you're pissing on the go! You puss pot! You ugly piece of meat!"

Morgat's features remained the same, unflinching in a barrage of the lowest and most insulting language that Rusk could command. The man had a face of unflinching ice, and his hooded eyes regarded his Right Koor like a person who knew he had fouled up. Two Knife kept on berating the Sujin, calling down the man's slut of a mother and his many fathers. The language was insulting enough that Sujins who did not think much of the tall, usually-quiet Morgat began to feel sympathy for the dog. By the sounds of it, Morgat would be clawing out all the latrine trenches with his bare hands.

However, Two Knife had no intention of doing such a thing. Instead of lessening his swearing at the man, he leaned in close to Morgat's ear and took a breath. "Good," he whispered, though his face was a terrible thing to behold. Those managing a peek in Morgat's direction noted how he didn't bat an eye in the face of Rusk the Two Knife, not once. Nor did anyone see how the man's downcast face lit up for only the briefest moment.

His message delivered, Two Knife pulled back and roared. "I hope you enjoyed your extra hours, because you and the other sleeping ladies will be working the land for three, since you have all that extra energy. After this day, Morgat, by Seddon's sunny arse, you'll wish you had perished in your sleep."

Morgat stared off into space, showing little sign of having heard anything.

"Get dressed," Two Knife hissed like a boiling pot. Morgat immediately did as he was told. It was one of the reasons Two Knife had approached him first. Morgat was a fully-fanged butcher, hiding amongst the sheep. He had no scruples whatsoever about taking a life, and Two Knife wondered if the man had a limit as to how far he would go. In the war with Nordun, Morgat had done many horrific deeds to strike fear into the hearts of the Jackals, and he had done so with the exact same stoic expression on his face.

Rusk whirled around and the watching Sujins quickly found something to occupy their attention. No one wanted Rusk down on them so early in the morning. The men took down the eight-man tents that they had used and folded them away. In the hustle of breaking camp, a ferocious-looking Rusk watched them all with frightful blue eyes. He raked his gaze to the left until he settled on the bulk of the koch they were protecting. Morning sunlight splashed over the frame, draping one side in shadow. Surrounding it were the Axemen, standing firmly at attention and appearing to need little of either sleep or food.

Two Knife studied them with a critical eye. Royal Axemen—he despised their very presence.

"Get moving you bloodless piles of guts," Two Knife suddenly roared at the Sujins. "This is going to be one of those days where you'll wish you never slipped out of that bitch of a mother's womb!"

6

With the sun coming up, Tarco wasted very little time in deploying the scouts ahead of the column. He rode at the head of the procession, flanked by the group of forty Lancers in bright battle dress. They rode in precise lines and kept their eyes fixed straight ahead. The Lancers were skilled riders in any army, and yet with his own upbringing and the training of the Cavaliers, Tarco looked upon them as little more than servants. They were a brave lot, he would give them that, but only brave enough to garner attention from him, perhaps hoping to be selected for the elite ranks of the Cavaliers. Let them hope.

The sky was a beautiful blue, but he paid no attention to any of it. The Plains of Evan, a billowing, narrowing sward of gold with a single dirt ribbon of a road parting it, were coming to an end. The approaching forest crowded in on the swaying fields, making them slowly disappear as if a dark curtain was being drawn across the land.

Tarco's scouts were somewhere ahead. They would alert him soon enough if anything was amiss. He spent much of the morning thinking about his episode with Bloor. He would accomplish this mission without error and report

Bloor's failure to properly discipline an officer. Tarco had other ears beside his father's that would listen with great interest to his report, and they would do him well when he succeeded Bloor in rank, naturally or otherwise.

The greater, thicker timberland drew closer. Behind Tarco and the Lancers, Bloor moved up and down the line, instilling unease wherever he went. It did not slip Tarco's attention that he stayed near the swaying koch as it moved along. Whenever Tarco looked back, he could see the dark figure of Bloor riding alongside the Axemen and their charge. He looked for only a short moment, for he hated to lay eyes on the man.

Ahead of him lay the deep green woodland known as the Hrand Forest, where Tarco sometimes had gone with his teachers and father when he was a child. The hunting there was plentiful, and these days, the depths of the forest could hide any number of unseen dangers. Childhood is blissful ignorance, the Cavalier thought, for now a place that was once a delight to explore was a place he would prefer to avoid. However, speed was a necessity in this journey and going around that dark place was impossible. They planned to go straight through. Tarco thought that if there was any place for an ambush at all, it would be there that it would be best sprung, but Bloor was willing to wager that they weren't going to be hit. *Idiot.*

"Sent the scouts out?"

Tarco swung in his saddle. Bloor did not notice the Cavalier's surprise, or if he did, he chose to ignore it. Tarco looked the man up and down. "Yes," he finally reported, not caring in the least how the man snuck up on him.

"I'm going to head north then. See if I can catch one of your men."

Tarco watched Bloor as he pulled on the cuffs of his metal gauntlets. "You? Riding out to scout?" The commander nodded solemnly.

"Decided to get a little dirty this day?" Tarco's humor was a thin veil of sarcasm.

The corner of Bloor's mouth hitched up in an answering smirk. "What would you know of getting dirty, Tarco?"

"I served on the front as often as you did," Tarco shot back loudly, disliking the attack on his service. He took any opportunity to announce his accomplishments in the field. "In fact, I imagine I would have served to an even greater degree if you weren't around to hold me back, day after day. There was a point when I could not even take a piss without you behind me," his back straightened, arrogant beyond Bloor's imagination.

"You can thank your father for that."

Tarco looked mortified for a moment, as if a great secret had just been revealed. He regained his composure in a beat. "You would like me to believe that. You did everything you could to keep me from earning my rightful place as a leader amongst the Cavaliers."

"By you taking a piss?"

"You know what I mean. Keeping me under watch. Not allowing me to head out on my own. Assigning me the least dangerous tasks."

Bloor shook his head, sadly. There was no talking to this idiot. "Another reason why I gave in and accepted you this time."

"Why exactly, Bloor?" Tarco's face crunched up in annoyed curiosity. "I'm getting tired of puzzling that one out. Did you hope that you could embarrass me again somehow? You won't, I'll have you know. I'm watching."

"Watch me leave, then," Bloor said, in a tired voice. "I'll be back later this day. With your scout." With that, he put his boots to his horse and the beast lurched forward in a rumble of hooves and dust.

Tarco watched the man ride off, quickly pulling ahead of the column. He couldn't care in the least when the bastard returned. If he was lucky, perhaps there would be several scores of Jackals out there waiting for a chance to pounce on a single Cavalier. If he was extremely lucky, he would see Bloor's head on a spear somewhere along the horizon. While thinking along the same vein, he realized that while the louse was away, he could command things his way. Louse, that was a good name for Bloor. Certainly much better than commander, which made Tarco want to feast on flesh every time he had to use it. He frowned. The image of Bloor's head on a Nord's spear shimmered before his eyes. If only he were so fortunate.

Two Knife also watched the shrinking figure of Bloor ride away. The Cavalier eventually disappeared out of eyesight amongst the distant trees. That was unexpected. Two Knife did not know that Bloor had planned such a thing. Where was the dog going? Even better, when would he be back? Leave it to that man to foul up a plan.

He stopped and studied the Sujins marching by. Here and there, some of them met his dark eyes and nodded. Rusk placed his hands behind his armored back and stretched until his vertebrae cracked. The koch and the ring of fearsome Axemen approached him, pole arms carried over their shoulders. Two of the legendary guardians gave him a scathing eye, wondering just what in Saimon's hell he was doing. Two Knife gave a unfriendly smile back, his thumbs playing with the hilts of his twin shortswords on either hip. They had gall, these royal bastards. Probably would talk down to him, too, if he gave them a command. They would definitely take their time in complying, arrogant toppers. He had never seen any of these prissy hardheads fighting the Jackals, and yet, they were held in the highest regards for protecting the king and his palace. He would wager that he personally had spilled more Nordun blood than the twenty Axemen surrounding that pile of lumber pulled on four wheels. And what was his reward? More fighting on the front, of course, but even deeper in the sweat and blood and shite of battle. Thinking about the unfairness of it all made the bile bubble up to the back of his throat.

The Axemen, Rusk seethed. The Axemen were supposed to be the best the empire had; unbeatable in single combat, or so they said. Rusk the Two Knife would see for himself.

Once free of the escort, Bloor rode hard, pushing his horse to its limits. He approached the thickening trees and looked back once he felt he was out of sight. The scenery he left behind him struck him as both empty and grand, and he appreciated the edge of the plains coming to an end. Since he was alone, he proceeded onwards at a much easier pace into the Hrand Forest. The timberland stirred up dark thoughts about what he would soon have to accomplish, distasteful but necessary as it was.

Everything relied on Two Knife. *Everything.*

He almost ran over the body of a scout and his horse. An angry storm of flies rose up, confused as to why their feasting had been disturbed. The warhorse stomped to a halt and Bloor directed his animal alongside the dead man and his horse, hidden by the tall grass. Reining in, leather creaked, and Bloor saw that the man was, indeed, one of their scouts. The ripe smell of blood assailed him. Flies buzzed around his eyes, yet he ignored them. Both the rider and his horse had been quilled with a fury of arrows, their combined blood staining the pristine prairie. Arrows had fallen around the bodies, their barbed heads nailed deep into the soft earth. The man had been caught napping.

Bloor looked about, wondering if the ambushers were still around. Flies continued their drone around the corpses. Flicking his reins, Bloor made his way deeper into the Hrand Forest.

Within the cover of the trees, an arrow was aimed at the approaching horseman. He was a shiny one and would not be difficult to hit. The archer knew the range and the strength of his horn longbow would easily punch an arrow through that shiny shell with an eye popping crack. His weapon quivered with the strain as he drew a bead on his target.

"Don't," a deep voice commanded him.

"What?" the archer asked, in surprise, his eyes widening in puzzlement.

"I said 'don't shoot.'"

"Why not?" the other protested. "He's coming right at us."

Alwan sighed heavily. Also a Cavalier, he wished they could have found more intelligent toppers for this task. As it was, he simply had to make do with what he had. He raised a finger.

"Who do you think that is?" Alwan indicated the nearing figure.

The archer squinted at the approaching Cavalier. A light of understanding came into his eyes. "Oh," he finally muttered, lowering his bow.

"Oh, indeed," Alwan straightened in his saddle. "You just saved your life, shagger."

"I wouldn't have missed," the archer rumbled.

"You might have. But I wouldn't." Without another word, Alwan snapped the reins of his horse and rode out to meet his friend.

7

The column of Sujins plodded onward in ranks of three. The early afternoon grew warmer, and a fresh breeze blew across the land and into their sweating faces. The men welcomed the wind, as a third of them were bone-weary from their lack of sleep, worsened by months of soft living in the Sunjan infirmary. For many of them, this expedition was the first real exercise since returning from the front, and their bodies complained.

Tarco pulled to the side and halted, inspecting the Sujins as they marched along. The koch came up, and from his driver's seat, Torham nodded in the Cavalier's direction. The Axemen, menacing with their fearsome pole arms held high and at the ready, surrounded the koch and barely acknowledged Tarco at all. That slight burned the Cavalier. He would like to see those tits march that wagon all the way to Marrn without him.

As Tarco sat in the saddle, transfixed by bloody images of Axemen being cut down by marauders, a figure moved against the march of the Sujins on the other side of the column. Rusk saw the Cavalier sitting on his animal, and kept his head down just enough to be unseen over the moving helmets of the Sujins. Watching the ground, he walked in a leisurely cadence towards the rear, and he believed, his destiny.

At one point in the road, a Sujin began a double-step to the head of the column. The movement caught Tarco's eye. He watched the man hurry along and recognized him as Toffer, one of the Sujin Koors. Tarco sighed in exasperation. What was happening now? He couldn't oversee every damn thing these dogs did. Tarco would make it a point to berate Bloor for his selection of these maggots, and he would make it known to his father, the minister, after the task at hand was seen to its conclusion.

With Tarco distracted, Two Knife strode towards the rear, nodding and flicking a hand at certain individuals in each rank. Some men returned the gestures while others scowled. Several men slipped hands onto their weapons. The Sujins, suffering from a lack of sleep, did nothing at all.

Following the koch, Gatesin marched on with Balto in the center and another Sujin named Hebrus on the far right, a grim, taciturn fellow. Rusk gave them all a nod as he went by. Only Hebrus nodded back.

"What in hell's name did I do to deserve that?" Gatesin muttered under his breath.

"Perhaps he likes you?" Balto responded casually.

"I truly am cursed then," Gatesin groaned back.

"Seems so," Balto said. He raised the back of his hand to stifle a yawn. It was contagious.

"Obviously he's been getting some sleep," Gatesin also yawned, and he cast a red eye around the countryside. "Seddon help me! What a sight. Not a damn thing to look at."

Without a thought, Gatesin turned and noticed Hebrus with his hand on the hilt of his shortsword.

"Hebrus," Gatesin said, "you've served under Two Knife before, right?"

"I have," Hebrus said. His breath rankled Balto's nose, even in the fresh air.

"You'd best stop washing your mouth out with dog piss," Balto commented, without looking at the man.

Gatesin waited for Hebrus to elaborate. When Hebrus did not, he rolled his eyes. "I guess you have," he finished in a sour tone. He clamped down on another yawn, making a face as he did so. It was going to be a long day.

Two Knife made it to the end of the column. There, wedged between two other Sujins, was his man, Klytus. Klytus was a mountain and often mistaken for a barbarian Tun. Klytus' murderous eyes met Two Knife's. In his breast and calves, that nervous energy that Rusk had come to expect before a fight began to build. This was a gamble of epic proportions. He had dreamed and schemed of such scenarios for a god's age it seemed, and to be finally given the opportunity was incredible. There would be no hesitation here, and no second thoughts. Two Knife made his decision in the name of Two Knife. He dropped into line with the Sujin on his left. Almost absently-mindedly, he drew one of his twin shortswords. The Sujin marching alongside the Right Koor did not suspect a thing. They were all Sujins.

Two Knife plunged his free blade into the Sujin's throat. The man staggered and fell to his knees, blood spraying, his flesh already paling. Klytus grabbed his own blade and gouged it into the ribs of the Sujin on his left. The man hopped up and down as if he had stepped barefoot on broken glass. Two Knife drew his second sword and drove it into the back of the Sujin ahead of him. He gasped like an old man and fell like a stone.

The Sujin next to Two Knife's victim stabbed the man next to him. He screamed in shocked agony and fell backwards, trying in vain to avoid the blade slipping into his guts. On that exact mark, a deadly chain reaction ripped up through the ranks and a chorus of howls from the dying and their killers went up throughout the procession. Traitorous Sujins pulled their blades free and stabbed at the men beside them, killing or wounding the first victim and then striking out at the other man in the rank. Heads were taken clean off in some cases, or shield arms were slashed useless at the shoulders. The ranks dissolved as if dipped in acid, and in a blink, the survivors desperately tried to place distance between their attackers and make sense of what was happening.

Screams resounded and cut through the air, adding terror to the confusion. Of the four hundred Sujins, the surprise strike of Two Knife's Sujins claimed almost a third of the number.

Two Knife flicked his sword across the face of a man who had survived the initial cut. The loyalist Sujin buckled backwards in pain and crashed into another behind him. Two Knife stepped in as if pouncing on an insect. He stabbed the first man through the belly and slashed the other's throat, his twin swords striking as if possessing minds of their own. Klytus grabbed another man by his helmet. He yanked the head down onto his sword and felt the steel punch through skull. He unslung his shield and plowed it into another victim, ramming its edge upward into the man's nose. A dragon's roar escaped Klytus and he kept close to the back of Two Knife. Together, they advanced though the scrambling knots of confused men, cutting and stabbing the loyalist Sujins seeking to fight or flee.

Tarco's head whipped around at the first cry, his fingers already clutching his sword. Before him, the entire column fountained blood and chaos. Some of the Sujins broke ranks and ran off to save themselves from their attacking brethren, while others struggled to clear their own blades. Some of the attackers missed their first strike and found themselves caught between two suddenly-furious Sujins, loyal to the crown. Guttural cries of terror and pain rang throughout. Rancid curses flew.

What was happening? Tarco's mind shrieked. Then, even as he was thinking, a Sujin charged him. *Him!* The man's shield went up, the tip of a sword pointing out from underneath like a great thorn. Tarco yanked his blade free and hauled on the reins of his horse. The beast swung sideways. The Sujin's stabbing sword took the animal square in the chest, and in a breathless rattle, it collapsed, taking Tarco down with it.

The Cavalier threw himself away, lucky to have become entangled in the stirrups. He landed in a roll and rose slower than he should have. The noise of fighting was in his ears. He whirled about and knocked aside the thrust for his heart. Snarling, the Sujin before him stabbed again, but the Cavalier had recovered.

Whatever Bloor might have thought of Tarco, for whatever reasons, none of them was about being a slouch with a blade. A scowling Tarco parried and stepped inside the man's guard, hacking off the extended sword arm as he went along. He spun out of the man's spraying embrace and faced another.

Tarco quickly dispatched his attacker with a short stab to the man's throat. The steel tip punched in and out as fluid as a sewing needle, dropping the man as if the very ground rose up to bite his legs off. Tarco looked to his horse and saw the bloody froth falling from its lips. Its dark eyes beheld him, frightful over the rictus of a mouth. Rage blossomed inside of the Cavalier. When one of the Lancers came at him, he ducked under a slash and sheared off a horse's leg. Man and beast crashed to the ground, half-landing on one of the corpses behind Tarco. The Cavalier deftly stepped over to the rider and stabbed the stunned man through the back of his neck. Vertebrae popped.

Sujins and Lancers killing Sujins! No one came at Tarco for the moment, and so he took the time to gauge what was happening. Even the Lancers hacked at one another. While there weren't so many instigating a fight, Sujins following from close behind ran forward and stabbed at the warhorses. Some horses kicked out and sent armored men flying through the air. Obviously, not all the men were treacherous, but that did nothing to lessen Tarco's disgust. This would never have happened if only Cavaliers were delivering the koch. Oh, how Bloor would burn for this!

However, then his mind hitched on a single thought. *The koch.* Tarco's eyes widened with understanding. He began making his way to the koch, heading into the thick of the fighting. Beyond clumps of fighting men lay the stalled koch, the Axemen's lines unflinching. Tarco snarled, and with each step his face grew even more furious, as if he had found worms in his morning's bread. These maggots had shown themselves now, and he would root them out by himself if he had to, one by one.

Gatesin heard the first thrust on Balto before he saw it. He heard Balto grunt, and then the scrape of metal on metal. "Dog balls!" Gatesin swore. Movement. Hebrus drawing his sword back for a second thrust. The Sujin ahead of him ran his blade through the ribs of the man on his left, spinning and whipping the steel across the throat of another. Gatesin got his shield up and blocked a thrust from the Sujin behind him. He parried another thrust and deflected yet another with his shield.

"Dog balls!" he hissed, louder this time, and pulled his sword out. He killed his attacker with one thrust, splitting the man's helmet and the face underneath.

Hebrus tried to stab Balto again. He rushed his thrust, and Balto, instinct leading his body and arm, twisted his shield into the weapon. His blade leaped out and up and cut Hebrus from chin to forehead, whipping the man's head back and sending a fine line of gore into the air. Hebrus sank to the ground, and Gatesin stood there.

Balto readied himself for an attack and for a split moment the sword brothers locked eyes, swords at guard. Before and behind them, Sujins tore into Sujins with a savage intensity. These were not nervous conscripts fighting. These were tried and true hell pups that had seen battle and lived to talk about it.

"Are you... you?" Gatesin yelled at the man.

Balto's face twisted up. "What do you mean?"

"What's happening, then?" Gatesin flung at Balto. To his right, a man reared up with bloodied sword. Out of instinct, Gatesin sided with Balto. The attacking man blinked, sizing up two ready warriors instead of taking one by surprise. He retreated, looking for easier meat.

"Run," Balto said to his companion, and bolted for the distant tree line. Without a word, Gatesin ran after him. Fleeing this mass of confusion where he didn't know why he was cutting up Sujins seemed the best course of action. They could size up the situation from a distance.

Towards the koch, the fighting intensified, while behind them, the bodies began to pile up in earnest. As soon as Gatesin had escaped the line, he glanced back. Tungang burst out of the furious combat, leaving a dead Sujin falling and split like a grisly ear of corn. The Tun had shunned his shield and held his battle axe two-handed as he pumped his legs for whatever they were worth. Shouting out curses in his native tongue, he spotted the fleeing pair and made for them.

"What's happening?" the Tun roared at the partnered men.

Neither of them wasted breath in replying. They ran on. Grimacing, Tungang followed. However, as he ran along, Gatesin suddenly knew why Sujins were hacking at Sujins. He slowed to a stop and turned around, mouth hanging open in amazement.

The koch. Seddon above. *Money!* It was for whatever riches were inside that box on wheels that the battle had been staged. Already, he could see the Axemen ringing the transport, pole arms hewing at all who attempted to reach it. They were not overly-concerned with who they killed. In their eyes, this was a Sujin matter, and they, the elite, were surrounded by Sujins all gone insane. In a torrid river of death and dying, theirs was an island of sanity and safety, and one that they would defend to the death.

"What are you about, then?" Tungang yelled at Gatesin, as he neared.

"Trying to make sense of it all. They want the koch."

"Who?"

"Someone," Gatesin replied, grimly. "Follow me."

"To where?"

Gatesin pointed with his sword. "Beside me, and not behind."

Tungang's eyes became livid for a moment, but he did as he was told. Both men broke into a run then, following Balto, who now had placed a sizable gap between them.

"And try not to get pig-stuck," Gatesin warned.

It looked as if his curse was working wonders, yet again.

8

Two Knife parried a sword to the outside and stabbed over the blocking shield. He pushed and felt bone. The Sujin behind the barrier gasped and fell backwards. Two Knife moved on. He stopped to cut downwards at an exposed knee, taking the leg off below it. He pushed his victim into the rabble ahead and strode forward, his eyes on the prize of the koch. Behind him, Klytus brained the fallen man with one powerful chop of his sword. Two Knife could see the Axemen. The nut had presented itself, but first they would have to cut through its shell. Surprise had worked well, it seemed; however, they would still have to work fast. The real chore was approaching rapidly. Two Knife again cursed Bloor for bringing these bastards in at the last moment. If the Axemen weren't here, the koch and the treasure within would have been theirs already.

Morgat appeared, ashen-faced, trading blows with a bear of a Sujin. Keeping his eyes fixed ahead, Two Knife plunged a sword into the bear's back. The warrior twisted around at this betrayal, howling, and Morgat swept his blade down, splitting the man's head in two. Two Knife moved on; Morgat followed. The plan to stop the march from both ends, roll up the loyalists, and meet in the middle was going like a tear in an old shirt. Bloodied Sujins fell in step behind the trio of men, disengaging their defeated comrades and leaving them either dead or dying. Together, a growing mass of Sujins marched on the stalled koch and the Axemen waiting there.

Tarco stopped a sword on his shield and stomped on a foot. A girlish scream pierced the noise of the battlefield. The Cavalier diverted another shield to his left and jabbed his blade into the shoulder of a Sujin. The man fell, wailing. Then, in the sun of the day, a shadow crossed the Cavalier.

Tarco spun, sword licking out. He cut the charging Sujin across the cheeks and noseguard, stopping him in his tracks. Stunned as he was, the Cavalier quickly made meat of his attacker and flung him to the dark red ground being churned into a frightful mud. Another Sujin crossed his path. Before attacking, the man saluted. Tarco gnashed his teeth. A salute from a traitorous snot? He'd make this one suffer, Seddon piss on his soul.

Coming up on where Tarco fought, Two Knife watched the Cavalier quickly step aside and to the rear of the challenging Sujin. His sword stabbed downwards into the hollow of a bent knee. Blood sprayed. The Sujin dropped to his knees, flailing as if trying to swat a pesky gnat. Tarco covered the man's head with his shield and stabbed again with the other.

Tarco.

Shortswords twirling like wild teeth, Two Knife increased his stride. Today would indeed be a good day.

Another war dog challenged Tarco, screaming as if he had just been yanked from between his mother's legs. Tarco smashed him with his shield, slipping his blade up into guts. Chain mail links popped. Tarco wrenched his weapon free and shoved the dying body aside.

The Cavalier turned about then and saw Two Knife approaching with his whirling swords. A pack of hard-faced Sujins followed him. Several of the men Tarco recognized with a growing sense of disbelief. How many were there? Over Rusk's shoulder, Kyltus grinned evilly at the approaching fight. Now, there was one man that Tarco was not surprised to see going over to another side.

The Cavalier scowled. "The dogs are tired of their masters?"

Two Knife came on. "I'm just tired of you."

Tarco attacked. Two Knife caught the man's blade on his left hilt and twisted it down. The Sujin Koor swung his right blade and smacked it halfway into the Cavalier's neck. Tarco's eyes popped open at the blunt connection, not really feeling pain but aware of something dead-wrong, like a cautious swimmer no longer able to feel the bottom of the lake. Only a moment ago, his body and mind were one, responding to every threat perceived and meeting it with deadly force. However, now Tarco's mind was suddenly alone, his awareness fading. He slowly sank to his knees, sword and shield falling.

Two Knife bent in close to Tarco's dying ear. "I'm *that* good, maggot. I'm that good."

Two Knife placed his boot on the dead man's hip and pulled his sword free. Blood splashed—an almost impossible amount of it. He wanted to foul this arrogant bastard even more, but there was still work to be done.

Before him, the fighting subsided. Most of the loyal Sujins were dead, although some had taken off during the fight. Some had even tried approaching the ring of Axemen surrounding the koch. To Two Knife's amusement, two of them were hacked down immediately. *Axemen*. Two Knife shook his head in appreciation. It was unfortunate he could not win over any of their order. If only he had known they were going to be here. In truth, it was useless to even try to convert them. The elite guardsmen were fanatical; it was unfortunate.

However, that also meant he would have to fight them. Tarco was a disappointment, but Two Knife was becoming increasingly aware of his own ability. He was that good. He suddenly wondered just how good Sunja's fabled reapers, the royal protectors themselves, would be. Without a word, Two Knife and his growing group of Sujins strode towards the ring of Axemen.

"Sweet Seddon!" Primo roared at the Axeman named Sallo. "I just killed three of the bastards, right before your eyes! That should be proof enough."

Tall Sallo stood with his hands strangling his pole arm. Like all of the royal reavers, he was a bear, scrubbed clean of anything resembling weakness or fear. The Axemen were a unit unto themselves and all others were regarded as beneath them. They were selected and hardened at handling potential assassinations from all angles, even from within their own army, yet not from within their exclusive group. That this revolt came from within the ranks of Sujins only strengthened their belief that they were unquestionably superior to them. Admitting any of these weaklings within their ring of protection could be disastrous. The man ranting at them could be a traitor. How could one tell? It was not too difficult to close ranks when Sujin fell upon Sujin. Some had sought refuge within the Axemen's ring, but they were driven off. The Sujins did not attack them, and the Axemen did not break ranks. Loyal or not, the elite dealt with any of them coming too close with glares or killing strokes.

Two Sujins had actually challenged them. The first lost his head in one overhead chop, and the other was laid open and twitching on the ground, split open from chin to bloody navel.

"Do not come any closer, Sujin," Sallo warned in a surprisingly calm voice. Primo could almost believe he was talking to a corpse if it weren't for the bodies marking the edge of the Axemen's boundary.

From atop the koch, a pallid Torham fidgeted and twisted at the reins of the horses. His orders were clear: Stay with the koch, but stay with the koch behind a wall of Axemen? Torham was glad he was sitting, for he doubted he could stand. When the Axemen slew the two Sujins, he felt only a drop better. They had not killed him yet, and thus, they did not suspect him as one of the traitors. No one had prompted him to move the koch. Or they had merely forgotten about him. Either way, Torham sat as quietly as possible, not even wanting to breathe for fear of attracting their attention.

"What are we to do, then?" Primo demanded.

"As you like," Sallo said, eyeing the mass of Sujins approaching from the front and the back of the now destroyed line.

Primo looked about him. The fighting had died down it seemed, and the positioning of the survivors had begun. A few Sujins he knew ringed the perimeter of the twenty royal terrors, but he knew where their loyalties lay. To the east, behind the koch, he saw some men fleeing towards the far-off forest. Watching them go, his stomach turned over. There were a handful of Sujins on guard behind him as well, visibly aware of being caught between the traitors who they once trusted and the Axemen.

"What about them?" Primo gasped.

"What about them?" Sallo didn't bother looking where the man was pointing.

"They're against you, as well!"

"Obviously."

"Then, if that's plain to see, isn't it just as plain to see that we're not part of their lot?"

"No," Sallo replied, with a stoicism that made Primo want to smash the man.

Sallo saw the man's feature's twist up in anger. "I'll grant you this," the Axeman's voice became louder, "go now. If any of you are truly loyal to our liege, then return to him and tell him what has happened here. Tell him and greet us when we return with the head of the leader of this rabble."

Standing no more than fifty paces away from the Axemen, with the koch now in the center, Two Knife's Sujins heard the words aimed at them. Rusk shook his head. The Axemen were a distrustful lot, but he supposed he would be as well, if their roles were reversed. He signaled his Sujins to stop, allowing stragglers to join the circle. He would need all of his dogs for the legendary Axemen.

Primo cursed, again, and motioned for the men about him to follow. The small band moved, unchallenged, around the fortress of Axemen, and beat a path towards the distant few, almost lost in the far-off tree line.

Desso looked to Two Knife, who shook his head. "Let them go," he said. He wasn't concerned with them in the least. He was concerned with facing the last barrier protecting the riches of the koch. He motioned for his Sujins to spread out and surround the Axemen, giving them a wide berth. It pleased Two Knife to see that the majority of his dogs were still alive. He wondered how many would still be when the day was done. However, first they must try what he believed would be futile, but would try nevertheless.

"Who is in command here?" Two Knife yelled out, and waved a single, shortsword.

Sallo acknowledged the hail, and looked at the Sujin Koor.

"I salute your loyalty here, so I'll give you a choice," Two Knife shouted. "Walk away now. Just walk away. Leave. Or, stay and join us. But if you *stay* and raise arms against us, you will all perish to a man...and *that*, I guarantee, will happen. So you have your choices. Two of them are wise. One is stupid. So, choose."

Sallo watched as something was handed to Two Knife and he showed the Axemen his back for a moment. Sallo had heard of this Sujin Koor, but did not know much other than that the man was dependable. He also had the reputation of being a troublemaker. Sallo felt loathing coil up within his breast.

The Sujin spun about and heaved the head of Tarco at them. The grisly trophy bounced once and dribbled a short distance before stopping at the feet of the Axemen. Sallo considered the head as if it were a melon gone bad. That was a mistake. If there were any choice to be made, Two Knife had just made it for them.

The grim Axeman drew breath. "Any salute from the likes of you is an insult, no more welcome than a bare-handed slap across one's own balls. I offer you this in return: Leave now, and if you are lucky, perhaps you will find your way back to your Nordish piss-pot spawning grounds. Maybe they will have more liking for you and give mercy. Any mercy will be *more* than what we will offer if you stay. Set upon us now, and we'll wound as many as we can and later stretch you out on these plains. Nail you to the ground with whatever is nearby. Those who die quick will be the lucky ones. Those who hold on will regret each passing second they threw in with the likes of you!"

The words were delivered with such sureness that none amongst Two Knife's Sujins found the offer the least bit amusing. To each man, all were suddenly aware that they now were branded forever as enemies of their birthplace. The slaying of their fellow sword brothers had changed their path, and there was no going back from this point on, not ever. Even Two Knife, once drunk on the rush of felling Tarco, sobered up immediately. He appeared to think on Sallo's words for a moment.

"There is enough coin in that box you are guarding for all of us," Two Knife threw out, finally.

"Is *that* what this is all about?" Sallo yelled back. "*Coin?* Is not service to the king privilege enough? The thought that his very own Sujins would steal from him is one I cannot begin to dwell on! The thought sickens my guts."

"But…"

"You're talking far too much now. You had the balls to cut down Tarco, but you hesitate to take us? You waste time here. Come and get killed, all of you. And know that when we are done butchering you like the fat sheep you are, we'll find the bitches you think of as mothers and make sure no more of you are born into this world. And if they can remember the names of your fathers, we'll find them too, and castrate them with wood saws."

Two Knife's back straightened as if he had been slapped. "Righteous bastard," he hissed. Behind him, the unmovable gloom that was Klytus stood with his weapons ready. His Koors, Desso and Toffer, were also nearby. His Sujins thinly surrounded the Axemen's ring.

However, how many would remain after the Axemen?

"You won't turn them, Rusk," Toffer said, wearily.

"I'd be surprised if you did," Desso added.

"You both turned," Morgat hissed nearby, his hooded eyes moving from one to the other. "And you didn't have riches in your purses, either."

"I wasn't talking to you," Toffer sneered. He didn't like Morgat at all. He had heard stories of the man, and he thought Morgat to be not right in the head. The man liked killing too much.

"You were talking to me," Two Knife said, "but you called me by my old name. Don't do it again, else I slap you across the face with a mace. A tickle you won't soon forget, I imagine."

Toffer frowned and nodded his understanding. It was only a slip, but Two Knife's tone carried a warning, and Toffer did not need a man capable of killing a Cavalier becoming harsh with him. Two Knife didn't just kill the Cavalier; he *executed* him.

"Morgat," Two Knife commanded, "have everyone with bows string them up, quickly and quietly."

The renegade Sujin leader kept his eyes on the Axemen as Morgat melted into the ranks of slayers behind. Closing with them would be costly, indeed, but a part of him wanted to test himself on the Axemen's metal. However, filling them full of arrows as they were would not be so bad though, he admitted to himself.

Two Knife thought of Torham, briefly. "Hurry," he said.

"It has been done," came back the words.

The Royal Axemen selected Sallo when he was twenty. By twenty-two, he was a veteran of the unit. He was big, a hellion with a broadsword, and dedicated to his king. In time, the king actually addressed him by name and promoted him to the rank of Right Koor amongst the elite protectors. Perhaps some would not consider it much, but given the high status of already being favored by the Axemen, it was as good as being promoted to commander in one of the five Klaws of Sunja. The move further bound Sallo in his devotion to his king and the royal family. He would forfeit his life to save any of them.

When Sallo was asked to protect the koch, he never thought that the threat would come from Sunja's own army, and Sujins, at that. As coarse as they were, Sujins were still thought to be utterly loyal to the king. Any other thought was unthinkable, and yet, here they were, as mutinous as if they were on the high seas. The traitors were demanding that which had been entrusted to him by royalty. The very thought stabbed him to the core. *Let them come closer then*, he thought blackly, *and we shall see who lives to see the evening sun.*

"Hold your ranks, all of you," Sallo ordered from behind his pole arm, the butt of the long, two-handed weapon braced against the earth. Sallo did not carry a shield, nor did any of the other Axemen. Broadswords of the highest quality were strapped to their armored forms.

"They are doing something," said an Axeman on Sallo's right. That they were, but what?

From atop the koch, Torham thought the same thing.

Then they guessed it, even as they heard the thrum of arrows and saw the black wave flashing at them, enough to turn their knees to liquid. The Axeman on Sallo's right gurgled as the flight of arrows struck home, knocking him off his feet, pole arm flying from his fingers. Two arrows pierced Sallo and forced him to the ground. Five other Axemen were struck in a flurry of iron barbs. Armor deflected some of the arrows, bouncing off steel plates, but several arrowheads punched through. Some Axemen whose helmets offered no facial protection at all dropped to their knees to cradle their bleeding features. One man fell to his knees, as three arrows almost magically stuttered into his chest.

Seven Axemen went down in the first barrage.

Two Knife fought down his glee when the Axemen on the edges of the koch managed to duck behind its armored bulk. The arrows had ripped through the first wall of Axemen, and even better, none of the horses had been hit.

"Again," Two Knife commanded. Morgat relayed the order.

Sallo rolled over onto his stomach and crawled back towards the koch. An arrow stuck out from his left bicep, but the one in his right leg snapped off when he flipped over. Pain exploded a second time.

"Stay behind the koch!" he heard someone yell. He believed it was Rover. Rover was a good man. If he survived this day, he would go far. Sallo got his head into the space under the koch when he heard the snap of bowstrings. Several of those beats ended in Sallo's lower body and legs, and he bared his teeth with each impact. The Axeman collapsed under the koch, arms outstretched. Hands gripped his forearms, and he was pulled through to the other side. Rover rolled him onto his side, for fear of causing his Koor even greater agony. Sallo's legs resembled bloody skewers of meat. The color drained from Rover's face.

"Kill...them," Sallo grunted through clenched teeth. Spittle, spawny-red, seeped through them. "Move...the wagon...and kill..."

Sallo eyes became glassy, and he went silent.

Rover closed the man's blank eyes. His face twisted upwards. "Torham!" The driver stuck his head over the edge of the koch. The fact that the driver had not been touched did not occur to Rover. "Move the koch! Go! We'll follow!"

Torham nodded and his head withdrew. He fidgeted in the driver's seat. In front of him and on his right, the remaining Axemen huddled together. A field of dead and rabid Sujins lay just beyond, and Rover wanted him to move?

Torham thought fast. If he moved, he would outpace and expose the Axemen, giving the Sujins a clear shot at them. He clutched at the reins of the horses and snapped them into movement. They started out slowly. Torham cracked the reins again and again, cursing them to hurry. He heard the Axemen shout at him to slow down, and he grinned in fright. *Not likely!* Not when he was away from them. The koch jumped and bucked with gathering speed. The shouts became lost in the thunder of the horses, and he saw the line of wilderness to his right.

Then two punches nailed Torham from behind, and the reins fell from his fingers. He suddenly could not draw breath. His head rolled. His body sagged and fell. The last thing he saw was the cloudy blue of the sky. Driverless, the koch bumped and swayed to the right, towards the forest line. The horses began running as if their reins were on fire.

From the cover of the timberlands, a group of Sujins watched.

"That bastard," Gatesin said.

"He's one of them," Balto stated with cold authority. "The driver's one of them."

"I'll take care of that," said a hard-looking Tavan. He barely escaped the traitorous attack. He gauged the distance and brought up a long bow. As he aimed, the bow string stretched audibly.

"You'll never make the shot," Primo panted from nearby.

"*You'd* never make the shot," Hatch retorted, fixing the officer with a knowing eye. "That boy would shoot an arrow up the eye of your prick."

"That good, eh?" Tungang said in mock skepticism. Primo gave the Northman a warning look.

"You'll never make the shot," Gatesin said.

"Never make it," Primo echoed, watching the Sujin archer measure the rapidly-closing range.

Then Torham tumbled from his perch and disappeared under the wheels of the koch. The Sujins were speechless and all turned to Tavan, who lowered his bow with its unshot arrow.

"He made it?" Primo said, unbelieving, not bothering to look.

"Not him," Balto said.

"Didn't need to make the shot," Tavan muttered. "That came from *them*."

"Guess the driver wasn't with the bastards at all," Gatesin observed. The koch, driverless now, raced towards them, bouncing in unseen hollows. "And look what's coming our way."

"Aye, and making fine good time too."

"At least those devils won't get it," Primo said. "Try and slow it down once it gets here."

"Slow down a charging koch?" Balto asked him, inclining his head doubtfully.

"I said *try!*"

"Let's see what…" Gatesin shut up then, as at that very moment, he heard the words that turned his own knees to juice.

"*Help! Someone, please!*" came the scream, a woman's scream.

Balto met Gatesin's disbelieving face. It was suddenly clear now. Royal Axemen, the massive escort, and the Cavaliers. Money, be damned! They were escorting royalty!

From where he stood under the thick greenery of the trees, Primo's jaw dropped. His surprise did not go unnoticed.

"Sweet Seddon above," Balto mumbled, breaking into a run for the koch. "Why didn't they *tell* us?"

Gatesin followed, as did the rest of the Sujins, having heard the same shrill shriek.

9

Two Knife's reaction was one of pure delight. He watched as the Axemen were slowly left behind by the speeding koch. Behind him, Morgat gave the word and a flight of arrows flew into the air, showering down on the elite guardsmen where they stood. The men were too big to miss. They appeared like a poor rehearsal of players on a stage, trying to catch a receding curtain. He laughed as an Axeman spun about, an arrow taking him in the shoulder. Two more arrows punctured his chest as if his armor were cloth, punching him to the ground. Another missile plunged downwards into the neck of an Axeman, dropping him to his knees. All was going better than planned. All that was needed now was for Torham to…

Then he saw it. Two arrows lanced Torham through the back. To Two Knife, it seemed as if the man was in the seat one moment and the next he was diving for the ground. His teeth clenched as the driver disappeared. In truth, he would have killed the man himself, but not until the maggot had brought around the booty.

"The horses!" he suddenly roared. "Kill the horses!"

Morgat fixed him with a confused look.

"Would you rather pick up the koch in Marrn?" Two Knife bawled at him.

Morgat bellowed for his archers to ready their arrows. Then came a scream, a scream that suddenly became a terrible chorus of men getting ready to kill. Morgat's hooded eyes widened. Two Knife's surprise matched the killer's. Together, they looked in the direction of the new voices. At that moment, the single shriek of a woman's voice was swallowed up and unheard by the traitorous Sujins.

"Hold!" Two Knife barked, and his archers dropped their sights. The rogue leader whirled about to Toffer. The man was shrugging helplessly; this was beyond him.

"Two Knife!" Desso yelled out. "Riders! Ahead of us!"

Two Knife's brow bunched up in sudden confusion. Riders? He and his Sujins struggled to see, the Axemen momentarily forgotten. There, erupting from the tree line on the left, was a solid line of horsemen. Screams of war tingled their ears.

Doubt clouding his face, Desso looked to Two Knife. "Visigar!"

Perhaps a hundred of the barbaric horsemen thundered across the plains, lances held on high like fearsome flag poles. Two Knife's eye flared open. What were *they* doing here? A glance told him the koch had almost made the cover of the forest. It would be easy to find, but first...

"Morgat!" Two Knife shouted. Morgat and his archers turned to face the new threat. Two Knife then whirled on his other two Koors. "Form up a battle line. Shields out and up!"

"We'll be ripped apart," a nervous Toffer quavered.

Two Knife silenced him with a look. "Then we'll be ripped apart!" he roared. "Get on with it!"

Toffer and Desso scrambled through the muddled mass of Sujins, roaring and swearing to get them into formation. Klytus turned, a dark mountain with the sun at his back, baring a yellow-tooth snarl at the thought of taking Visigar heads. The entire body of Sujins rippled, shifted, and fluidly transformed. Some of the Sujins gathered up lances from the fallen Sunjan Lancers and pointed them outwards. Desso glanced left and right from behind the line and looked back at Two Knife.

"*READY!*" the lesser Koor roared.

Riding ahead with his Visigar allies, Bloor saw the wall of shields butted into the ground before their charge. Another row of shields clamped down atop the wall like a slanted roof. There were a few spears poking out. He knew them to be those of the dead Sunjan Lancers. The Sujins themselves did not carry spears with them on this trip; Bloor had made certain of that.

With Alwan at his side and his Visigar mercenaries close behind, Bloor rolled his shoulder and loosened up his sword arm. Something had already happened with the koch; he could see it charging off toward the forest. Had Tarco somehow detected them and sent the vehicle away? Possible, but something else struck Bloor as the gap between the two forces began to close. There were corpses littering the ground. The Cavalier commander ground his teeth. Bloor knew this was the way it had to be, had accepted that there would be lives lost. He hoped, again, that his plan would be accomplished and vowed to remember the dead. He then set his mind on killing every black-hearted Sujin standing against him. It would be difficult. The Sujins were trained to withstand Lancer charges. Bloor scowled behind his helmet's visor. It was time to see just how well they had learned.

The gap closed.

The Sujin wall loomed up, their swords and spears gleaming.

The Visigar began to sing a battle hymn. The low-pitched sound slowly swelled over the thunder of hooves. Faces were set.

And they lowered their lances.

The surviving loyalists watched the koch tear into the forest. In a crackle of snapping branches, the trees swallowed it whole. The vehicle disappeared from sight. The sound of its crashing through the forest began to lessen in the din of another sound. Balto was the first to slow, upon hearing the new noise. Gatesin and Primo followed, and then the remaining men stopped in their tracks to look back at the field.

"Seddon piss on us all," Hatch muttered, shaking his head. It was not a good day to be a Sujin. They watched and heard the brazen smack of steel on steel, as a charging wall of horsemen plowed into the Sujin ranks. Cries of pain and rage exploded in the air surrounding the two groups. Even at this great distance, the loyalists cringed as the two forces smacked together like opposing mauls. Then the killing began in earnest.

Gatesin was glad he had gotten his arse out of there when he did.

"Them's Visigar," Hatch commented from where he stood, recovered from his jaunt across the field. "I can tell. The way they keep their line. And all that howling. They do that. Noisy bastards."

Balto looked grim. "Let's hope that's the only thing they do well."

"Damn hard thing to say," Hatch spat. "A bad day of it all around. First this and now that. The punces must have been eyeing us earlier. Just waiting."

"There'll be a lot less of whoever wins," Gatesin said.

"And they'll be looking for the koch," Primo said. "And us."

"Who is in that box?" Hatch wanted to know. Rank meant little to him at the moment.

Primo made a face. "I have no idea," he told them the truth. "And it's none of your concern. But we're moving after that box right now. Come on!"

Gatesin chanced a look at Balto's set face. The man said nothing. That was, perhaps, a good sign. It meant he had an idea. Gatesin had come to respect and look up to Balto as a thinker and even as family, dare he admit it. If the man had an idea, it was usually a sound one.

Without any further words, the loyalist Sujins turned and disappeared into the throat of the forest, clawing their way after the lost koch.

When Morianna felt the koch begin to move, a rush of relief coursed through her so strongly that she almost collapsed on the softness of her green satin bunk. She was moving, and hopefully escaping. Through the slits in the armor plating of the koch, she watched the terrible fighting outside. Never had she witnessed such raw carnage, as repulsive as a blocked sewer. *Worse* even, and the *blood*... She turned her thoughts to other things: Sujins. It shocked her to see Sujins fighting and killing other Sujins as well as Royal Axemen. It shocked her even more to hear the words spoken by the leader of the Sujin traitors.

Coin.

"Coin in that box."

As soon as she heard the words, she set about searching. She searched all about the cramped quarters of the koch and found nothing. If there was coin in here, where was it? She would gladly turn it over to end the killing. Did Bloor know where it was? Where was he, anyway? She glanced about the interior again. It was room enough for a luxurious green bunk, covered with equally-expensive blankets, filled with seductive down. There was the door exiting the koch, and at the foot of the bed, another smaller door that contained the toilet she loathed to use. A mirror was opposite the bed so that she could take the time to make her twenty-two years look sixteen. Underneath the mirror was a variety of jars full of powders and creamy pigments that she despised to use, but did so. The princesses of the East were reputed to pinch their cheeks mercilessly to obtain the rouge they desired, but not Morianna. She painted herself under the direction given to her by her mentor, Alora. She detested using the creams, but liked the scent of the powders.

She stooped underneath the bunk where there were cabinets and yanked them all open. Spare clothing flew out and into the air as if caught in the winds of a blizzard. No coin lay hidden therein. Near the front of the koch was a resplendent white gown that she was destined to wear. Its full length touched the floor, and precious stones decorated a modest neckline, setting off the silky material like the surface of the fullest moon. It hung near a small pantry. She preferred hanging it there instead of next to the toilet.

However, coin? Yes, there was coin here—there must be, she realized. Why hadn't she thought of it before—but *where* did they put it? Her eyes went to the floorboards then and widened. She pounced on them, tearing back the softest of furry rugs to expose the wood underneath. Where? She placed one hand on the surface of the floor.

Then the koch began to move. Morianna jostled to the right, crashing against the bunk. She tried to get her balance while on her hands and knees, and then the koch did a wonderful thing: It sped up.

She got to her unstable feet and pulled herself to the nearest window slit. The countryside raced by. She saw only far-swept fields and a dark ribbon of a road. She staggered to the right and peered out the other side. A forest could be seen.

The koch jumped. Morianna fell backwards, tangled in her dress. She hit and bruised her back on the wooden edge of the bunk. The pain dulled her one thought. Faster. They were going faster.

Something was not right. A voice laughed in her head. There was a *lot* not right, this day. She lunged for a window slit, and with whatever breath remained in her lungs,

screamed for aid.

There was another jump in the koch's flight. She fell back to the softness of the bunk, landing on it this time, and gripped the edges for dear life.

Just one month ago she had turned twenty-two and had the adoration of her servants and friends. She had developed into a young woman, and the dresses and gowns she wore announced her coming of age. Morianna, in the words of some of her servants, would be a pleasant catch for any prince: a rich meal and dessert, all in one. She was a slim girl, yet ample in the places that mattered to men. Her hair was grown long and dark, though she hated having to comb it out every night. Short hair was much more to her liking, yet she knew men preferred it otherwise. Her face was round and stuck with a sharp nose. Her eyes were a dark brown. Two dust-spot-sized moles lined up, side by side, underneath her right eye. If one had asked her father, the king of Sunja, he would be the first to admit that of all of his daughters—Morianna being the last—she was perhaps the most plain. Many of the household staff openly believed that the king had a tongue lathed with modesty. A far nicer thing to say was that the man was obviously blind, or stupid, or both.

Morianna was, in fact, just bearably cute with her country looks untouched by the creams, perfumes, and lotions her father had commanded her to wear, and which her older sisters used more and more often. She would never strike love into a suitor's heart on first contact. However, if exposure was prolonged, a particular warmness—likened to a mild fever but much more pleasant—would heat a man's heart. Only when they were away from her person would the true nature of her presence take hold. By that time, it would be much too late.

Several of the men around Morianna were affected in such a way, but because of their positions in life, they were forced to focus their attentions on more easily accessible women in the kingdom. The king had made it quite clear that all his daughters would be married, with their virginity unplucked, to princes of faraway kingdoms to secure alliances. All could dote on his daughters, but to go any further would invite peril. There was a penalty, as severe as they could come in Sunja, for pursuing any of the princesses.

No one really knew what the penalty was, for as soon as the king made the decree, all eyes were averted elsewhere. Given the nature of the ruler, the populace suspected the penalty would be quite bad. The king had a penchant for understatements.

Rumor had it that the daughters were also told the same: Do not play with the emotions of those who are below your station, lest they invite the wrath of the king of Sunja. They listened and obeyed their father. Morianna was the least of the king's worries. She always obeyed the wishes of her father, and knew that whatever had to be done was always done with the people's interests in mind. She was all for making the lives of those around her more bearable. Months earlier, a royal delegation from the distant kingdom of Marrn arrived in her father's court. Marrn knew of Sunja's struggle with the vicious Nordun. The king of Marrn suspected that if Nordun was successful in bringing its neighbor to its belly, it would not stop there. Marrn would find itself mobilizing to repel a battle-hardened Nordun army—if the Nords won.

Sunja respected Marrn's borders and kept its problems within its own. Trade flourished between the two countries naturally enough, even though no ruler had given much thought to a formal peace treaty. Treaties could be unpleasant business at times, and why ruin an affable relationship?

However, in these times, Sunja was not adverse to an alliance. Secret couriers were dispatched back and forth between the two countries as the Klaws of Sunja grappled with Nordun Jackals. Letters bearing official royal language were written, read, and sent, along with a few words of informal banter. Both kings discovered that they shared a taste for wine, and took particular pride in what their wineries produced. An agreement was reached concerning the marriage of Sunja's youngest daughter to a prince of Marrn, the second of three princes. The marriage would not be a major affair, as the children betrothed were not first-born, but it would serve the rulers' mutual purpose nicely enough. As tradition dictated, a dowry from the father of the Sunjan to be married would also be given.

So it was agreed upon and written. The king informed Morianna of her fate in a less-than-sugary manner. She took the news well, if not stoically, perhaps thinking that her future was one that she would control. It was not every day that a young lady was lectured about her duty to her people and homeland, and told that marrying a complete stranger in a faraway land she had never visited was completely acceptable.

At twenty-two, Morianna was far more mature than her years allowed, and she had learned from Alora, her mentor of so many years, how to hide her emotions when needed. She took the news of her impending marriage well, but without a glimmer of joy or apprehension. There would be a period of time for the princess to visit Marrn and become acquainted with her future husband. It was meant to further her understanding of her role as both wife and ambassador for Sunja.

Morianna agreed to all of this. She accepted her duty to her father and her people. She understood that her own interests did not matter. She pushed the one man she was becoming more than fond of from her mind, and tried to replace him with the image of the prince from Marrn. She believed that, once she was away from Sunja, and given time, something resembling love might possibly do its silky dance in her heart. Now, however, it was impossible to focus on anything.

Morianna screamed as the koch struck something hard, its side bouncing into the air. It hung at the apex, the vehicle still moving forward, and a great whip-like snapping of timbers rang out. There was a groan of wood on metal. Horses cried out in panic. The koch crashed to a stop, turning over onto its left side. The air filled with falling objects inside the compartment. Morianna was flipped onto her back and hit her head on hard wood, dazing her. Her personal effects rained down on her. The green mattress flew off the bunk and covered her, protecting her from the clothes and smaller objects that fell. She felt things hit the padded material. It was all she could do just to listen and breathe in darkness. She heard the team of horses outside. Some were in pain or scared out of their wits. Their cries became even more frantic, the princess noted, as if they were exposed to fire. She closed her eyes in an attempt to shut out their noise. They were all right. That was what mattered. They would quiet soon enough.

The princess found herself drifting, her consciousness slipping away from her. While her mattress protected her from flying objects, she still hit her head hard on the heavy wood of the koch. A moan escaped her, as her fingers prodded at a goose egg of a bruise on the back of her head. Darkness descended once more, but she regained her aching senses after a short time. Morianna groaned and pushed the mattress back. She looked about and saw her wedding gown piled up on the floor, which had once been the left side of the vehicle. The cabinets had opened, their doors swinging in the light, and baubles of various sizes spilled out, thankfully missing her. Her powder floated about the air, and a whiff of it went up her nose, sparking a violent burst of sneezing. The crash had shattered the jars of cream and their oily contents covered the interior of the koch and a good portion of her clothes, making Morianna hate the stuff even more. The pain of her head, the potential ruin of her garments, and the fact that she felt another barrage of sneezes coming on made her scream out in frustration.

Only one horse could be heard outside now, screaming in its own way. Morianna believed the thing must have broken its legs to be making such a sound. Pity welled up inside her. Perhaps, if she got out, she could see to the animal. She tried to move and found that her limbs responded. Hoisting herself up, she cracked her head into the corner of one of cabinet doors hanging down. The new pain drove her to her knees. After a moment, the princess looked to the door. It was on the side on which the koch was resting. It offered no exit. She looked up. There was a single, horizontal window slit above her, over the bunk. She could reach it easily enough, but there was no way she could get through. *Sorry*, she thought to the horse outside.

The slit suddenly became dark as a shadow passed over it. Morianna cried out for help, out of reflex, but there was no answer. She then realized how quiet it was outside of the overturned koch.

There was a tapping, like a fist, on the outer shell of the vehicle, near the front, but then it raked across its length. The loud scratching made Morianna clamp her mouth shut. Someone had silenced those horses, someone perhaps not altogether friendly. She looked to her fallen gown, which now resembled a dazzling cow paddy.

The tapping began again. It was a sinister probing, moving along the length of the armor. The noise bounced into another long scratch, like nails across wood, and the slits in the plating darkened again as whoever it was outside passed by once more. Where were the horses? There was a fumbling on the hull of the koch. The unseen visitor began pulling on the framework underneath, picking at the wood like a gouging chisel.

Then, she heard the breathing, deep and labored, like someone breathing through a nose filled with a cold. The princess' own breathing quickened. What had found her?

There was a loud, frightening splintering and the floorboards that she had searched buckled outwards ever so slightly.

Morianna's heart crashed and banged. She wanted to scream but did not. Something had found her, something *strong*. The sound of wooden planks snapping reached her ears. The koch shook violently and even jerked off the ground. She flashed her palms out to brace herself, and an awful crackling and twisting of wood shot throughout, as if the thing was attempting to make a new doorway in the floor. Then something was ripped from the bottom in a shriek of wooden fibers. There was a distant clattering of wood, but the sudden lurching of the koch took Morianna's attention as it was rolled over like a toy box.

A scream flew from the princess' lips. She tumbled along the ceiling and onto the side, staring up at the door that was now exposed to light. Debris showered her again and the powder went up in a ghostly plume, sparking another round of sneezes. When she subsided, she gazed at the iron locks and sliding bar on the inside of the door with wide, fearful eyes. The bar was as thick as her wrist. Nothing could get inside, not through that.

The thing rocked the koch back and forth for a few moments, to the sound of someone breathing through a stuffed nose. Then it released the koch and she tumbled back against the bunk. The tapping began anew at the crease of the door and went up along its length. A low moan came from the depths of Morianna's throat.

What was out there? There was an intake of breath, the likes of which she had never heard before, and something slammed down on the door, rattling it its framework. A huge splinter of iron punctured the lower crease of the door and sent wood chips flying. The iron worked the wood, forcing it apart like an unwilling mouth. Morianna shrieked. The iron bar squealed back and forth, opening the mouth a little more with each movement. Another shriek from the princess, and the whole frame shuddered with the penetration.

The bar withdrew. The princess of Sunja held her breath. She would not scream again. Whatever was out there, she would not scream again, she ordered herself. Her hands found a sturdy knife she had used to cut her food, and she thrust it out before her, aiming it at the door.

A shadow filled the splintered crack in the doorframe. The shadow became flesh. A huge eye, black and red-rimmed as if it had downed tankards of ale the night before, peered in. Spotting her, the eye opened wider, in delight. Morianna pressed herself against the wall of the flipped koch, her bottom lip trembling uncontrollably. She honored herself by not screaming. In truth, her fright froze the breath in her lungs. She could not tear her gaze off that single baleful eye. She dropped her knife. An axe might have been better.

Fingers, thick as spikes and clawed with serrated nails, slipped into the opening like the legs of an immense spider. They flexed as they came in. Heavy gasps of breath bellowed from the outside, as if a woodsman was readying himself to fell a tree with one chop. Morianna braced herself against the floor, her vision full of the invading fingers. Terrified whimpers began squeaking from her throat.

The fingers reached down, finding purchase. Knuckles came into view, knuckles that tightened white and pulled.

The doorframe whined in protest of this unfair siege, but it refused to give. The pressure increased. The whines became pops, yet the sliding bar securing the door held. It would not give, Morianna hoped to Seddon above, ever. She convinced herself between the hammer beats of her heart that it would never give. Nothing was stronger than iron.

The edges of the door, however, *mooring* the iron…

One powerful yank ripped the door from its frame. With it came such a roar of triumph that Morianna's own terrified scream was barely audible.

10

Just as the ground beneath his feet began to tremble, Morgat loosed his arrow and a barbed sheet followed his lead, slicing into the ranks of the charging Visigar. The barbarians were ferocious fighters and only their tribal bickering kept them from uniting under a single banner. If they ever did, the old folks said that the rats plaguing Sunja's east lands would be too many to manage. However, that day was far off, and in the meantime, the Visigar clashed with the Sujins and Lancers only when one or the other meandered too far into the other's territory. Now and again, more ambitious knots, such as the ones charging, chose to rake the countryside for loot and fame.

The front line of horsemen absorbed the arrows and several fell. Some animals rolled over, head first, taking their riders with them. Men, once astride their mounts, suddenly found themselves on the ground as the killing weight of their animals squashed the life from them. Pain-filled cries speared the air as riders and animals alike disappeared into the tall, yellow grass.

The rest came on.

Roaring out one last battle cry that was as barbed as any lance, the Visigar smashed into the Sujin shield wall.

Except for one.

One horseman jumped *over*.

Morgat's black eyes nearly popped from his skull when the horse flew up and over. He threw himself wide, hitting the earth hard. The beast landed where he had stood, its rider rearing the animal up. Iron hooves flashed out and a Sujin's head broke open with a chalky crack. The rider swept his long sword down and cleaved open another head. The horse pranced about in a circle, kicking, biting, and clearing the space about it.

Morgat got to his feet with a growl and unsheathed his sword. No one had ever driven him to the ground, and he was not about to let some Visigar horse shite claim that he had.

Sujins near the animal ran from it, throwing their bows to the ground and reaching for more personal weapons. Their comrades buckled and heaved and collapsed in places from the Visigar charge. The barbarians punched through in some places, driving dead and dying Sujins to their knees. Worse still, riders swept around the shield wall entirely, forcing the edges of the line to wheel inwards to deflect the attack. The formation tried to hold, but broke down. Screams, battle cries, and the stink of the fight filled the air, and Morgat filled his lungs.

A Sujin came up behind the Visigar that had jumped the line and hewed a rear leg off his horse. The animal went down with a shrill scream. The rider somehow rolled free and managed not to have any of his own legs broken. He rose up, bulky and covered in coarse animal hides that had slipped in places. Sunlight flashed off the shiny armor underneath. The rider slipped into a fighting stance. A conical helmet shook.

Morgat's mind raced. *Armor? Heavy armor on a Visigar?*

A rallying cry went up from the embattled Sujins. Here and there, pockets of them knotted together and swept inward to seal up holes made by the attacking Visigar. Other Sujins caught notice of the lone Visigar on foot amongst them. In ones and twos, they charged the armored horseman. In ones and twos, they died. Swordplay, dazzling in its mastery, hummed in the air and in and out of defenses like a silver needle stitching. However, instead of pieces being kept together, men flew apart.

The man cleared a space around him in a matter of seconds. He reached down and pulled up an ownerless shield. A Sujin peeled himself away from a dying Visigar and charged him. The swordsman, as this was no mindless Visigar, twisted his shield to parry the thrust. He spun across the back of the man, his long sword cutting into the Sujin's back. As the man went down, the swordsman swung about towards Morgat. The visor on the man's helmet fixed on the Sujin, the sun making it gleam. Grunting, Morgat advanced with his shortsword, gathering up a shield as he went. He could see the man's eyes narrow in recognition within the slits of the helmet. *Does he know me?* Morgat briefly wondered, and feinted. Morgat's intention was to drive the swordsman to the left or right, to get him moving.

However, the man did not move.

Morgat's blade stabbed upwards. The swordsman's shield met it and sent it off at a harmless angle. A long sword punched in and through Morgat's stomach. He hit the ground three heartbeats to being dead, his eyes wide with amazement.

The swordsman whirled about. Before him, the Sujins' wall was actually reforming in the face of the Visigar assault. The charge had been costly for both sides. Several of the barbarians lay dead or dying while the Sujins stoically hacked their way back into a superior position. The professional Sujins assessed the Visigar horses to be the key to the fight. They began gutting the horses at every possible chance. Sujins on the edge of the Visigar charge were reaping in earnest. Two Knife's forces began pooling together, shaking off the crush of the charging horses. Two individual blocks began to take shape. Koors bawled out orders above the din of battle, drawing stragglers to their growing mass. The Visigar were quick to pounce on men reacting too slowly to rejoin their sword brothers.

Behind his visor, Bloor scowled. The Sujins were too sound and were re-forming their ranks with an unsettling ease. At that exact moment, a riderless horse came running towards him. Throwing his shield away, he grabbed the reins of the horse as it went by, the weight of the animal nearly pulling him off his feet. He hauled down on the reins, digging his feet into the bloody earth, and quickly brought the animal under control. He hauled himself into the saddle when the animal allowed him, grimacing with the weight of his armor, and felt a twinge of pain in his back. He ignored it. Righting himself atop his new mount, Bloor waved his blade above his head. "No prisoners!" he roared.

The Visigar roared back and drove into the forming boxes of the Sujins. The horseman slashed through their lines, their swords clattering off the upraised shields. One Visigar plowed his horse into the middle of the box before him. The animal died with a blade in its throat, and the rider flew forward, smashing into a head of a Sujin. Both men went down, but Sujins standing around the horseman hacked the Visigar to pieces before he could rise.

A warrior ran at Bloor. The Cavalier parried the sword and stabbed back, taking off an exposed ear. The man screamed. His hand covered his wound and he fell back out of sight. Letting him go, Bloor kicked his horse into motion. He wanted to get to the koch, which was nowhere in sight. It had gone into the forest. Bloor fixed on a possible entry point and steered his horse for it. From the corner of his eye, he saw the last of the Royal Axemen moving towards the melee. There were still some alive and eager to lash out with their pole axes. He saw one Visigar take the full blade of a pole arm square in the chest. The dead man flew from the saddle, amazingly still in one piece. The Axemen heard Bloor's command to the barbarians, but none could reach him as he rode by them all. There was no time to waste on any of them. He wanted the koch, and he galloped free of the bloody ruckus, bending low in the saddle and urging his new horse onwards.

Only one of the Visigar followed him.

Two Knife stabbed and slashed. With every step he took, something fell, be it man or beast. They meant nothing to him. Two Knife was of the same mind as Morgat. He could not believe that these savages were ruining his plans, and the thought of it drove him into a killing frenzy. There was more important work to be done than dealing with these maggots. In his fury, he hacked down one of his own by mistake, but bloodlust made him forget the incident in a blink. Of the formed blocks of Sujins, one failed to completely close. A wedge of Visigar drove into the gap like an iron boot in a closing door. They broke upon the Sujins like waves on beach rocks, fighting savagely. Warriors were thrown from dying horses and the Sujins fell upon them.

Two Knife saw Klytus, nearly as tall as a horse himself, throwing away his shield. The man grabbed and yanked the bit of one horse down with one arm before it could kick him, stabbing the rider through the ribs. Then he held onto the horse as he stabbed it through the neck. There was no stopping that one. Two Knife darted out of the way of a charging horse, cutting the legs out from the animal as he went by. Rider and animal crashed into the ground. The Visigar found himself pinned underneath his mount when Klytus loomed over him. Pragmatic, the big man plunged his sword into the fallen horseman's face.

With that, the Visigar horsemen abruptly wheeled about and fled. Two Knife ran after them for only a bit when he realized what foolishness it was. He watched them go with grim satisfaction. There were significantly fewer, perhaps no more than twenty or thirty.

"Axemen!" he heard Desso cry out.

Two Knife spun about. Sure enough, the Axemen were on the move, aiming for the box formation of Sujins that had held. There was only a handful, only half of their force perhaps, but with each step they took, something fell. Two Knife saw a Sujin damn near chopped in half by the lead Axeman, and then the elite slammed into the Sujins' formation like a maul. There was a metallic clash of axes and armor. The lead Axeman left his pole arm in a dead Sujin, producing a shorter axe for more personal work. They pushed like charging bulls and trampled over any unprepared Sujins. The formation bulged at the edges and exploded into confusion as Sujins tried to distance themselves from the attacking Axemen. Then, one royal guardsman took a sword to the chest and the rush of the spearhead suddenly died. Another faltered, tripped by something unseen. The remaining Sujins threw themselves upon them, and a feral battle marked the earth.

When the fight neared its conclusion, the Sujins drew back. They discovered a field of dead brethren, sprinkled here and there with the massive frames of dead Axemen.

"Wait!" a furious Two Knife barked. There were heaps of dead around, and too many of them were his. In the middle of the slaughter, only two Axemen remained, standing back-to-back, reduced to swords. On Two Knife's roaring, cursing orders, the Sujins pulled farther back from the two guardians, eyeing them from over shield edges. Klytus wanted to tear into the last Axemen. He had already killed one with ease. They were far too arrogant for his taste, but Two Knife's word kept him at a distance.

Defiant, bleeding from unheeded scratches, the last two Axemen leered at the ring of traitorous Sujins.

"Why wait?" the one called Rover challenged. "We're not going anywhere. Or are you going to kill us with arrows, instead? Surprise me and do otherwise. Show me some balls and do otherwise."

"You want us to do otherwise?" Two Knife yelled back. "We could fill you with arrows right now!"

"You could," Rover yelled back, "and I expect nothing less from a traitorous rat bastard like yourself! Go on then. It would save us from being stunk to death from your maggot shite innards. You call yourselves Sujins? You are the lowest maggots to ever breathe! Betraying one's own, and for what?"

"Coin!" Two Knife sputtered back. "The likes of which you and I have never seen before. The riches of a king that cares shite for either of us! Who are you to fight for one who cares nothing for you? Who will ask about his fortune first before the fate of you, his precious Axemen? You're like blind dogs! I've been on the Nord front, and I've seen our brothers hacked to pieces *if* they're lucky. If they aren't, they get sent back to a paltry pension that's supposed to make up for lost limbs, or even worse! I've seen men that killed for him who are now begging in the streets! All the while, our king commands even more of us into the bone grinder while having grapes fed to him!"

Rover had no immediate answer. The moans of the almost-dead filled the silence. "We gave our word to him!" the Axeman finally shot back. "Freely! You do what you want, for anything else I have to say will be nothing more than sounds aimed at maggots. Brainless, spineless, white shite-making *maggots!*"

Hearing the words and standing a few paces from where Two Knife stood, Toffer held a dark, blood-drenched cloth to where his ear had once been. He considered himself lucky that the damn Visigar had missed his head. He winced at the gravity of the Axeman's words, rather than his own personal pain. Then, he saw Two Knife's back straighten.

The Sujin Right Koor stared at the defiant Axemen in the middle of the dead. His face blanched, and those near him actually felt the temperature of the air rise. Two Knife took the Axeman's words straight to whatever black heart resided in his breast. Who were they to judge him? None of the Axemen were ever on the Nordish Front, nor were any of them ever assigned to patrol the backstreets and gutters of

Sunja where the stricken Sujins begged for any coins thrown at them. They knew not what they talked about. Two Knife had had enough of these righteous bastards, and decided that arrows were too good for this pair.

He stepped away from the surrounding Sujins and pointed a sword at both of them. Two Knife appeared to want to speak, but his face became tight with fury. He said nothing. He marched towards the two Axemen, alone. His swords flashed in the afternoon sun. Knowing the disposition of their leader, not one Sujin dared to move without his command. They stood and watched. This was to be personal.

Rover stepped away from his sword brother, a big Axeman named Kagle. Kagle, feeling Rover step away, glanced over his shoulder and spied the approaching warrior. A quick look informed him that no other Sujin made to charge. Not a missile weapon was in sight.

Kagle turned to face this one Sujin. Rover waited for the man to reach him, rolling his armored shoulders and holding his broadsword before him.

"I've killed two of you already," Two Knife said in a low voice as he drew closer.

"I've killed *ten* of you," Rover hissed, his sword sizzling for the Sujin's head. One of Two Knife's blades slapped it down while his other stabbed for Rover's body. The Axeman jumped back from the attack. Kagle moved in; the big man had two swords himself and both blades whirled and slashed at the Sujin like a great chewing machine, driving the Sujin backwards. Two Knife parried and dodged, the clash reverberating over the field of the dead. Rover darted in behind the Sujin, and Two Knife jumped to the side, placing Kagle between them. Kagle's swords retreated and he dropped back to gather his wind. Rover charged in, snarling. Two Knife locked up one sword with his own and felt Rover's free hand clamp down on the wrist holding his other blade. Two Knife leaned back, avoiding a butting head. He lifted his boot and drove it into the side of the Axeman's knee. The joint exploded like a hard plum. With a roar, Rover went down, pulling on Two Knife's wrist and refusing to let go.

Seeing his sword brother collapse, Kagle roared and charged in. He got only two steps when Two Knife abruptly spun and flung his free blade into the charging Axeman's throat. The blow snapped Kagle's head back. Swords flew from his nerveless fingers. His roar became a frothy gurgle. Two Knife whirled back on the fallen Rover. The Axeman slashed for a leg, but the Koor was too nimble. Two Knife jumped over the sword, breaking the man's grip on his wrist. Rover rolled over to his knees to face his opponent and Two Knife's sword lanced in. Rover stopped the thrust, but he did not stop Two Knife's boot. Two Knife had learned long ago that it mattered not how you killed a man, only that you lived to tell of it. The Sujin kicked the man square in the face, laying him flat on the ground. Rover's head bounced. Two Knife kicked again and felt face bone shatter. A third kick and the Axeman's body went limp, his sword dropping to the ground. Two Knife could have stopped then, but the fury had a tight hold. He kicked again, driving his boot into the man's face, and kicked again, and again.

After a short while, he decided to stomp, with both feet.

Two Knife kept on stomping long after his foe's features had disappeared. He finally stopped, his breast heaving, and looked down at his handiwork. Baring his teeth, the Koor hoarked and spat on the dead man at his feet. Satisfied that he had made his point, he moved to retrieve his sword sticking out of the other corpse.

The Sujins watching their leader were speechless, to a man. In the aftermath of the fight, some of them grinned and shook their heads with evil mirth, while some struggled not to vomit. The remainder looked on with mixed feelings of fascination, awe, and fear.

Two Knife was not a man to make angry.

11

As the beaten Visigar were retreating, the group of loyalist Sujins delved deeper into the forest. They ran as hard as they could in their battle dress, puffing and sweating. Hatch somehow had enough breath to curse the traitors behind them, curse the forest they now were in, and curse the tangles trying to trip him. The shade offered by the forest cooled them to a point. The men were thankful for the cover it provided. In here there would be no horsemen, and they would have the advantage in the thickness of the vegetation.

They came upon the road that had swallowed up the wildly rolling koch. Old as it was, it twisted off into the halls of the woods. Thick branches, heavy with foliage, seemed to grow together overhead, forming a ceiling of lush color. The road sprouted grass from neglect, making the trail of the passing vehicle easy to follow. Primo scowled when he saw it. He took the lead and hurried down the throat of the forest. He ordered two men to drop back and keep a rear watch. The dogs that had set themselves upon the column would be heading this way soon enough. Primo knew who led them; he had seen the man with his own eyes. The raiders preoccupied Two Knife for now, but Primo knew he was persistent, a snake of a fighter, and cunning. Primo could add a few more words to describe the man, and if he lived to see the heights of Sunja again, he would do so in his report.

"Stop here," he commanded the men after a lengthy run. They stood, some with their hands on their knees, in a narrow corridor of timberland. The road had been covered in yellow and orange needles from tall spruce trees, and the passing koch had smashed aside several low branches trying to stitch up the road altogether. Some broken limbs lay here and there and the wheels had torn up the earth, leaving tracks of fresh dirt winding deeper into the forest.

"They went in far," Primo observed, taking in a huge breath. The scent of the spruce air filled his senses. He would be more than content just to sit and inhale the aroma of the woods. "Just our luck."

"We should keep moving," Balto threw in.

Primo nodded and started walking down the trail. "Let's. Come on. Where's that Sujin fortitude you're all so proud of? What's a walk in the trees? Or would you rather stay and wait for those tits back there?"

"I would stay," Tungang said. "I saw who was leading them."

They all stopped. The sudden attention of having knowledge others didn't made the big man feel good.

"Well then?" Gatesin demanded. "Or are you waiting for the lad to come by and introduce himself?"

"It's Two Knife," Tungang said, glowering at Gatesin for robbing him of the stage.

"Aye," Hatch said with scorn. "I can see it in that hell pup. A right nasty one, he is."

"I saw him as well," Primo confessed.

"What about Tarco and Bloor?" Gatesin asked. "Where are those two in all of this?"

"Bloor took off before the fighting started," Primo told him. "He'll probably be cut down when he returns."

"Have my doubts on that," Gatesin muttered to himself. Balto silently agreed.

"And Tarco?" Hatch asked.

"I don't know what happened to him," Primo reported.

"I do," Tungang said. "He was cut down by Rusk. Two Knife took him on, one on one, and took his head. Proper, too."

"That true?" Balto asked of Primo. The officer sighed and nodded. So much for keeping secrets.

"Then this has all gone to piss," Hatch mused.

"No doubt," Gatesin said, scornfully, "seeing as I had to kill the topper walking next to me before he stuck a sword in my gullet."

"A thing he missed, seeing it's so big," Tungang smirked.

"Speaking of big things, it's a wonder you made it out. The target you make. How did you manage that anyway?"

Tungang suddenly sobered. "That was not funny, little man. I could ask the same of you. Question my loyalty again and I'll gut you. Just remember that."

"I remember everything," Gatesin snipped back.

Balto shot Primo a meaningful look and the officer took the message. "No one's questioning anyone here. Not while I'm still about. We made it and, seeing as there's only a handful left, I think we best watch each other's backs instead of trying to flay them. Let's get moving."

"I could stay here and kill a few as they came," Tungang offered.

"And die yourself?" Gatesin asked. *Or perhaps show the way they had gone.* He did not like the way his mind was working. He would keep an eye on the Tun.

"I don't think you'll miss me."

"Nonsense, Tun," Balto said and flashed a smile. "Every farmer knows the value of a good bull."

Tungang pointed an axe at the veteran. "I'll gut you later."

"You'll come along," Primo said.

"Good idea," Hatch said. "He'd only make Two Knife fight all the harder. And catch us quicker."

"A damn sorry thing," the man named Tavan said. He had been quiet up to this point, no doubt as stunned as the rest of them. "That he turned as many of us as he did. The power of gold to turn a man back on his oath."

"Aye," Primo said, leading his small band deeper into the forest. "They'll be hunted down and butchered for it. Guaranteed."

"*If* we get back and report them," Gatesin said, in a low voice.

Balto fixed him with a frown.

"We'll get back," Primo said from the lead, supporting his own belief, "as long as we're careful."

"We'll get back," Balto vowed to himself, taking his eyes off Gatesin and studying the halls of the forest. "I have no doubt of that."

"I saw some running in the direction of Sunja," Tavan reported. "The speed they were going, they're probably there by now."

Balto took a quick count of heads. There were eleven of them, thirteen including the men trailing behind them; a fighting force at any time, but not against Two Knife's Sujins.

"How many?" Gatesin saw his sword brother counting.

"Thirteen of us, counting the ones behind us."

"Aren't there scouts supposed to be about?" Hatch glanced about as he walked beside Primo. The officer nodded.

"Somewhere. Hope to find them as well. Our chances of getting out of here would be that much better. And getting whoever it is in the koch. And that's what's got my curiosity right now. Who is in that bloody box?"

"You really don't know?" Gatesin asked. He did not believe the man earlier. The admission surprised him. Primo was a Koor under both Tarco and Bloor.

"I never asked. Neither did Two Knife. Wasn't proper. Just knew there was a king's ransom on board. Never said it was a woman. They didn't tell us anything."

"Strangeness," Balto said to himself. He was thinking with a full head of steam now.

Primo took another deep breath as he marched along. "We'll find out soon enough."

"You sure we will?" Gatesin said with doubt. "Those horses were moving fast last time I saw them. Without a driver as well. I wouldn't be surprised if they were on a rocky beach by now."

"I'm surprised you're all still talking," Primo didn't bother glancing over his shoulder to address the man, "when we should be quiet. So shut up." Gatesin lapsed into a faithless silence.

Primo was more than right. They found the wreck of the koch by early afternoon. The sight of the vehicle was a sobering one. It lay on its side, wheels still, just beyond the mossy dome of a boulder, lodged deep into a ground gone from being soft and earthy to hard rock. The single track marring its surface told the loyalists that the koch was not slowing in the least when the wheels rumbled over it and the entire bulk tipped and crashed. The body lay on its side like some great beast, but the disturbing thing was the absence of the reinforced door. Something had ripped it off the koch. The image of a cow having its ribs pulled out lingered in Gatesin's mind, except this was wood and iron. The Sujins rushing to reach the koch slowed and moved about its grounded shell with an air of caution.

"See there," Tungang growled and pointed. They could smell the blood before they found the source, and it silenced them all. The horses were not far away from the koch, twisted, torn, and lifeless.

"They came this way," Primo said, slowly sweeping his sword in the direction he meant. "And flipped. Hit the rock there and tipped. Then something found the horses as they were still in their harness and killed them."

The Sujins ringed the site of the crash. "Ate them, looks to me," Gatesin commented. "Or at least two of them. And how about this one with its head torn off? What's strong enough to do that to a horse?"

Balto was close enough to offer his agreement. Hatch stood nearby, his hand straying to scratch at his crotch. The Sujins, to a man, were hard-disciplined, fighting men who had seen their share of battlefield oddities. Steeled through countless campaigns, they had shared strange sights and yet, for all of them, this was something new.

"They didn't bother burning anything," Hatch said, examining the exposed under-koch. His eyes stopped on the recess. The frame about it had four separate hinges, all ripped away and dangling raw splinters. "Seddon above," he breathed.

Primo hoisted himself up onto the koch and peered into the compartment. He expected the worst, but was relieved when he found only a ruined mess of splintered wood, clothes, and powder. The pleasant smell of a woman's creams and perfumes drifted across his nose, and he felt the pit of his stomach fall away.

"Well?" Balto wanted to know.

"Nothing," Primo answered. "There are a lot of clothes in here. Woman's clothes," he eyed the flop of a truly beautiful gown, "some very fine. And perfumes."

Gatesin moved ahead to take a better look at the horses, eyeing the fringes of the road and the woods in case something lurked. There were six heavy horses, big, strong animals. Only the one had its head removed. The others were mangled in other ways. Their wounds were all ragged and deep, clawed. He knelt down beside the deflated body of one of the horses. It had been disemboweled, before or after its head had been twisted around. The brutal stench of raw gut filled his senses and he lifted his forearm to his nose. He had seen worse in his time, and in truth, after seeing the bodies of people, the killing of animals did not bother him as much as the smell, but these horses…

"A hard way to die," Tavan said from behind him, causing Gatesin to stand. "Gashed open like that. Wonder what did it?"

Gatesin surveyed the shadows of the forest. "I wonder if it's still around."

Tavan's eyes widened a little at the admission. The young Sujin scanned the gloom around him, hoping that they were, indeed, alone.

"Something missing here," Balto said, nodding towards the recess underneath the koch. "Something was fixed there solid, but it was taken. We all heard Two Knife shouting about coin. I wager this was a strongbox full of it and something took it." He turned about and began watching the long shadows of the timberland. "Something very strong."

The veteran Sujin met the eyes of Primo. "And we have to find *her*."

"I know," Primo said grimly. "Though truth be known, I'd much rather be going in the other direction."

"Where? Back there is Two Knife."

Primo allowed a smirk. The whiteness of his teeth was startling. "I think the odds are better with him."

Nearby, Hatch hoarked and spat into the ground. "Seddon almighty! I'll say the odds are better. Look at these!"

They crowded around where the Sujin was gesturing. Off the hard road and between the spaced trees were two large footprints, as fresh as if the owner had stepped onto a hot loaf of bread. The feet were crowned with three toes apiece. At the end of each was an uneven mark in the earth, like a wide jagged knife.

The men stared down at the marks, quietly wondering just how bad things had gotten.

In that moment, with the stench of blood thick enough to make a regular man dizzy, they heard the approach of horses. Primo signaled the Sujins to make a line and directed Tavan and four others with bows to the cover of the trees. Gatesin stood, shoulder to shoulder, with Balto and Primo.

He didn't like being placed in the middle of the open like they were, no matter how narrow the road was.

"Shields out," Primo instructed them. "Make the wall and make anyone pay dearly for it if they try and get past."

The Sujins waited. They heard the horses again, somewhere back along the road with their hooves clicking off rocks. The scuffling increased gradually until the lead horse showed its head around the bend in the road. Then its rider appeared out of the shadows. Another horse and rider joined the first. Both halted when they spied the koch ahead and the wall of Sujins behind its wreckage.

Primo recognized the features of the man on the horse just as the two Sujins he dispatched earlier ran up behind the riders. The man had discarded the helmet before entering the forest. It was too tight a fit for him.

"Lord Bloor!"

Bloor nodded and nudged his horse closer. He didn't hear the questions fired at him from Primo. His face became hard as the koch transfixed his attention. The koch had been cracked open like an egg. He caught the aroma of blood on the air as the corpses of the horses came into view. Though he did not show it, relief flooded through his person.

"Where is she?" Bloor said in a commanding voice.

"Who, Lord?" Primo wanted to know. He was relieved beyond words to see the Cavalier, but why was he wearing hides over his armor? He presently looked more like a bulked-up bandit than a Cavalier.

Bloor did not answer him. He rode forward and drew up beside the koch and examined its husk with a solemn face. The other horseman dismounted and removed the animal hides covering his armor. The plate mail placed him as a Cavalier, which struck Balto as curious, as he knew there were only Bloor and Tarco on this march, and this obviously was not Tarco. Why were both of them looking like Visigar?

Sensing he was being watched, the man turned and stared directly into Balto's face. There was a wildness there, controlled, but there nonetheless. Black eyes held Balto's own for a moment and the Sujin tried hard not to show any unease, not to this one. There was something there that would feast on Balto if he showed even a drop of doubt. After a moment, the man's face slowly split in a sly grin and he glanced away. The grin irritated Balto, and steeled him even more against the newcomer.

Bloor inspected the wreckage for a moment more before declaring, "She is gone."

"She is that," Gatesin muttered, wondering who "she" was.

Bloor heard him. He straightened in the saddle and swung his horse over to the man and glared down at him. For a moment, Gatesin believed the Cavalier would strike him.

"You," Bloor said in a voice full of loathing. "I should have realized it sooner. Once again, Gatesin, you're a bane to anything you are a part of and to the company you keep. I should have banished you the morning I saw you, before we left Sunja." Gatesin's face flushed with chagrin, but he maintained discipline. It wasn't his fault all this had happened.

"Even the dowry is gone," Bloor's scowl deepened.

"Lord," Primo said, "who are you talking about?"

Bloor's armored shoulders slumped with fatigue. He looked over the Sujins before him. They were obviously loyal and did not suspect him of anything. That was good; he needed them now. His face became set again. "What happened back there?"

Primo blinked. "It was Rusk, Lord. The one they call Two Knife."

"I know the man."

"Yes," Primo said. "My apologies, Lord Bloor. There was a plot to take the money within the koch and looks like it was led by Two Knife." Primo gave the rest of his report of what happened to the escort and Tarco. Bloor exchanged a dark, knowing look with the unknown man at the mention of Two Knife's involvement. The motion made Primo pause.

"Is there something else, Lord Bloor?" Primo asked.

"No," Bloor said. "I'm surprised any of you lived at all. The dowry is missing. It was a gift, honoring the marriage of Morianna, Princess of Sunja, to the Prince of Marrn. That is what you were all protecting: money and Morianna."

The gathered men were stunned into silence.

"But we'll find her and the dowry," Bloor announced to them all. "Before the others."

The news caused Primo to slowly nod. Royalty! The thought of an abducted princess shocked the remaining Sujins. Who would have thought, *and* a dowry?

And Two Knife's Sujins.

"They're the least of your worries," a voice informed them all. The Sujins whipped around, ready for action. With open hands, a man stepped out from the behind the trees where the footprints were discovered. It was the tall, scraggly fellow Gatesin had wondered about only a morning ago, the scout that looked to have fought tooth and nail for whatever possessions he had. A heavy ax was slung across his back, and a shortsword hung in a scabbard at his waist. Faint ribbons of silver ran through the man's greasy black hair, and from behind its weedy length, one eye regarded them all. That one eye, black as pitch, glistened with a malevolent knowledge. The other socket was a dark pink hole.

"You're one of our scouts," Bloor recognized the man, as well.

"I am," he nodded. "I signed on as a scout. Scouting is only side-work, really. Pays for my other work."

"Which is?" Bloor asked, without waiting.

"Hunting."

"Can you find Morianna?"

The scout looked him in the eyes. "I can. Though I doubt she's still alive."

"She's alive," Bloor stated in a dangerous tone. He would not accept anything less.

The scout appeared thoughtful, but he did not rebuke the commander.

"And you will find her," said Bloor, filling the silence. "You will do everything in your ability to find her. Understood?"

The man nodded. "We better get moving then, and you'll need to bring your horses, as well."

Bloor frowned. "Did you think we would leave them?"

"I don't know, but we'll be needing them."

"Why?"

"Bait." The single word made a suddenly uncomfortable Gatesin and several of the Sujins size up the girth of the warhorse. *Bait?*

The hunter was already leaving the road and moving for deeper woods. "Do as I say and I'll find you the woman."

"Princess," Bloor corrected him, annoyance in his voice.

"Try and be quiet. And be mindful of where you're stepping," said the scout and hunter, ignoring Bloor, or just not hearing him. He stopped between the two trees, forming the entrance to the inner halls of the woodlands. "And keep those horses quiet. At least until I say otherwise."

Bloor would let him have his say for the time being. He despised men who did not know their place in the order of things, but a thought suddenly occurred to him. "You," Bloor said, louder than he had intended. "You said you were a hunter. What do you hunt?"

The man peered towards the way to be taken. He heard the question and glanced back at the Cavalier high on his horse. The smile on his face was both sympathetic and dreadful.

"Trolls," he answered.

The word fell into the midst of the Sujins like a boulder, causing them all to stop thinking. They regarded the carnage around the wreckage with a new respect. Some thought of their childhood and the tales told to them to frighten them off to bed. Others remembered haunted stories when they were traveling long distances through swampland, stories full of creatures of faerie lore and things that would devour bad children in huge bloody bites.

Trolls existed only in the fringes of their minds. None had ever heard of a man seeing a troll and living to tell the tale. Seeing the destruction before him, Gatesin did not feel particularly confident in his chances. Balto also felt doubt in his stomach. He had heard the stories as well. He had even told a few to children and delighted in their awe-filled faces, and now they were about to go hunting for one of those stories.

From atop his horse, a determined Bloor held the reins in one hand while his other clutched the hilt of his long sword. He looked at his unnamed companion on his own horse. The man nodded in answer.

Bloor looked back to the troll hunter. "Lead on."

12

Toffer's ear, or at least the place where his ear had been, had slowed its bleeding. He regarded the fourth rag he held to it, admiring the amount of blood running down his wrist in slow beads. He had seen enough blood, in his time. A long, loud ringing went through his head. It was one continuous chime that was both distracting and infuriating. It placed Toffer's already-high-strung nerves on edge. If someone got on his bad side or asked one too many questions, he would strike them down and not think twice about it. Except, of course, *him*.

"They went this way," he reported from where he knelt, touching the earth at the rim of the forest. The ringing seemed to bounce off the inside of his skull. He winced. "There're the tracks."

"Not that many men," Desso commented to Two Knife as he sized up the edge of the woods.

"Don't talk so loud," Toffer grated.

Desso looked down at the Sujin Koor, noting the bloody bandage he held to the side of his head. "I wasn't talking to you."

"He was talking to me," Two Knife said, and Toffer became quiet. Toffer had no fear of Desso. He could take him easily, even though Desso considered himself to be no slouch with a blade. The man was capable enough with a sword, but not quite up to Toffer's ability. Two Knife was another matter.

"Well, anyway," Toffer continued in a not-so-brave tone. "They went in here. We'll catch them soon enough."

"The Sujins you mean. Not the horses," Desso said.

"Of course I meant the Sujins, you idiot."

"Watch who you call an idiot, else I make you blind by lopping off that other ear."

"How would that make him blind?" Two Knife asked.

"No ears," Desso explained, as if it were obvious. "Nothing to keep his helmet up." The joke did nothing except make Two Knife wonder if he should kill Desso.

"I'm not interested in any of them," Two Knife said after a while, deciding to continue making use of Desso. "I want that koch. I want that coin. And I only care about those running bastards if they get to it first. Besides," he took in the towering heights of the forest and felt a light breeze on his face, "we are many. And they are few."

For a moment, the Sujins simply regarded the forest. "Let's be off then," Two Knife announced. "There's work to be done."

Two Knife marched into the forest. He was riding a high wave of confidence from the day's trophy kills. A handful of Sujins would be nothing to him. His Sujins followed, grim and with weapons bristling. They had already spilled the blood of their sword brothers this day. None among them felt any hesitation at spilling a little more. Within moments, the forest absorbed them all.

13

They were spread out in a wedge behind the scout, feeling their way through the pillars of the forest. Sunlight spilled down through the shadowy canopy above in thin beams. Bloor had dismounted and thrown off his Visigar garments. On foot, he led his horse, keeping the animal's face close to his ear.

Gatesin suspected that the scout telling them that the horse would be used as bait had struck a chord in the Cavalier. The thought amused him. Bloor obviously did not have much use for people, but perhaps horses were a different matter. The man probably preferred them over the company of women. That particular thought soured Gatesin's stomach.

"What's your name?" Bloor asked the man leading them.

"My name?" the man repeated, and glanced at the Cavalier.

Bloor did not ask the question a second time.

"Jace," the man answered and suddenly stopped. "By the way, I forgot something. This way."

"We don't have time for this," Bloor said. He did not want to stray far from the trail of the princess.

"You'll have time for this," Jace informed him. The troll hunter turned to his left and began weaving his way in and around tree trunks, between the shafts of sun that lit up the gloom. He led them for a little ways, until the mossy ground beneath them began to shine and twinkle.

Gatesin's eyes popped wide when he stepped on something hard and felt it press into the soft earth. The ground was covered in gold and jewels of unimaginable value. It was as if a star had fallen out of the sky and shattered into a thousand pieces. Hatch drew up next to him and let his breath out in a stunned whistle. The other Sujins stared in wonder at the scintillating ground.

"Here and there," Jace pointed to the splintered wood of a strongbox smashed against a tree. Rivers of wealth sprayed to either side, while a pool of riches lay glistening at the base. The precious metal and stones twinkled dully in the sparse sunlight, mesmerizing all that beheld them. Just a handful secreted away would ensure a life of leisure, and more than just a few of them felt the tug of temptation. Primo swore a vile oath completely out of his character, while Gatesin agreed with him. Both men wondered, for a brief moment, if Two Knife needed any new recruits.

"If your eyes were shovels, that damn mess would be scooped up by now," Bloor rumbled at them. His solid voice shook the Sujins from their fantasies, and they straightened up where they stood. Bloor scowled at them before he studied the treasure with a dour expression, clearly not as impressed as the rest. "Looks to be all of it."

"Didn't take anything," Balto commented, moving around the area. He showed a marked interest in the spilled treasure.

"Trolls aren't interested in coin," Jace said, reproachfully. It was clear to him that none of these men had any idea of what had grabbed the princess. "It's only interested in eating. Anything it can get its claws into. Look above you."

Jace pointed to a place higher up. Branches had been snapped and the flesh of the tree recently scarred. The hunter spat into the ground. "That box of yours was thrown against the tree. You know how much strength it would take to do that? About all of us combined, perhaps."

Bloor scowled. Next to him and still on his horse, Alwan made a face, as well. It was obvious that the creature was strong, but it would not be a match for them.

"How much of a start does this troll have?" Bloor asked, in a hard voice.

Jace thought for a moment. "Hard to say. It has eaten, though. Those swipes taken from the horses were filling, I wager. I imagine it's just walking at leisure now. It doesn't suspect us. There's no wind to carry our scent to it, so it has no reason to hurry along. But…"

"But what?" Primo asked before Bloor.

Jace smiled unpleasantly. "The trouble with trolls, see, is that they're gluttons."

Bloor's features darkened again.

"It'll be eating again soon enough," Jace went on. "And I don't mind telling you that it left behind a lot of meat back there. I don't know why it stopped when it did. Sometimes the smell of blood causes a troll to eat too much. If that happens, it purges itself, and eats again. Sometimes it wanders off somewhere and sleeps for a week. Either way, it'll stretch its stomach as far as possible. Doesn't know when it'll eat again, I suppose, so if it has something handy, it'll bring it along so it can devour it later. If it took your princess, it did so just for that. She's small and easy to carry, and still alive."

"Still fresh," Balto whispered with an expression of horror. The treasure on the ground held no sway over him now. Jace nodded at the man, thinking him a quick one. He'd seen it happen before when he was younger and still learning the signs and habits of the beasts. It was necessary to tell these men everything now. It wasn't a myth they were going after. A part of Jace wanted to show the Sujins that he knew what he was talking about, wanted to drown them in grisly details, especially the commander. He seemed a serious one. Jace knew troll tales that would make a man's heart freeze as if dipped in a winter's stream.

"So this troll of yours," Bloor abruptly spoke, "will be hungry again soon?"

Jace nodded. "A meal goes through it faster than shite through a goose."

Bloor regarded the man for a moment without a flicker of humor in his face. "I wouldn't know anything about that," he said in a stoic tone. He then addressed the others. "Primo, you'll take six men and pick all of this up. Into your packs. Leave nothing for Two Knife. Gatesin, you'll go with him, and if you bring misfortune to us this time, I'll personally stab you though the heart. When you're done, follow us at best speed. We'll have caught this troll and killed it by then." Bloor spotted Jace's brow furrow with amusement. "You disagree?"

"Lord, not at all. I'm confident in your men. I just never had this small a group with me before, is all. Not when hunting, anyway. When you're after trolls, having as many as you can is a good thing. It'll be interesting to see how the troll likes it."

"I imagine so," Bloor said in a menacing tone. "I'll see to it personally that it doesn't have chance to *like* it."

Jace supposed the man would do just that. He was a dark one, this Bloor.

"May Seddon smile on you, Lord," Primo wished aloud.

"Seddon," Bloor said, staring off into the forest, "can kiss my sunny arse."

Primo's face went slack with surprise and more than a few chuckles bubbled from the surrounding Sujins.

"See to your orders," Bloor said, gesturing with his sword as if he would have no problem taking the heads of anyone slacking. "Alwan," he said, and the man riding the horse came to attention. "And you few," Bloor waved at six Sujins, "with me. Lead on, scout."

Jace got moving. Bloor followed with Alwan just behind on his horse. The other Sujins made a line behind the two

Cavaliers. Primo did not waste any time watching them leave. He regarded his remaining few, still smarting a little from Bloor's blasphemy. He would say a prayer for the man later, and hoped that he would not be late with it.

"Let's get busy, then," he ordered, sheathing his sword. He took off his pack and spilled its contents onto the ground. Dropping to his knees, Primo began scooping up treasure.

"They could've left us a horse," Hatch muttered.

"They left us Tungang," Gatesin said.

"I'll let you live," Tungang pressed Gatesin, "if you tell me about this curse of yours." Gatesin flashed the Tun a look of contempt.

14

The monster moved fast.

The troll plowed through the woodland, ripping out lesser branches seeking to slow its passage, and stepping over fallen timbers being absorbed by the ground. It stomped on green beards of moss and splashed through glassy streams. Anything within earshot of the rendering and snapping of timber took flight, terrified of the approach. A huge fist gripped Morianna's thin ankles as it carried her on its back, slung over its shoulder like a sack of dead brush.

With every step, her head bounced like a child's doll. Her face was pale and her arms slapped like lead weights against the thing's lower body and legs. The creature did not think of her as a burden. In fact, it barely felt her weight at all. Its belly was full at the moment and its thoughts were set on moving deeper into the forest, away from the wreck of the little ones. When the time came, and it would come before night fell, it would remember that it carried a little one over its shoulder. Then it would devour her.

The troll stopped, for a moment, and sniffed at the air, its great nostrils flaring. It gazed about the forest. While not intelligent, it was cunning. Its head, covered in a long, flowing mop of sewage-colored hair, reared up, and great black eyes, rimmed blood red, narrowed and then widened.

There. The troll's mass of fat, rubbery, green-grey flesh, like that of rotting cabbage, plunged ahead. It bashed aside smaller trees and elbowed the larger ones. In moments, the thing found the stream it smelled. It splashed into the water and squatted, great knees cracking like ice in an early spring thaw. With a flap of its arms, it threw the little one against the dirt embankment with a solid thud. Snorting, it dropped to its knees and began lapping at the water with a yellowish tongue, black eyes narrowing and closing in pleasure. A wide mouth housed two pointed tusks, which were visible even when, on the odd occasion, the thing's mouth was closed. The tusks almost touched the outer corners of the troll's eyes. It guzzled the water, not in the least bit afraid of being discovered, as the air carried only the scents of the water and the little one nearby. There were no other smells in the air and nothing to be wary of. The little one beside it was motionless, and if it suddenly ran, it would be an easy thing to catch. Content for the moment, the troll allowed itself to gulp down the cool flow of the stream. Once its thirst was satisfied, it would continue on to its den.

Its territory was still far away, but it would get there, eventually. It was a monster of legend, this particular troll, and had seen many seasons come and go. Time was a human measure, and of no concern to the beast, but it had outlasted several of its kind, and had witnessed endless seasons, from cold to hot and back. It had feasted on all manner of flesh, and had lived long enough to know the difference in flavor amongst different living things. Young flesh was the sweetest and most tender, often squirting its juices when bitten into, but old flesh had its qualities as well and often held more flavor. It had made meals of just about anything wandering into its territory, to the point where nothing ventured into its hunting grounds anymore. This forced the troll to seek sustenance outside its boundaries. Its hunger was as monstrous as its size and as it consumed, it moved farther and farther away from its original home. It now believed it had a considerable breadth in which to hunt. Sometimes, the things it caught chose to fight, or tried to fight, especially the little ones. It discovered it liked it when the things tried to resist. It had learned, long ago, that the meat seemed much more flavorful when they did. Why this was so remained a mystery, but it knew that fighting was good, so let them fight.

Let them struggle.

They tasted better when they did.

15

Two Knife reached the koch. The sight of the vehicle made his heart jump in his chest. Then, he remembered the loyalist Sujins still unaccounted for. His own minions swarmed the area and quickly established that the prize they sought was gone. Staring hard enough to scorch the underside of the koch, Two Knife saw for himself that the strong box had been taken. As he was in a rush, the manner of its removal did not enter his mind. Klytus and Desso lurked nearby. Side-by-side as they were, the picture gave Two Knife thoughts of a vicious dwarf standing in the shade of a mountain. Both of them expressed an eagerness to find the remaining Sujins. Two Knife would have been content to let them go if the treasure was where it was supposed to be. However, it was not, and that presented a problem.

"They have it," Klytus rumbled, dark eyes fixed on his leader.

"Well," Two Knife remarked. "It isn't here, is it? Damn them."

"They can't be far," Toffer said from nearby. He had tied a thick strip of cloth around his bare head. A rosy flower stained the cloth where his ear had been, and sweat began turning the white cloth dark. "They would have to carry the thing. The horses are dead."

"The horses are ripped apart," a man observed with a disgusted face. "What, in Saimon's hell, could have done such a thing?"

"Whatever it was is a friend," Toffer decided. "They would've been farther down this road if they had horses. If the koch stayed on the road…"

"Whatever then," Two Knife scoffed. "Horses don't concern me now. That box is what I want. Anything inside?"

A Sujin's head popped up from the upturned doorway. "Nothing. Mostly gowns."

"Gowns?" Two Knife repeated, exchanging looks with a puzzled Toffer.

As proof, the warrior handed down an extravagant evening gown decorated with precious stones about the neckline. Klytus took it from the man and held it up before his face. Its silky length bounced down before his interested eyes. Two Knife snatched it away, staring hard at his henchman. Dismissing the brute, Two Knife inspected the gown, the fine fabric becoming knots in his fists. Clothing? *Women's* clothing? He stretched the gown to its fullest. Tumblers began to fall in his mind: the Axemen, the treasure…The treasure was just that, but the *real* treasure…

Two Knife looked to Klytus. The man was holding up a lady's undergarments now, his rough face piqued with an even greater interest. Two Knife snatched those away as well. "Royalty!" he announced and spun on Desso with wide eyes. "Royalty! *Now* I understand!"

A grimacing Toffer stepped back, ever wary of his leader. Two Knife held the clothes up for him to see. "A woman! A princess, I wager! A princess that's to be married. The treasure was her dowry! A dowry for some idiot in Marrn! We were escorting a princess! A bride, Toffer! A *bride!* That bastard Bloor! He fed us the story about riches but he was hiding the real treasure! A princess!"

Toffer nodded his understanding. His head still rang from his missing ear, but he was much quicker to catch on than Desso. Anyone was faster to catch on than Klytus, but Klytus was not recruited by Two Knife for his thinking skills. Other Sujins standing around began muttering their revelations.

Two Knife calmed himself. He was grinning widely when he faced his killers. "We were after a fortune and we still are, but now there is an even greater fortune waiting for us. It will be dangerous. Have no doubts on that. But if you accept the risks, you will live like kings in distant lands. We have something here of even greater value!"

Desso's weapons came up in a gesture of "What?"

"Ransom!" Two Knife cried out.

For the briefest of moments, Toffer's wounds ceased to hurt, and his face broke out in the slyest of grins. He knew he wasn't wasting his time with Two Knife. The man thought big.

Jace moved through the tangle of the forest, while the rest of the men followed behind. Light and shadow dappled the ground as the afternoon made its relentless march. Jace had no desire to hunt trolls at night. He considered himself brave, but intelligent. Daylight was best. It was a fact that as big as trolls grew, the things could remain as still as stone when they wanted. So still that, under the proper conditions, people could walk right by them. More than once, hunters had their heads twisted from their shoulders by huge claws reaching out of the shadows. Nighttime would be hellish if a malicious troll was about the area. He had seen it happen, and it wasn't pretty.

Following a troll did not take much skill, but who in his right mind would do such a thing? Jace frowned as memories and feelings flooded his mind. The men behind him were becoming noisier, and he shot them a scornful look. At least the horseman companion of the Cavalier had dismounted to better keep his beast quiet. If the troll heard them, it could turn back on them just for the sport. Trolls spoiled for a fight during the right seasons, and ripping something apart would be a thing of delight for them. However, with only a handful of men after it, the beast might decide to press on with its prize. Jace scowled again. The princess was as good as dead in his mind, if she wasn't already. If the troll felt threatened, it just might fling her at them to ensure its own escape. The shattered strongbox came to his mind. A princess would make a mess amongst these trees. Then again, the thing just might bolt her down its gullet and run for the nearest marsh or swampland.

He just hoped the thing hadn't eaten half of her already somewhere along its path. That would be a sight he wasn't certain he could handle. Jace's scowl deepened as if he were being cut with jagged glass. None of the possibilities were favorable for the girl. Still, he would press on. He did not think Bloor would give up until he had her, or her remains.

"Wait," Bloor said, looking about the woods. Jace stopped walking and regarded the Cavalier with an unhappy look. This one was too used to giving orders.

Bloor continued sizing up the terrain. They were actually walking up a steep rise in the land, and the Cavalier saw the brush thinning and the sun making a stronger appearance up ahead. Light reflected off his armor. He gave the area a thought. Bows could be possible here, to a point. There was a natural corridor to let arrows fly without too many trees to slow them.

"Alwan," Bloor said, as he looked back the way they had come. "What do you think?"

The other man, quiet up until now, inspected the area for a moment. The slope went from north to south. The embankment was a small one, but for a determined defender, and one that was hiding as well...

"Workable," Alwan said with a professional air. "Good for a stab."

"Everything is good for a stab with you."

"Everything is," the black-bearded man said quietly, still inspecting the terrain. Jace did not like him. He had a bad feeling about the man, and his feelings were rarely wrong.

"I hope you get the opportunity then," Bloor informed him. "You and the rest will stay here. Bleed these maggots after us." He faced Jace. "We'll move on."

"Just you and I?"

"And the horse," Bloor answered.

An unpleasant expression came across Jace's features. Did he truly mean they were to hunt the troll alone? A full-grown troll? The hunter felt his knees tense up.

"Follow us when you can," Bloor said directly to Alwan. "The trail shouldn't be too hard for you to find."

Alwan's black eyes glittered like a cat. He smiled, knowingly, and cast his attention towards the earth he stood upon.

"And don't get killed." Bloor warned him.

This final order made Alwan grin wider. It brought his teeth into view. The shadows made his expression all the more unsettling for the men ordered to stay with him.

Bloor turned his attention to the six remaining Sujins. "He is a Cavalier, as I am. You obey him as you would me. Do as he says, and you'll live. Understood?"

As one, the Sujins stated that they did. Bloor studied the faces of the gathered men. He wondered if they were still in shock at the wicked attempt on their lives by their sword brothers. Maybe Seddon would grant them the opportunity to settle the score. Then Morianna entered his mind. These Sujins would have to fend for themselves and buy him time enough to rescue her. Two Knife's Sujins would be coming this way, and soon. Dividing his forces was a risk, but given the circumstances, it was one that he had to accept. Bloor turned his back on them and faced the scout.

"We go," he said.

"Just the two of us?" Jace asked, barely suppressing the doubt he was feeling.

"For now," Bloor replied. "Find this thing, scout."

"Oh, I'll find it," Jace responded with confidence. "But what are you going to do when I *do* find it?"

"Kill it." Just like that. The man spoke the words with an edge as threatening as any blade. Jace considered Bloor for a moment, wondering if the man really knew what they were in for. This one struck Jace as having a sizeable pair of balls. However, this was a troll they were pursuing, and balls would only get one so close to the beast. There was an old a joke amongst the troll hunters: Those with the biggest balls regretted it the instant a troll had a hold of them.

"We need more men," Jace said quietly.

Bloor fixed him with such an unfriendly face that, for a moment, Jace believed he had done something incredibly wrong, like cursing in the face of Seddon.

"We go," Bloor repeated in a hard voice. Jace smiled gently at the attempt of intimidation. The man obviously did not know what he was talking about.

"We need…" and the hunter paused. He wanted to tell the Cavalier that he had hunted these monsters for ages. He wanted to tell him that a *pack* of warriors was needed to bring down one of the beasts, and that a lesser number was plain foolishness. He wanted to tell him of his own folly when he went after a troll for the first time. He remembered when he beheld one of the creatures in all its destructive glory and how his own awe nearly killed him. In the end, he wanted to tell the Cavalier that if he really wanted to save the woman, he would need whatever manpower he could muster. Two dozen Sujins would be best, and a handful *might* do it, but two? *Two?*

Bloor cut him off before he could lecture him on any of this. "Now!" he said.

Disbelief in his eyes, Jace shook it off as if he were airing out a dusty blanket. Contempt curled his features and he turned away without another word. There would be no showing this one. He was poisoned with the convictions of his own ability. There would be only one way to show him the error of his judgment, and Seddon help them all when the time came. Without another word, Jace lead the Cavalier into the forest. The thoughts lingering on the hunter's mind seethed with black anger. The thing they were pursuing was not a forgiving sort, nor was it mindless enough to simply flee like a wolf or similar predator. They had something of an advantage in that it did not know it was being pursued or how many were pursuing it. However, once it did, it would no longer be a hunt. For one side, it would be a massacre.

Alwan watched them leave and stood staring even after they were long gone. The black-bearded Cavalier said not a word to any of the Sujins standing around. He idly patted the face of his horse and ignored the men waiting on him. One of the Sujins, restless in knowing that the day was moving on, glanced at his companions before speaking out. "What shall we do now, Lord?"

Alwan did not say anything. He kept on comforting the horse, as if it was dear to him. The Sujins fidgeted. Was the man deaf? Didn't he hear Bloor's instructions? What was wrong? When the time for an answer had long since gone by, the man who had posed the question moved to ask it again. Alwan faced him, pursing his lips. His black eyes shone in the rays of the scant forest light. "We kill." Then, the Cavalier smiled at them all, a maniac's smile. "Or be killed."

Gatesin wished Bloor was dead. As he scooped up loose treasure into his pack, he envisioned a giant troll grabbing the Cavalier by the neck and twisting it off. It would be a messy ending to a long career, but Gatesin believed that it was just. It would be blindingly painful for an instant, and then nothing. Yes, if Bloor did fail in his chase of the troll and the Sunjan princess, Gatesin would scarcely be able to conceal his delight. The man had accused him of being a traitor and the reason behind the Field of Skulls. Gatesin felt he had proven his innocence and his loyalty to Sunja in the months that followed the massacre, yet the Cavalier was obviously not the forgiving kind.

"Over there, Gatesin," Primo pointed out a clump of gold coins near the base of a small tree. The gold sparkled in the sparse light. Gatesin nodded shuffled towards the small pile of wealth.

"I'm too honest a man," Tungang growled nearby. He finished stuffing precious stones into his own pack. "Look at all this. No wonder they want it. Riches here to buy anything a man wants. Anything a hundred men want."

"Keep at it," Primo ordered, placing a hand on his lower back and arching into a stretch. He cast a watchful eye on the way they had come. The dark part of his mind suspected Two Knife's Sujins were massing in the shadows, ready to overwhelm them. He wanted to be off soon. "Hurry."

Then Primo crouched just a bit, straining to see anything through the shadows, one hand on his sheathed sword, the other held his shield. On his back was his own full pack. Gatesin scooped up the small handful of coins, wondering if the gold would be missed at all if he left it. The Sujin glanced up, his face glistening with a light sweat. He saw the pose struck by Primo against a backdrop of grey-green and dark shades. The image opened his mind and a memory tumbled out.

"What are you thinking about there?" Balto said, nearby. The man's voice brought Gatesin back and he looked about to find his comrade standing next to him.

"About Makko."

"Oh."

"And Delk."

Balto's lips tightened. "Ah, I see. Brave lads they were."

"They were," Gatesin agreed.

"Who's Makko?" Tungang wanted to know, finishing stuffing gold coins into his back pack. Some gold fell back to the earth, yanking a curse from the man.

"You hear everything, do you?" Balto asked.

"Not as much as I want," Tungang admitted. "Especially when it comes to our friend here, and his mysterious past."

"Ask anyone and I'm sure they'll tell you of the field," Balto said.

"They'll tell me a tale of the field," Tungang caught him. "Most of men who were there are dead now, Balto."

"Ah," Balto frowned. "So they are. And my own memory isn't what it used to be," he admitted, with a sly eye in Gatesin's direction.

"If you ever do remember," Tungang said, much too loudly for everyone's comfort. "Tell me."

"I'll tell you to shut up," Primo snapped at him. "And I'll not tell you again, else I'll slap you hard enough to make the other two of you run back to their tribes."

Tungang shut his trap and ground his teeth. His officer was right, but the anger in him still wanted to dare the man into trying just what he promised.

However, then Primo's hand went up, and all the Sujins paused in their work.

The forest air hummed with silence. Balto and Gatesin exchanged looks. Sound had an interesting way of carrying in the halls of a forest, but the absence of sound in this one was unsettling. The woods carried not a single call of birds. A pretend stillness gathered about them, like a thick blanket trying to deaden a quiet step or a child holding its breath until the moment to cry out. Something was trying with all its might to stay as quiet as possible, and its approach thundered in an unnatural silence.

"They're coming," Hatch whispered, eyes steady and peering into the gloom.

"They're here," Primo corrected him. Balto nodded. He caught a scent on a scant breeze, as bare as perfumed flesh. Sweat. Of course, he thought, it could be his own sweat.

"Balto." The Sujin looked to Primo.

"Lead everyone else back to the others. Take this," he shrugged off his backpack, heavy with treasure. Balto took it with one hand and promptly gestured for Tungang to take it. Primo handed his shield to another Sujin and took the man's bow and arrows.

"Tavan, you're with me." The man nodded and handed his own pack over to Hatch. The Sujin took it, watching Tavan readying his own bow.

"Go now," Primo instructed Balto. "We'll slow them down as much as possible. Move fast and run when the screaming starts. Drop off our shields somewhere behind us. We'll use them later." Primo hefted his new bow and tested the string. He looked out into the forest. "And don't look back."

"Understood," Balto said in a low voice.

With baleful looks, the departing Sujins left. A grim-faced Hatch gave a curt nod to his sword brothers staying behind. Seeing their bravery made him momentarily forget the itching in his nether regions. He knew both men from two campaigns against the Nordish Jackals. Tavan was an excellent archer and, though capable enough, Hatch wished Primo had ordered him to stay and watch their backs, as he had done so many times before. However, Primo was there, and Primo was very good. Taking a breath, Hatch adjusted the pack he carried and left them.

No sooner were the treasure-encumbered Sujins out of sight than Primo drew Tavan close. Both men checked the quivers on their backs and sheathed their blades. Primo strummed his bowstring with two fingers as if it was an instrument instead of a weapon that could easily punch through armored plate at short range.

"You really think you would have hit that driver?" he asked the younger man.

"Through the eye," Tavan informed him.

That made Primo pause. "Ready?" Tavan nodded. "Then move over that way. Shoot the first target you see and move. Never stay in one place too long, but don't give ground until they press you. I'll do the same from my side. An arrow and then I'll move. Listen for the screams. One or two arrows and move. Understood? Keep at it until you have nothing left to shoot. Maybe we'll bloody their noses enough to make them pause. Maybe even draw them off the others."

"What if they charge?" Tavan asked. Primo stared into the face of the man he ordered to remain behind with him. Their chances were not good, but this Sujin was going to stand with him without a word of protest. That kind of loyalty, of sense of duty, inspired Primo.

"Did I ever tell you," Primo said, slipping around the question, "that I was once very good with a harp?" Tavan cocked his head in mild surprise. "Well, I was."

"Never tried to play it myself."

"Don't," Primo told him. "Try a wind instrument instead. Easier on the fingers."

"I will do that," Tavan said, and meant it.

Primo nodded. That was all the time they had. He pointed with his bow. "You're there. I'll be over there. And try not to stick an arrow in me."

"You won't know it if I do," Tavan said, and tapped the tip of his bow to his eye. Smirking, Tavan moved away from his officer. Primo darted off in the other direction. He stepped lightly where he could, in moss patches where he found them. He finally knelt down behind a large tree, his bow held low, arrow pointing to the ground. Sunlight flowed past him. Primo watched the gloom of the forest and waited.

16

Desso moved like a cat through the brush. In fact, he envisioned himself as one of the great predatory cats. It was said that huge black ones lived in the south lands, where the night was every bit as hot and sultry as the day. When he was younger, he had been in the service of a merchant that made a business of selling rich rugs picturing animals and creatures of all sizes and legends. Desso's job at the time was keeping the dust and grit from the material. As a boy, he would struggle with the great handmade weavings, hoisting them up to the roof of the merchant's building. He would hang them over bare wooden beams and brush them out carefully.

Sometimes, when the merchant was not looking, Desso would punch the rugs. He liked the way they buckled under his fists. He liked the sound of his fists against the rugs' hides. He would have liked to hit them with something heavier, but he feared damaging the merchandise. It was a game to him, a secret pastime he enjoyed that eventually went on to luring stray alley cats. He would feed them, feign tenderness, and bring them close enough so that he could stroke their backs. He wondered if the animals were shocked at all when the hands massaging them suddenly snatched them up and pummeled them. Sometimes they managed to draw blood, but after a while, he learned to wrap his hands in rags.

When he worked for the merchant, Desso could care less what he saw on the rugs most of the time. One day, a picture seized his attention. It was a dark rug, with a bare moon in one corner and an ebony jungle stretching out below it. In the jungle, a pair of animals resembling horses grazed. The creatures were sleek and their bare backs gleamed with moonlight. To the right of them, edging its way down a rocky cliff, unseen by the feeders, was a great black cat. Desso had heard of lions and tigers, but this was neither. Its hide was as black as pitch and its eyes shimmered, as green and restless as a sea. It was a night hunter, and he believed it to be a particularly dangerous one, strong and silent and striking with both fang and claw. The beast had a made such an impression on the young lad, that a week later, the picture still on his mind, Desso joined the Sujins. He would become the great cat in the picture. He, too, would be a feared hunter of the night, and not only to stray animals in alleyways.

Perhaps when he had made his fortune, he would buy that very same rug from his old master, or beat him within an inch of his life and then take it from the old man. Desso thought of owning a villa and having every arch draped with pictures of all the great cats, but not the black one. That one he would hang over his bed. An expensive wish, and one he soon realized was not to be had on his meager wages.

It was not difficult for Two Knife to win him over. The prospect of snatching a fortune from a king that cared little for his Sujins and making off with it to parts unknown struck a chord of adventure and daring in Desso.

Moving forward now with his shortsword and shield, Desso became the great beast he idolized. Somewhere ahead, his prey waited. The signs were all around. He scoured the ground and bush and went the way they led him, taking him off the old trail and into territory now spoiled by fleeing men. He would find these Sujins soon enough. When he did, he would kill them with fang and claw.

"Here," he drew up and pointed. On the ground before them, half-hidden by a small woodland flower was a single gold coin.

Toffer came out from behind him and picked it up. He bit into it. "Tastes like gold to me!" he exclaimed, excitedly, and stuffed the piece into a belt pouch.

Two Knife and the rest of his Sujins gathered round. The renegade Right Koor saw the broken shards of the strongbox. The men they hunted had not wasted time on hiding the smashed wood. The loyalists knew they were coming. He wondered how far ahead they might be.

"Only the one gold piece, though," Toffer said. "They have the rest. Lapped it up like dogs at their own balls."

"You just took the first piece of your cut," Two Knife directed at Toffer.

"One gold piece more than I ever had," the pale man answered him with an unpleasant smile.

"How far along are they?" Two Knife swung back to Desso. The dark mass of Klytus moved behind the man, like a whale just under the surface of the sea, poised to swallow him whole. Desso did not like having anyone standing behind him anymore than a great cat liked being on its back.

"Not far," Desso told his commander, stepping away from Klytus. The big man watched him go.

"Get to it then," Two Knife ordered.

"We should look for more," Toffer said.

"For what?" Two Knife threw back at him. "Scraps? Go ahead and pig about then. The main prize has been carried off already. I want to get it before they begin having thoughts of taking it for themselves."

Klytus wore an expression of dark concern.

"I wouldn't be surprised if someone amongst them decided to 'lose' whatever they were carrying. This much wealth has an effect on maggots. Just look at us," Two Knife explained. "Look at what we're doing in the king's service, sworn to defend his name and honor," an evil chuckle escaped him. "Saimon only knows what we would do to anyone else."

He gestured for Desso to get moving, and the man did so. The rest of the Sujins, a wave of warriors, followed him through the forest.

The trail was still fresh. They had not been gone long, and perhaps were even closer than he suspected. He would have to be careful; they may try something. Part of him doubted it, as they had the greater numbers, but the men they hunted were Sujins. Harried and hunted, they would do anything but what was expected of them.

Toffer muttered something behind him, but his words were lost sounds to Desso. His ears were tuned to listening forward, not behind. Toffer said something again. Then Two Knife.

With an annoyed sigh, Desso ceased hunting in his great cat mindset. Instinct retreated to reason. He straightened and half-turned to the men behind. A look of loathing hung about his features, as if the men had ribbons of noisy chimes fixed to their behinds. Desso's arms went wide as if to say "What?"

From where Two Knife crouched, Desso was framed between two trees. A sharp hiss of wind perked his ears, and in that instant, an arrow shot into Desso's back and half emerged from his chest, stretching the front of his chain mail vest. Desso inhaled sharply, as if being doused with freezing water, before dropping his sword and shield. He fell to his knees, one hand cupping the straining bulge in his chest, while the other reached halfway behind his back. Desso finally rolled over onto his side, wondering why the pain was suddenly not so bad.

The men behind him bolted for the protection of nearby trees. "*Dog balls!*" Toffer exclaimed, landing hard on his elbows behind a fence of brush. His missing ear ached dearly when he hit the ground, and he put a fist to the bloody bandage, willing it to stop and only making it worse.

Two Knife raised his head above the rock he hid behind. Desso lay dead to his right, gone from the world, with an arrow through his middle as if it were a hardened apple. Two Knife let a string of curses loose and thudded his forehead into the soft ground. He should have been more careful than this!

"Seddon Almighty," Toffer said, harshly. "Bastard got dead good and proper. Straight through the middle. Damn fine shot at that."

"Yes it was," Two Knife had to agree, peering at his officer with accusing eyes. "Why couldn't we have gotten *him* to join with us?"

"I did what I could with the time I had," Toffer said defensively. "We did well for ourselves, I'd say."

Another arrow hissed through the halls of the forest, and another grunt of pain. "Stay down," Two Knife yelled. Only two arrows thus far. Shooting in a forest was difficult, to say the least. There was at least one archer, perhaps more, but he doubted it. There simply weren't enough Sujins remaining. They were somewhere close by. The woods were thick, and straight lines of fire would be difficult to get. All they needed was to find a long corridor and they would find their archer at the end of it. However, they would have to circle around to take him, and that meant time. Times like these, Two Knife despised archers. Behind him, sprawled out and kissing dirt, were his remaining Sujins. It was like Bloor to do something like this. The man was keeping him from his prize and it galled him.

"Toffer."

"Yes?"

"Get our maggots ready."

Tavan hurried back twenty paces after sticking the lead man through the chest. He skipped to and fro, ducking and weaving behind tall pillars of timber. He darted in behind a large tree trunk, putting his back to it. Breathing hard, he glanced back to see if he was being followed. He saw that his field of fire had been greatly reduced. No more than twenty paces out now. Too close. In the dim light, it would be even more difficult to catch a man unprotected, now that they knew he was about. He smirked. Too close for some poor dog. Tavan reached behind his ear and felt the feathered shaft of an arrow. He extracted the missile and nocked it. Placing his shoulder against the tree, he looked back the way he had come, searching for targets.

Primo retreated a similar distance before dropping down onto his belly. He lay behind a mound, framed on either side by spruce trees. He peered over the crest of dirt and rock and could see the treacherous Sujins ahead, grey black wraiths amongst the trees. One stood up, placing a tree between himself and Tavan's aim, but exposing his side to Primo. If he stayed that way a few moments more…

The shriek jerked Two Knife's head around in time to see a Sujin flop into view only paces away, a buried shaft in his ribs. The dying man hitched backwards, gripping the killing arrow and staring at where it caught him. He dropped to the ground a moment later, one leg shivering in death.

That was enough for Two Knife. He looked about and signaled for Klytus. The man barely hid his bulk behind a tree trunk. Two Knife chopped a hand in the direction from which the arrow had flown. The big man nodded and left, gathering up a handful of Sujins as he went.

"At least two of them now," Toffer observed from where he took cover behind a tree.

"At least," Two Knife grumped. "But not for long."

"It could be a trap."

"Our money is that way," Two Knife reminded the man, not caring in the least how Toffer cringed and pressed a hand against the bandage of his head wound. "And I think this is about all there is to their trap. Remember, Toffer: They are only a few. We are the many. And these toppers have slowed us enough."

Two Knife crossed his chest with his swords. He thought for a moment, then shoved one of the blades into a scabbard at his waist. He groped for the shield near Desso's corpse and pulled it to him.

"I've had enough of this," he growled to the Sujins around him. "Shields up."

Tavan waited for a target. The traitors were wise to him now and weren't taking any risks. He hoped to be able to wreak more carnage amongst their ranks, but the odds of that were shrinking. With a huff of breath, he turned and ran, dead brush snapping with each step. He ran for several heartbeats, leaving the Sujins far behind him. He darted behind a tree and glanced back. He had run through a short corridor, an excellent spot for a ready archer. He studied the huge spruce he stood behind and considered climbing it. His shoot and move tactic would be useless if he did. No, he would stay grounded. With that, he crouched to one knee and readied an arrow. It was a short alleyway he had run through, but he would nail the first maggot he saw on the path.

His patience nearly spent, Two Knife barked, "Up and forward!" A line of Sujins rose and linked shields with a practiced ease. A second line stood behind the first, raising their shields and linking them across the tops of the Sujins in front. With their roof and wall in place, the line was now protected from arrows from ahead and above.

In the middle of the line, Two Knife gave the order to advance.

Primo heard the crunch of underbrush. He leaned out from behind his cover and saw the line move off in Tavan's direction. He decided to break those formed ranks with a few well-placed arrows. A snap of brush nearby snatched his attention and he turned to see a loose knot of men approaching cautiously. They had managed to come up behind him. A curse tore through his mind. There were too many, and he should not have hoped a man like Rusk would leave his dogs in one place for long. Primo's stomach flashed cold and he willed the fear away. He stepped a few paces to his left, knowing they had not yet spotted him; however, that would soon change. He smoothly extracted another arrow, took aim, and released.

A short grunt sounded and a man flew backwards, an arrow sticking out of his face. The others cried out and charged. Primo readied the next arrow, the feathered end pulled close to his cheek. The shields went up. Primo lowered his aim and released.

A charging man fell flat on his chest, his right shin punctured. The others came on. Like a well-oiled machine, Primo nocked an arrow, aimed, and released. The range was much shorter now, and the missile smashed through a raised shield, nailing the forearm it hung upon. The owner cried out in pain and fury, dropping back behind those who continued their charge. Perhaps twenty paces away from him. Primo drew again, refusing the temptation to rush his aim. He loosed. The impact of the arrow on shield rang through the forest gloom.

Ten paces.

Primo turned and ran.

Like hounds on a deer, the remaining Sujins yelled out in fury when they saw the archer take flight.

Klytus saw the escaping man and dropped his sword. He hauled out a dagger and flung it at the man's back. The blade spun through the air, cutting for its target, and Klytus' heart leapt in his chest. However, at the moment of impact, the man darted to the right and the blade whacked into the wooden flesh of a tree. The man disappeared into the brush with four Sujins on his trail. Klytus watched them give chase for a moment. They would catch him. Not giving another thought to the matter, he casually retrieved his sword and his favorite dagger.

The wall of shields before Tavan extended well beyond what he could see. He didn't think that was a good sign for him. One bowman was not going to be much of a threat against a disciplined advance of Sujins. He chose to fall back, drawing them after him, and maybe circling behind if possible.

If he were going to do that...

Tavan shrunk back from the shield wall.

Through a crack in the shields, Two Knife spotted a figure moving deeper into the brush. "He's moving," the renegade leader said sharply. "After him!" The wall broke down and the hunt began.

Tavan could hear the clatter of shields as they came apart and decided to run. Clutching his bow and head bent low, he began sprinting though the woodland, leaping and ducking as the landscape blurred by. He weaved in and out of the trees looming before him, slowing somewhat as he dropped down a low embankment filled with a stream with water the color of black glass and stones like robins' eggs. Breathing hard, he crossed the water in two splashes. He barely felt the chill of the water through the thin material of his boots. He came up to the opposite side of the sharp rising embankment and threw his bow up. Tavan hauled himself up after his weapon. Flipping his legs up and over, he snatched his bow and flung himself behind the protection of an old tree. The hounds were chasing him, but Tavan wasn't going to run all day. This fox still had some bite. The hunters came closer.

Tavan waited until he heard the first boot hit the water. Then he stepped smoothly out from behind his hiding place. A line of Sujins filled the small channel. They spied the lone archer as one.

"Swee..." one Sujin began.

Tavan shot him through the mouth.

Then a dagger crashed into his chest. Tavan staggered back a step, staring at the weapon sticking out of his chest and feeling only a buzz of pain as blood swelled about the dull metal. His back hit a tree and he slid down its base. The forest began to spin and he was at its center, his eyeballs being forced back into his head. By that time, a Sujin had climbed the bank and yanked the helmet from his head. A shortsword was poised at Tavan's throat. He felt the pointed tip. He looked up, and the smile that greeted him was that of a hyena.

"Should've kept running," a voice said, and the sword pushed home.

Toffer handed the bow of the corpse to Two Knife. The rogue Right Koor considered it for a moment. This rabbit was dead, and he deserved it for the chase he led them on. Two Knife sawed at the bowstring, snapping it in two, and tossed the ruined weapon onto Tavan's body.

"A waste," Two Knife snarled. "A damned waste to have come all this way after one man."

"There's still the other," Toffer said. "But our boys'll catch him soon enough."

Two Knife shook his head and peered back the way they had come. "Damn me for a fool, but I was taken. Running after this rabbit has only let the others widen their lead over us. Damn me to Saimon's blue hell if I let that happen again."

Toffer nodded quietly. His wound began buzzing anew with pain. Somehow, ending the life of this one Sujin caused him a brief moment of clarity. He focused on Two Knife's words; the man was right. Chasing the one man as they had! It was embarrassing to be diverted.

Two Knife cast a poisoned look in the direction of the escaping Sujin. The wasted effort left a taste as foul as bile in his mouth. He would not be fooled a second time.

While Tavan was dying, Primo was growing tired of running. Behind him were only four hunters. The thought of running from their likes was galling. He steamed up a low hill and reached the crest. He paused at the top, spinning around and standing tall in the grey gloom of the forest. Beads of sunlight speckled the ground about him as he readied his bow. Primo did not wait long.

He shot the first Sujin to appear out of the shade, the arrow razoring into mail and breast bone with a pop of metal ringlets. The impact took his life, and in the time it took for him to drop to his knees, the three others behind him were fanning out, seeking to flank the archer. Primo readied another arrow, its feathered end near his cheek. He concentrated on only what needed to be done. His patience was rewarded when one man stepped out from behind a tree and darted behind another. The tree granted his body protection, but the man's lower calf lay exposed. Primo released and the arrow zipped through the meat of the calf, bringing the man down with a roar.

Then there were two, and the two charged the hill.

Primo hurried one arrow, and it drove into an up-raised shield instead of a throat. Then there was no time for anything else. Primo threw his bow aside and yanked his blade out, parrying a lunge as he did so. The officer danced backwards, avoiding a slash from the Sujin on the left. Then both men were on the hill. The first man threw aside his shield and charged in, hacking at his former officer's head. Primo stopped the attack at high guard and chopped down at the exposed knee of an over-extended leg. His blade bit bone but did not cut through. The man's face went ashen and he dropped to the ground. Primo darted back, yanking upwards and pulling his sword free. The second Sujin waded in before Primo could deliver the killing cut. The two men stood at arm's length for a moment, studying each other for weakness. Primo recognized the man who fought him, but he could not put a name to his face. Behind him, he could see the other man with his leg half sheared off, vomiting onto the ground. On that cue, both men attacked.

Slash and parry, jab and circle, the two men whirled about each other. The first breath Primo had, he looked into the eyes of the man he fought and said, "Quit now and I'll spare you. I'll forget all of this and you can be a Sujin again. Lower your sword."

The other man smiled and the flash of teeth was as friendly as a skull's. "I've already killed two sword brothers to get to you, men I ate and drank with. I gutted them, and I'll gut you."

The man lunged.

His sword held two handed, Primo deflected the blade coming at him and stepped in close to the man. His elbow pistoned into the other's face once, then twice, mashing the Sujin's nose and driving him backwards. Wasting no time, Primo punched his sword into the man's guts. The traitor's eyes flew open.

"Like this?" Primo asked, and shoved the dying man back down the hill. The Sujin fell and rolled only a short distance. Primo looked down on the body with disdain. How could the Sujins have maggots like these in their ranks?

Then he heard the noise. Primo looked up. The other warrior was still holding his leg. His face was a pasty grey from blood loss, his eyes hooded and sleepy looking. Primo casually stepped over to the man, noting his sword lying on the ground. The wounded man followed his gaze, but did not move. Without a word, Primo took another step and stabbed the man through the throat. The Sujin gurgled a cry and collapsed on his back.

Primo regarded the man and the dagger he had hidden beside his thigh. He had spotted the blade's tip and noted the out-of-sight hand, readying for a quick thrust for when he was close enough, no doubt. Primo sighed. These maggots were truly the lowest form of life amongst the remaining Klaws of Sunja. The man should have surrendered. Had he done so, Primo would have spared the man.

The thought made Primo think long and hard, longer than perhaps he should have. He exhaled and heard the moans of the last hunter he had wounded. He searched the woods, and there, in the corridor of the forest, he spotted the first man holding his lower leg with the arrow still in it, his back against a tree.

Beyond him appeared another Sujin. The wounded man quieted when the new Sujin emerged, but became animated once the man came closer. The man—a big one—paused and listened to the wounded one's report of the battle he just witnessed on the hill. The big Sujin hunkered down, and as Primo watched, drove his sword through the wounded man's gullet.

The newcomer waited for a moment before pulling his blade free. In the hush of the woods, the disturbing sound reached Primo easily enough. When the man finished, he stood and turned to face Primo on the hill. He studied the officer for a moment. Then, without a word, he walked forward, the brush snapping underfoot.

Primo's mouth screwed itself up as if it were full of raw lemon. He should have recognized the brute as soon as he saw him: Klytus.

"If you throw… down …" Primo began, and then let the words die. He realized how ridiculous he must sound. Klytus had just killed one of his own, and not because he was a traitor, but because the man could no longer walk. He supposed the man might be a loyalist, but something in his quiet approach told Primo different. The officer glanced about his person and spied a shield from the one whose nose he had flattened. Taking his time, he walked over and picked it up.

Klytus reached the base of the hill and began walking up it, dark sunken eyes fixed on the man before him. Primo never realized just how black those eyes were until they were glued on his person. The gleam in them—it wasn't the light of a professional soldier who did his job and hoped to get off the field as soon as possible. The light in Klytus' eyes was malicious and eager. The eyes were those of a butcher who enjoyed his trade, enjoyed inflicting pain, and was confident in his work.

Sword and shield in hands, Klytus walked to within three paces of his former officer. Primo waited.

"Only you?" Klytus spoke, abruptly, his rough voice low but carrying on the quiet hill.

"Only me," Primo answered him.

They sprang at one another.

Back and forth they moved for seconds, testing and probing each other's defenses and ability. Primo realized with frank regret that the ogre before him was more than capable with a blade. Klytus realized, as he hacked at a head that was suddenly no longer there, that Primo probably earned his rank on sword play alone. Neither made any mistakes to end the fight early, but that would change as the battle wore on and their arms began to tire. Primo was tiring quickly. Klytus was the stronger of the two, and he rained blow after blow down onto Primo's shield. Sensing that the man was weakening, he began hammering at him with both sword and shield. With each connection that Primo could not dodge, his arms ached more and more, and he became more aware of how Klytus was watching him over the edge of his shield, like a ravenous monster would a trapped child. Overhanded now, Klytus brought his sword down on the other's shield, hammer stroke after hammer stroke, driving his foe back.

Primo stumbled. Klytus barreled in and realized the trick. He twisted suddenly, and the sword seeking his throat slipped along his jaw instead, opening up a terrible gash as if it were a bursting seam. Primo cursed at how his gamble almost ended the fight, but now he was practically underneath the bigger man. Klytus swung his heavy shield over Primo's guard, and its edge connected with the man's temple. Primo collapsed onto his belly, and Kyltus brought his shield down across the back of his exposed neck, driving the man against the ground. Primo's sword flew from numb fingers.

Standing with a foot on either side of the fallen man, Klytus drew back his blade and drove it through the small of

Primo's back. Other than the sound of steel shearing through mail links and vertebrae, Primo made not a sound. Kyltus stood over the man for a few moments, inspecting his kill, blood from his chin spattering onto Primo's back. He finally wrenched the blade free and stabbed again, just to make certain. Finally satisfied that the man was dead, he pulled the weapon out and wiped it across the body. He gingerly felt the cut along his jaw and grimaced at the sting. He would need stitching for this one, and he had killed the only nearest comrade who might have done the service. The big man cursed himself. He sometimes killed too quickly, and something usually bit him in the arse when he did. Cursing, he lumbered over and sawed away some cloth from the corpses surrounding him. He balled the material up and pressed it against his chin. Still bleeding, he turned about and decided to find Two Knife and the others.

Perhaps they had located the money, and the wench.

17

The man called Jace took the lead, letting the task of leading and quieting the horse fall to Bloor. Jace had no real use for the animals except as slaves, and in cases like this one, four-legged bait. Cavaliers, Lancers, and anyone else taken up with horses were all equally fools. They should get dogs, if they needed companions so badly. At least dogs were more manageable, and more tender, too, if one got caught on the trail without anything to eat.

The forest floor flattened out and thickened in areas. New trees the height of little children flourished in the gaps between older ones. Jace listened to how the sound of their passage carried for only a short distance and then thankfully died. Bloor was behind him, and he could feel the man's gaze on his back. The Cavalier was a cold one, but determination fired him to his core.

For Bloor, it took everything he had to keep from bolting into the woods, screaming out Morianna's name. If it were another man, Bloor would have beaten him senseless for such an unforgiving lack of discipline, for even just thinking it, and yet here was Bloor himself, having those very thoughts. He drew a breath. He hoped this would be all over and soon, but something warned him otherwise. He pushed the feeling from his head and heart.

Jace stopped abruptly in his tracks, bent over at the shoulders, and stared to the right, like a deer unsettled by something unseen. Bloor froze and followed the hunter's gaze. He saw only more trees and shadows, and nothing of the woman he sought. Why did the hunter stop?

Jace was suddenly beside him. "It's near," the man said, his lips barely moving, his breath foul.

"Where?" Bloor demanded in a hiss. To this, Jace raised his flat palm, invoking silence. The horse snorted. Jace moved to the animal and stroked his neck. It was a beautiful animal. A full sixteen hands high and well-muscled, well cared for.

Jace patted its neck gently and whispered in its fluttering ear. Then he cut the animal's throat in one quick movement. He held onto the reins as the horse jerked back and brought the dying beast to the ground. In the stillness of the forest, the blood lathered the soil like spilled soup. Jace dropped to a knee and stroked the head of the horse, watching its eye become glassy. As an afterthought, the hunter looked to a stoic Bloor. The horse had been with the Cavalier for perhaps all of a year. It was the longest time Bloor had ever owned a mount, and yet, in that time, he never named it. It was a good horse, but it served its purpose. He would sacrifice a hundred more like it to help their present cause.

Jace waited for the protest that never came. The grim-faced warrior said nothing. That was good; the man was in control.

"Horses are the best bait," Jace explained in a low hiss. "This will bring the monster on. It'll smell the blood. Seddon help us all."

Under granite eyes, Bloor's mouth moved. "You don't seem so confident anymore."

Jace regarded the man while trying to listen to the forest. For a moment, he said nothing. He measured the Cavalier standing before him and reminded himself that the warrior had no inkling of the might of the thing for which they searched.

"Don't you worry, I can do what I said I'd do. But there is a point where we won't be hunting the troll anymore. It'll be hunting us. Bringing down one of these things is a job for a group of men. Not two."

"We'll manage."

Jace smiled unpleasantly at the ignorance. "Oh we'll do *something*, I imagine. We'll do something." He stared Bloor in the eye. "When I was younger, I had a pack of lads to hunt these things down. A pack. Biggest, meanest, *bloodiest* bunch of bastards you ever laid eyes on or heard tell of. Ten men, and each of them as strong as you and me put together. They'd be a choice for your royal spearmen back there."

"Axemen."

"What did I say?"

"Spearmen."

"Oh. Well, whatever. They'd still be a choice."

Bloor did not tell the man that if he said the same in the company of Axemen, one of those blades would probably cleave his skull like so much soft cheese.

Jace went on. "The point is that I had a pack of the most able brutes for hunting back then. Six of them died during hunts. Two had limbs ripped out so they could never hunt again. One had been thrown into a cliff wall and was never right in the head afterwards. The last one retired. He tried to get me to retire. I told him, 'No, not while there are still trolls out there, not me!' And he called me a fool and one that was just walking around dead and didn't know it yet. Times like these, like now, with me and you, and you looking at me like you are now, times like these make me think…why didn't I listen to that tit?"

Jace broke out into a hiss of a laugh then and tried to suppress it. Bloor did not share it, and Jace sobered up upon seeing the man had no sense of humor. It was just his luck.

The hunter suddenly had a thought. "You ever been fishing, Lord?"

"No," Bloor admitted, which caused Jace to roll his eyes in exasperation.

"Well, say if you did. If you took time off from killing people, that is. Say if you did. What would you do if you went fishing for trout with your pole and line, and ended up hooking a whale? You think you could land it? Saimon's arse—you think you could even make the thing *pause?*"

Bloor did not answer.

"That's what we're fishing for this day, knowing full well that we only have a pole, line, and hook. That's exactly what we have here, the wrong equipment for the wrong kind of fish."

"Why didn't you mention this back at the wagon?" Bloor asked in a controlled tone.

"I did. I said, 'Just the two of us?' And you said nothing. What would you have done if I said anything more back there?"

Again, Bloor said nothing. They both knew what would have happened. Jace nodded, mild victory shining in his eyes. He especially knew what would have transpired and the command to find the beast would still be the same. Bloor was as hard as he was stubborn.

Jace stood up and stepped away from the dead horse. "Don't get any blood on you. We stink enough as it is, but the blood is the sauce it wants. Sort of like a big roast, drowned in its own juices."

If he meant it as a joke, Bloor was not amused. Jace frowned and gave up. "Once it gets wind of it, it'll be heading for us. Usually, we used ropes to snare the thing, but even the strongest ropes will not hold one for long. That's where you have your pack of men come in. You snare it and try to hold it long enough for the others to come in with their spears. Never get close to the beast. Stick it from afar with spears, not arrows. One can never trust an arrow to get through its hide, but a good iron-tipped spear…" Jace was nodding to himself, lost in a tide of memories. "Get one on a spear and you'll know it. A ride you'll not want to take twice, I tell you, if you decide to hang on to the spear once it's in."

"Why not use heavier weapons, like axes? Pole arms?" Bloor asked.

"Always used spears," Jace admitted, his brow crunching in puzzlement with the idea. "Never tried them things. You could, I suppose, but I prefer to jab at the things. Even the spears are no guarantee that you can take one down, but you have to start somewhere. Stick it in and run. Stick the bastard with as many as you are able. Stick it in his eye if you are lucky to get the shot, or the legs. The legs are a good target. Trolls hate to bend over. They're like old men when they do."

An unpleasant chuckle left the troll hunter then. "An old punce that will rip your arms out if it gets a hold of you."

"The eye, then," Bloor said to himself.

"I said if you are lucky to get a shot at the eye. The thing isn't going to stand still blinking at you. And then if you miss, well, the skull is as thick as any helmet. You might split the skin, but you'll not crack the skull with only a spear. Get a leg first. Take away its legs so it won't be able to run away, and even better, it won't be able to chase you. You can kill it from a distance. Burn it even, if you want."

Bloor was looking into the distance. "I see," he muttered.

Jace wondered if the man had listened to him at all. "You will eventually," he finally said, and when the Cavalier did, the hunter was willing to wager that he would be full of questions, if he lived. Jace studied his own weapons, an axe and a shortsword that he could almost laugh at now. It was just his fortune to be caught in a hunt without the right tools. His scowl was brimmed with ironic mirth. He had the worst possible weapons, short of being armed with only knives. In his ears, the ghosts of long-dead companions jeered and joked.

"We need more hands for this," he complained in a whisper. He shook his head and became quiet. That was fine by Bloor. For a man who wanted them both to be quiet, he had done plenty of talking.

They waited for moments, neither of them breaking the silence now nestling over the forest. Bloor's thoughts centered on the task ahead and rescuing Morianna. Things truly had taken an unfortunate turn, but he was certain he could make things right. His determination to accomplish whatever needed to be done was one of his greatest strengths.

Jace held up a hand then and moved to a tree. He motioned for Bloor to come close. Bloor did not move, and Jace gave him an annoyed look, his one eye glaring, but Bloor remained where he was.

The troll hunter scowled, turned about, and stepped over to stand directly in front of the Cavalier, nose-to-nose. "You want the girl, right?"

"Yes."

"And you say you've never hunted a troll before?"

"Not until now."

"Then, just so you don't get us *both* killed and her *eaten*, you do as I say. Rank means nothing here. Not to me and not now. Understand that?"

Bloor regarded the man with hard eyes, seeing how his empty eye socket shined. "I do."

However, Jace could see that the man did not believe. "Then listen to me," he continued on, "there are only the two of us. With a group of men we might have a chance to slay the beast. We go for the legs. Get the girl, scatter, and run. Whoever gets the girl runs with her. The other one leads the troll off in the opposite direction. There are no heroics in killing these things, only survival. Remember how it took the wagon apart? The horses? It was only hungry then. Think of what an *angry* troll would do. A *wounded* one. Think of it. We have only one chance to get the girl. Get the girl first and then maybe we kill it. But we get the girl first and get her away from it. Agreed?"

Bloor studied the man's face. "Agreed."

"Then listen. You will stand over there, behind those trees. Stay out of sight. I'll do the same over here. The blood will cover our scent and it'll go for the horse. When it does, we'll take it from the sides. Whoever can reach the girl first will take her before the other strikes, and that one will be the rabbit to run. These pig stickers," Jace held up his sword, "should cut it. Go for the legs. The knees. If either of us can get the knees, then the fight is won. If we can slow it down, we can get away from it, and that's the next best thing to killing it."

"Won't it be *angry* then?" Bloor asked with the barest sarcasm. "*Wounded?*"

Jace's good eye squinted at him in annoyance. "You want to do this alone? I think not. Just remember what I said. Whoever is able to get the girl grabs her, while the other baits the troll. Go for the legs. I figure they should be big enough for even you to hit. And don't slash them. *Stab* the topper. Stabbing's the best way to pierce the hide."

Bloor stared at the man. Legs be damned if he had a sure strike at the head.

Jace met the other's stare. Arrogant ass, his one eye projected.

Both men heard a noise then, a sound that made both look as one. Heavy and hot, like a blast from a metalsmith's bellows. Jace's face became hard and he shooed Bloor to move into position. The Cavalier quietly did as he was told, yet burned just a little with the resentment of taking orders from one obviously beneath him. Both men moved away from their bait, poising themselves just out of sight of the carcass. It came closer. Branches began to snap and the sound of breathing grew louder, harsher. The Cavalier edged further back behind his curtain of trees, placing his back to them and bringing his sword up. Was the thing circling them?

When he believed it to be feeding at the horse carcass, he craned his neck around to see. The bleeding carcass remained untouched. A louder cracking shattered the air, followed by the deflated squeal of *something*.

Bloor looked again, and still the horse lay untouched. Seddon above! How big was this thing?

The breathing came like the rattling of a fire now. Bloor wondered offhand if the beast breathed fire, though the hunter had said nothing of the sort. He found himself disliking the man. The hunter admired the monster too much for Bloor's tastes. What was a wild thing to the steel and training of Sunja? The notion irritated Bloor. To think that one troll would make a man fret so. Perhaps it was the rareness of the creature that convinced Jace that he was an authority on trolls. Well, Bloor would allow him that much, but he refused to be intimidated by the old hunter's stories.

Bloor's features darkened. *Fishing for whales, indeed.* Then he was aware of the footsteps. The troll approached slowly, each step a crunch of branches.

Then something heavy hit the tree Bloor hid behind, or punched it, and the forest trembled. He shuddered and pressed himself up hard against the bark, eyes narrowed in concentration. The breathing became deeper still, and no longer did Bloor think of standing near a bellows. Now he felt as if he were being sucked inside one.

Then there was nothing.

A pause, as if the thing was considering something.

There was the unmistakable movement of flesh, of joints cracking, then the snapping of tendons and ligaments being bitten and torn: the wet sounds of an animal feeding on the recent dead. A smell reached his nose and wrinkled it, a fecal smell, raw and strong and mixed with another stench that Bloor could not identify. Fingers flexing on his sword, Bloor inched out from behind his cover of trees.

He froze.

Side on and hunched over as the troll was now, it was equal in height to him. Standing, the troll was perhaps three or four heads taller than Bloor, and he was not a small man. It was huge in girth as well, perhaps three times the size of an armored Axeman. The arms of the thing were as thick as the body of a grown man. Bloor watched as muscles coated in a thick layer of fat shook and shivered. He caught a glimpse of tusked jaws, flexing and tearing into the horseflesh. A red maw worked noisily on its meal. Seddon above, the troll was huge!

Hunkered down, the thing ripped the flesh apart with bloody claws. Blood sprayed up the length of its forearms and face, speckling it. Bloor realized the truth behind Jace's words. Attacking the head was risky because the thing was too tall, out of an ordinary blade's reach. However, now the head was within range. The thing shifted, perhaps feeling the weight bearing down on its tree-trunk-sized knees, and showed Bloor its back. His eyes went wide. There was Morianna, unconscious and hanging over the thing's shoulder. Her dress was in dirty tatters. A bare white arm shook as the thing moved. A leg and bare foot fluttered and waved like a doll's limbs. Her head bounced on the troll's back. The Cavalier's heart stopped beating. Was she dead? She couldn't be! Not after all his careful planning! She had to be alive! She *was!*

Then, the thing did the unexpected. It dropped her to the ground, wanting a better grip on its latest meal. Morianna fell to the cone-and-needle-covered earth, landing on her back. One arm fell across her chest, while another reached out towards Bloor as if somehow sensing he was there and imploring him to help.

Breathing in a lungful of air, he adjusted the grip on his sword and stepped out from the protection of the trees. A great chunk of horse flesh was ripped free like deeply grown flowers being uprooted. Blood geysered. The troll shoved the dripping meat into its maw and began chewing in earnest. The smell of blood and excrement was now so strong that Bloor's eyes watered. He focused on Morianna. He could grab her. Jace would be the distraction; he would be the rabbit.

One strike, the words formed in his head as he gazed at the bull-like neck of the troll. Turned as it was now, with its back exposed, Bloor had the chance to take the head from its shoulders. Then he remembered Jace's advice to go for the legs. He ignored them. The hunter probably never had the opportunity Bloor had now. One stab, one thrust, that was the best way. Strike hard at the base of its skull, through the mess of black hair covering it. Stab it and it would be dead. Bloor could not reach the legs anyway, or so he told himself, not the way the monster was positioned. The neck would be the softest, the easiest.

The troll ripped another chunk of horse free. Bones snapped. The air about its head appeared pink.

The neck. Bloor moved nearer. Morianna lay at his feet, but he did not reach for her. In one strike, he could end this thing's life. The back of the thing was at least the width of three men. It was enormous. Jace was right; a pack of men was best to take on a beast like this. However, Bloor edged closer, focused on doing the impossible. The thing shifted again, its great knees cracking. On the ground, Morianna's dark hair had spilled over her face.

The neck. Stab it. A slash would be no better than a lick. He could see how enormous the beast was. A slash would annoy it, alert it, and endanger Morianna, but a stab through the neck would bring it down.

The troll shifted again, its great knees cracking. Morianna was on the ground within reach. Her eyes were open.

Her eyes!

Bloor froze. Morianna's mouth opened to scream.

Jace roared from the other side. The troll's head jerked about and it stood up in a surprised rush, dropping its meal. Horse flesh quivered in its jaws. Jace screamed and howled at the beast, infuriated that it stood before him, and finally turned and ran. The troll tensed and did nothing for a moment, wonderment filling its brain.

Bloor grabbed Morianna's hand and began hauling her out of the troll's shadow. Then, one of the troll's massive fists swept about and Bloor stumbled while dodging it. He pulled Morianna back, just as another mighty claw swiped over his head, turning the bark of a tree into a peppery mist of chips and fragments. He landed on Morianna and felt her arms clasp around his neck. The troll towered above them both, and a leg moved as if it had decided to crush them both with one stomp. Its red teeth were bared in fury.

Then it howled in pain.

Jace ran only far enough to realize that the thing wasn't following him. He backtracked immediately to find the thing clawing at the skin of a tree, the Cavalier and princess at its feet.

Without thinking, only knowing what had to be done, Jace did it.

He took three running strides and swung his axe. The blade, strengthened with his momentum, crashed into the side of the troll's lower right leg, driving the troll to its knees, and catching its full attention. The thing spun about and swung at Jace. The troll hunter released the axe, dodging the claw singing for his head. He backpedaled, and saw Bloor spring into action, getting the woman to her feet.

"RUN!" the hunter screamed at him.

Showing him how it was done, Jace did just that. The troll roared, drowning out any other words. It grabbed for the hunter again, but the man was too nimble and was already out of reach, ducking behind a thick tree. He remained there only a second before the tree shook from the ground up as the troll's claw slammed into it. Jace flung himself forward, placing distance between the troll and himself, going deeper into the forest. He ran only a short way, before checking to see if the troll had pursued him.

The troll had taken two shaky steps before stopping to inspect its wounded leg. It roared furiously at the axe embedded in its limb, attempting to frighten the weapon out of its flesh, but the stinging thing remained until the troll reached down and plucked it free as if it were no more than a splinter.

"Good," Jace breathed.

As if hearing him, the troll reared back its arm and flung the axe in his direction. The result was like a full-grown man throwing a spoon with all of his might. Jace didn't have the chance to flinch as the spinning weapon ricocheted off a nearby trunk. The axe could have killed him where he stood, if it had found him. The sound of the connection startled him badly, yet it was of no matter to the troll hunter. He lived, and he had done what he wanted. He had hobbled the monster.

Almost with an eerie understanding, the troll rose up. Jace took a step backwards instinctively, prepared to run, but there should be no need to run. He had crippled it. He cut the muscles there in half. The thing should be *crawling*.

Instead, the troll took a single step. Claws opened and closed. Huge blood-rimmed black eyes searched for and spied him. A calm voice advised Jace to run, just as those inhuman eyes flared wide with wrath. He tensed. The troll charged, pounding through the forest, roaring and gripping tree limbs, pulling itself along on legs that tried to keep up.

Jace fled.

Once again, he had underestimated the rage of one of these beasts. Behind him, the sounds of a forest being torn apart filled his ears, and that familiar feeling of having done something totally beyond his abilities flooded his mind. The feeling made him run all the faster.

Bloor struggled with Morianna for several steps before he realized the troll was not pursuing them. He paused in an area where the ground was carpeted in white wildflowers. When he looked back, the way was empty. The sounds of a chase echoed throughout the forest, a chase that took the monster away from them. Jace had saved them. His action made Bloor reconsider the hunter in a new light. He hoped the man could run. Then he turned back to Morianna; for the moment, they were safe.

He settled her against the base of a tree trunk and swept the hair from her face. The brush of his fingers against her face caused her eyes to open dreamily. "Bloor," she whispered, still weak from the terror of her ordeal. "Where is it?"

"It's gone," he said, still brushing her face, gently touching her cheeks and forehead. She closed her eyes at the contact, and sighed in relief.

"It was..." she suddenly grimaced in memory and her body began to shake. Her eyes welled up. "It was going to..."

Bloor shushed her. If any Sujin saw him then, they would have been surprised at the depth of tenderness. He placed a single finger on her chin and quieted her trembling, easing the hitchings of fright in her voice. Her skin was surprisingly soft to touch as he caressed the curve of her face.

"I thought I was dead," Morianna whispered in a squeak of a voice, tears rolling down her face. The scene moved Bloor's heart like nothing else did. He moved in closer to her face.

"Not while I breathe, Anna," he promised softly. "Not while I breathe."

The princess' breath quickened and the tears continued to fall. She leaned forward and nestled her head in the shallow of the Cavalier's neck, inhaling the comfort of his closeness. Her arms came up to her chest, and she began shivering. Bloor stiffened for a moment. He was in unfamiliar territory, yet his armored arms rose up and wrapped around her. His body welcomed the closeness of her own. He looked down at her, and smelled the wondrous scent of her hair. Then, with a boyish shyness, he kissed her forehead and held her tighter.

SEVEN YEARS EARLIER...

The village still burned in places. Try as he might, Bloor could not block out the smell of burning flesh and hair. It was the first time he had ever caught the scent of such an overpowering stench. He remembered the scenes of people ablaze when the Nords unleashed their fire arrows into the palisade and the dwellings beyond it. The sun had almost disappeared behind the horizon, as if it had no stomach for the terrible carnage about to transpire, when the blazing arrows hissed up into the young night sky. The missiles hung there with the stars, as if indecisive, before slicing down like hot razors. He remembered a mother running with her baby; the bundle caught an arrow and flamed up in an instant. He saw the woman drop to the ground, shrieking as she slapped out the flames, heedless of her own cooking flesh, when a pair of burning arrows sang out of the black heavens and buried themselves in her back. She caught fire just as quickly as leaves, and the way they flailed about begging for help chilled Bloor's spine. In battle, ordinary civilians were like uncut fruit, with about as much intelligence.

He did not move to help any of them. It would have meant leaving his post on the palisade walls. If he did that, they would have lost the village to the Nordun Jackals. The Jackals would have overrun the palisade in moments, gutting anyone defending it. In the end, they lost the village anyway, and practically a third of the people living there. The siege was going fine from the defenders' side until that hellish rain of fire.

So much for Bloor's unblemished record. He fought down the bile of disgust and wrenched his eyes from the efforts of the townspeople and warriors combating the dying blaze. From where he stood on the wooden battlements, some ten feet up from the muddy ground, he could see the destruction wrought. Dying ribbons of flame shrank back in a mist of rain, yet there was still enough light to see. Thankfully, the granary escaped the blaze, and because of the deaths of so many, those who survived would not starve in the winter. Shelter for the survivors would be a problem, as many of the dwellings had been destroyed. Perhaps it was Seddon's will that opened up the clouds moments after the battle and drenched the buildings in a late-summer downpour. Bloor had his doubts. It was enough to save what remained of the place, yet not enough to save a mother and her child. Bloor's eyes lingered on their blackened corpses. After a somber moment, he wanted something to drink.

He looked out over the battlements, across a dark field of grass and scattered trees, and the blackened bodies of dead Jackals. Even in the growing darkness, the curs gleamed like murderous beetles. Alwan had suggested a raiding force of perhaps five or six hundred, yet they had fought like several thousand. It was not Seddon's hand that helped them survive at the most critical moment, when the Jackals' arrows of flame were falling from the heavens and incinerating them within the palisade. If the priests wanted credit or to extend blessings to Seddon for that, then they could kiss Bloor's saddle-hided arse, and kiss it right in the crack.

The exhausted Cavalier regarded the horsemen, dismounted now and moving, with torches, amongst the dead raiders. They seemed more than content to ravage the dead. Bloor saw a wagon being hauled up by two horses. Men walked amongst the corpses with a wary step. Bloor watched the men haul up weapons and throw them in the back of the wagon. There were survivors of the Nordun force. If there were officers, they might be saved for ransom. Their commanders might pay for them as well, good coin, too, and Bloor wondered if the stories of the Nords executing ransomed commanders were true. The men rooted through the dead raiders like pigs in filth and made no move on the village. The Cavalier wondered who they were. The enemies of his enemies were not necessarily his friends, but in this case, an exhausted Bloor was willing to make the exception. He did not have the strength to fight off another siege.

It had been a strange week, to be sure. The fifty-man patrol of Cavaliers and Lancers, riding in the far northeastern corner of Sunja on a bright, late summer afternoon, had come across a previously-unknown village of several hundred people, nestled comfortably in the valley known as Devil's Gullet. The valley was a forgotten one. It was a hard, rocky land, unsuited for growing anything, or so the stories went. It was a long, narrow dredge of a valley, as if Seddon grabbed it once by opposite ends and stretched out whatever appeal it might have held for people. Sunja claimed it on their maps, but none of her people populated it just yet. It was quite removed from the farthest inhabited region. In fact, the Sunjan force was in the area only to ensure against Jackal strikes in the territory. It was also an opportunity to give some raw recruits a safe exercise before throwing them into the stalled meat machine on the front.

The people living there were quite surprised when the Sunjan force rode into their midst. Bloor recalled how the children, dirty and clothed poorly, stared up in wonder at their shining armor and assortment of weapons, before bolting and scurrying away. They fled before them like mice, towards the open hole in the wall that was their gate, squealing all the way. The village had been established by the normally nomadic Visigar. Perhaps three hundred families lived there. When they approached the palisade walls, walls that appeared to have been there for ages, the sudden line of archers appearing made his stomach turn cold. Only a handful, but from a distance, each archer made a man feel as if they were aiming only at him. The reception had even turned chillier when Bloor asked the Visigar if they had any idea that they were squatting on Sunjan territory. A man appeared on the walls (the village the elder Bloor later discovered) and informed the Sunjans that it was *they* who were on *Visigar* land, yet the elders would be open to talking about the matter.

Alwan was against it from the beginning, saying that they were scared for their village, and if they were scared at all, it meant that the archers they saw behind the palisade were the only defenders. The man's reputation for blood-letting was emerging. It made Bloor ill. He would bring it up with Lord Maullus when they were back in the city. However, looking back, Alwan was right about the archers being the only fighters. Bloor knew that Alwan was keen to rip into a Visigar village, *any* village, but he wasn't about to indulge him. Against Alwan's advice, Bloor accepted the invitation to dinner that very evening. Only one man would enter to discuss the terms of Sunja and the interests of the Visigar. That one man would be Bloor, while the others would stay outside, camped out of arrow range.

After that, oh how things had quickened.

The meeting with the village elders was pleasant enough, given the circumstances. The people with whom he dined with did not seem overly concerned. In fact, the elders talked carefully about how long they had lived in the valley and debated Sunja's claim to it with the Cavalier. They ate roast pork with a generous helping of vegetables and drank Visigar mead. It was all going along well enough when Alwan had appeared at the table and delivered the report of a scouting Lancer. Moving in the direction of the village was a powerful Nordun raiding force. The Visigar were considered to be the wolves of the north, but the Nords were hellions, and their raging hordes were a match for the iron-disciplined Five Klaws of Sunja. Some even whispered they were superior.

The elders' fear could be sensed around the table when Alwan gave the news. Whatever they had hoped to achieve in the talks with the young Cavalier commander was tossed to the wind. Fierce they were, but realistic as well. The Nords were moving towards their village while most of the Visigar fighting men were elsewhere. There were only a dozen warriors amongst them, with the rest being only old men and young boys. They were capable enough to hold a bow, but if the Nords got inside the palisade, they would be ripe for the cutting. The women would be ravaged, and the youngest of children would be taken as slaves. One could not negotiate with Jackals. One elder said it best, then, at the table, "Two men from different peoples can learn to understand each other, but no man can understand a mad animal."

The Visigar did not like Sunjans, but they *hated* the Nords.

An alliance was struck. The elders wanted the Lancers and their Cavaliers inside their walls quickly to help them protect their women and children from the butchers. In return, they would listen to any demands the Sunjans made of them. The elders had no other options. They knew that one fat village was far too tempting a parcel for the ravenous Jackals to overlook. The presence of Sunjans was wine with the meal. Bloor told them not to worry. Though they were only a small force, the Sunjans would defend the women and children from the Jackals to the last man. His words drew the barest look of interest from Alwan. Then the elders, seeing the seriousness of the commander before them, quickly began talking amongst themselves. One man came forward then, almost shyly, and informed the two Cavaliers that, not to insult the promise just given, perhaps all was not as dire as it would appear. A secret then was revealed.

THE TROLL HUNTER

When the Jackals arrived at the palisade early in the evening, whatever meager defenses could be mustered were ready.

Bloor remembered how it went. The Nordun force that confronted them was not just a group of raiders, it was a well-trained battle group and their commander had not been blinded by loot. Seeing before him only a village only made of sticks, he ordered it to be razed from the land by fire. Bloor supposed that the man believed the flames would distract the defenders from the Nords, or even drive them out from behind their walls.

The sun dipped behind distant mountains, arrows fell, and buildings went up in flames. People died, while behind the gates, Bloor's fifty Lancers waited for the order to charge, waited to be unleashed while the village turned a fiery orange. The Jackals loosed wave after wave of flaming arrows, and with each blazing volley, Alwan himself swore that this particular group of Nords hated the Visigars' guts. However, Bloor waited and watched as the Jackals advanced on the walls. They were halfway across the black field when the returning Visigar, the fighting men of the village, struck the exposed archers and horsemen from behind. The foot soldiers wheeled about to face the charge of the returning horsemen, and Bloor released his fifty into their backs. The battle was short, bloody, and thirty-six Sunjan lLancers returned to the palisade gates. They slew perhaps three times that number of Nordish Jackals. The returning Visigar warriors, the warriors the village elders were waiting for while stalling a single Cavalier commander, killed the remainder of the Nordun Jackals to a man. Bloor did not think Seddon liked him. The entity probably hated his guts for all the curses and snubs he threw in his direction. How many slurs could a god take before finally taking action against the offender?

On that day, Bloor could only believe that as much as Seddon disliked him, the god obviously *despised* the Nords.

Bloor watched the Visigar horsemen as several detached themselves from the scavengers. He knew who they were the moment they started for the wall. Proud, haughty, and extremely unpredictable, the warriors of the Visigar were as renowned as the Cavaliers when it came to horsemanship. As wild as they were, it was known that they needed only a single threat to bond the individual tribes together, and a single leader to drive them across the known world. They had fought both Nordun and Sunja for land before, and Bloor knew that there was no love lost among all sides. With the village burning, he had already directed half of his remaining force to aid in saving smoking homes. The rest stayed with him, faces grim, to square off against the returning Visigar warriors. A large force rode up to the opened gates, their armor and weapons dark and bloodied. One man held up a fist and stopped just at the threshold, studying the waiting Sunjans. He was a big Visigar, black of beard and hair and pale of flesh. The hilt of a sword peeked over his right shoulder. Bloor thought the man looked quite threatening. Although he did not show it outwardly, Bloor *felt* threatened.

"You are not Nordun," the man said to him in a rumble of a voice.

"No," Bloor replied. "We're from Sunja."

"I see. Since when does Sunja help Visigar?"

"Since today. Since they," Bloor nodded his head at the heaps of Nordish dead, "were Nords."

"Are you to fight us, now?" the man wanted to know.

Bloor hid his annoyance. "We can talk about that *after* we save what's left of your village from the fires."

It took most of the night to stomp out the flames, but the combined forces of Sunja and Visigar did just that. The next day was one of rest for all. The following evening, the officers of both groups, along with the village elders, shared a meal. They sat around an open fire pit, outside and underneath a brilliant canvas of stars, as the common hall was one of the buildings lost to the flames. It did not bother the people gathering around the cooking fires. The building would be rebuilt.

"My name is Prong," the big Visigar introduced himself from where he sat, nodding at the seated outlanders. "And I'm too tired to fight Sunjans this night."

Bloor nodded, glad to hear it.

"So," Prong went on, "for this night and this night only, we will share food together, drink together, and talk. We will do this because of this man," he clapped the shoulder of the village elder who Bloor had talked with the day before. "He tells me that you did not know of our returning, and pledged yourselves to the defense of our homes. You came to our homes peacefully, and that alone saves you from my slayers."

Alwan, sitting next to Bloor, rubbed at the corner of his eye. It was strange how things unfolded.

Prong went on. "He also tells me you were talking about us being on Sunjan land."

"We were," Bloor said. There was no sense in stretching any truths here.

"Sunja is on *our* land," Prong warned the two men. "But we have thought about what has happened here, this day." He looked around then. The darkness of the night covered most of the damage wrought by the fire. "We will move. It would be the wisest thing to do. The Nords are more organized than you think, and they'll send another force this way to look for their maggots. And you also know where we are. Too many now know of us. This makes us uneasy. So we'll find someplace new. Not because of you telling us to go, Sunjan, because we wish to do this. Understood?"

Bloor thought about the word *understood*: not agreed upon. In his position, with the remaining men he had, an understanding was perhaps the best he could presently manage. "It is," he said.

"Good." Prong said. "Now let's eat. Killing Nord maggots is a tiring thing. They're as hard as rocks. But to kill them and then put out a fire is exhausting. I can sleep for a week, I think."

Bloor nodded his agreement. He could smell the huge slab of beef being roasted over the flames.

"I'm glad we are not at war with them. The Nords are devils. Or as you call them, hellions?" Prong asked the two Cavaliers with an amused grin. A flask was handed to him, and flagons followed.

Bloor agreed again with the man. He spoke the truth, and such words from the Visigar made the young Cavalier think about their fight with Nordun.

Prong took in this Cavalier leader. He was a young man, and Prong had been around long enough to be a quick and sound judge of character. Oh, he had made some mistakes, but he had killed those eventually. However, for some reason, he liked this particular Sunjan. The man had saved his father, the same village elder that Prong had praised earlier, and who first parlayed with the Cavalier. Bringing his force inside the palisade had made the Nords pause and grant the Visigar warriors extra time to arrive. There had been losses, but Prong was enough of a man to realize that anytime one could speak about defeating and killing Norduns, this was a good thing. Prong felt no need to inform the man that he had saved his own family as well, but as the night went on and mead and wine flowed, Prong disclosed it to Bloor anyway, in a dragon's breath that could have ignited another blaze. He sat close when he did so, so that no one else could hear.

Equally as drunk and just barely holding onto control himself, Bloor's eyes still flew open when he heard the news.

"For that alone," Prong slapped him hard on the shoulder, "I'm grateful."

"Then," Bloor said to him, the alcohol numbing and slurring his words, "please move your people far from here. For Sunja's military will come this way again, and when it does, I cannot guarantee I will be in command."

Prong nodded his understanding, drunk enough that his head might fall off, and promptly fell asleep.

One month later, the surviving patrol returned to the sprawling city of Sunja. Alwan once commented that the cityscape reminded him of a fish peeled open from the belly, the innards sunbaked and hard. Bloor was not sure he saw the city exactly like Alwan, but a little part of him was relieved to return. He wanted to make his report promptly.

Bloor and Alwan left their horses in the barrack's stables. They reported to their commanding officer, and having done that, returned to their own personal quarters. After four months of border patrol, it would be strange to have four walls and a roof again. Even sleeping on a pallet would be strange, and then there were the bathhouses. Four months without the opulence of Sunja's bathhouses was torturous when one was used to daily baths. The men nearly died when they entered the heated waters. They did not know how bad they smelled until they saw patrons screw up their faces.

Within two hours of being cleaned up, a summons came. They were to appear before Lord Winter, who wanted to hear their tale firsthand. Almost immediately, they stood in Lord Winter's office. The walls were covered with detailed maps of Sunja, her borders, and the realms beyond. Each map or set of maps was separated by worn-looking scabbards nailed to the wooden timbers, and each scabbard still contained a weapon. It was said that they were the weapons of long-gone commanders fallen in battle or retired. Four personal aides, tough looking sub-officers, stood nearby, one in each corner of the room. Another man wearing bright robes of red and gold stood off from the right corner near Lord Winter's desk with a quill and parchment as the commander listened to his officer's report. Bloor gave a more detailed account of what had transpired at the Visigar village, while Lord Winter barely gave any indication of listening. Alwan stood at attention a few steps behind Bloor. He listened to the young man, and realized that depending on the commander's mood, Bloor would be either commended for his actions or damned.

As he sat behind his desk, Lord Winter's face made nary a twitch. His short cropped grey hair sparkled in the light and made his grey eyes gleam. He was one of those frosty men who seemed to be always attired in battle dress. Lord Winter was every bit as frigid as his name suggested. The lines of his face seem to deepen every time Bloor saw him. The man had an imperious air about him, gained in twenty-two years of military service to his country. Even the king himself took care in addressing the man as "Lord." It was said that anyone fixed upon by those glowering eyes would carry a curse into Saimon's hell.

A court fop once made a jest of the Cavaliers while in the presence of the king and Lord Winter, something of how it would take more than a hard winter before the Jackals would let up in their attacks. Without leave from the king, Lord Winter strode over to the jester, whose cheery confidence was sapped the closer the warrior came. Lord Winter broke the man's nose with one thunderous slap of a leathery hand. The man collapsed to the floor, unconscious.

"*Lord* Winter," the commander had stated in a rumble that carried across the hall. It amused the king greatly, and the fop was said to have never opened his mouth again while in the presence of *any* military man.

Lord Winter wore a well-cared for vest of leather. The shoulder guards were decorated with several resplendent badges of honor. His suit of plate mail was in an adjoining room if he needed to don it, dousing tales of the man wearing it while he slept. Both of Lord Winter's elbows rested on his broad oak desk as if he expected Bloor to feed him. His mouth twitched every so often as he chewed on the renewable corner of his mouth, but the remainder of his face was frozen, his icicle-like stare judging. Bloor, as with all other Cavaliers, found that they could never look Lord Winter in the eye when giving reports. There was something terribly blasphemous about meeting his glare, as if one were urinating in a temple in front of a row of priests.

Bloor finished by addressing the man as Lord. Lord Winter said not a word. Then the man slowly blinked as might a bear just emerging from hibernation. He sized up this young man before him and one set of fingers did a slow tattoo on the desk's surface.

"Interesting," Lord Winter finally allowed. His growl sounded hungry.

Bloor kept his unease hidden behind an unflinching face. He stared directly over the commander's head. *Interesting* coming from Lord Winter could mean many things: *interesting* how one lets a horse tribe escape Sunjan justice for squatting on Sunjan territory, *interesting* how things sorted themselves out in the end, or *interesting* to see if Bloor's story would change after a month in a cell no bigger than the desk the commander now sat behind.

Lord Winter's eyes sought those of Bloor's, but the man kept his gaze over his commander's head. Bloor could feel the man's eyes, and that was enough for him. The man continued his slow drumming, making the indentations already in the wood's surface even deeper. Bloor had glimpsed the shapes in the wood like a scattering of coins, but did not dwell on them. Only now did he realize that Lord Winter's fingers had drummed them into the wood with their powerful beat.

"Interesting," Lord Winter repeated and took a deep breath.

With his unease growing, Bloor felt that the man was about to reprimand him.

"What of the Visigar, then?" Lord Winter asked. "Do you think they will move?" His voice was low, as if the man talked from within a deep well, yet clear enough as if he stood right at Bloor's ear. The words came slow enough for one to suspect the man was becoming senile, but one wrong glance at Winter and his feigned numbness would be thrown off.

"I don't know, Lord," Bloor answered truthfully.

Behind him, and not unnoticed by the four aides, Alwan closed his eyes as if in mortal pain.

"Lord, if there is fault there, it is mine alone," Bloor went on. "Their war leader gave me his word that his people would leave the area. They also believed that the Nords would return to investigate what had happened to their Jackals. They seemed to have more concern for that than of returning Cavaliers and Lancers."

A skeptical chuckle stabbed the air then, coming from the man dressed in red and gold robes. Bloor did not look at the man, not while in the attention of Lord Winter.

However, Lord Winter did just that. His lidded eyes slid in the direction of the laugh, without moving his head.

"Something…amuses you, Schull?" he inquired in a dry-wood tone.

"Only that the king's Cavalier took the word of a Visigar. The gullibility damn near struck me off my feet, Lord Winter. Gave his *word*, indeed. Really?" the man asked with a sarcastic smirk. Bloor did not move. He disliked this robed man.

Lord Winter's baleful attention swung back to Bloor like an executioner now faced with the decision of who to dispatch first. "Why do you believe this man will keep his word, Cavalier?"

"Lord, the battle was over. The elders vouched for our honor. We would have had to confront the returning Visigar warriors. In fact, it was the intentions of the elders to delay our actions on their then-defenseless village until their warriors could return, which they knew would happen shortly. We knew not about this. With the appearance of the Nordish Jackals and our pledge to save the women and children, the Visigar decided that, at the time, we were not the greater threat. That went to the Nords."

To this, both Lord Winter and the robed man named Schull gave agreeing grunts.

"We did delay the Nords long enough for the horsemen to return and strike at their rear, Lord," Bloor went on. "We saved a village. If we had not been there, the Nords would have razed the village to the ground. Our actions granted us a respite with the Visigar. I also talked to the leader afterwards. In my judgment, he is an honorable man."

"Oh, your *judgment?*" the man named Schull smiled and flicked a knowing look at the Cavalier commander, inviting him to say something. Lord Winter said nothing. Instead, he leaned back and took a breath, his nostrils flaring as he did so. The man seemed like a great bear, deciding whether or not it was worth the bother to eat one of them. His head turned ever so slightly, his eyes downcast so that he did not look upon the robed man.

"Guarding our frontier," Lord Winter drew out. "We're at war with Nordun. Not a single clan of Visigar. This man did the right thing. The right thing, I say," in a tone that was not to be questioned. The commander never looked directly at the robed man, but rather pointed his head in the direction of the man's feet. He did this not because he respected the man. Perhaps he did, but Bloor believed Winter did what he did just because he felt like it. "I've got a score of captains who will defend the border on a word or even a dirty glance. By Seddon's rocks, I've got *Maullus* who will ride out on a word and put any *nation* to the sword on my say so. Seddon knows I have to talk that one down just to keep him here. Then there was Tallus, when he was alive. But this one thought things out before he acted. For that, he'll be commended. That's what separates us from those Seddon-damned toppers squatting in that shite pit called Nordun."

"I'm sure they would have done the same," Schull replied.

That caused Lord Winter to fix the man with dangerous eyes. "Are you comparing my Cavaliers to those maggots, Lord Schull?"

Lord Schull's face slackened, as if he might have bitten into something that looked quite different than how it tasted. He cleared his throat. "Not at all, Lord Winter. I've praised our Cavaliers and Lancers just as much as the king. I'm very impressed with their history. Please don't read too much into my words. I just find this pup's inexperience amusing. I imagine that Visigar leader has already spun the story across a dozen clans by now."

"A dozen clans not fighting us," Lord Winter's deep voice carried, his eyes returning to the floor stones. "Did you know Lord Tallus? A hard man by all accounts. Not as hard as Maullus, by Seddon's mossy arse. Thank whoever you want for that one being on our side. But Tallus now, a hard fighter and a good man to take orders when there was a commander around to give them. He only got his command because he did what he was told, and shortly after that, he rarely did anything worthwhile at all, right up until a Jackal stuck a lance in his chest."

"I heard it was an axe."

"I heard that one too," Lord Winter nodded once. "But it was a lance. Anyway, Tallus was the kind of man you wanted at your back. He followed his orders straight. You couldn't get any straighter. But as for thinking? No. He wasn't a thinker. He let *us* do the thinking. He was more of a…" Lord Winter's drumming filled the space of silence. "Killer. Not as hard as Maullus, if you can believe that. Yet he was good enough at killing to impress my commander at the time, who eventually gave him a command. And we all know how that ended."

They all did. Tallus had been killed in a sizable skirmish with the Nords. Lord Winter let the stillness swell just a little before continuing. He flicked a finger towards Bloor. "I hear you're capable enough with a blade."

"I am, Lord."

"Well," Lord Winter said. "I see no scars or missing limbs. Not yet, anyway. And you *seem* alive. And you seem to think as well. Family?"

"None, Lord."

"You're not one to stay close to your horse, are you? I've enough of those shaggers."

"No, Lord," Bloor said. He suddenly wondered if he had unknowingly served with any of those shaggers.

"No, eh?" his commander seemed to contemplate something for moment. "This Prong fellow. Did he seem trustworthy to you?"

"As I've said, Lord, his village was half-destroyed. To stay there would risk another meeting with roving Nords. He struck me as an intelligent man, and yes, I would trust his word. If he proves me wrong, then the fault is mine."

"You'd trust a Visigar?" Lord Schull wanted to know.

"I'd trust the *man*, Lord." Bloor returned. Another smile crossed Lord Schull's face as he regarded the seated Cavalier commander. It was obvious to him that this one was full of virtue. For a quick instant, so quick Lord Schull was not certain if he saw it himself, Lord Winter's brow jumped once in plain amusement. Then the silence was back in the chamber, but nowhere as intense as before.

"Go on, then," Lord Winter finally said. "Get a meal into you. Get some sleep as well. You'll be contacted about your future duties. Dismissed."

Bloor bowed smartly and retreated two steps before pivoting on a heel and exiting. Alwan did the same and followed the man out.

The lords watched the men leave. Lord Winter's fingers began drumming on the table again as the door closed and they were alone. He had already made his decision, and Bloor would be his man. "What of him, then?"

Lord Schull shrugged. "He's a serious one."

"They're *all* serious ones."

"What do you think, then?" Schull threw back.

"I think he's the type you want. I've talked to some others who know of his character. Maullus knows of him, as well, says he's a quiet one, hard, steady, and he thinks. That's from Maullus, and *he* doesn't say much about anyone. I believe those are qualities you're interested in. He could've charged into that Visigar village and killed the lot, probably with losses, but he didn't. That other one with him? He's a killer, like Tallus. He *would've* charged in and been up to his elbows in blood. You don't want him. But Bloor, now, he's a different animal. He chose to parlay, to talk things through, and it worked for him. I could look for some others that have the same qualities and more experience than he does, but to tell the truth, I don't want to. I need them at the front."

"He is still a pup," Schull pointed out.

"All the more reason to give him to you. I need my experienced Cavaliers at the throats of the maggots warring on us. Or ones skilled at killing, ones like that Alwan there. Bloor will suit your needs, well enough, I think. He'll do what he's given to do, that's for sure. What say you?"

"So you've made your decision then?"

"I have," still speaking to the robed figure of Lord Schull, Lord Winter stabbed a finger at the door. "He'll do."

"Fine then," Schull said, secretly relieved that he would have the rest of his afternoon free. "I'll make the recommendation. There shouldn't be a problem at all. The princess will be delighted with her newest protector. What are you smiling at?"

In a rare instance, Lord Winter showed teeth. "Maybe you want Alwan instead?"

18

"Morianna, this is Lord Bloor," the king's servant Barlow announced with a flourish of his boney hand. His eyes twinkled with false kindness. This was a part of his duty he seemed to be doing more of these days, and he did not like it in the least. No civilized man should have to burden himself with having to take care and heed of such a little priss. Brown, fourteen-year-old eyes stared up at the shining figure of a man dressed in polished, plate mail armor. Bloor was not the tallest man Morianna had seen, nor was he the largest, yet dressed as he was, the impression he planted in the mind of the young princess of Sunja was that he was *huge*, and intimidating.

"I don't like him," the princess said to Barlow, and turned her little nose back to her book.

Barlow's aged face frowned ever so slightly and his eyes fluttered as if struck by a dust cloud. He looked around the chamber of the palace library, taking in the walls lined with shelves, heavy with all manner of books. He needed a moment to weigh the little one's words. Nearby, the librarian, a thin man as tall as Bloor, smiled feebly at

Morianna's words. His smile vanished with one look from Barlow.

The advisor took in Morianna, bent over some history tome or something else pertaining to her ongoing education. Sunlight from windows set in between the shelves of books illuminated pretty motes of floating dust. The young princess sat across from her personal nursemaid, a thin, middle-aged woman with dark hair. Barlow believed her name to be Alora. Morianna's remarks surprised her as well, and her back straightened from the rawness of tone only a child could manage when he or she had just embarrassed her teacher.

"Anna, dear," she began timidly. The princess' head came up.

"I don't like him. Send him away. Father said I could choose who I wanted, and I don't want him. Look at him. He's too mean-looking. I don't want him around me all day long. Bring me someone else."

Barlow inhaled. He did not care for the tone of this child. It smacked of insolence. "This is Lord Bloor, Princess," he repeated. "And I'm afraid he is the one your *father* selected. Lord Bloor is a respected Cavalier and he does his duties very well. You'll barely notice him about."

Morianna appeared not to have heard, continuing to be deeply absorbed in her reading, but then her shoulders heaved as she took a deep, dramatic breath.

Bloor kept silent, not knowing how to react. Orders were orders and yet how could a mere child, even given the fact that she was a princess, defy the words of her father, the king? Orders were to be obeyed, and that was the one rule above all that his taskmasters had beaten into his head. There was never any questioning of them, and certainly no defiance. Though he would deny it, having his orders ignored by a young girl of fourteen bothered him.

Morianna turned a page and wrinkled up her little nose in resentment. "What's this word, nanny?"

Alora's features softened as she leaned in close to her little girl. She had been assigned to her by the queen eight years ago and instructed never to be far from her side. Alora tried to do her job as well as possible, as her mother had done before her with the young king. She had seen this pattern of behavior before: the princess' tendency to ignore something she didn't like. The nursemaid and teacher hoped to stave it off before something unpleasant took place. Perhaps, a few moments' distraction would smooth over the acceptance of the Cavalier.

"Sound it out, dear."

"It's too big."

"Try please."

"I can't. It's too big. You read it."

"Acquiesce," Alora supplied it for her. Morianna continued on without a word of thanks, puffing her cheeks out when she came upon a word she disliked. Every now and again, she would shoot a black look in the direction of Bloor. Each time she did so, her eyes became darker and darker still with annoyance. The men were *not* listening to her. She was a princess, and these men were not listening to her.

Barlow chewed on the inside of his mouth, screwing up his face as he did so. Twenty years of dealing with court politics, upheavals, baronial squabbles, and border wars, and here he was, being ignored by a young girl. He had heard that the king rarely visited his children. Barlow could understand why.

"So I'll leave you here," he announced to them all, meaning for Bloor to stay. "You know your duties. You shouldn't have any troubles."

"Take him with you," Morianna commanded, without looking up. Her eyes darted to the edge of the table, but no farther, in Barlow's direction.

"And if you do have any trouble, you're empowered to act accordingly," Barlow went on, ignoring the young princess' words and feeling a guilty smack of pleasure in doing so.

"Barlow." Apparently, Barlow was not the only one who disliked being ignored.

"But reports are to come to me. Understood?" Barlow continued as if he had not been interrupted.

"Barlow!" Morianna stamped her feet as she yelled his name.

"Yes, Princess?"

"Take him with you. That is a command!" She raised her chin, impudently.

Barlow sighed heavily. "I'm afraid I can't do that."

"TAKE HIM!" she shrieked, striking her book from the table in a flash of fury. Alora jumped in her seat, as did the librarian, but not from the princess. His book! He scrambled in and scooped the precious tome up off the stone floor before the pages could settle down.

Morianna stuck her chin out and stood up, red-faced. Her chair went over in a clatter. Her little chest heaved with anger. "He's mean-looking! And ugly! Take him away or I'll tell my father! He won't like you bringing him here, disturbing my studies."

Alora moved to touch the girl's shoulder. "Leave me alone!" the princess shouted and twisted away from the fingers. Alora shrank back. Morianna stomped her feet again, trying to punch a hole in the floor. "Can't you hear me? I don't want him around me! I don't like him! I don't like him at *all!*"

She stepped away from the table and stormed up to Barlow, tiny fists ready.

The old man wondered if she meant to hit him. "After this display, I'm certain Bloor doesn't like you much, either," he stated calmly.

"I DON'T CARE!" she shrieked and stomped. Across the table, the librarian quietly retrieved his book.

"In any case," Barlow said in a steady tone, "you can be certain I'll be informing your father of *your* behavior today."

"Go tell him, then," she countered brazenly.

Barlow managed a smile. "As you command, Princess. You," he directed at Bloor, "will stay here."

Bloor nodded, waiting for another outburst from the child, but Morianna said nothing. Her temper, in furious bloom only a moment ago, now simmered. She stared at Barlow with slitted eyes, her mouth a tight button.

"Carry on with your studies," Barlow advised her a little too sweetly, as if celebrating a round won. Morianna picked up on it right away.

"I'll have another! You'll see! I'll have another! I don't take orders from you! I don't have to *listen* to you! My father will hear of this!"

Turning to leave, Barlow glanced at the stoic Bloor. He gave the Cavalier a sympathetic look. Barlow made it clear in that one look what he thought of the princess, and of the task given to Bloor directly by the king. The old man left the library, robes swishing in his wake.

Her little chest heaving, Morianna glared at the doorway. Her mouth was a stitched line of hate. She stomped again, one last time for good measure. The thoughts traveling through her mind were as terrible as a young child could conjure. Feeling his gaze, she suddenly glared at Bloor. The scorn in her eyes was so shocking that it took an effort to mask his feelings. She really *did* dislike him. If she had a dagger, Bloor would have expected it thrust into his heart at that very moment.

"I don't like you," she hissed at him. "Not at all."

Alora touched the girl's shoulder to calm her down, and the princess twisted away from the woman's fingers as if she were diseased. "Why does Father make him stay here? Why? I didn't ask for him. I don't want him. So why is he here? Stop trying to touch me! Stop it!"

A tired-looking Alora attempted to say something, but Morianna cut her off as shockingly as a frozen axe. The child's words spilled out like a rush of chilling ice. Bloor did not care for the way the nursemaid withered and shrank back under the onslaught. The woman had no fight in her at all, or perhaps the child had worn her down long ago. She let the princess rant as if she were caught in a flash rainstorm.

Abruptly, Morianna stopped shouting. "I'm hungry," she declared. Thrusting out her chin, she ignored everyone and marched straight out of the room.

With a face full of worry, Alora went after her, hitching up her dress as she did so. Not knowing what else to do, Bloor turned and followed, beginning his new service as protector of the king's youngest daughter. His armor rattled as he moved along. The three of them marched along the swept corridors of the palace, through numerous stone arches to the kitchen. All along the way, Morianna screeched and blared at any servants in her path. Not one person dared look directly into her face. The servants pressed themselves up against the stone passageways to escape her, causing the Cavalier to think of ghosts. It somehow wasn't enough for Morianna to pass by peacefully. She screamed and threw a fit at almost all of them, scorching them with cruel words about their clothes, their lack of work, or even facial features. One lady possessed a large wart on the side of her nose, and Morianna pointed and jeered at the thing. A young man was accused of smelling like the rump of a horse. Another woman was told she was fat enough to be three. All the while, Alora simply followed and said nothing, though she winced at every barbed comment. Bloor noted how the woman's shoulders slumped and her head sagged a little lower at each berating. He wondered what she had taught this young princess, and then wondered if she was thinking the very same thing.

The princess marched into the kitchen and sat down violently at the head of a large wooden table. By the time Bloor entered behind Alora, he wanted to cuff the young bitch soundly behind the ear, twice for good measure.

The cook was a heavyset woman in her later years. She flittered about like a bee in a field of the prettiest flowers. At a glance, the kitchen was spotless, the hearth burning low with a neat pile of cut wood stacked nearby. A counter and preparation area with hung knives and pots of various sizes gleamed with readiness. The scene impressed Bloor immediately. He wondered if the woman caring for the kitchen had a military upbringing.

Alora drifted in after the princess and strayed to her side, not daring to sit. Her eyes were embarrassed when she looked at Bloor stopped in the doorway. Morianna also saw him, and her lips curled up as curdled as milk touched by vinegar. Her eyes were full of fury.

"I want pudding and cream!" she announced loudly, banging her fist on the table. In a moment, a bowl and spoon were brought to her. A milky sauce covered a small hill of dark pudding. She gouged a wooden spoon into the dessert and snapped up the first bite.

Expressionless, Bloor glanced away. He looked down the corridor they had traveled, not expecting to see anyone. In the second his eyes were off of her, Morianna scooped up the bowl and threw it across the room. It bounced off his breast plate. Chunks of the dessert splattered his armor, and sauce dripped to the floor. Bloor crouched into a fighting stance and his hand found the pommel of his blade, while his eyes met those of the princess. He blinked at her as she set her face, ready for a fight.

"Don't you like *pudding?*" she asked him with an evil scowl.

Alora's hands had come up to her mouth to mask her shock. She looked ready to die on the spot. The cook scrambled for a cleaning cloth.

"You don't shine as much now, do you?" Morianna teased him. "That's a good thing, don't you think? Don't you? Of course, you do. You don't say much, do you? That's a good thing, too. My nanny can't shut up at times, but if you don't say anything, maybe she'll learn from you. She's not so stupid. Or fat. Not like her. She's like a big grub." Morianna pointed at the cook trying to clean the front of Bloor's armor.

"Don't do that! Get me more pudding!" the princess yelled at her. The woman's face dropped. Her dark, button eyes darted fearfully from Bloor to the princess.

"Sorry m'Lord," she whispered, handing him the towel before hurrying off to do Morianna's bidding.

Bloor was speechless. He dabbed at himself. He personally cleaned and oiled his own armor, scrubbing it to a polished finish. He scolded those in his charge if they ever fell below his standards, and even punished some to push his point home. However, now… his thoughts teetered as if on the edge of a cliff. He dearly wanted to punish this *child*.

He could not touch her, as badly as she needed to be disciplined. Perhaps there would be an attempt on her life? He allowed himself that notion. If there was, he could beat the life out of the assassin. There was some relief in that idea, and he hung onto it, managing to keep his face only a shade of red instead of the full, raging crimson. He wiped at his armor. *Willpower*. This would be a test of willpower. That was suddenly very clear to him.

Like a surly hound on an unwanted leash, Bloor followed Morianna and Alora around the palace and its grounds for the remainder of the day. He endured the princess' trilling and kept a stone face when Alora offered him looks of sympathy. Bloor believed she had seen this treatment many times before. What she didn't know was that he was made of sterner stuff. They moved around the royal grounds, through wondrous gardens home to several large copses of beautiful timber, the kind a woodcutter would cut off one of his own limbs to sink an axe into. The trees basked in the nearby glow of carefully sculpted beds of blue, yellow, and red flowers. As they walked, they appreciated the sounds and vibrant scents that the carefully-groomed grounds had to offer; at least, Alora did. The princess seemed to gripe at everything: gardeners who passed them by and didn't bow fast enough, servants slow in delivering her freshly-squeezed fruit drinks, stone cutters labouring with ivory statues not yet polished up to the grounds' standards, and, of course, Bloor.

The princess even subjected Alora to her cutting tone. To his continued dismay, the lady said nothing. Bloor wished the woman would turn and slap the child to curb her incessant bitching, but she never did. Alora was obviously made of even harder stuff.

The afternoon slipped into dusk and Alora guided the young princess through the palace and back to her quarters. Waiting for them at the huge oak door was a trio of armored men. One opened the door and quickly stepped back. Without a word of thanks, the princess marched in.

However, Alora paused and turned back to the men. "Thank you for your time today, Lord Bloor."

Somewhat surprised, Bloor took a brief moment before tipping his head.

"I would like to say that this was one of her bad days," Alora continued in a little voice, careful of being heard.

"Alora!" Morianna bellowed from within, causing the woman's face to wilt just a little.

"I'm sorry," she offered. "These men are part of the watch and under your command. You are the day commander of Morianna's watch. In his haste to leave us, I didn't hear Barlow inform you of this."

"He did not," Bloor said.

"Well, they are." Alora informed him. "You will have some time to collect yourself after each day. I must go now. The princess must prepare for dinner with her father." Another little smile and she closed the door. The sound echoed in the corridor.

Bloor stood back from the oak door, gazing upon its surface. From within, he heard another shout from the princess. The girl still had breath to spare.

"A treasure she is," one of the men smirked to Bloor. "I'd pay Saimon himself to take her."

Bloor looked at the man, his eyes cold. "Those words are all I need to take your head from your shoulders."

The guard paled.

The second man came to his rescue. "He didn't mean anything by it. He only said what we are all thinking, Bloor."

The Cavalier turned his killing glare onto the second man. "Do I know you?" he said in a voice as disturbing as the scratching of fingernails on slate.

"No, Lord," the man said quickly, coming to attention.

"Then you'll remember to address me as *Lord*," Bloor warned the man. "You call me by my name again and I'll yank your tongue out from that bird's nest you call a head."

"Yes, Lord," the man said promptly.

Bloor continued to stare at the soldier, placing himself directly in front of his face, eye-to-eye. The man lowered his gaze immediately. Bloor continued to stay where he was. The silence was an incredibly fragile thing, and both guards felt that if they even released their breath this Cavalier would take their lives, and they were right.

Only inches away from the man's face, Bloor simmered. The unvented rage from the day with Morianna threatened to overwhelm him. He reminded himself that these men were protectors as well, though of a lesser kind. He also reminded himself that killing them outside the door of the princess would not be looked upon favorably. He might even be released from his duty.

That single amusing thought let the steam out of his anger. He stepped back and surveyed them both. The first man had sleepy eyes. Mud-brown hair peeked out from under his helmet. The second man had a round face with a hawkish nose. Bloor thought he might even have fangs. Both men were large and well-muscled, wearing mail armor and carrying swords and shields.

"What are your names?"

"Borus, Lord," said the sleepy one.

"Lyan, Lord," said the second. "And, Lord?"

Bloor looked to him.

"Begging your forgiveness, Lord. Neither of us meant any insult."

"Then keep quiet when I'm around," Bloor told him. Both men promptly did so, standing so hard at attention they might have had meat hooks driven into their backs.

"You're giving them a hard time, Bloor."

Not recognizing the voice, Bloor turned to see a man standing in the corridor in a Cavalier's battle dress. The glare returned, and the newcomer, a Cavalier himself, felt a twinge of intimidation. He hesitated for a moment, and then remembered who he was—and who his father was.

"You're in command of the night watch?" Bloor asked.

"I am."

Bloor sized him up and scowled. "I don't know you."

"No, we've never met," the man admitted. "Though I've heard about you and I'm impressed."

Bloor's scowl did not slacken in the least. If this pup was actually trying to flatter him, he would *flatten* the man.

Tarco read as much on the other's face. "Well, in any case, I dare say, you won't forget who I am. I'm Lord Tarco, a Cavalier, like yourself." Tarco had indeed heard of Bloor, and knew the sickening type: big, dumb, and blindly devoted to the king.

Bloor's first impulse was to question just how Tarco got this duty, but he kept quiet. He would ask Alwan who Tarco was. He kept his hard face, and then nodded to the guards.

"Then you'll remind these two that making jests about the royal family while on duty isn't something they should be smiling about."

The two men appeared even more uncomfortable. One Cavalier was trouble enough. Tarco nodded his understanding and studied the pair. "Seems you've given them something to think about."

"I think they should think about it while they pull the night watch with you."

Neither man showed any reaction to the punishment. Tarco smiled, but it did not reach his eyes. He had heard that Bloor could be a bear about enforcing regulations. Tarco just didn't want to be bothered with the extra men. He cared even less about the princess, though he could keep a guarded pretense up in the company of those who did. Bloor was one of those of whom he would have to be wary.

"Alright then, Lord Bloor," he agreed. "An extra watch will be fine by me as punishment. What about the two lads coming here shortly. Their replacements?"

"Keep them on. Five sets of eyes will let the princess rest easier, don't you think?"

Five men to protect one girl? She wasn't even the first-born! Tarco did not say this. Instead, he forced a smile. "Of course. I'll take care of it." He looked down and noted that his leather boots did not reflect his face, as they usually did. He would take a strap of wood to the back of the servant responsible.

"But I'm curious, then," Tarco faced Bloor, "what does amuse you, Bloor? I see stains on your armor. Not exactly the shining example of regulations yourself, are you?"

Bloor's scowl deepened. "The princess did that."

"Did she sling something at you? Word has it she has quite the arm. Did you find that funny? If you did, I can guarantee you that the princess—this princess—has a real wit about her. A real wit. You'll cherish it after a while."

The Cavalier said nothing and it disappointed Tarco. He could not fully exploit this brute's dull wits if he kept quiet.

Bloor did speak after a while. "Am I relieved, then?"

"Of your duty here, yes," Tarco said in a dismissive voice, assuming a superior tone. "I'm in command of the night watch. You are the day. This duty really isn't that important. I'm surprised that they need both of us to oversee it."

It surprised Bloor as well, but his face did not show it.

"After all," Tarco went on. The man obviously liked to hear his own voice. "The princess is the last of a long line sired by the king. And Morianna's...unique personality, shall we say, doesn't require a complement of royal Axemen about her. But some manner of professional is required. That is where I come in. And you, of course," Tarco granted with a feigned, good-natured frown, studying Bloor's figure.

"I'm certain that, after a while, the king will probably require only one of us. But for now, you are the day while I get the tedium that comes with the night. You must be quite the hellion to win the day watch. She apparently had one guardian before, but the king decided on a much larger watch. I'm surprised no one has bothered to tell you all this."

"I didn't ask," Bloor stated.

"As any good Sujin. My apologies, Lord Bloor. I meant Cavalier."

"No offense taken. I know the Sujins."

"Do you, now?" Tarco said with a coyote smile. "You'll have to tell me about them. I rarely get a chance to converse with the men I'm overseeing."

Bloor was sure the Sujins were upset about that. His face betrayed his thoughts, just for a flicker, but it was enough for Tarco to pick up on. He studied Bloor's face for any further hints of sarcasm. He was about to have his say when he realized that potentially starting an argument outside of the royal chambers was probably not a wise course of action. He smiled again. Bloor did not.

"Come back at dawn, then," Tarco told him. "You'll have the honor of chasing her down to breakfast. And, of course, the honor of dodging it."

Giving a curt nod that was only ceremonial and not at all friendly, Bloor left Tarco to his duties.

19

Before being introduced to his new charge, he was shown to his quarters inside the palace, one level down and away from those of Morianna's. The palace was huge, as each successive king added new towers, chambers and walls to its bulging mass. The king himself was supposed to reside here, as well as the rest of the royal family, but Bloor heard it once said that if someone did not want to be found in the palace, it was an easy thing to do. The palace kept a force of men at arms within its cavernous bulk, as well as two hundred handpicked Sujins, in addition to the hundred or so royal Axemen. Bloor considered himself lucky that his new room was not near any of the other military staff. He followed a servant to his quarters through a dimly lit but well kept stone corridor with high arches of red wood. He passed several closed doors, presumably of other household staff, and more than a few storerooms. His chamber was at the very end of the corridor. He faced the heavy wooden door and sighed mightily, suddenly tired from the day and the idea of several more like it. The door was not locked, but Bloor felt confident that his privacy would not be intruded upon. There was practically nothing inside besides an all-too-soft-looking bed covered with thick blankets. The blankets puzzled Bloor, as summer was not yet finished. There was also a wooden table and chair, and a single tall dresser. All were of a better quality than the ones he possessed within the ranks of the Cavaliers, but Bloor did not own much beyond his horse, weapons, armor, and three changes of spare clothes.

The door swung open and he saw there was light within, and saw a long shadow stretched out on the floor.

A pensive Bloor stood on the threshold for a moment, studying the dark shape.

"Evening, Bloor," an easy voice greeted.

Alwan.

He stepped inside the room and beheld the man in plain clothes sitting at the table and waiting for him.

"Hard to recognize you without your armor and blades," Bloor muttered, moving across the room to the bed. A bare pallet for his armor lay nearby. "Since you are here, help me get out of mine."

Alwan moved to do so. "I feel like I could catch a horse without my armor. It's unsettling sometimes. Until one gets used to it."

Bloor cocked a brow. He knew Alwan for a short time, but only on a professional basis. There was always a gap there that they both seemed reluctant to cross. Alwan had a reputation with a blade, and from what Bloor had seen, the reputation was well earned. He rode a horse as if his mother's own arse had been afire when birthing him. However, what Bloor remembered about Alwan the most were the tales surrounding him. If even half the stories were true, then Alwan was Saimon himself. While most men talked openly of heroics and noble deeds performed by renowned Cavaliers, they whispered when they talked of Alwan. It was said he took no prisoners if he could get away with it. Before he turned twelve, it was said that his father, a wealthy landowner, had killed his mother in a fit of dementia one winter's night before splitting his own skull open with an axe. An uncle supposedly sold whatever possessions his brother had and took any coin the banks held. He kept a third of the total sum and used the last to pay for Alwan's schooling within the Cavaliers' ranks. Rumors depicted a troubled boy stabbing animals with knives stolen from the kitchen. There was a rash of killings involving beggars and homeless people that were somehow connected to his name but never proven. It was said that the boy excelled in the military arts and that he never backed down from anyone or any challenge thrown at him. Another tale suggested the Cavalier had killed a hundred men by the time he was twenty, and those were only the known ones. If there was a charge at a spear wall, Alwan would be at the front of it. He seemed to delight in catching his sword brothers unawares at drinking occasions, holding daggers to men's throats and scolding them for dropping their guards at any time. Another tale had Alwan catching a fellow Cavalier napping while he was off-duty, amongst sword brothers, and well within the safe confines of Sunja. The warrior elite woke up to a knife at his throat and the fist fight that followed left him and three of his comrades unconscious on the floor.

Bloor could believe that story. He did not doubt Alwan could fight.

Some said the man was fearless.

Some said he was suicidal.

Most all agreed he was unbalanced.

Alwan would at times openly laugh at scenes that would break another man's heart. He would sneer at children bawling beside the corpses of dead parents, and he would swear openly in the churches of Seddon, daring the god to strike him down...if he could.

Bloor had seen the man's feral nature in battle. He was ruthless, better than all those he killed, and yet he took orders as Bloor gave them in the battle of Devil's Gullet. He pondered that, as the man helped him out of his armor, and he decided that he didn't care for the rumors, as long as Alwan did his duty, and Alwan always did his duty. They never talked much out on patrol, but they did seem to work well together for some reason that escaped Bloor. Bloor then remembered overhearing one Lancer commenting on how he "rode along Saimon himself." Bloor didn't care. Alwan could handle himself and that was all he could ask for in a Cavalier, but a part of him wondered if the stories were true.

The man helped him out of his armor without much to say. In a pair of white leggings and under tunic, Bloor indicated to him to sit. Alwan did so, sitting back at the table. Bloor remained standing and leaned against a wall, his sword within reach. One could not be too relaxed around the man.

Ask anyone. Alwan was *evil*.

In the glow of the lamplight, Bloor regarded this evil man and waited, letting the stillness grow.

"I heard of your new assignment," Alwan finally said. "Guarding a princess. Lucky you." He smiled, and the light made his dark features look hellish. "Is she pretty?"

Bloor frowned. "She's a girl."

Alwan's smile lingered. "She'll grow up."

"What do you want?" Bloor demanded. He was tired and wanted to both think and sleep. He didn't need Alwan keeping him from either.

"Does she smell pretty?" Alwan asked quietly, his smile disappearing. A twinge of unease went through Bloor. Perhaps the man *was* unbalanced. The man's eyes were on the table and his hand shifted, reached out, and touched the base of the lamp.

"I would not know," Bloor said stoically. "Now say what you have to say and be off."

Alwan's smile reappeared as slowly at the sun coming out from behind stormclouds. "The others talk about you, you know. How you care for your horse more than people. Personally, I don't see a problem. Caring for people is a waste of time and effort."

"Yes, well," Bloor interjected. "This was pleasant. Do come again."

"And just as much of a talker as I."

"You've said enough."

"When I have things to say."

"Then say what is on your mind. For the last time," Bloor said in menacing tone.

"Very well then," Alwan nodded. "How was your first day?"

"Long."

"Do you enjoy the position?"

"It's my assignment and my duty to see it done," Bloor said indifferently.

"What would you say if I could get you back out there, at the front?"

"I'll go where ordered," Bloor said truthfully. Here or there. It really did not matter to him.

"*Devoted*, aren't you?" Alwan smirked.

"And tired."

Alwan said nothing to that, so Bloor went on. "Is that all then? You're asking for my thoughts on returning to the front?"

"Yes."

"Then we're finished. Lord Winter has given me the charge of this girl. I don't think you can change his mind that easily."

"He hasn't met me privately yet," Alwan said. "But I do know of Lord Maullus, and he is sending me back to the front. He asked me to pick my men. I'm picking you, if you want it. I carry some weight with him, it appears. He might be able to sway Lord Winter."

This was news to Bloor, and he considered it carefully. "I wonder why you have Lord Maullus' ear? Been doing some work others have no stomach for?"

"I do what I'm told."

"Devoted, aren't you?" Bloor countered thinly, drawing an irritated scowl from the seated Cavalier.

"This is the kind of banter I'll miss, Bloor."

"We hardly talked at all."

"When we did, it was good," Alwan said. "There was a pureness there. No nonsense, all business. I enjoyed it. When I heard about your reassignment, I admit I was surprised and disappointed. Of them all, I trusted you to keep my back. Of them all, I knew you to be the only one *capable* enough to watch my back, the only one that wouldn't die. When Lord Maullus told me of my next assignment and to pick my companions, I gave your name right away. He told me if you desired it, he would try and persuade Lord Winter to assign another to watch the princess. As to what I do for Lord Maullus, either here or on the front, well, I only do what he expects of me and nothing less."

"Keep that in mind when I say I expect and owe you nothing," Bloor told him. "You aren't doing me any favors."

"I'm not?" Alwan's brow rose in puzzlement. "I've heard about the princess. She's charmed you, has she? Already?"

Charmed would not be the word Bloor would use, but instead he said, "I'm sorry to disappoint you, Alwan, but I have no desire to leave this task so soon after receiving it. It would be bad form."

"Bad form? Protecting a girl is good form?"

"A princess."

"The seventh child of the king?" Alwan retorted. "Or is it the sixth? But what does it matter?"

"She is still royalty."

"Are you hoping to get invited into the Axemen, perhaps?"

Bloor made a sour face, and Alwan breathed a sigh of relief. "At least that much is good news," he commented. He rose to his feet. "I won't press you any further then. Think on the offer. I'll give you a week. Perhaps even a month, but I doubt it'll take that long. I've heard about the princess, Bloor. And if you still wish to stay at her side, then I'll choose someone else. Lord Maullus has given me the authority to recruit whoever I want."

Bloor held up a hand, "One thing. What do you know of a Cavalier called Tarco?"

"Tarco?"

"He told me he was one of us. He wore the armor."

Alwan thought for a moment. "I don't know anyone by that name."

"He shares the duty of protecting the princess."

"Two protectors?" Alwan feigned being impressed. "Soon she'll have royal Axemen. If they can be spared from the other children, that is. There are so many. The king's busy in the spring."

With a smile thick with sarcasm, Alwan turned to leave. He opened the door and paused. "But then again, I supposed if I were to assign a man to watch over one of my daughters, I would choose you as well."

His words came with a smugness that left Bloor wondering if he had just been insulted or complimented. It could be difficult to tell with this one. He would so often hide his distaste behind a smile. Bloor did not say goodbye to the departing man and stood with his back against the wall for long moments after Alwan had closed the door. Return to the front, to fight the Nords again, to be up to his chin in blood, but to give up his assignment here, and to have Lord Maullus pull on Lord Winter's arm to do so, left him with a unpleasant taste in his mouth. It would not do. It simply would not do to ask for another, as much as a pain Morianna might potentially be. He beat down any remaining doubt in his mind. He had made his choice. There would be nothing else except protecting Morianna. That was his focus and duty now.

Having made his decision, Bloor considered the door. He stepped away from the wall and quietly locked it, remembering all those tales of the evil one delighting in catching men off guard.

One could never be certain with Alwan about.

20

Bloor slept like dead wood.

In the morning, a servant brought him a more-manageable leather cuirass, a shiny helm with an open face, and bronze greaves for his lower legs. Bloor considered it all, ruefully, as he washed and shaved himself. He cared little for the opposing black griffons pawing at each other on the front of the armor, but he was impressed with the weight of the armor after slipping it on. It was much lighter than his regular battle dress, though he felt the vest would stop very little if he were pressed into a fight.

Despite that one misgiving, he was thankful for the change in armor. Wearing full battle dress throughout the day was not necessary while within the palace and on its surrounding grounds. Because it lacked the lustre of his plate armor, he decided that it might not attract bowls of pudding. However, there were always other desserts. He strapped on his shortsword and left for breakfast; he would meet the princess after eating.

Or so he thought.

He heard her petulant voice on the steps leading to the kitchen. It was only his second day in the youngster's presence, and yet her voice pierced through him like a frozen arrow. Was it too late to take Alwan up on his offer? He paused on the stairs, thinking it through again while the princess complained incessantly below. What was she doing down there at this hour in the morning? Wasn't he supposed to meet her at her chamber doors?

A groan came from the direction of the kitchen. It was a girlish groan, full of frustration at why something wasn't exactly the way she wanted it. Taking a breath as if he were about to charge into battle, Bloor continued to the kitchen. He would be on guard this time for thrown food. The princess would not catch him napping a second time.

"Why didn't you get any cream?" Morianna bellowed at someone. "You know I *loathe* strawberries without cream! I like the sweet cream! You were supposed to get the ingredients from the market and make it yesterday! Yesterday! I was even *here* yesterday and you didn't say anything? Are you stupid? You are *so* stupid sometimes! Why do I put up with you? Why are you so stupid? What's wrong now? Why are you so stunned? Tell me! And fat too! Maybe there was cream, but you ate it all yourself. I suppose you usually do sneak a taste or two. Maybe I'll tell my father that the reason you're shaped like a barrel is because you're eating everything. Isn't that right? It is, isn't it!"

Standing in the doorway of the kitchen, Bloor cleared his throat. Morianna whirled upon him as if caught doing something incredibly guilty. Chagrin flashed in her dark eyes and her face screwed up. Bloor thought she was preparing to spit, but when she recognized who it was, hatred darkened her already-angry features. It shocked Bloor to see how a young face could manage to look so *evil*, so full of raw hate.

Behind her, the heavyset cook, the same elderly lady from yesterday, looked at Bloor for a moment with eyes rimmed with tears. The relief in her face was identical to the expression Bloor would expect to see on the faces of villagers being saved from Nordish Jackals. She was about to break under Morianna's assault. Something in her face told him that much, but his appearance bolstered her.

"What do you want?" Morianna seethed, her chest working in and out like hot bellows.

"Breakfast, my Lady," Bloor answered her.

"It's too early for *your* breakfast," she decreed. "You can eat later."

Seeing her little fists balled up at her hips, Bloor stayed where he was and battled the temptation to walk over and smack the little tit. Willpower, he told himself. "I have my duties to perform later. That is to protect you…"

"You can eat later. Go on," Morianna cut him off, dismissing him further by wiggling her fingers at him as if he were a troublesome curl of hair sticking to them. "I don't want to see you now. I'm talking to this servant."

Willpower, he stressed to himself, though he still felt the heat rise in his face. Before it could come to full bloom, he bowed curtly and left the kitchen. He marched back to his quarters, remembering the scalding incident, and wondering where Tarco was. The night Cavalier should have been with her. Arriving back at his room, Bloor entered, closed the door, and sat at his table. His fingers spread over its surface and he took a deep breath. He relaxed. After a moment, he began to feel the cold energy in the wood curling up into his hand like a shy thing, and rolling up his arms. The memory of the princess faded. The sad face of the cook faded. The angry words became a whisper, and his mind drifted: the countryside, his horse, a clear duty to fulfill.

A whining Morianna to discipline.

The knocking at the door broke the image and his eyes popped open. He lurched to his feet.

Tarco.

"Good morning," the young man said pleasantly enough.

Bloor stared. He was dressed casually in a fine white shirt, green vest, and black leggings, the standard clothes for an off-duty Cavalier. Tarco was also weaponless.

"I heard you in the kitchen. I should have told you earlier the little one likes to eat in the kitchen sometimes, whenever the fancy takes her. I imagine she just likes torturing the poor woman doing the cooking. Poor old Sera. She does her best—a damn fine job, too—but it seems there's just no pleasing the princess. She's a fickle one. I'd be tempted to spit in her food if I were bringing something up to Mori…"

"Why aren't you battle dressed?" Bloor interrupted the prattling.

Tarco paused. "I…she told me to go early last night. Told me to go to sleep."

"She told you to go to bed last night?"

Tarco nodded uncertainly, and Bloor's face became stern. Those who knew the Cavalier would say that stern glare was only a shade away from being murderous.

"I've been with the princess for a day only, and in that one day I can't remember a single word of kindness she has said to anyone. Anyone," he stressed, while looking directly into Tarco's offended features.

"Are you saying I'm lying?" he shot back, daring Bloor to say the words aloud.

Who was this man? Bloor wanted to know. Why was he so sure of himself?

Bloor stepped in close to the man, right before his face. For an instant, Tarco's resolve shook, but he did not move back.

"I'm *telling* you, you're lying," Bloor breathed into Tarco's face with repressed rage. "And if you try it again, I will inform Lord Winter and let him address you, personally. Do I make myself clear?"

At the mention of Lord Winter, a spark of insolence came to Tarco's eyes. "I know my orders. If you speak to Winter, it will be your word against mine."

"*Lord* Winter, to you," Bloor corrected him.

"I know his name," Tarco sneered.

"Then address him as such. Think of it as practice."

"You are a righteous one, aren't you?"

"That I am. As a *Cavalier* should be. Or do you just wear the clothes?"

That struck something. Tarco stretched his neck and his mouth became an angry line. "You're a brave one, I'll give you that."

"And I'm judging you," Bloor said, tasting bile on the words and liking the flavour as much as he liked this idiot before him.

"There were four guards at her doors. I felt I could retire early," Tarco told him, his face a hot scarlet.

"Our orders were to be around the princess constantly."

"Those are Lord Winter's orders."

"His orders are to be ignored?" Bloor asked.

"I know my orders, Bloor. And Lord Winter isn't around her as often as we are."

"As often as you are," Bloor corrected him.

Tarco smiled evilly. "Whatever you like, Bloor. I see what kind of man you are now. I imagine you will enjoy your time with the little treasure."

"You mean the princess?"

"Of course," Tarco's mouth opened as if he had been slapped.

"Then address her as such," Bloor warned him. "I don't like your tone, Tarco. I don't like your attitude. If we were on the front, your four limbs would be stretched out and nailed down on a hill for such dereliction of duty. How long have you been a Cavalier?"

"Is this because of what happened in the kitchen? Are you misplacing anger here? Because if you are..." He stopped talking then, for Bloor's face was blooming murder. Tarco had never seen such fury in a man's face before. It cut his words from his throat, and in truth, he wasn't sure if he was safe in the man's presence, anymore. He wished he had brought his blade.

Bloor spoke in a controlled voice. "Answer my question."

"Five months," Tarco answered immediately.

"In the field?"

"No, only here."

Bloor's brow crumpled into disgusted puzzlement. "How is it that you got this post without first serving your year on the borderlands?"

Tarco's face became colorless then, and he kept staring at the sword at Bloor's waist. What did the man mean to do with the blade? Would he have to fight for his life here? Not here. Not in the palace. Not with another Cavalier. "My father is the Minister of Defense," he admitted in a rush.

Bloor kept silent. He studied the man's face and saw no lie there. So much was becoming clearer now. "Did you serve with the Sujins?" Bloor demanded.

An exasperated "No," escaped the man, as if such a thing was beneath him.

"So you only trained with the Taskmasters?"

"Yes."

A heavy sigh left Bloor. He had all the answers he wanted, for now. Any more would probably just ruin his appetite. He would have thought that the life of a princess, no matter if she was the last of the line, would be guarded by men with more experience. He remembered the haughty attitude of the man earlier and sighed again. Tarco had a set of balls; that much could be said for him. Balls *that* big had a way of being removed quickly though, and not always with a knife. "You should be on patrol somewhere," he finished. "This is not for you."

"That's what I told my father. Really, I did! But this is what he wanted. He didn't want me to go out there with the others. He didn't want me to work my way up. I would have, but it was *him* that wanted it this way. He made it happen this way. I would have gladly gone to the front, Bloor, but he insisted that I do this," Tarco's shoulders slumped, as he blurted out his tale, surrendering to Bloor's judgment. However, Bloor suspected that Tarco had done this many times before and had perfected it, to admit to being in the wrong without really believing it, throwing himself on another's mercy and getting off lightly because of it. He didn't appreciate the performance. It might have worked on his father, but not on Bloor.

"So you do as you're told, do you?" he asked the young man firmly.

"Yes," Tarco said, relief in his voice. He hoped that the man before him would understand his position.

"Then," Bloor began, "you can get out of my doorway. I'll see you later in the evening, in battle dress and with weapons. If you do not relieve me in an orderly fashion, I will inform Lord Winter of your dereliction of duty. Do you understand?"

Tarco's mouth fell open, "I was doing as I was told."

"Then you'll do as I tell you now. Understood? Take that from an experienced Cavalier and one who is above you in this duty."

For a brief moment there was poison in Tarco's eyes. He might give in to his father's wishes, but it was obvious that he disliked being ordered around by anyone else. Bloor thought he was going to remind him of his father's position in a feeble attempt at regaining some measure of control. Instead, Tarco kept quiet.

"Understood?" Bloor demanded.

"Yes," Tarco answered.

"You can go. And rest this day. You will be on duty this night until the dawn."

Tarco turned to leave.

"And Tarco?"

He looked back questioningly.

"Salute."

There was the briefest of pauses, and again Bloor thought Tarco was going to refuse. However, Tarco saluted instead, his right hand going across his breast and bowing at the hips.

Bloor closed the door and sat down again. A deep sigh lifted his shoulders and he exhaled at the gall of the younger man. How much younger, Bloor really didn't care. He possessed the greater experience and that was enough for him to keep Tarco in line. Officially, there was no law for Bloor's assumed command, since they were both on equal footing in the guarding of the princess, but his experience did give him an edge in matters. The younger man might still invoke the name of his father to ward off some of Bloor's commands, and if he did, Bloor would be hard-pressed not to clout him for doing so. Perhaps he would anyway. Bloor had no doubt that Tarco was probably on his way to check into Bloor's records, if he hadn't already. His records should be enough to cock the younger man's brow in interest, if not respect.

The Cavalier drew a long breath again and hoped that things did not get any more complicated, and it was only the second day. He could not help but feel an urge to locate Alwan.

Willpower.

Focus.

The words did not help this time.

He returned to the kitchen an hour later and found a plump Sera moping over a simmering pot. She glanced up when Bloor entered the room and sat down at the main table.

Her face showed nothing of the verbal lashings from the princess. Button-brown eyes sparkled at him. "My Lord," she gushed. "I've been waiting for your return. What would please you this morning?"

So many things would please him, and all of them were beyond Sera's power. "Anything you have ready would be fine," Bloor said to her.

The woman looked more than happy to serve him, flittering off and carrying her weight with a nimbleness Bloor would not have thought possible. She moved about the kitchen, hands gathering up this and that and depositing several good things on a wooden plate. She brought him peeled apple halves and warm bread with honey butter. She brought him dried beef from the night before, still tender.

"Thank you. It's all very good," he told her. The words put a crinkle around her eyes and she gave a pleased nod before moving off to do her other kitchen chores. Bloor saw how her face softened when he thanked her. When was the last time she had heard a kind word? Maybe not as often as she should. As he chewed, Bloor's thoughts turned to his own childhood. It was so nice to have someone prepare something good to eat and then give it to you, and all that was required was a kind word for the gesture. He believed it was the best bargain in the world. He wanted to speak to her, but she moved so diligently around with her work that he did not. He appreciated what she did, but in truth, he was not ready to become a friend, not even an acquaintance.

Bloor was not sociable. He lowered his eyes and went on chewing. She said nothing to him in turn, recognizing that he was a Cavalier, and realizing that as one of his position, he would speak to her when it suited him. She thought no ill thoughts towards him for this. It was the way of the land, and it would remain so long after she was too old to carry on her work. She kept on with her chores. She wanted to make fresh bread this day, and set about preparing to do just that, checking off items in her mind.

Bloor finished and went to start his daily duty in the service of the princess. He arrived at her chambers where he met the attentive faces of Borus and Lyan. Both of the men seemed to be quite eager to please him this morning. Bloor showed no emotion whatsoever as he inspected them. They kept their armor and weapons in reasonable shape. He finished gauging them and his eyes flicked from one to the other. He said nothing, which he felt was compliment enough. They would have to call on Seddon's help if he found something lacking.

"The princess is inside?" he asked them.

"She is, Lord," Borus replied promptly.

"Did you see her return from the kitchen?"

"We did, Lord."

"Was she alone?"

"She was, Lord," Borus said, almost apologetically, to Bloor's suddenly-sour face.

"Don't ever leave this post unless you have orders from me or someone of higher rank," Bloor warned them. "Don't let the princess wander from her room by herself if I'm not with her. That part should be easy to obey. I'm supposed to be around her at all times during the day. Understood?"

"Yes, Lord," Borus said.

"Clearly, Lord," Lyan added.

Bloor studied them both again. They seemed to mean it, and that was good. He potentially had a pair of able soldiers here. He hoped he did. He did not want to have to pommel either one. It would not be good for morale. Without a word, he turned to the princess' door and rapped its surface.

"*Go away,*" Morianna yelled from within. Bloor frowned and drew breath. It was still early morning.

"Alright then, come in," Morianna suddenly grated. Not really expecting to be invited inside, Bloor cautiously allowed himself in. He sought only to announce himself and stand outside with Borus and Lyan, but the princess flicked her fingers at him again, as if fixing him with a spell.

"Stand over there and be quiet," Morianna told him. The princess sat at a white cloth-covered table. Alora sat across from her and gave him a little nod in way of greeting.

Bloor did as he was ordered, fighting down a flare of resentment towards the child. He glanced at a tapestry hung on the wall depicting a scene of woodland elves prancing about. Scowling, he put his back to it, and watched the pair play their game. He couldn't recall the name of the children's game, though he had seen it before. He hardly ever played games while growing up in the company of Cavaliers. Beyond the table stood a magnificent bed, draped in a fine silky mesh to keep insects from the sleeping princess. Extravagant blankets shone through the dreamy mesh and smothered the bed. The curve of a white bed pan peeked out from underneath one corner of the frame. Bloor sized up the bed again. The thing looked big enough for three people. Bloor supposed the king expected his daughter to put on some weight as she grew. Beyond that, the chamber of the princess was spotless, with clothes out of sight in closed, handcrafted closets of expensive-looking wood. Bloor did not see any toys about, though he did spy an impressive rack of shelves filled with books. It appeared Morianna was starting a collection of her own to rival that of the library.

"That was a stupid move," Morianna announced loudly, giving a triumphant look at her protector to let him know it was a stupid move. When Bloor did not acknowledge her, she pouted.

"Yes," Alora agreed quietly, with all the patience in the world, it seemed. "Seems it was."

"*Really* stupid," Morianna insisted. "I suppose I should let you take that move back, but if I do, I think you'll only do it again. So I won't. You'll remember it next time, won't you?" she said, not expecting a reply. "Now I can do *this*."

She did just that. Alora removed her captured piece. She then inspected the board of black and white pieces, and eventually made her move. "I wouldn't do that," Morianna told her. "Because if you do, *I'll* be able to do this. Why would you ever think of making such a move? Aren't you thinking? See? You'll lose these pieces here and here and here! See? Do you see?"

"I see," Alora said, chin in her hand, reconsidering.

"I'll only help you once and that's it. Next time, I'll let you do it and you'll be sorry." Alora made her move. Morianna shook her head in undisguised loathing. "I *hate* it when you do that," she fumed. "Take this!"

Alora quietly watched the next move, removed another one of her pieces from the board, and countered with one of her own.

Morianna shrieked. Bloor jumped, having let the flow of their exchange dull his senses. He regained his composure. Before him, Morianna screamed again, a raw sound straight from the back of her throat. The princess glanced at him, looking worried about something, and went right back to the game. His dislike for the girl grew.

Morianna countered Alora's moves with loud grunts to convince both Bloor and Alora of her superior play.

Until "Aha!"

The tide had turned.

"I *knew* you would try something like that," the princess said, color in her cheeks. "I just *knew* it. You always do that, you know. You're *so* predictable," she glanced over at Bloor again to see if he was listening.

"Do I?" Alora asked, innocently.

"Yes, you do. Always the stupid play. I don't know why I play with you at all. There's no challenge playing you. Maybe I should play him!" Bloor did not meet her gaze.

"But that would mean I have to look at him and who wants to do that? Not me. Maybe I'll teach you how to play better, Alora. Then you can beat anyone. Except me, of course. You'll never be able to beat me. Never, never, never," she trilled, prancing her fingers along the edge of the table. She went on about Alora's lack of skill, not in the least concerned about being rude. The lady did not flinch under the barrage, as if she was caught in a sudden summer downpour without a shawl and helpless to do anything about it.

Tiring, Morianna got up and ordered Alora to follow her. "This day, we'll go to the market. I wish to shop. Except you," she directed this at Bloor.

"I'm sorry, my Princess?"

"You aren't coming," Morianna repeated, stepping up to him, fearless. "You have a much more important thing to do."

"But..."

"Listen to me, you idiot," Morianna cut him off, sharp enough to draw blood, stamping a foot as she did so. "I don't care where you do your duty, but while you serve me, you *serve* me!"

Bloor blinked at her. For a moment he was speechless. Then he collected himself. "But..."

"SHUT UP!" Morianna shrieked at him. "Just SHUT UP! I'm sick of you already! I don't care what you think. You see, Alora? I told you he was a proud one! Well, now you serve me! I'm your princess and you have to do as I say. So proud, this Cavalier is. Well, you'll do as I say because if you don't *I'll* tell my father!" She cast the last few words at him like spears.

"Do you like that idea, horseface? Horseface!" She clapped her hands with evil delight. "That's what I'll call you from now on! Horseface! Do you like your new name, horseface? Do you remember who my father is? The king! That's who, horseface! Ugly horseface! Are you getting mad yet, horseface? I can see red in your cheeks! Look Alora, horseface is getting angry! *Soooooo* angry! HORSEFACE!"

Morianna abruptly became pensive. She studied him for a moment longer. "I know exactly what I'll have you do. You'll stay here, just like you are, standing with the elves there. You stay there until I say otherwise. And I'll have someone check on you to make sure you do as you're told. You'll stand here just like a statue. A horse-faced statue!" She beamed at her brilliance. "If you stop being a statue, I'll see to it that you work in the stables with the rest of your friends, the horses. Understand? And you'd better say 'Yes.'"

Bloor hesitated, wanting oh so very much to reach out and smash the little bitch. Instead, he said, "Yes."

"Good. It's nice to see horseface obeying for a change. Maybe I'll keep him after all. Try being more like a horse, will you, horseface? Look at me." Bloor met her eyes.

"DON'T LOOK AT ME!" Morianna yelled at him. "EVER!"

"Morianna," Alora said quietly, her hands folded in her lap. The princess whirled about to face her teacher. "Leave him alone," the woman told the child.

"He *looked* at me, Alora," she pleaded.

"You know why he did," Alora said, her voice firm yet gentle. "Stop it now."

Morianna did, for a moment. Incredibly, she paused for exactly a moment, the eye of the storm. Then the clouds rolled in again, and the wind picked up. She spun about to lash at Bloor again, and instead marched right out of the room.

"Stay right where you are, horseface!" she warned him, from out in the corridor. "You stay right *there!*"

Alora got up from where she sat. She did not look at him when she left the chamber. She had pulled Morianna off him this one time, but she made it clear that it was only the one time. Bloor wanted to curse her for allowing the child to grow in such a way, but he held his tongue instead. Willpower, he growled to himself. *Willpower.*

21

There he stood for four long dreary hours. In that space of time, he memorized just about every detail of the room before him. Large ornate clay pots hunkered down in the corners of the room, gushing unknown flowers of green. When the sun shone in, dust motes floated by his eyes and disappeared beyond the light. A thick rug lay on the floor, spiraled and coarse looking, warm to bare feet on cold mornings. Books on shelves, and the abandoned game on the table, the pieces standing in their last play. Somewhere out and beyond the open doorway—no one had bothered closing it—he heard a loud clatter of something falling. Twice he heard people call out to one another, their cries echoing briefly. Then nothing.

Bloor was still young enough to be spiteful, spiteful enough to prove to the little bitch that he could follow an order. He thought about several things while he stood, to remove the dull ache of boredom. He thought of Devil's Gullet, replaying the events as they happened in his mind. He remembered the night of drinking with the warrior known as Prong. He remembered leading a troop of Lancers through rolling foothills vibrant with tall green grass and cut in places with streams that looked like shiny ribbons. He thought of sunny skies and tall dark forests. He thought of how fresh the wind could be when he rode against it.

Then he remembered where he was: in the lair of a hellion princess.

Time drew the day on, pulling it along like a sick mule. His thoughts went from the majesty of the plains and hills of his travels to exacting revenge upon Morianna. Revenge went from elaborate schemes ending in public embarrassment to sharp, open hand clips across her head. The faces she made in his mind's theater pleased him wickedly, and he felt no guilt in conjuring them up. He knew he would never do any of these things to her, but it took some of the boredom out of simply standing there.

However, boredom won in the end.

A servant came into the room, cleaned it, emptied the chamber pot, and dusted around the Cavalier, much to Bloor's amusement. She was a young lady, fair, and wore a white shawl over her head. At first he thought she would speak, but when it became obvious that she wasn't about to, a part of him became suspicious. Did the princess give her instructions to act this way? Perhaps she simply saw him for what he was, a brief two-legged addition to the room. Not once did she look at Bloor, and she left upon finishing her duties, without saying a word. Not even an attempt at dusting him off, the thought of which lightened his mood. Sometime afterwards, Bloor felt the need to relieve himself, and he left his post to do so. No princess could keep him from that, and the notion of using her bed pan made him smirk. He walked past the silent figures of Borus and Lyan. He only left them long enough to urinate in a latrine trough outside of the palace, and he returned soon after. The Cavalier slowed when he neared the two men again, staying out of their sight and hoping to catch them in a whispered conversation, but he didn't hear a word between them. He looked for signs of smugness when he went past, but both men kept their faces earnest and watchful.

Bloor liked what he saw.

Then he was back in the room. The whole little foray did not last long, and yet it was just enough to shore up his resolve.

Then he thought about the men outside.

Bloor walked over to the open doorway. "You two," he spoke to them. "Take a walk about. Find a latrine. Then return here. Don't dawdle."

"Yes, Lord," the men responded, relief in their voices. Bloor reminded himself that while he suffered, he did not have to allow his men to do the same.

He heard them when they returned, not having been gone long. That was good. They were dependable after all.

By late midday, another servant, a man, entered the bedroom. He looked to Bloor immediately. He stood back and studied the man for a moment, quietly taking in his armor, shortsword, and stance. Bloor ignored him.

"She's forgotten about you, you know," the man said. "She does it all the time. On purpose, we believe. Gives meaningless chores and forgets about them. She's probably gone all day."

Bloor looked at the man. He was middle-aged and had the look of someone that worked hard for what he possessed in life. Appearing clean but worn, he was dressed in a flowing white shirt that stopped at the knees. Green leggings continued on after that. The shirt's neckline was open, and grey chest hair peeked out.

"If you need to take a piss, go ahead," the man said.

"I did."

"Drinks are fine as well."

"I'll wait," Bloor said to that.

"Look," the man began. "She's gone. There's no one about but servants. Go and relieve yourself, get something to eat, to drink, and come back. No one will say anything. We know what she's like. I'll even stay here if you like, until you return."

Suspicion flared up in the Cavalier, narrowing his eyes. "No."

The man saw Bloor's face and read it right away. Sighing, he left the room, leaving Bloor to wonder if he had just passed a test. While he thought, he stayed exactly where he was.

The day went on. The light waned in the windows, and gradually grew dark. Bloor kept on standing. His back ached, as did his feet, surprising him. It wasn't the first time he had done a long watch. It might have been from standing in the one spot for the day, and his body nagged him about it. None of his commanders in the past had submitted him to such weary guard duty. Fear of Morianna kept him there, fear of admitting defeat to her. Then there was Tarco, the Cavalier of name only. If Bloor left, he would have lowered himself to Tarco's level, and without the benefit of having a powerful patron to support him.

Sometime, after the sun had gone down and the sounds of the day had disappeared, Bloor heard footsteps approaching. He heard Morianna yelling at someone. Her voice echoed through the halls and caused him to scowl. He would show this youngster what it meant to do one's duty, but she did not appear.

Tarco entered the room instead, a shadow against the dim light of the corridor beyond. He shook his head.

"You've been here all day? Like this?" he asked.

"Yes."

"You're a fool, Bloor," Tarco said sadly.

"Am I?"

"You know what she did today?"

"No."

Tarco straightened his shoulders. "Do you wish to know?"

"No," Bloor said truthfully. It did not matter to him. Tarco kept quiet for a moment, his features shrouded in darkness.

"I spoke with my father, and he informed me you have no authority over me. We are equals here. I'll grant you your experience, but that's all. You don't have any authority to command me."

"Why are you here, Tarco?"

"To relieve you," Tarco answered simply. "Your duty is over."

"You'll stand here?"

The Cavalier chuckled. "No, I won't. I'll go to her library, where she is now, and I'll stay with her until dismissed."

"Then I'll stay."

Tarco leaned forward ever so slightly, as if he did not hear correctly. "You'll what?"

"Her last order to me was to stay here. One could argue that since you are a continuation of the watch, you will continue standing here."

"Stand here?" Tarco grated. "In the dark? Foolishness!"

"Then you are ignoring your duty."

"What duty?" Tarco demanded. "Stand in a bedroom all night?"

"Is my watch finished?"

"It is."

Bloor relaxed, ignoring the whining of his joints and back. "Then do what you want. I'll return in the morning of course, whether you are here or not."

He left several things unsaid, leaving Tarco to fume about his course of action. He would figure things out for himself. Disregard of a command from a royal figure, even one as young as Morianna, brought about severe consequences, even if the command was a pointless exercise. However, there was something else Bloor counted on, and that was his original command from Lord Winter to protect the princess, speaking on behalf of the king.

"This isn't our duty, Bloor," Tarco pleaded.

"I know that," Bloor agreed, "And I'll mention it to Lord Winter. Perhaps even Lord Maullus if I see him. After that, we'll see how often we have to repeat such commands."

For a moment, Tarco said nothing. Then the man smiled impishly, understanding flooding his face. "You are a bastard, Bloor."

"No," Bloor said. "There are rules here and someone did not explain them to the princess, or they did and the princess has forgotten. All she needs is to be reminded."

"So shall I stand here?" Tarco asked eagerly.

"I'm not ordering you to."

"But I'm to continue your watch," Tarco said, catching the scent of a plot. "I understand that now."

"Then stay here."

"Good. For how long?"

"Until she returns," Bloor told him. "Or someone notices."

"We could get into trouble for this, Bloor. There is a line," Tarco warned. "She is only a child."

"We are following the *Princess'* wishes," Bloor explained in a calm voice. "How could we, a pair of Cavaliers, be wrong in that? Besides," Bloor rolled his eyes, "she shouts like a full grown woman."

A tight smile crossed Tarco's features. "I will stay here, then."

Bloor left him to it. He wondered if the king would even hear of it. He stopped before the four men standing outside of the doorway. Two were the replacements for Borus and Lyan.

"A good watch today," he informed them.

"We're used to it, Lord," Lyan commented.

Seddon above, Bloor thought. What manner of princess is this?

They saluted him as he passed and he made his way back to his chambers. He caught a servant in a hallway and requested something to be brought to his quarters to eat. He retired early, struggled out of his armor, and ate a late supper. He undressed entirely after finishing his meal, but not before placing the wooden plate and goblet outside his door for the servant to retrieve later.

Bloor was asleep as soon after his head struck his pillow, and it was deep enough that he did not hear the utensils being picked up outside.

On the next morning of the continued watch, Morianna once again commanded Bloor to stand where he was while she moved freely about the palace. Lord Maullus, of all people, marched into the bedroom. Lord Maullus was the kingdom's legendary terror, the kind of man whispered about in awe and dread. Maullus was the right hand of Lord Winter, and together in their youth, the pair had torn a huge chunk off any and all of Sunja's enemies. His head shaved bald, Maullus stood like an angry ogre about to storm off to war. He glared at Bloor as if his eyes could blast lightening. A frosty beard coated the lower half of his face, completely concealing his mouth. His hands were clasped behind his decorated cuirass. Bloor stood in the same place where he stood the day before.

"How long have you done this, Cavalier?"

"A day, Lord," Bloor answered immediately.

"A day of this?" the commander seethed. "Upon whose orders?"

"The Princess Morianna, Lord."

Maullus' features darkened then. "You've been stationed here all that time?"

"Only yesterday and until now, Lord. Tarco had the night."

Maullus said nothing, chewing on the offence to his Cavaliers. To have a child circumvent the standing orders of his men galled him. That fact that both men stood here as they did greatly pleased the commander. "You are a solid man, a shining example of our order. And, as of now, you are relieved of your duty for the remainder of the day. Those are my orders. I'll take care of this *Princess*."

Though his eyes suggested otherwise, Maullus spoke in a very calm voice.

Bloor knew Maullus would indeed take care of everything. Fierce in the field and in his loyalty to the king, he was also quite protective over all the men he had collectively christened as maggots. The maggots *he* commanded. In his youth, he had clawed and sucked up a Seddon cursed canyon of farm filth in earning his title of commander. He had performed all of the dirty tasks on and off a battlefield in service to his king and country, and he hated to see good men giving good effort put to waste or sacrificed needlessly, knowing firsthand what happened on the borders and on the wartime fronts. He gave hard orders to the maggots under his command, but nothing he hadn't done when he was in their position. They were *his* maggots, and no one, excluding the king, had the power to abuse their loyalty or question their honor, and Seddon above, any civilian doing so would be dealt with harshly. Maullus was as unpredictable as Lord Winter when it came to his Cavaliers and Sujins, whom he also commanded. None of the court notables would cross words with him when it came to the reputation of the Five Klaws of Sunja. Where Winter could be compared to a bear at times, Maullus was a rutting wild boar, and he was not afraid of mincing words in the presence of the king.

Those thoughts and others crowded into Bloor's mind as he returned to his quarters early. He could not but help think what Maullus would say to the king, if, in fact, he did go to the king. Eventually, he went to sleep with an untroubled expression about his face.

22

The next day was different.

When he opened his door, both Borus and Lyan stood waiting for him. The princess summoned him directly to her study. They delivered the summons with an air of fear, which caused a twinge of worry in Bloor. He dismissed it right away. There was nothing that the princess could do to him, or so he thought.

When he entered the study, he had different thoughts. There were all manner of things to throw at him in here. The princess sat behind a fine table with a polished crystal ink well at one corner. She wore an exquisite white dress, though somewhat fluffy looking. A quiet Alora sat off to one side with her eyes downcast, but her features were relaxed looking, as if suppressing a pleasant idea.

"My Princess," Bloor addressed her and saluted. Then he waited, his eyes fixed on a window glowing with morning light. Morianna sat there and glowered, her eyes blazing like the twin tips of forge pincers.

"You think you are smarter than me?" Morianna finally asked him.

Bloor decided not to answer.

"I asked you if you think you are smarter than me?" she repeated, her voice rising.

"No, my Princess," Bloor said.

"You got me into trouble. With my father."

"I did?"

"Yes, you did. You stayed in the room," Morianna accused him.

"Didn't you instruct me to stay in the room?"

"No, I did *not*," she lied with a child's wounded disdain. "You purposely stayed there to get me in trouble."

A part of him wanted to paddle this girl, but instead, without looking at her, he said, "Perhaps you should take greater care in how you instruct your household staff."

"You got me into trouble!" Morianna fired again, louder.

"I did not."

"SHUT UP! I'll *tell* you when you can talk!"

Bloor noted that Alora did not jump at the outburst. The princess' frequent tantrums no longer seemed to affect her.

"If you get me into trouble again with my father, I'll send you far away from here. *Far* far away. Somewhere where you'll not see Sunja for a very long time."

Bloor wondered if this angry child knew what she was talking about. It was not his place to contradict or lecture her in the presence of others. He reminded himself that his duty was to protect only, and Morianna went on to explain this to him in great detail, even repeating herself in places, until Alora reached out with one hand and placed it carefully over one of princess' hands on the table.

It was then, at that exact moment, that the tears began to flow down the princess' cheeks. Her mouth twitched and her cheeks became a frustrated red. Her words became hoarse, and she began wiping her nose on the sleeves of her fluffy white dress. The action made Alora gasp in horror, and a cloth appeared almost instantly in her hand. She practically jammed the handkerchief into Morianna's unhappy face. Someone knew the true worth of the clothes the girl wore.

Then the girl abruptly stopped talking, turned towards her teacher, and buried her crying face in the shoulder of the woman. Great wracking shudders went through the young princess, and her head jerked to and fro ever so slightly, causing Bloor some concern for the girl. Alora gently reached up and placed one hand on the back of her head, steadying her.

"My Lord Cavalier," Alora then addressed him for the first time, and not unpleasantly. Her words surprised Bloor, and left him at a loss. "Please wait outside. We will call for you if you are needed."

Bloor nodded and removed himself from the room. He closed the door behind him, and regarded the wondering faces of Borus and Lyan. He told them nothing, not knowing what to say. He was glad of being excused from the embarrassing scene, and though he imagined punishments much worse, a part of him felt a pinch of shame at causing a young girl to cry. He told himself she deserved it, but he failed to convince himself. In one instant he was being barked at, and then the princess was being consoled as if a relative had died. He thought about it, and in those quiet moments, he heard nothing from the study. He heard nothing from further down the corridor. The palace could have been deserted.

A peal of protest from behind the door broke the illusion, quickly smothered by Alora's gentle voice.

Then nothing.

Bloor waited.

In the days to come, Bloor began to watch the princess more carefully. As he and the other guardians rarely left her side, it became an unconscious habit. He made her a study in character. Perhaps it was the display of emotion that had shattered his preconceptions of a spoiled child. He told himself that a spoiled child's greatest weapon was tears that could fall as easy as a sword being drawn. In the possession of a princess that could have almost every wish granted, it would be a very deadly weapon indeed. However, the more he watched her and listened, the more he began to think otherwise. The day-to-day life began to take on a distinct and rigid pattern, and what he did not see, he overheard in conversations between the princess and Alora.

Morianna would wake early in the morning and have Alora and other palace servants bathe her, dress her, feed her, and generally fuss around her while she barked and snipped at them all in annoyance. She was like a living doll to them it seemed, and Morianna often rebelled against the image. Nothing was left to her to do for herself, and Bloor wondered if that somehow affected her behavior. It certainly would affect him, being constantly swarmed over and adjusted and pampered from the time of waking to bedtime, to be perpetually picked at and fussed over, but did it allow her to lash out at her servants? He supposed he would if he lived as she did. In the end, Bloor decided she should not. It was easier to simply brand the girl as evil and leave it at that. As time went on, even that thought began to change.

Then there was Morianna's education. Her learning was paramount to her father, and Alora instructed the young princess mercilessly through volumes of education every day within the confines of the palace library. When the walls of that place became too much, she studied in her bedroom: reading, writing, calculations and problem solving, geography, known science, etiquette (which both surprised and amused Bloor), and a wealth of other subjects Bloor only distantly remembered or never studied at all. The sheer ocean of information surrounding her senses was overwhelming. It bewildered Bloor that Morianna could remember any of it. He believed his upbringing had been difficult with his own adequate schooling and physical training, but what Morianna underwent amazed him. Alora reviewed materials often and would regularly set out tasks and goals that Morianna would snap at like a caged animal not wanting to be bothered. In the end, she bent her head and concentrated on what was needed to be done, just to get it over with.

However, it was never ever truly finished. There was always something new to learn. Morianna studied and toiled for most of the day, with the exceptions of her meals, daily walks around the palace grounds, and other interludes that Bloor was not privy to and could only assume were for females only. She sat through lectures given by scholars in astronomy and alchemy that Bloor found difficult to follow at times. Politicians and merchants who offered their insights and experiences in the world beyond the palace were also brought before her. She would listen to them all with an equally tired Alora, though Bloor could see the teacher's effort of maintaining a look of interest for the princess' sake. The speakers would lecture until it was time for Morianna's bedtime, and she would retire to her chambers. There, she would read something pertaining to the next day's schooling until sleep took her, only to wake up to do it all again.

After the first week, Bloor realized that the princess never saw any of her other sisters. There was a rumor there were brothers, but Bloor was surprised to find this untrue. She had only sisters, and she never spoke to any of them for reasons beyond the Cavalier. She did not have any friends to speak of, other than the books placed in front of her. No other child of her age came near her. Bloor eventually came to view Alora as the only person he could actually consider a friend to the princess. The older woman shared much of the day with the princess and seemed as resigned to her rigid routine as Morianna.

Time marched on and Bloor began to understand many things. For the princess and even Alora, the palace was in fact a luxurious prison, and they were released from it only a few times during the week. For one afternoon each week the princess was permitted to venture out into the city under Bloor's guard and several stoic royal Axemen. On those days, the excitement in Morianna burned almost uncontrollably. With a beaming smile, she would jump into her waiting koch surrounded by a dozen guardsmen and royal Axemen, and then was taken into the depths of Sunja's city. However, the king had rules for these outings: Interaction with the common people was not permitted. If it happened, she would be denied her excursion the next week. Morianna watched the people on the streets from the designed lattice windows of her koch. If she saw something she liked, a single guardsman would buy it for her. If she saw a merchant's store that caught her interest, she could enter it only after the store's regular patrons were flushed out into the street like frightened rabbits. Most things, especially food, were inspected and checked with a critical eye before the princess could touch them or even take them aboard the koch, and no food from the stalls along the street was ever allowed at all.

To Morianna, the children in the city were much more fortunate than her. Sunjan children played and worked. They walked freely about and they had friends, true friends. There was never a mountain of books for them to study, at least as far as Morianna could see. There were no instruments to master, and no boring lectures to bear. There was only a child's existence until one day they woke up and found themselves as adults.

On the first day of accompanying the princess into the city, Bloor studied the clever designs of the latticed window, behind which Morianna's form could be just seen. He saw the heaviness of her head against the window, and could imagine the longing in her eyes. Her brown eyes that Bloor at first thought to be full of insolence, contained only a frustrated longing. She was outside the palace, but still leashed.

After several such trips, she would return to the palace and the royal grounds, grudgingly accepting her fate. Bloor believed she would be impossible to pacify or contain on the way back, but in truth, she was usually only sullen and reflective on what she had seen in the city. Within the grounds, she would be allowed some time to get her daily exercise. She would walk and think on what she had seen or items of interest she might have had a guard purchase for her. She would dally within the copse of trees, and sometimes she would have the opportunity to venture into the royal stables and exercise her horse, a beautiful and docile gelding that Morianna seemed bored with. She was not permitted to run the horse, as her caretakers and father feared for her safety, so she trotted it throughout the parade grounds, around and around, with a bored expression on her face. Bloor supposed it was not like a ride in the city with all the people to watch, but it was still better than being indoors and her routine studying.

In the evening, Morianna would be ushered back to the palace and into her private chambers with guards watching all the while.

The life of a princess.

It struck Bloor that she lived for those moments when she was allowed out of her palace shell, if only for a few hours. The more he thought about it, the more he believed it to be a miserable existence. He wondered if Morianna had ever thrown a fit if her schedule was somehow changed, preventing her from leaving the palace. He wondered what she would do if allowed six days in the city with even greater freedoms and only a day of study. Would she know what to do with herself?

One of those afternoons, in the shade of the stables and standing before the parade grounds, Bloor stood beside the stablehand in charge of the princess' magnificent gelding. They stood side-by-side as they watched the unimpressed princess stroll about the beaten tracks on the back of the animal, around and around.

"She doesn't seem too happy with the beast," Bloor commented to himself. The man next to him took it as a signal for some idle conversation.

"Naw," the stablehand said, chewing hard on something. "Never is. Hates it, I think. If I had a pony when I was her age, I'd piss myself evra day t'get on it. But she rides it like it t'were a dirty dress she has t'put on."

Bloor glanced sideways at the man. He appeared to have missed shaving that day, and had a round, tanned face. He was missing three teeth in front, giving a flash of the gaps when he spoke. His worn clothes were clean, and the sleeves of his white shirt were rolled up to the elbows. He didn't bother looking at Bloor when he spoke.

"But she's a princess," the man sighed. "And I sure as Saimon's hell wouldn't want her life."

"Why?" Bloor asked, curious.

"Naw," the man said, keeping his eyes on the horse and princess at all times. "You should know. You keep an eye on her evra day. Would you want a life like that?"

Bloor considered it: everything provided for, except freedom. All the advantages of the world except being able to come and go as one pleased. He thought about the open plains and being able to ride over them with a horse underneath, the wind in his face and the sun beaming. He knew then what choice he would make.

"Naw," the man spat out again. "Not for me. Not me. Not good to be wishing for another's place in life anyway. Seddon knows I pity the girl."

Pity the girl? He wanted to ask why a stablehand would pity a princess, but then he knew the answer. Did all the servants feel the same way? Did Alora? Did the cook Sera, after being eaten alive by the princess when something was not prepared quite the way she liked it? Did they all pity her? Was that the reason they endured her?

That night in bed, Bloor thought about the people around her. None of them were left unscathed by the princess, as she took equal bites out of all of them. They were red cheeked with chagrin at times, but they never said a word back. He supposed that they never would say anything against the girl with him about anyway, the protective hand of the king. They probably believed he had permission to limb them if they ever did. He thought about it some more.

The palace servants performed their tasks and were allowed to return to their quarters or homes at the end of the day, to their friends and family, to no doubt talk about the lonely princess that they served. Bloor supposed that they were luckier than the princess in that they had greater freedom, and perhaps they knew it. Would that not lead them to feel pity for the princess? Perhaps that was why they endured her cutting tongue as often as they did, in addition to the privilege and security of being on the king's staff.

His feelings slowly shifted out of focus and shifted into something else.

Where were the king and queen? Where were her sisters? Relatives?

Why was Morianna always alone?

His thoughts followed the same pattern, night after night, nipping at the tails of the previous nights' conclusions. Time trekked on, as heedless as ever, dragging them all with it. Bloor became more and more thoughtful about the fourteen-year-old girl he served. He began feeling pity for her, which only infuriated her if she saw it in his face. The lashings that he endured at times were almost as bad as any rain of arrows.

The time came where the day's events took an unexpected turn. In a subdued tone, Morianna announced to him that it was her birthday. She said it with such boredom that Bloor scarcely believed her. What child didn't become excited at the time of her birthday? Morianna was not, but her attitude changed when Alora informed her of a special surprise in store for her that morning. Circus performers were allowed into the audience hall and all manner of acrobatics were witnessed by Morianna and a small audience. Balancing tricks and juggling acts of various objects entertained her for all of an hour; whereupon she was brought to another hall to listen to a small group of musicians perform several selections that Bloor had often heard Morianna practice on her instruments. The musicians played with energy and vigor and dedicated each tune to the princess. It was one of the few times that Bloor believed that she was happy.

Shortly after the concert, lunch was ready, and they dined in the formal hall where the princess rarely ate. Therein, four other young women sat waiting, straight backed and staring ahead. They were all carefully groomed and dressed in exquisite colors. They varied in ages, perhaps by a year each, with the oldest being perhaps nineteen or twenty. Behind each of them stood their own personal servants, and it was then that Bloor realized that these young women were the older sisters of Morianna. The excitement of this meeting took the princess off guard completely, as did the presents they presented to their little sister to celebrate her birthday. Bloor watched and listened to these young princesses talk. These young women, he realized, were every bit as isolated for each other as Morianna, and excited conversations quickly became boasts and arguments. Even the oldest argued, and the littler ones countered with a ferocity that ran in the family. Though taught the necessity of manners and courtesy, they failed to even perform the simplest of social interactions with each other. Please and thank-you's were nonexistent. They snapped at each other, and it surprised Bloor that no fistfights broke out. The food was lavish and rich desserts followed, yet the combative mood continued throughout the affair. The king and queen were absent from the gathering. A magic show began after the empty dishes were cleared away, and the children were diverted from each other for an hour. When it was finished, the sisters departed without goodbyes, leaving unopened gifts and a testy Morianna.

"It was almost perfect," Bloor heard her say to Alora, "Until *they* came."

The king granted her a rare treat, an evening visit into the city. That trip made her forget about her sisters. Bloor and a group of soldiers and Axemen protected her as always, and Morianna rode about in her koch, watching everyone from behind her special latticed windows; a dark figure watching the street lanterns being lit. Ever so often, Bloor would glance in the direction of the princess. It occurred to him that perhaps the greatest part of her birthday was the total absence of having to concentrate on anything.

So ended Morianna's fifteenth birthday.

23

Two months after her birthday, Morianna became increasingly irritable towards her servants. Bloor witnessed her throw a tantrum over a meal missing a dessert. She lashed out at the stablehand for holding onto the reins of her horse as she mounted. She verbally attacked Alora for pressing her to study harder. Even Bloor became a victim when catching her eye at times. He later learned from Alora that the youngest princess had an academic recital to perform before both the king and queen. With the approaching date of the recital, Morianna's stress increased tenfold. Of all the people, it seemed, she did not want to appear inept before her parents. Bloor could appreciate the girl's feelings, and he could see the extra effort that she forced into her studies, memorizing detail after detail from the volumes of information spread out before her. It was not known to Bloor why she had to do such a thing. Perhaps it was a test, or perhaps a reward was promised if she did well.

Inwardly, Bloor hoped she would be allowed greater freedom from the palace or even a reduced time for studying. The more he guarded her, the more he saw a young woman whose childhood had been robbed. He felt he understood, not having much of a childhood himself. He felt great pity for her, and it armored him against her accusing rants. He came to realize that her attacks were not really directed at him, but in effect, were veiled rants against her existence. She wanted more from her life. She wanted to see parents who clearly did not want to have anything to do with the girl, for reasons unknown to him. She wanted more than only glimpses of the world beyond the walls of the palace, beyond all of the fine foods and the countless servants at her beck and call, beyond the fine clothes and the private tutors.

How many people from Sunja's lower classes would give anything to possess what the princess had under the exact same conditions?

Perhaps all.

However, Bloor still pitied her. It was a strange feeling for him. He had gotten used to despising her far too easily.

Days went by, and Morianna went from being easily flustered to solid confidence. She memorized every single bit of information she was supposed to, and in her practice sessions with Alora, smoothly began and finished her recital on the history of Sunja. She even managed to smile when she did so. Bloor discovered the princess had an engaging smile when she bothered showing it. It brightened her face and made a person forget about her character.

"I'm ready. I don't need to do this again," she informed Alora, when her teacher wanted her to repeat her recital.

"Do you want your parents to hear you say such a thing, and then you stutter in error? And in front of him?"

"No," Morianna admitted, eyes downcast.

"Then again, please. You must do well, as it not only serves you, but reflects on me favorably. Do you want me to be banished?"

"No," Morianna repeated, her shoulders slouching. It amazed Bloor. For all of Morianna's ranting at her own teacher, of all the vicious ravings she threw at the older woman, she did not want to have her teacher removed.

Bloor earned a new appreciation for the quiet Alora. She never raised her voice to the princess, and though Morianna gave commands, it was slowly dawning on the Cavalier that it was Alora who was truly in control. With a careful frown, she could persuade the young princess to do as she wanted. With a well-placed word, the princess would become attentive, and more than once, Bloor noticed Morianna looking expectantly to Alora for that frown or word. It was heartening to see the teacher holding some sway over the girl. It was incredible that Morianna could be brought to bay by such subtly. Even he began to learn from the teacher. As few words as possible sometimes carried as much weight as a roar, and a roar, when finally used, could truly terrify. Bloor tried to imagine Alora if her anger was ever roused. She would be a terrible sight to behold. Morianna's anger was commonplace enough, but her servants, Bloor included, were hardened against it. However, if Alora were to become furious, perhaps the very walls of the palace would split with her thunder.

Bloor would remember her long after he left Sunja and the palace. In those days, Morianna wasn't the only one that learned from Alora.

The day finally arrived when Morianna gave her recital before her parents. The princess was nervous, her face drawn and perhaps a shade paler than usual, but controlled. She had prepared long enough that even if she did perchance slip, she had a "pardon me" ready on her lips, and would be able to move on with barely a ripple. It was a far cry from when she would stomp her feet and swear. Morianna was ready.

Bloor did not witness the recital, as it occurred after his watch duty. He heard of it from Tarco the next day, who was more than delighted to retell the evening. Morianna did a wonderful job in recounting all that she had learned in the past weeks, and not once did she stumble in her speech. Even Tarco was impressed with the amount of information she managed to pack into her head. However, it was unfortunate that the king barely noticed her effort, and the queen was absent for some unexplained reason. As Morianna delivered the history of the kingdom to him, well-dressed aides would approach him, bow low, and whisper things into his ears. The king listened to them with far greater interest than he did his youngest daughter's recital. He gestured Morianna to continue on each time she paused when a new aide appeared, until he ignored her completely. His eyes were on her in the beginning, but were drawn away to other matters entirely by the end. Morianna could have mispronounced every word she had memorized and talked about fantastic creatures of fairy lands, and the king would not have blinked.

After finishing, the princess was red faced and quietly sullen with the wasted effort of the past weeks. The king's feigned gratitude and praise for her at the end was a far greater slap across both her face and Alora's, who stood off to one side. To her credit, the teacher controlled her disappointment of the king much better than Morianna. Tarco reported that the woman did not say much, but one could tell from her face that she was indignant. Their audience had shown barely a whiff of genuine interest in what they had worked so hard on. All of their energy was spent for nothing. How would Alora motivate the princess to have a care for any future task?

The day after the recital, Bloor stood with his back against the door of the princess' study, listening to the faint voices inside. There were sobs in the morning, and then there was a long unsettling silence. Morianna took her meals in her room, Sera bowing to Bloor when she carried a silver tray to the princess' door. Alora came and went with the day, but said little to the guards outside the door. Bloor stood with his men at arms like unhappy statues until he was relieved by Tarco and his watch.

In the passing months, Bloor had gone from tolerating the young inexperienced Cavalier to wary acceptance. Tarco would often ask him for stories of Sunja's frontier, and after a while, Bloor relented and shared one or two experiences. Tarco listened with great interest and disturbed Bloor with his questions, like how much blood there was if one was beheaded, and how soon a corpse lost its color. A Cavalier should not ask such things, and Bloor told him just that. Bloor later reflected on what manner of man would even ask such things, or would have such morbid fascinations? Not a Cavalier that had served in the far ranges. Bloor suspected Tarco had read too many overly heroic accounts or seen too many dramatic stage enactments. One campaign would cure him of that. One campaign would cure anyone.

Then came the day when Bloor was summoned to the chambers of Lord Maullus.

He arrived at the quarters of the fearsome commander and was surprised to see a serious looking Tarco also present and standing at rigid attention. Bloor wondered if Tarco had persisted in knowing about the life of a Cavalier with Lord Maullus. Lord Maullus would be more than willing to grant the man's request. Bloor stood next to Tarco, not daring to meet the eyes of the commander. A stillness settled over the room as he took his time sizing up his men. There was a rumor that the man could be like a frozen stone at times, and this was one of those times. He seemed content to make the Cavaliers wait. In the lamplight of the room, Maullus' bald head shined.

"You will both be going to the Nordish front," he announced to them. Tarco's breath hitched in his chest at the news as if he were a boy again, being hoisted up onto the back of his first horse. "You've been assigned to the First Klaw in the West. The commanders there need additional Cavaliers, and there have been strong requests for you, Bloor. Someone remembers you. As for you, Tarco, I've decided to send you along. The experience will be to your benefit if you manage to stay alive. Bloor will see to that. He'll be right next to you at all times. Understood? Don't bother answering. I'm telling. You'll both go together and give those Nord sheeplickers a proper paddling across their balls. Understood?"

"Yes, Lord," both men answered, with Tarco shouting out his reply. His eagerness was embarrassing. It made Bloor uncomfortable.

Maullus regarded the young man for a moment. There was something in the way Tarco answered that bothered him as well, but he let it pass. "Watch your own out there," he said to Tarco. "The Jackals have had a good bite of Sujin, and have tasted Cavalier as well. The bastards weren't trained by me, whoever they were. And if you die out there Tarco, I'll personally go to Saimon's hell and paddle your balls with a horseman's flail. A tickle you won't soon forget, I guarantee. I get invitations all the time from Saimon and it isn't because I'm such a charming guest, it's because I have a side profession of paddlin' maggots. But enough of that. You'll both leave in the morning. I suspect you won't have any complaints considering the duty you've had for the past year or so. After the princess, this should be easy."

Tarco allowed himself a grin at that.

"What are you smiling at, you stupid-looking knob sucker?" Maullus inquired with a disgusted face. "You think I'm here for your amusement?"

"No, Lord," Tarco said quickly, his face reddened.

"Lord Maullus," Bloor asked, coming to the other's rescue. The commander regarded the man with an evil eye. "How many are going to the front?"

Maullus looked to the far wall. "All of you. Every last bastard that can hold a blade. All personal guardians will be replaced by royal Axemen. A strain on them, but damn them anyway. If I had my way, I'd have them all at the Jackals. All told, a hundred Cavaliers made up of healed veterans and new meat will be riding out in full battle dress. A Cavalier from the front will be arriving tomorrow, supposedly, and lead you back to the First Klaw. A lad of reputation. I believe he even put in a request for you, Bloor."

Bloor stopped the urge to roll his eyes. Alwan. Who better to lead them back into hell but one of hell's own?

"You know the man?" Maullus asked, seeing the recognition in the other's face.

"Yes, Lord. His name is Alwan."

That drew a snort of amusement from the commander. "I'm not a thankful man by nature, but I am thankful for having that one on our side. He is a hellpup. A bloody handful. The Nords would trade a thousand of their own for his head. We need lads like that. Put some fear back into those bastard Jackals. They've been too damned inspired for too damn long. You stay away from Alwan, Tarco. He'll wind up getting dead before long, and whoever rides by his side will too."

Maullus stopped for a moment, thinking on his own words. "But not before paddling some Nordish balls. Good and proper too," he purred in a murderous tone.

"Aye, Lord," Tarco said promptly.

"No need to shout boy. I'm right in front of you. Unless you think I'm older than I look. The beard fool you, boy?"

Tarco paled almost comically, "No Lord," he said.

Maullus remembered who he was speaking to, and decided to let the young man off his barb. He didn't need any visits from that pompous tit of a father. It would only lead to charges of murder. It wasn't the charges of murder that bothered him, it was the thought of having only Lord Winter coming to his cell to visit him.

"That's one way to kill Nords, I suppose," Maullus commented. "When they're puzzling over what you mean. Course, that means you have to get close enough to get your meaning across. And I've never known a Jackal wanting to just listen to what any of us had to say."

A dark chuckle rumbled from Maullus' throat, as if he were clearing it of cranky phlegm. "Any real questions then? No? Good. Off with you both then. Get a good night's sleep. Get a good meal. Find a wench too, if any will have you. Do all of that and gather up your weapons and gear and be ready to move when Alwan gets here. I'm told he's a terror when it comes to riding, and he'll probably only stop long enough to report in, replace his horse, and gather you up. Hell driven. A fine example to us all."

Both men turned to leave. "On second thought, you stay for a bit, Bloor. We'll have ourselves a smile."

The Cavalier nodded. Tarco hesitated for a moment, but he left the room with only a quick questioning look at Bloor.

Lord Maullus waited for a few moments. Satisfied that they were indeed alone, he motioned for Bloor to have a seat. "Now for that smile."

"A smile, Lord?"

From behind his desk, Lord Maullus pulled out a drawer and produced an ornate bottle with purple and white lilacs etched upon its surface. Two wooden cups followed, not as fancy as the flask, but looking well-used. The commander uncorked the bottle and began pouring, eyeing Bloor as he pulled up a chair to the desk. In the lamplight, the liquid sparkled.

"This," he indicated with a nod, "is very good wine. Made by a master. Well, almost a master. But it is still very good wine. Not too sweet and not so dry. I dislike drinking alone, Bloor, and I wanted to talk with you personally. I worry about this Tarco character. You know who he is, of course?"

Bloor nodded as the commander handed him a full cup.

"Good," Maullus muttered. "See that no harm comes to that pup's head. Keep him close by at all times and keep him out of trouble. His father wants it that way. Tarco jumped at the chance to fight the Jackals, and his father, as much as it turns my guts, loves his boy very much. Shouldn't have let him become a Cavalier, if you ask me. Anyway, while he is out there, his father requested me to assign a guard for Tarco, a bodyguard. You don't fight Tarco's battles for him of course, but keep him alive. Do you get my meaning?"

Bloor nodded.

"And make no mention of this to Tarco. The minister wants it that way. I suppose Tarco can twist his father's balls any way he wants, and his father, in turn, gets to twist mine. A fine example of life in the royal court."

Lord Maullus sniffed at his wine and sighed with content. "You'll be back in your element soon enough, and for that I envy you. This court life isn't for me, Bloor. It's much too dull. The longer I stay, the older I feel. You can't see your enemies here. Out there it's much easier, but if I were where the fighting was the thickest...well... I'd be worm food quick and proper," he chuckled and raised his cup. Bloor matched him, and together they drank in silence. Maullus was right about the wine; it was very good.

The commander smiled.

Bloor returned it, and understood the commander's earlier meaning.

"Can you not return anyway, Lord?" Bloor asked of him. "You would be an inspiration to us all."

That brought a pleasant expression to the old commander's face. "No," he said. "The king wants me here nowadays. I believe it's to compliment Winter sometimes. We both give him guidance, he says. I feel like I'm perched on one of the king's shoulders while Winter is on the other. We're like two old vultures. I trust you won't mention to him that I didn't call him 'Lord' when talking about him. Taking things to the extreme that is, I figure."

"I won't, Lord."

"No ranks here now, Bloor. Just two men. You and I sharing some wine before one of us goes off to war. Can you do that for an hour or so?" a sigh left the commander, and he took another drink of his wine. In that instant, Bloor could plainly see the man and his desire to ride off with them in the morning as he once did in his younger days, with companions now long gone. He wanted to ride off to war one last time. He remembered what it was like as Bloor remembered what it was like to ride free along the frontier.

Bloor would return to that soon enough, while the other could only sit and carry on remembering.

"I will try…" Bloor said, subduing the urge to address this man as his rank dictated.

"Good."

Understanding, Bloor drank with him. He would recall the commander and his smiles later in the week. The wine released both of them at the time, and they talked of simple things: about being a Cavalier, of battle, of companions lost and remembered, and the trials they all endured. It was a pleasant conversation, and it made for a comforting memory, one Bloor would remember in the days and years to come.

24

Alwan arrived two days later than expected. He had encountered a pack of Nords believing he was carrying something of importance back to the capitol. Perhaps he was—he did not say. However, he dealt with them all the same. He killed twenty Jackals in the past two days, all left dead along a forested path in twos and threes.

"How did you manage that?" Tarco asked him blatantly when they were saddling up and preparing to leave Sunja. From his horse, Alwan flicked a look toward Bloor, and ignored the younger man altogether.

"I asked…" Tarco began, and stopped when Alwan fixed him with a stare cold enough to freeze water. The Cavalier continued staring at him long after Tarco dropped his own gaze. After a while, a thin cruel smile split Alwan's features, and he shook his head at Bloor, who didn't say anything. Alwan rode off a moment later to inspect the remainder of the Cavaliers leaving Sunja.

"I thought I was dead then," Tarco whispered to Bloor after the man had gone.

Bloor considered the open gates ahead of them. "So did I."

He then thought of leaving Morianna. It was not an assignment that he relished in the least, and yet, he found himself hoping that the young princess fared well in her life. He hoped that she would somehow change, and wondered if such a thing was possible. Then he remembered the Jackals, and his mind came back to the task at hand.

A hundred Cavaliers rode out of the capitol city that day, towards a war-torn front where the First Klaw of Sunja fought tooth and nail with an enemy as unforgiving as the mountains and as numerous as raindrops in an ocean. No one really knew why the war began, though the king declared that it was Nordun wanting more territory, and it was they who struck first. The conflict was in its fourth year, and the Nords were gouging into Sunjan territory. The armies of Sunja pushed them back when they could, only to be forced back themselves by hordes of Jackals. The two seesawed, back and forth, and the front to the east had become an arena with blood-soaked sands. Sunja believed the Nords had more warriors but lacked any real fighting skill. No one cared what the Nords thought, as long as they died. They had begun the war, and Sunja was determined to finish it.

At the end of the first week, Bloor strove for a private meeting with Alwan. In the days riding east to the front, he had avoided speaking with him, having no stomach to talk with him at all. Seeing him again brought back memories, and none of them pleasant. Alwan enjoyed killing far too much for Bloor's tastes. Warfare was only a part of being a Cavalier, an unwanted chore that Bloor had a duty to perform to the best of his ability. The trouble was, he was *good* at doing his chores. He did not relish it like Alwan. He told himself he did not; he *knew* he did not.

The party of Cavaliers stopped on the trail to the front. They settled in under the leaves of the forest, under a black night sky where no stars came out. Watches were set, and a moving patrol was assigned. Though they were nowhere near any action, it was known that the Jackals delighted in slipping past their watch points to execute night raids on remote villages.

"You got your wish," Bloor told him that night while sharing a campfire. Alwan raised an eyebrow. "I'm back."

"I had nothing to do with it," Alwan said.

"That's not what I heard."

"What did you hear?"

"I heard from Lord Maullus that someone remembered my work."

Alwan shrugged. "You flatter yourself, Bloor. That's not like you. You've been guarding little girls far too long. It wasn't me who said such things. You'll have to search elsewhere if you want to find this person."

They became silent, and the night crept on with sounds of men speaking in low voices and the crackling of their fires.

"What of this boy with you then?" Alwan asked.

"He's a new Cavalier."

"I can see that," Alwan retorted. "The shine hasn't left his eyes just yet. But I hear this one has political connections as thick as chains."

"He does." Bloor saw no reason to hide the truth. He would only sniff it out later anyway. "His father is the Minister of Defense. He hasn't even been outside of the walls of Sunja. Never on a patrol. This will be his first war."

Alwan made a face. "Just what we need. He better not bring a jinx down on our heads. I'll cut his throat myself if that happens. Seddon above, a pup! Perhaps we'll see some action before we get to the main force. Bleed some of that juice out of him. Color his blade."

"Lord Maullus made it clear that I was to stay close to him."

"Did he now?" Alwan said acidly. "He attached the likes of you to him? What a joke. You attract trouble like blood does flies. If you get *half* as much attention as when you did on the frontier, how do you think you'll be able to keep both of yourselves alive? Protect him? Seddon above, it'd be safer to cut him loose."

"I'll keep watch over him," Bloor pushed back. "He won't be killed while I'm around."

"I wonder who will."

"You're one to talk," Bloor accused. "The number of men that have died around you."

"It's war, Bloor," Alwan said simply. "Men, women, children, animals die all the time. Has a year minding some little girl made you forget that? And we're waging war against an enemy who asks for no quarter and gives none. Men carrying banners of truce to the Nords were allowed to approach well within their territory only to be hacked to pieces. Under flags of truce! This is the kind of enemy that we are fighting here, Bloor. We simply can't bloody their noses and make them surrender. We have to take the whole head off."

Alwan paused for a moment. He flicked a rock into the fire. "And you think you can protect the boy from the Jackals?" he exhaled deeply. "Best of luck to you then. You'll need it."

Alwan waited for a rebuttal, and when none came he rose and peered up into the night. He lingered a moment longer before walking off into the darkness. Bloor let him go. He was too busy thinking on the man's words. Alwan was right. Against the Nords, it was kill or be killed. How was he going to manage to keep himself alive, let alone Tarco? The weight of it made his shoulders slump. No, he would do it. It was a task given to him. It was something that had to be done.

They joined the First Klaw later that week. The Klaw's commander of the combined forces of Sujin, Cavalier, and Lancer was a man named Kadon. Kadon had served under Lord Winter at one time, and it was said that he recognized the man's leadership qualities immediately. Kadon was tall, devoid of fat, and wiry with taut muscle. With a wintry moustache and beard, and blue eyes that always looked bloodshot, one could mistake the man to be older than Lord Winter instead of only in his forties. Lord Kadon welcomed the Cavaliers back and quickly placed them into smaller units that would scout the wilderness, scour any roads ahead, and keep watch over the First's flanks. The Nordish Jackals were naturals in gathering information, and they wore light black leather armor than enabled them to move quickly and quietly. They preferred sending men out in webs of individual scouts rather than units. The Cavaliers were used to thwart them. They would find the Jackals and kill them before they could detect the First Klaw and reveal their presence to their masters. At this stage of the war, positioning the main battle groups was critical, and to have a body of troops discovered before they moved into position for a greater scale attack risked having them killed, lopped off like a groping hand.

Kadon placed Alwan in charge of the Cavaliers and he matched his replacements with the remaining units as best as possible. Alwan then broke the units further down so that the scouting Cavaliers operated with greater maneuverability. He arranged it so that Bloor went out with Tarco, and the relief in the younger Cavalier's face was unmistakable.

The first time.

In the following weeks, Tarco's relief was slowly replaced by puzzlement, followed by resentment, and finally, anger. They were still moving about the wilderness together, detecting and killing any lurking Nords, while most of the other Cavalier scouts eventually operated alone. The Sujins began to joke about the Cavalier with a nursemaid. Some even wondered loudly if the men were simply overly fond of each other. No one would say anything while Bloor was about, but when Tarco was alone, words were spoken loudly and meant to taunt.

On the eve of a patrol, both men were preparing once again for an expedition that would take them deep into Nordish territory. They were in the Sunjan war camp, standing before their horses and going over each other's supplies and weapons. Words between the two men had dwindled away into only the barest communication, and most of that was initiated by Bloor. He could feel the tension in the air, and waited for Tarco to speak his mind. He didn't wait long. Tarco abruptly stopped inspecting Bloor's horse. His face became hot and he flung down the reins. "Why are you doing this, Bloor?" he demanded.

"Keep your voice down," Bloor warned him with hard eyes. They were alone with their horses, yet voices could carry far enough for any lurking Sujins to hear. In a war camp of several thousand, someone *would* hear.

"Why are you doing this?" Tarco repeated in a harsh whisper. "Why? Do you think I'm weak? I'm the only Cavalier now that has a partner. All others go out alone except me. Do you think I'm stupid? Useless? We've gone out a dozen times now and I *know* how to scout!"

Bloor nodded. Tarco was a fast learner. He remembered his lessons from the Taskmasters and quickly learned from experience. Tarco was no slouch with a blade, either. He had proven that to any Nordish Jackal crossing his path, as well as any Sujin speaking with too sharp a tongue.

"So answer me then? Why do you hang off me? I'm beginning to dread this duty. When we leave camp I can feel the eyes of the others on me. On us! What must they be thinking? Already the campfires are burning with jokes about us. How am I to prove myself with you constantly around? How?"

"Tell me who jokes about you," Bloor said in a dangerous voice.

"I will not!" Tarco choked out, chagrin roasting his features. "I can handle anything anyone throws my way. What I can't handle is having a nanny! I know why you are doing this. It's because of my father! He probably ordered you to do this, am I right? But you can't shield me all the time Bloor. In the beginning, perhaps it was necessary, but not now. I can handle myself. Only by doing this by myself will I prove my worth in this army."

"Tarco," Bloor said quietly. "This is not war yet. This is only rooting out the rats. We're looking for dangers against the whole of our army and we've been lucky. Most of the time scouting is uneventful, but one needs to be always wary, always alert. You know your way about the wilds, I'll give you that. But what if you run into a pack of Jackals instead of one or two? I'm around just in case something happens beyond your ability. Don't even think of me as being here. Ignore me."

"I wish I could," Tarco seethed, still red in the face. He threw the reins of Bloor's horse at his hands to show his displeasure.

Bloor let him. *Willpower*, he reminded himself.

25

The next day, Bloor and Tarco made their way through the activity of the war camp. Alwan waited until the pair were right in front of him before he hailed them to stop. Tarco reined his horse in and tried not to look too nervous. While he was convinced of Bloor's nature, he wasn't wholly certain of Alwan's; the man unnerved him. He gathered from the other Cavaliers and Lancers that he unnerved them as well.

"Bloor," Alwan said, "this day I'll be heading out with Tarco."

"Why?" Bloor asked, controlling his annoyance at being kept from his duty to Lord Maullus.

"Because," Alwan stated, nodding at the other man, "the lad will kill you, I daresay. I can see it in his eyes. Tell me you can't?"

Bloor said nothing.

"I'll go this day. You stay here on my orders."

A frown clouded Bloor's features but he nodded his acceptance. Alwan said nothing more on the subject and Bloor did not pursue it.

This time.

Bloor did not think of what he was going to say to Lord Maullus if something happened to Tarco. He only hoped that they both returned alive and unscathed.

They returned to camp before nightfall with blood on their armor and blades.

"What happened?" Bloor demanded, pushing men out of his way to step up to Tarco's horse. Tarco dismounted from the other side, glaring at the man who had been ordered to guard him.

"Nords," Alwan said calmly. "About a dozen or so, wouldn't you say so, Tarco?"

"Aye, Lord," Tarco expelled in a tired voice. He looked exhausted. He took off his helmet and hooked it to the bridle of his horse. Spent excitement flushed his face and sweat soaked his hair flat to his skull.

"What of them?" Bloor wanted to know.

Alwan smirked. "We killed them, of course."

"We killed them all," Tarco said with a new edge to his voice. Bloor recognized it at once. He had heard it before, though not often, but hearing it only a few times was powerful enough to imprint it in his mind. Men who had never been in a real fight where other men died were sometimes fearful of how they would ultimately fare. When they finally found themselves in a fight, when there is no time to think, but only to act or die, they usually did one of three things afterwards: they grieved for killing another man, became sick or simply numb with gratitude for being alive, or, as in Tarco's case, they came to accept it, to even *welcome* and relish the furious rush that comes with a life or death battle, and long for more.

It disturbed Bloor to hear the edge in Tarco's voice, one that hinted at a belief of invincibility. The man was smiling at him, gloating, to think that he was once worried about fighting Jackals. In Tarco's eyes, there was the look of a man who now felt those about him should be afraid. He wanted to be feared.

Bloor knew then that Tarco was forever lost to him.

THE TROLL HUNTER

"I killed five men this day," the son of the Minister of Defense said loudly, for all gathered around to hear. There would be no more jokes or smiles behind his back. "Five men I sent to Saimon. *Five.*"

There were some muttered words of encouragement from Lancers and Sujins. Alwan gave instructions to some other scouts concerning their patrols, as the Nords he and Tarco killed that day were either deserters or advances for a larger force, and Alwan had never heard of Nord deserters before. "If they are scouts, that means the Nords are looking to flank us, or wanting us to think that they are flanking us. And they're damn close." Alwan gave further orders before dismissing the riders. All the while, Tarco glared at Bloor, daring him to talk down to him. In his mind, the day saw Tarco become a Cavalier, an equal to Bloor. He would no longer have Bloor watching over him. His arrogant smile said as much.

As Alwan walked away, Bloor caught up with him. "You knew there were Jackals out there."

Alwan said nothing.

"You knew and you still lead him into harm's way," Bloor accused him.

"I did what you could not do," Alwan retorted. "There is no easy way about this. You know that. He would have either died today or lived. Just so happens he lived. And he did well. He did indeed kill five of the ball lickers. He was something to see."

"I'll be with him next time," Bloor informed him.

"No, you won't."

Bloor scowled.

"Bloor. The pup's been bled now. He's tasted it. He's gotten his wish and there's no going back. You saw him this day. You should have seen him on the ride back in, the way he was searching the forest with his eyes. He was *wishing* for more Jackals to kill. The boy has become a man."

"It's my duty to Lord Maullus."

"You don't think Lord Maullus will understand? He had you watching over him and Tarco hated you for it. Today he fought hard and lived. Now he's like the rest of us, and he'll serve as the rest of us, as you will. Unless otherwise ordered to, he and you will scout alone. I'll be pressing that to Lord Kadon as well, and you *know* what he'll say." Alwan's face became reflective for a moment. "I'm just glad he wasn't bad luck for us. An untested man in battle is the loose brick in the wall. One only needs to tap it the right way…"

Alwan waited for Bloor to say something, and when nothing came, he went on his way. Bloor watched the officer stride away, and his argument died in his throat. Why did he want to argue anyway? He was relatively guilt-free of Tarco in this way, and Alwan was right about Lord Maullus. The commander would care little if his orders for Tarco were overturned in the field; it was the fortune and nature of battle. Bloor wondered what Maullus might say to the man's father, and then he shrugged that off as well. None of it concerned him anymore. He was free of his duty now. He could concentrate on helping rid the land of Jackals without having Tarco at his heels, and the timing could not be better.

26

A week later, the two armies found each other and bloody war erupted, the likes of which the two nations had never witnessed before. War that leached youth to a battlefield that chewed up flesh and bone by the sloppy tonnage. In the years to follow, Sunja and Nordun would wrestle each other back and forth, tearing and biting at each other like men consumed with a hatred beyond reason. Sunja's five separate armies, her Klaws, were composed of Sujins and armored cavalry consisting of Lancers and Cavaliers. Within each Klaw were the usual military sappers, armorers, weaponsmiths, and the necessary supporting staff that only fought under dire times. Although Sunja had strength of arms and finesse, Nordun had raw savagery and numbers. The Nords displayed a frightening level of skill as well, one that the Sunjans would never have expected from their ilk. Regardless, the Sunjan king believed Nordun to be an insignificant threat, and one that would be contained within a year.

In the long years that followed, the Jackals caught and destroyed two of Sunja's legendary Klaws on two separate fields of battle. The first demise of an entire Klaw left Sunja reeling in the knowledge that a force of five thousand had been crushed by a pack of barbarians. The Fourth Klaw faced a swarm of Jackals on an open plain to the northeast of Sunja. The land was ripe for Sunja's Lancers and Cavaliers to reap havoc with their heavy chargers. The Jackals played on this, and the charge of the Lancers met with a line of hidden spears the Nords plucked up from the ground at the last possible moment of contact. The Sujins rushed in, but were too late to save their companions. They only met the blood-high Jackals waiting for fresh meat. There were survivors from the Fourth, including the commander of the force, and their tales of the day left a somber mood in all that heard it. Lords Maullus and Winter called it overconfidence on their commander's part, and said that they would never be caught sleeping again.

They swore to avenge the loss of the Fourth.

A year later, the First Klaw met its bloody end. The five thousand on the western front were smashed to a man, and woke an otherwise indifferent king to the possibility that his realm was truly in danger. The tale of that horrific night captured the attention of all living in Sunja and made them look at their children with worried eyes. The destruction of the First was unlike the Fouth. There were survivors from the Fourth numbering in the hundreds, but the story of the First would go down in Sunja history as being the worst defeat ever suffered. The First Klaw was set upon in the night, caught unawares for reasons still unknown, and many a Sunjan died in their sleep, stabbed to death by Jackals. Only a handful escaped to tell of the madness and confusion of that hellish night, as black-leathered Jackals, like shiny beetles against a sheet of rising flames, ripped through the army of five thousand and gutted them all while they struggled out of their warm bedrolls. Stories were told of how the Nords used long spears and spiked head after head of whatever Sunjan Cavalier, Lancer, Sujin, and supporting staff they found, creating the Field of Skulls. The subsequent retelling of that dreadful time would instill the hardest man with awe and fear of the Jackals.

With the destruction of the First Klaw, Nordun sent a clear message to the Sunjan king: Defeat was nowhere in minds of the Jackals.

Doubt began to chew on the confidence of Sunja's commanders. How could one force be slapped, punched, stabbed, and bitten, and rise up on two separate occasions to fight back with even greater savagery? How does one finally pry open the jaws of a mad dog locked onto your leg? Estimates placed the Nordun army at best at twenty thousand men, but now the number seemed only a wistful dream. The Nords seemed to be innumerable.

Worse still, all were mobilizing.

Two Klaws were destroyed, and while there were some survivors being directed into the remaining armies, it took time to fully train a Sujin to a Klaw's standard. It took even longer to train a Lancer or Cavalier. The Nords appeared to be born with blades in their hands. Some even joked that Nord offspring cut their own way out of their mothers and slapped on armor the instant they were out of the womb. The remaining three Klaws were deployed as the king saw fit under the guidance of Lord Winter and Lord Maullus, his two prime military advisors. He ordered two Klaws to stay at the crumbling front, to try and lure the Nordun spearhead between the armies who could then crush their flanks. It was a strategy that would take a very long time to realize, and with an unwilling adversary. The last Klaw was designated as the home guard. It was comprised mostly of the wounded and recently healed. They were granted a brief respite before being circulated back into the true fighting to the west. After the two horrific defeats, Sunja no longer glowed with confidence in being able to deal with Nordun. They became reluctant to engage the Jackals without deep debate on terrain, tactics, and strategy, and security at night was rigidly enforced.

No one wanted another Field of Skulls.

It was because of this thinking that, from the fifth year on, major battles with Nordun were avoided completely, and skirmishes became commonplace. Sunja needed to gather her strength and while she was loath to do it, she danced around the Jackals whenever possible. The only danger realized in such a strategy, as a dour faced Lord Winter informed the king, was that it also gave the enemy time to gather their strength, and the Nords already seemed infinite.

After a time, the growing friction between Bloor and Tarco came to an explosive head, and Tarco left the First Klaw with the aid of his father's signature. He missed the Field of Skulls.

Bloor did not.

The Cavalier became a man of legend then as he and a handful of Cavaliers and Sujins fought through a wilderness echoing with the sounds of Sunjan dead and dying and whooping Jackals hunting for the living. They survived for a week in the timberlands as they made their way back home. During that time, Bloor encountered the man called Gatesin. The man he felt was responsible for the destruction of the First.

Gatesin was something of a loner in the army, and it was easy for him to slip under most everyone's notice, until the bad luck started. The man was a Sujin in the First Klaw with the dubious distinction of being plagued with terrible luck, and that ill fortune seemed to spread throughout the army. It took little for the Sujins, a superstitious bunch at any time, to place blame on Gatesin, who bore the knowledge with a sullen demeanor. It started slowly, with Gatesin always drawing the most unfavorable duties within the Klaw, or injuring himself in routine training drills. It was just enough for the other Sujins to believe him to be afflicted with a curse. However, Gatesin's reputation grew as he was present for the greater ills of the First Klaw. During the winter, a terrible cold rendered almost the entire army helpless and exhausted; a virus spread throughout the camp resulting in a day of sickness that took its toll on several Sujins; and a supply train got delayed in a blizzard and did not get to the army until the fighting men were eyeing each other as food. They called it chance and all of it bad, but there were those that began to suspect that Gatesin did have a curse on his head, and that curse was affecting the First Klaw.

In the spring, another virus hit the recovering Klaw, and the leaders suspected that the water supply had been poisoned by Jackals. Several men within the ranks came down with a monstrous bout of diarrhea. At the same time, the supply trains were being raided, and for a week the rations were stingy, bowels were thunderous, and morale was low. Some suspected the Jackals were behind them now and nipping at them as a small mobile force. This bad luck was stuck on Gatesin's head like an unwanted hairy mole. The fact that in both cases Gatesin remained healthy while those around him suffered was not lost to those around him. Bloor was given the task to ferret out any traitors within the Klaw's ranks, and questioned a petulant Gatesin at length, as he was one of a handful guarding the water wagons. Despite not finding any real evidence to suggest anything underhanded, Bloor found Gatesin's quiet skulking demeanor incriminating. He questioned others on the same watch, and to a man, no one accused Gatesin of being anything more than a jinx. Bloor left him alone, though his suspicions remained. Could a single man be cursed so badly?

Then came the Field of Skulls.

Bloor and Gatesin were amongst the fleeing survivors. It was at that time, running through a dark wilderness and being pursued by Nordish Jackals smelling blood, that Bloor became convinced that the man was indeed ill fortune on two legs. He even considered killing the man, wondering if perhaps, with the man dead, their luck would somehow improve. Bloor was sorely tempted to try.

In the end, only a handful of men got away with their lives.

In the reassignment of the survivors, Gatesin went to the Third while Bloor was reassigned to the Second. For a long while, Bloor waited to hear of any disasters befalling the army. When it did not, Bloor believed that Gatesin had somehow been killed, perhaps even killed by fellow Sujins when they realized who was in their midst.

In time, he forgot about Gatesin.

Bloor stayed with the Second Klaw and was taken into a light skirmish group comprised of fast-riding Cavaliers and Lancers led by Alwan, a group that cut the Nordun Jackals like a razor time and time again. Like wraiths, the Sunjans would slip out from a treeline or emerge from behind a hill, drawing a line of corpses from whatever war parties they would find, and galloping away before the Nords could retaliate. They were so successful that Alwan began leading them further behind established Nordish lines, often ignoring orders not to advance. They continued such daring attacks until Alwan was replaced with a leader that followed orders to the letter, and kept the Sunjan riders back beyond the Nordish borders. In one instance, the war party apparently gained a measure of infamy with the Jackals, as one strike on a small group of raiders turned out to be an ambush. The Sunjans escaped, though they lost half of their riders, including their newly-appointed leader. Alwan was given his command back, and his first request was for replacements; there were none to be had. Instead, they received orders to strike even further into Nordun territory.

Alwan smiled at the black irony of it all. At full strength, they were being held back by the commanders, but now that their force had been crippled by half, they were ordered onwards.

It was thought that either Lord Winter or Lord Maullus had somehow developed an open dislike for Alwan. He guessed it was Winter. Maullus he thought of as a swordbrother he could trust.

Each foray out into Nordun territory became increasingly more dangerous, and it seemed that each time they went out, one less returned. They were eventually given a handful of replacement Cavaliers and Lancers, to move their numbers up to twenty, but even these men were gradually bled away by the Jackals. Bloor thought of a king ignoring his daughter's recital, and wondered how much attention was given to the battles they fought and died for. It seemed as if their unit was being used as a cavalry longsword, to cut and bleed the enemy as much as possible before riding away, until the sword was blunted enough that it could no longer be used, or it was torn entirely away from Sunja's grasp.

Over time, Bloor slowly became darker, brooding. Comrades died in the field. Missions became even longer, with even greater odds of having one's head stuck on a spear. He hardly ever spoke to anyone, and when spoken to, he would answer with a nod or a shake of the head, perhaps a surly grunt. The one constant was Alwan, and somewhere, amongst all the chaos and death, Bloor became what he didn't want to be: He became like Alwan. He became a remorseless slayer of men. He could never keep his hands clean of the blood, and he eventually stopped trying. Nightmares no longer plagued him, as if realizing that no more terror could be sown within his sleep.

Perhaps his commanders took notice of the bloody state these riders were returning in. Perhaps they took notice of the dead gazes of men that had been fighting for too long and yet needed to fight longer still. Their cadaver expressions mirrored the emptiness they felt, and not a man wondered how much blacker their souls had become or would become before they died. A rumor began that the unit might be disbanded; it never came to be.

When, after seven years of war, the order came for Bloor to return to the capital city, he had to think hard to remember what and where Sunja was.

"I've been ordered home," he told Alwan quietly.

This amused the other man. "You *are* home. Where are you really going?"

"Back to Sunja."

"Sunja is still back there?"
He was not the only one to have forgotten.

He traveled alone, back to the city, through a countryside that he had not seen in years. He preferred it that way. He would sometimes see advance guards for a wagon train bearing wounded men back to the city, but he stayed clear, wanting nothing to do with them. The people traveling with the wagons sometimes saw the rider in the distance. The Cavalier was nothing more than a thin silhouette on the plains' horizon, always ahead of them, leading them away from Saimon's kitchen. The captain of the wagon train knew of Bloor. He did not see a man ahead them, only a hellion that was on Sunja's side.

Bloor had to think hard on what path to take. He saw the roads, yet wondered if they led to the city. It had been a very long time since he had been back, so long in fact that the word *home* seemed dusty to him. When he finally beheld the capitol city, he felt a strange elation that leeched the strength from him. There, the city lay out before him, high on a bluff overlooking the Plains of Evan. He sighed as he urged his horse along, up a rocky incline towards the plateau where Sunja's formidable walls rose up, her tall watch towers glinting in the sun like ivory teeth. His eyes searched the battlements of the walls, expecting to see lookouts, and marveling at the stone structure. The ordinary things he never noticed at one time now jumped to his attention. He led his horse through the main gate of the city, inspecting the murder holes above him and the sunlight checkered cobblestones below as the hooves of his animal clopped along. Bloor greeted the men guarding the main gates with a stoic nod of his head.

"Returning from the front?"
"How goes it out there?"
"Glad to be back, I wager?"
"Did you happen to see a fellow named…?"

Bloor ignored them all. He was not interested in making friends. He didn't care if the speakers thought him aloof or pious. Let them think what they wanted behind their safe walls. They would not be so talkative out there. They would not make a sound in the dead of night, where a Nordish Jackal could cut the throat of your companion from ear to ear without you knowing. He registered in the city's ledger, reported in to the gate captain, and made his way to the barracks of the Cavaliers.

Home.

Along the way, he noted the streets and how nothing had changed. He might've gone back in time for all he knew. Merchants hemmed in the sides of a road crowded with people. A smell of unwashed flesh smacked him in the face, the dull noise of voices on top of voices could be heard, yet only a smattering could be understood, and every so often someone would bounce off his legs or dart out of the way of his horse. Above, he saw buildings and women hanging out of open window, shaking blankets. He scarcely saw a man between the ages of fifteen and fifty and it disturbed him. There were some about, but with limbs missing. The war was stealing away Sunja's men. What would happen if the war continued for another seven years? Perhaps, if he was fortunate, Bloor would not be alive to see that come to pass. He wasn't seeking his own death, but he had become so tired of everything, so weary of carrying on the fight, that the final punch of a killing blow was beginning to seem like a blissful release from his own exhaustion.

When he reached the barracks of the Cavaliers, he stabled his horse, not listening to a word of the boys working there. He went from the stables to the training area, seeking the building of the paymaster, a miser by the name of Varner. The king chose well when he employed Varner. It was rumored that he knew the location of every gold and silver coin in the kingdom, and if he didn't know about it, he was close to finding out. Bloor found the pear-shaped man in his office. There were two men at arms outside his door, and another pair just inside. All were dressed for battle and looked ready to eat dogs raw. Bloor gave them little attention. Inside, the wooden building was a line of men leading up to a barred window. There was another pair of guards on either side of Varner's window. They studied Bloor as he approached, even though he wore the armor of a Cavalier. Bloor wasn't offended. He would have worried more if they ignored him completely. He eyed the line of men and assumed them to be Sujins either on leave or heading back to the front; probably heading back to the front and checking on their accounts before leaving. He took a breath and a strong smell of something hit him. He was reminded of pine cones, and a healer's ointment. When the man standing at the window turned to leave, Bloor saw that his face had been badly burned and an eye was missing. The burns glistened with a thin sheen of ointment that everyone could smell. Bloor's eyes flicked casually away before the man felt his gaze. He hoped the medicine helped ease the pain. The one-eyed man walked by, and Bloor's gaze settled on the floor between his feet.

"Step up there," Varner's hard voice instructed him. Bloor looked up from having drifted off in thought and saw that he was four strides away from the window. A grey-looking Varner was scowling behind the bars and his hand scratched at a full head of hair the color of silver coins. "What's your name?"

"Bloor."

"No last name?"

"That is my last name."

Varner hummed to himself as he searched his ledgers and eventually found the name. He glanced up to take in the man before him. He did not appreciate the tone of Sujins or Cavaliers in general, hearing too many of them gripe and complain about how easy he had it behind his bars. Varner's scowl deepened. His job was every bit as important as theirs. See them try maintaining the bookkeeping of a kingdom, and they would treat him with a little more respect. Some even scoffed openly at him, swore at him. Seddon above if he ever got any figures wrong, then not only did he have it easy, he was incompetent. Then there were the ones that demanded to see the numbers for themselves, those that could make sense of figures, thinking that money was missing from their accounts.

Not on Varner's watch.

He was an honest man, and he despised being accused of anything, especially cheating a soldier of his wages. The one before him looked like a scraper, and he wondered if he was going to make any trouble for him this afternoon. Varner could see that the man was a veteran, but in his experience, the ones with a few cantankerous lines in their faces could be even more irksome than the strutting recruits.

"Just got back, did you?" Varner asked, opening another ledger. His finger went down a column of numbers.

"Yes."

"How is it out there?"

"It's war."

Varner looked up from his numbers, giving the man a hard scowl, wondering if he was being smart or not. A stoic Bloor met the paymaster's eye, and after a moment, it was Varner that looked away. This Cavalier was just lucky he was in a pleasant mood. He checked the amount Bloor had accumulated in his years of fighting. It was an impressive sum.

"How much do you want to take out then?" Varner asked him.

"How much is there?"

Varner snatched at a quill and jotted a number down on a piece of paper. He jammed it through the narrow opening at the bottom of the bars. Bloor's expression lightened considerably when he saw the number. Varner thought he came very close to smiling, or whatever it was these bastards did when they were happy.

"I'll take out fifty."

"Fifty," Varner repeated and caught Bloor's affirming nod.

"Heading to the harlots are you?"

"No."

Right, Varner smirked, but he asked no further questions. "I'll keep the rest here then."

"Your reputation is well known, Lord Varner. That would be best."

Varner straightened. It was rare he got a kind word from a Cavalier. He grunted and went about counting out Bloor's money. He counted twice. After a moment, he pushed a little blue cloth purse out through the narrow slot. Bloor swept it up, without bothering to count. That little gesture pleased Varner. He had spent a lifetime counting and perfecting numbers without any error, and it pissed him off when some of these brutes stood before his window and recounted what he always counted out twice. This one at least had some sense, and trust.

"Staying in the barracks, are you?" Varner asked, his tone changing to almost pleasant. Bloor nodded.

"Should be plenty of room then. Half-empty, from what I hear."

Bloor spoke with a touch of sadness. "My thanks, Lord Varner."

Varner's hand came up in a wave of "Don't mention it." He watched Bloor leave his building. He noted the worn look of the man's armor and the care that had been put into preserving it. The Cavalier looked weary, he thought, but seemed well enough. With that, he went back to his ledgers.

Bloor went back to the barracks. He gave his name to the attendant there, and strolled about the large room while waiting for a cot and a foot chest to be prepared for him. There were cots covered with grey cotton blankets every three steps, and a foot chest lay at each base. All were in clean condition, and no dust could be seen. The air inside smelled fresh, and Bloor remembered his own training within these walls. No man was allowed inside unless cleaned up first. The taskmasters would make a man pay for stinking up the room, smelling and coated in the day's sweat and grime. The chambers were probably even cleaner than before, as Bloor suspected that only half of the bunks were being used. Through open windows, sounds of training could be heard, and he felt a touch of nostalgia. Perhaps he would wander by later.

"Bloor?"

He turned about and greeted Captain Belsarus. Belsarus had trained and conditioned Bloor and forged him into the Cavalier he was today. Belsarus had twenty years on his old student, and rivers of silver ran through his dark mane of hair. His skin looked like tanned leather. However, he was still in solid shape showing nothing in the way of extra flesh around his face. The lines around his eyes were deeper than Bloor remembered, and a little darker.

He didn't allow his pleasure at seeing the old man to show.

"When did you get back?" Belsarus came closer, his broad smile brightening his eyes.

"Today, Lord."

This pleased Belsarus. Bloor had not lost any respect over the years on the front. Several did, thinking that once they had experience on the battlefield they were equals to the taskmasters, and could dispense of formalities as they wished, but not this one. Bloor always was more rigid than the others, and it made Belsarus happy to see he hadn't changed. "When will you return to the front?"

"Eventually, Lord."

Belsarus nodded. "Perhaps you'll be taking some of my students with you then?"

"Perhaps, Lord. How are your recruits these days?"

"Younger than you or I, Bloor," Belsarus smiled again. "But they are ready to go into battle. I can think of no one better than you to lead them into the storm."

It was strange for Bloor to see the man smile so much. He never did before. It was a little unsettling, but good to see. "I can," he said quietly.

"I'm certain you could, but let's talk of that another day. I've arranged an officer's quarters for you as well, so you won't have to sleep with the pups. No one who's been away as long as you have should have to sleep with the raw meat, eh? You'll get your own room with a good bed in it. Not too soft, of course, but not the ground either."

"I don't mind sleeping here, Lord."

Belsarus waved a hand. "Bah. Saimon will suck on my arse if I allow that. You'll see that the luxuries of the room would make a king bark, but it's enough for you, I wager. The taskmasters have no better when pushing recruits through the ball wringers. Anyway, you'll take it and like it."

The familiar words made Bloor almost smile. He remembered hearing them often, usually right after Belsarus had ordered them to perform some strength training routines, exercises that left more than one man in the sand on his hands and knees. Belsarus smiled at him and clapped him on the shoulder. He wanted to talk more, but he had work to do as the day was not yet finished. However, he had wanted to see this man, to clear his wondering if it was the same Bloor that he had punished so long ago.

"Get a good rest, Bloor, before you go back to war," he told him.

"Thank you, Lord. I will try."

Belsarus nodded. "Bjarni will show you to your quarters," he pointed to an attendant who had materialized behind Bloor.

The Cavalier nodded and took his leave. Belsarus watched him go. It was good to see one of his lads returning. He had trained so many for so long, the faces becoming like far-off stars in the night sky: there, but featureless. However, he did not forget Bloor. How could he? The taskmasters still talked about him from time to time. What the man did in training had not been repeated since. It was good to see him alive.

Without a word, Bjarni led Bloor to a room filled with only a cot, a table and two chairs, and a wash basin. There were two books on the table, which Bloor ignored, and a hanging rack for his armor. Bjarni helped him out of his heavy gear and hung it on the rack. Clothes were stripped. He handed Bloor a thick towel and a bar of soap and led him to the bathhouses. Bloor gasped with pleasure when he slipped into one of the deep pools, submerging himself in the hot water. The bathhouses alone were worth coming back to Sunja, and he wondered how he could have forgotten about them. When he surfaced, a pitcher of mead with a single cup was poolside. Bloor sampled it and found it good. He drained the first cup, poured a second, and luxuriated in its taste. He sipped on the second while he sat in the pool, looking about the empty chamber. It was strange not to see anyone here, but the recruits would come after their day's training. He let his guard down, and sighed when he did so. The sounds of water lapping up against the pool relaxed him, as did the pressure of the water against his chest. He closed his eyes for a moment, and dozed in between sips of his mead.

There was something to being home after all.

27

Bloor returned to his quarters that evening. He dined alone, declining an invitation from Belsarus as politely as possible. The taskmaster did not press him. Bloor sat quietly in his room. Bjarni brought him a feast on a platter: a roast chicken with warm, honey-buttered bread, jugs of mead, and water. Bloor considered the food and drink for a short time before eating anything. He thought of the men fighting in places far away and the thin stew they would be spooning to their mouths with chunks of stale bread, the same meal they ate almost every day when no fresh meat or vegetables were available. He ate only half of the chicken, leaving the rest for breakfast. He stashed his cloth purse full of money underneath the cot. He went to bed after that, stretching out, and realizing that for the first time in a very long time, there would be no one shaking him in the middle of the night for a turn on the watch. The cot was soft, and after years of sleeping anywhere it was dry, it slowly brought him back to life away from the war. He wondered how long he would sleep for, and then reminded himself that there was no reason to wake in the morning. He cast a look at the half-eaten chicken on the table, the jugs rising up like fat towers beside it.

There was little noise outside of his walls, and the absence of it buzzed in his ears. He turned his head. There, at the head of the cot, was his shortsword, well within his grasp if he needed it.

Before sleep took him, he wondered if he would.

He slept almost twelve hours. Chagrin flooded him when he stuck his head out of his shuttered window and saw the sun almost at noon. He devoured the rest of the chicken as if it were a stolen thing, went through his morning toiletries, and dressed in the clothes given to him. He strapped on the shortsword and headed for the door. He froze on the threshold.

Where was he going?

He *had* no place to go.

Should he see Belsarus? He decided no. The man would be busy at this time of day, and truth be known, Bloor did not want to see the young faces of his recruits. He felt like relaxing again in the heated pool, but not until the later part of the day. Maybe in the evening he would go there, but what to do between now and then?

He remembered the cloth purse full of coins.

Bloor decided on reacquainting himself with Sunja.

He walked aimlessly throughout the streets, lingering where he wanted and watching people go about their ways. He brought with him all the gold coins in the cloth purse that Varner had given him. He didn't think he would buy anything this day; however, but he brought them anyway. It was always best to be prepared. It was that frame of thinking that made him bring along his shortsword. He had strapped on a blade every morning since he could remember, and to walk about without one hanging at his hip was unthinkable. He wore the casual clothes of a Cavalier, the white and green shirt and vest, with black pants and high leather boots. A black leather scabbard held his sword. While he walked, some people greeted him. At first he did not return their greetings, but he gradually warmed to it. The people were reacting to the clothes of a Cavalier, and when he realized this, he felt a little foolish, then annoyed at feeling foolish at all. Even though people did not know him, they knew he was a Cavalier, and the sight of him perhaps made them feel a little better. Perhaps greeting them back was a good thing, a reassuring thing. Thereafter, he greeted all that threw a smile his way or a respectful hail. It made him feel good.

A merchant in the market square handed him a cup of water. "You look thirsty."

"I'm not on duty," Bloor said, wondering if there was a reason behind this kindness.

The merchant smiled. "It does not matter. Take it. We know you are a fighting man of Sunja. Take it. Go on. Think of those who cannot drink at this moment yet wish for it."

Bloor took the water and drank it. "Thank you."

"Have you been in the city for long?"

"Not long," Bloor moved away with the slightest of bows. He did not want to talk to the man. He did not want to be pressed for war stories. He did not want to remember what it was like to be thirsty for days, to have one's tongue and throat swollen, to see one's flesh become yellow and dried out.

Not this day.

His path led him through the streets and further into the merchants' square. Sunja had many such places. He wandered by a three-story inn with its doors wide open. Laughter chimed out from within and the wonderful smell of roasting meat went by his nose. He stopped for a moment, wondering if he was hungry enough to go inside, but he continued on.

He walked by street entertainers—jugglers of knives—and remembered a Cavalier who could do the same and bury the same blade into the head of an oncoming Nord. The man ended up with his head stuck on a pike in the Field of

Skulls. Bloor could not remember his name, but he could remember the man's face. Merchants sold cloth of bright colors, vegetables, and seasonal fruit. People haggled and bought and sold. Children ran freely through the square. Smells of honeyed and garlic bread assaulted him. Cooked skewers of meat also tempted. Old men stood and talked and drank flagons of ale. The smells of perfume, animal fur, unwashed flesh, and hair rallied around and made him dizzy. He smelled blood, the coppery odor cleaving through his haze, and he saw a man butchering chickens on a wooden block. He saw children play. A man and woman pulled along a mottled cow. A young girl, perhaps seven, with blond hair streaming down to her gowned waist, pulled on her mother's white dress. The mother led her away. Bloor watched them all go, disappearing in the tide of people.

While he watched, an unseen woman, in turn, watched him.

For the rest of the day, he wandered about the city, seeing it, smelling it, watching its citizens interact with one another. He often stopped in one place and simply watched, moving along when he felt like it. Walking in whatever direction he felt like. When the sky darkened and its edges became orange, he decided to have dinner. He remembered the tavern with the wonderful smell of cooking meat. He returned there and made his way through the swinging doors. The interior was just having its lanterns lit by a woman dressed in a simple grey dress, and she moved between tables and chairs constructed of heavy wood. Pleasing to the eye, the furniture looked incredibly heavy. Bloor thought it would take several men to move any of the tables, and probably a good many more to actually throw one. No doubt the owner liked it that way.

He sat down with his back to a wall, well away from the tavern's patrons gathered around the bar. Bloor placed his elbows on the table and studied the people over his laced fingers. The serving woman approached him as he idly bumped his fingers against the ridge under his nose.

"What can I get you?" the woman asked.

"What do you have to eat?"

"A garlic roast. Beef. Fresh killed this morning."

"That will be fine."

"Drink?"

"Mead."

She nodded, thankful that this one didn't seem to be a troublemaker, and went to the kitchen. Bloor thought she was pear-shaped and not unattractive, and that was as far as his thoughts took him. He thought about the owner of the tavern instead. After a life of fighting, Bloor wondered what it would be like to simply get up in the morning and work at something so...safe.

He thanked and paid the woman when she brought the food. It was a luscious pile of meat and vegetables, and when she placed it before him, he stared at it for a time.

"Something wrong with it?"

Bloor took a moment before answering. "No."

He savored every bite, made every sip linger. He thought of many things while he ate. He tried to forget the front. He did not want to remember the times when they were starving in the winter. He did not want to think about the fear of having their drinking water poisoned. He concentrated on just eating and making it last. He left soon after finishing his meal. It was a good place, that tavern, and he would return there, or perhaps he would find another place. He had the time, had plenty of it in fact. Or did he? He did not know when they would call him back to duty. He pushed it from his mind and wondered about the next day and where he would walk in his city, hearing the music of the remaining coins in his pocket.

Bloor continued to live that way for three days. He tried to forget as best as he could.

On the afternoon of the fourth day, as Bloor found himself waking up usually around noon, things changed. He rose, washed, and dressed himself with the fresh clothes

Bjarni had laid out for him outside his door. Bjarni was a good man. He spoke very little, but nodded every now and again with the barest of smiles. Bloor liked those qualities. When he opened his door to leave, with thoughts on finding the old city fountain, a man stood waiting for him.

"Good afternoon, Lord Bloor," he said. He was older, with a full head of grey hair. His dark eyes were rimmed with lined baggy flesh. "Your presence is requested by the Princess Morianna."

Bloor's face went slack. As incredible as it sounded, he had completely forgotten about the princess.

"If you will follow me," the man said. When he spoke, there was an odd and potentially annoying whistling at the end of his words.

"How does she know I'm here?" Bloor asked, finally finding his voice.

The man smiled, showing he still had all his teeth. "She saw you in the market square the other day, Lord Bloor. She and the Lady Alora were there. She remembers you quite clearly."

Bloor felt as if he had been discovered by an unwanted person, and he had. It was just like Morianna to summon servants before her and lash their heads from their shoulders with screams and insulting reprimands. The peace that he'd become used to was gone. A sigh left him. He looked at the shallow chest of the man before him.

"Don't want to go, do you?" he asked him, a whistle in his words.

Bloor wisely did not answer.

"You really have no choice in the matter, I'm afraid," the messenger informed him with a sympathetic air. Then he smiled again.

Bloor did not understand why the fool was smiling. He found himself remembering all too clearly his dislike for the girl.

The man's smile faded. "Shall we go?"

The messenger's name was Korvik. He brought Bloor to the palace of the king and the chambers of the princess. He remembered it all, though the walls had been washed in white dye it seemed, lighting the gloom considerably. Servants moved about the corridors as stoic as ever, making Bloor sigh. Had Morianna's existence as a child become something even more pitiful as an adult? Had she become even worse towards people?

They arrived at the same door that he had guarded for months, where he had first met the princess. The guards posted were not the same men that followed his orders so long ago. He forgot their names, but he remembered their faces. No doubt Alora wanted to meet him in the same study as before. He doubted Morianna had any sense of nostalgia. Every day was the same for the girl who had no friends and barely saw her family.

The door opened and Korvik beckoned.

They entered, and Bloor's gaze swept over the shelves of books still where he last remembered them. Nothing had changed here. Sitting in the same chair, with an older version of Alora sitting beside her, sat the princess.

Morianna.

Her hair was longer. Her face seemed rounder now, and her eyes were those of an adult. Bloor could see that she did not use creams or the usual face paints like some other court royalty or nobility. Morianna's skin was untouched by such enhancements. She regarded him, her breath hitching in her chest, and Bloor knew then she was about to scream at him, maybe even throw something at him, perhaps even pudding, but she didn't. She sat where she was and regarded him with those deep dark eyes.

She had grown up.

"Hello, Lord Bloor," she said simply. A warm smile lit up her face.

It stunned him. He blinked and cleared his throat. "My Princess."

"How have you been?"

Bloor hesitated again. "Well," he managed.

The princess nodded. "We spotted you in the marketplace a few days ago. I couldn't believe it. The purest chance. I didn't know you had returned. I sent Korvik here out to ensure that it was you. When I found out it was, well, I had to see you again. It's been such a long time."

Her eyes dropped to the table and she flicked a glance at a quiet Alora. "I was a little worried, in fact. I wondered if you would come at all."

"You summoned me. I came," Bloor said.

"Did you say anything to him, Korvik?" Morianna suddenly asked the man behind Bloor. "Did you ask him as I instructed you to?"

"I did not, my Princess," Korvik answered in a calm manner. "I am completely at fault. I allowed Lord Bloor to assume that there would be dire consequences if he did not meet you. I told him he had no choice in seeing you. I am sorry."

Bloor swung about. His eyes widened at the messenger. Alora smiled at the Cavalier's expression and placed a hand over her mouth to hide a giggle.

"You look surprised, Lord Bloor," Morianna observed with a little smile of her own. "Was I really that bad?"

The directness of the question completely disarmed Bloor. He chose silence as his defense, but Morianna waited for an answer. He was not certain who he was dealing with here, but when confronted with the unexpected on the front, the best course of action was to push ahead. "I am surprised, my Princess."

"Korvik was only supposed to ask you to come, not order you. I thought that perhaps a request would be much more convincing than a command, though I did not have the courage to ask myself. I had to send Korvik. Now it seems that was a mistake? I only wanted you to come here by your own choice."

She sighed, her shoulders slouching. "Will you sit with us for awhile?"

Bloor almost did, and not because it was a princess asking him, but because it was the woman Morianna inviting him. There was something wrong here, and Bloor could not yet identify it. She was playing with him; that had to be the answer. She was lining him up for an arrow, and he hesitated.

She picked up on it immediately. "Please,' she added in a small voice.

However, like the half-wild animal he now was, he sensed a greater trap and it made him shake his head. His back straightened. "I would feel greater at ease, my Lady, if you would set about the task you require of me, and let me attend to it."

"There is no task, really," Morianna said, her expression frail, looking to Alora for support. "Does that mean you would rather go? I understand you are on leave from the war."

"Yes, my Lady. I would."

The disappointment on Morianna's face was genuine. "I understand," she said. "Another time perhaps? It was good to see you again, Lord Bloor, if only for a short while. I also wish that, in case we do not meet each other again…I wish to…apologize for my behavior all those years ago."

For the second time in the afternoon, Bloor's face went slack with surprise. However, this time his mouth fell open.

"That was the purpose of this meeting, you see," Morianna poured out. Alora placed a hand on the woman's forearm, but the princess kept on. "If you'll take it, that is. I don't blame you if you don't. I'll understand fully. I would be the same if our positions were reversed. I was a tormented and spoiled child with next to nothing in the way of social manners. I have changed. I just wanted to show you that. And then, maybe, put away one more painful memory."

She smiled gently at the end of her words, and if Morianna had disarmed the Cavalier before, she stripped him down now. His mind scrambled to say something. To think of something suitable to say, but having a princess apologize only made him blink in awkward silence.

"I...apology accepted," he managed, feeling stupid even as he said such a clumsy thing. "And I apologize as well, for being so..."

Morianna waved a hand. "You're in a hurry, I can see. Thank you again for coming, Lord Bloor. Please come again if you find the time and patience in your heart. Korvik, please show Lord Bloor out."

The elderly man bowed smartly. Bloor did not protest. He might have been hit by a mace, he was so senseless by what was happening. He thought it was a dream and that he was still back in his room. He would not touch another drop of mead while he was in Sunja. The stuff was sweet, but hit the senses too damn hard. Korvik gestured for him to follow. Bloor bowed to the princess, and followed the man out.

When they had gone, Alora's hand slipped down the princess' arm and rested over her hand. She gave it a comforting squeeze, and that helped Morianna bear the rejection she felt in the room.

Their footsteps echoing, Korvik walked along with a troubled expression. Neither said anything. Bloor waited until they were outside of the palace. "This is far enough. I know the way."

"As you wish," Korvik said, the final word ending with that odd whistling noise.

"Why did you tell me to come if she wanted you to ask?" Bloor wanted to know.

"If I had," the other replied coolly, "would you have come? No, probably not. I knew that as soon as you opened your door. I've been asking around about you and I must say, I'm impressed with the stories I've heard thus far. However, when I saw you this morning, I saw a man trying to forget the last few years, even the years with a princess."

"I would have come," Bloor rumbled. "I would not have turned down a royal request."

"Ah," Korvik said, "that is where you are wrong. She did not ask you as a princess. She wanted me to ask you as only Morianna, only as a person. Now, I ask you, would you have come knowing that? That Morianna the person had asked for you, and not the princess? I say again, you would not."

"So you twisted your meaning," Bloor squirmed in discomfort, wanting to be right.

"I did," Korvik said. "I did so that my princess would get her wish, even though I knew she asked the impossible. I know of her past, though I did not experience it directly. I know of her past. And...I know what sort of person she is now."

Korvik let the words hang in the air for a moment. He weaved a strong spell and he could see the concentration on the Cavalier's face.

Bloor did not care for the man's speech in the least. Somehow, Korvik made him feel badly about rejecting the princess. How he had done that, Bloor would have to sit and think about for a while. He suspected a flagon of mead would go a long way in helping the process. He did not like the way the man was smirking at him, either. He could see Korvik was a person that enjoyed being in the right. Bloor turned and walked away without a word of farewell. He had things to do, he sulked, and time available in which to do them. He did not want to visit with a girl that had once been a bitch to all she knew. A child who could only deal with her own misery by making all those about her just as miserable, or even worse if she could manage it.

He would think long and hard over the short meeting that morning.

He would forget about Morianna.

28

The week bore the sludge of the meeting along, but it failed to clear the bay of Bloor's mind. He sunk into a tide of indifference and forgot about the war. That surprised him a little. He had heard tales of young men waking up from nightmares, but where were his bad dreams? Did his drinking have a hand in his dreamless sleep? He was no longer a young man, but shouldn't he feel *something*? Had the years hardened him beyond what he expected, where cutting up another man was no more bothersome than cleaning a freshly-landed fish?

Had something happened to him?

What had he become?

He tried drinking mead and ale to unlock some deeper truth inside of him, but all he found was that he hated the painful echoes of the alcohol and the waste of the next day. From there on, he drank always in moderation, and he stopped thinking of what he had become. He believed that he never really changed at all, and that the fighting and killing never really bothered him in the first place.

He thought of Morianna instead.

Another two weeks went by, and Bloor began to feel the press of the barrack walls around him. He found himself edging closer and closer to the training grounds of the recruited Cavaliers, drawn to the loud instructions given by the taskmasters. He wanted to watch, to see what crop the taskmasters were sowing. He realized something else that day: He wanted to return to the front, to be living and doing what he did best. The calling was weak, but it was enough to warrant an afternoon drink. It sounded like a plan.

In the early summer afternoon, Bloor sat at the back of the tavern he had first visited weeks ago. He found out the owner's name was Toth, and the serving woman was Jilly. He visited often since then, and while the patrons and owner did not speak with him, they recognized the big man and quietly accepted his presence. When he was there, there was no trouble with anyone. One look at the colors the Cavalier wore was enough to keep the peace. He had shown his worth one night when he stepped in between two men about to fight. A few cool words from the Cavalier removed both of the arguing men from the premises. For that, Bloor received a free drink. They knew he did not drink too much, but when he ordered his second pitcher of mead, followed by a third, the women serving him knew something was on the man's mind. They let him be. There were other customers to tend to, and the Cavalier was not one to become a lout when he was drinking.

People came and went. The tavern went dark. Lamp lights were lit. The crowd grew. Bloor continued thinking and drinking. He wanted someone to come and speak with him. He wanted to listen. He wanted to feel like the patrons at the bar. He wanted to feel like he belonged, but no one sat down at his table. No one talked to him. Some people were even watching him. Bloor decided that he did not like being watched while he drank. He got to his feet, swaying just a bit. The next day would be lost to him for certain, but he didn't care. He was leaving, and the people parted for him like a flimsy dark curtain. Placing one foot before the other, Bloor made his way out. He got to the door, smelling the warm night air outside, and staggered against the doorframe.

Someone caught him and held him upright. Words went into his ears, promising to help him home. Bloor did not care. This night, a little help getting home was a good idea.

He was aware of blackness and realized his eyes were closed. Bloor opened them carefully, expecting pain. He stared at the ceiling of his private room. A deep breath escaped him, and he was relieved that he found his way home. There was no ache in his head. Not yet anyway, but his stomach did not feel like breakfast just yet, and his tongue curled at the thought. It would only shove the food back. Smacking his lips, Bloor wished he had the foresight to get a jug of water. He did not feel like moving.

He closed his eyes.

And jerked them open again. Sitting there across from him, watching, was Alwan.

"Good morning, princess," the Cavalier said quietly.

Bloor grimaced as pain twisted up under his brain pan like a trapped snake.

"I thought you died last night," Alwan said. "Feel like any of this?"

Alwan held out a cup, and Bloor smelled the water. He tingled with need. Alwan held it out at arm's length, then he drank it. He placed the cup back on the table, next to a pitcher, and looked at his feet with interest.

Gritting his jaw, Bloor forced himself to a sitting position. His head immediately began to spin, and he closed his eyes at the ride. The room still went round, so he opened his eyes anyway. He glared at the water next to Alwan. It was too far away. He got to his feet and shuffled across the room, noticing then that he was still dressed. He got the pitcher and drank and drank and drank. He finished with a gasp, and then drank a little more. He went back to his cot with the pitcher, casting a deadly look at Alwan. He placed the pitcher on the floor and lay back down.

For several moments, neither man said anything.

"You know," Alwan said. "That's something I've noticed about you, Bloor. You never ask for anything. Never. Not even a damn drop of water."

"Would you have brought it?" Bloor asked weakly.

"Saimon, no. But you still could have asked."

"That's why I didn't ask."

"But you never ask anyone for anything, Bloor. I've seen it. I've seen it more than anyone else, I expect."

Bloor grunted.

"I'm surprised you lived, to tell the truth. You drank enough to make me and five others sick last night."

"You saw?"

"I saw. *Everyone* saw. *You* should have seen *yourself*. The empty pitchers were like battlements around your table with the likes of you—and you're not easy to look upon in the first place—peering at everyone like you were about to grab them. You scared a lot of people last night. Damn impressive, actually. But then you left. Or at least got up to leave. And you could feel the hope in the place then. There wasn't one person in that place that thought you weren't going to kill someone. And then you grabbed that one poor bastard! The look on his face! I almost *died!* Haven't laughed like that—"

"Alwan. Shut up."

Alwan did so with an understanding nod.

"How did I get back?" Bloor finally asked.

"I carried you."

"I didn't kill anyone?"

"No. Far from it. Though they didn't know it."

"I needed carrying?" Bloor asked.

"You needed a priest," Alwan frowned. "But you vomited twice on the way back here, so I decided against it. In the street, no less. I was impressed."

Bloor propped himself up on one elbow and drank more water. "Is that why the bed is wet?"

Alwan appeared puzzled for a moment before exploding with laughter. Realizing what had happened, Bloor frowned, but Alwan's peals of laughter unlocked something inside and he began to giggle.

In the end, he roared.

When they both regained control, Bloor tried to lay in a part of his cot that he didn't piss on. "Why are you here?" he asked.

Alwan shrugged. "Got sent back. Like you. Only I managed to elude the messengers a little longer. But they got to the commander. He felt as if I had enough of the front for a while and that a rest was due."

"If they only knew," Bloor smiled at him.

Alwan's brow creased mildly. If only.

"How goes the front?"

"The same," Alwan reported quietly. "I felt I was killing enough Jackals to win it by myself. But they just keep coming, madder than before. I would like to sit around one of their campfires, just once, in their company, just to see what they get so angry about."

"That would be interesting," Bloor conceded.

"Tarco is also back."

Bloor's eyes rolled. "Tarco."

"He doesn't seem to like you anymore," Alwan said.

"I tried to keep him safe. I had orders from Lord Maullus himself. Tarco thinks I was trying to control him, when I was trying to keep him alive. Trying to save him."

"You never tried to save me."

Bloor made a face. "You are *beyond* saving. In any case, I couldn't care less about what Tarco does now. He's capable enough and I'm free of him.

"Just be careful if he is about. I've heard him talk."

"What's that supposed to mean?"

"He seems to have a special place in his heart for you. For all that time you spent nursing him."

"I was under orders," Bloor repeated.

"He doesn't see it that way."

"Punce," Bloor breathed and drank from the pitcher. "He never was all that smart."

Alwan looked about the room. "Mine is just like this."

"Is Tarco in the barracks?"

Alwan shook his head in disdain. "Far too hard for the likes of him. No, I believe he is with his father and the family's estate."

"A tough man, Tarco," Bloor commented, sarcasm in his voice.

"Enough of him," Alwan suddenly said. "So what else have you been doing in the city besides drinking and pissing yourself in your sleep?"

Bloor smiled once again, just barely holding back a chuckle.

They talked then for most of the day. At mid afternoon, they visited the bathhouses and relaxed more. Alwan would fetch pitchers of cold water for them both, and on the third trip, he brought back some fresh apples for them to munch on, along with a loaf of bread and honey butter. They ate, drank, and with the approach of evening, Alwan left Bloor to sleep in his room. The Cavalier made his way through the barracks housing the new recruits. Unlike Bloor, he had visited the training area twice now, and conversed with Belsarus while he was training a group of young men. Belsaurus remembered him, and smiled when he saw him. Here was another man that he had trained that survived the front and the onslaught of the Nordish Jackals. When he recognized that it was Alwan, he could not help but shake his head. No, he did not train Alwan. *Unleashed* would be a better word.

In the evening and well after his conversation with Belsarus, Alwan walked out into the deserted training area. It was a wide open arena, marked with equipment to both train and harm potential Cavaliers. Wooden swords and spears, heavy weights for training, wooden targets, and a running track encircling it all. In some places, the sands were fresh from being raked over spilled blood. They might train with wooden weapons, but they still cut. Alwan believed it to be a good thing. A warrior should know that he can bleed. It would take the shock out of him if it happened on the battlefield. Alwan suspected that Belsarus made certain that all of the recruits were wounded during training at least once, just to prove to them that it happened and that wounds healed.

Alwan remembered his days as a recruit as he strolled around the area. A moon drifted overhead, washing the place in night blue. He strolled in and around worn pillars and racks of wooden and iron weapons and recollected days gone to him.

When the sun came up, Alwan stood in the arena with Bloor at his side. They were near the cutting posts, large wooden practice posts scarred and chipped from the Cavaliers hacking away at them with weighted iron weapons. It was just past dawn when Belsarus emerged from the main barracks with his taskmasters and recruits behind him. He acknowledged the two men with a curt nod, then he turned on the young men he and his aides were about to torture, and roared.

"This," Bloor noted, out of the corner of his mouth to Alwan, "is the Belsarus I remember. Not the one that shook my hand."

"He shook your hand?" Alwan asked, surprised.

"He didn't shake yours?"

Alwan turned back to the morning exercises. "I hear he prefers boys anyway," he muttered.

Bloor smirked. He heard that one himself.

Belsarus had the hundred or so raw Cavaliers first run laps around the training area. They ran until he said stop. None of them dropped behind the pace or out from exhaustion. They were already well past that point. Bloor remembered men being beaten and whipped on his first day. Belsarus believed that ten or so lashings across the back would be a caress compared to what the Jackals would do to them if they were captured, and he screamed it at all of his recruits. The Nords preferred disemboweling a man, after they took a stone hammer to all of his fingers and toes, or so Belsarus enjoyed telling his recruits. Bloor could not recall anyone ever escaping the Nords once they were captured. He wondered where Belsarus got his horrific tales, or if they were only tools to make the men work harder. Bloor remembered it worked on him.

As the taskmasters put the recruits through their exhausting paces, Belsarus wandered over to the pair watching. "Well now, this is a rare honor. If only you could have lost the hellion beside you."

A sardonic smile stretched across Alwan's features. "My thanks, Belsarus,"

"For what?"

"Saving me the breath I would have wasted on offering you a drink later this evening."

Belsaurus waved his hand through the air as if clearing it of a stench. "When were you going to offer that? I wouldn't accept it anyway, for fear of you remembering each tickle I gave you. Could be poison!"

"Could be," Alwan allowed.

The mirth drained from Belsarus' face. "I'm glad that you are one of Sunja's, Alwan. If only because you would give us all too much trouble if you were with the Nords."

With a skull smile, Alwan looked to his feet.

"Well," Belsarus changed the subject. "Care to exercise with us? Shake some of the rust loose? Show these pups what real men can do? You both look fit enough, although you," he shook a warning finger at Bloor, "just might be red in the face after one lap."

"I just might. Thank you, but no. I'm content to watch."

"Alwan?"

"When you have sword practice, I'll be happy to join."

Belsarus frowned. "The day I let you practice swords with my lads is the day I wake up in Saimon's hell."

"Several things will get done on that day, I imagine," Alwan said. "And besides, the swords are wooden."

"Forget it. I hate to think what you would do with a wooden sword," Belsarus said.

"Then they're not ready for war then, are they?" Alwan countered simply.

"With the Nords, they're almost there. With you? No. I think not," Belsarus answered.

"How long have you had them?" Bloor asked.

"Only seems a few days. But almost four months now. I don't know where the last hundred went. I heard they were sent to the Third."

"Possible," Alwan said. "The Jackals against the Third are a bloody pack."

"I heard they were all rough. Like hellrock." Belsarus commented. "Makes one wonder whose back will crack first, ours or theirs? Seven years ago—*four* years ago, you both could give me answers as to how the war would go. Now I bet you both don't know. Seems like I've been trimming meat for the butcher for ages, and I can only do so much. They seem to be getting younger, too. The lads need more time to season. Against the Jackals, half of these buggers will probably die in their first meeting."

Both Cavaliers kept their opinions to themselves. Belsarus looked towards the young men running. "But no one listens to me anymore. Now it's just 'Do what you can,' and 'Get them ready.'"

"Do you still tell your stories to them?" Bloor asked, wanting to change the subject.

"Stories?" Belsarus eyes lit up. "Stories, you think? And you've fought the Jackals! Yes, I still tell my stories. Gets their juices boiling."

"I'll give you a story," Alwan offered.

"Let's hear it," Belsarus said.

"The Nords have a new way to get information from prisoners, it seems. They don't make examples of anyone anymore, as most of us now fight to the death to avoid capture. So, small groups of men aren't always taken. Perhaps one here and there, and that's about it. In any case, the Nords will place your head in an iron vice and lay you on your back. They then put a broad strap of leather across your forehead, and it seems almost impossible for a man to rise from the ground with it on. Then, a group of them stands around, just out of reach of your arms and legs, and slash at you while you lash out. That's just for fun, I believe. When they want you to talk, they strap on weights to your hands and feet and splay you out. Again, you can't move. Then comes in a cutter with a knife. Fingers go first, all from one hand. Then he cooks the stumps with a torch. He'll do this all without asking you anything, but the time he's slicing off the second finger, you are talking anyway. Can you imagine what a man's saying by the time the cutter is finished with that first hand? Let alone when the torch comes out? They don't even listen to what you might have to say, anyway, until this is all done. Then the cutter listens while the poor punce tells him whatever he wants to know. Then the cutter goes to work on the *other* hand. And then the toes of one foot, and so on."

Belsarus made a face. "And then they kill you?"

Alwan shook his head. "Then they open up your stomach."

That made Belsarus grimace openly. "How do you know all this?"

Alwan did not blink. "I saw it. Scouting at night. Found a skirmish party too large to deal with and too far from the Sujins to do anything. Didn't even have a bow to put him out of his misery. All I could do was listen—and I heard everything—and report back anything that the Nords found out. You learn some things you don't want to know sometimes."

"Seddon above," Belsarus swore softly. Bloor's expression was grim. This was a new story to him as well. "You couldn't do anything for the poor topper?"

Alwan shook his head. "Not unless I wanted to join him."

Belsarus regarded him for a moment. He did not quite believe the Cavalier, not this one. Alwan might not have wanted to save the man, but not for that reason. It was no mystery that there was a side to Alwan that was as scary as a bare knife in a moonless night. He just might have been content to listen and watch the torture session. Neither Belsarus nor Bloor asked any further questions. Alwan would unsettle them more by telling them what they wanted to know. It was instances like these that made Bloor not want to become too sociable with him. That side of Alwan distanced him from more than just a few Cavaliers and officers. More than a few said that it was a good thing Alwan was fighting on their side. Alwan *frightened* people, and Bloor suspected that he liked it that way.

The conversation ebbed and Bloor stared ahead, noticing a figure entering the training area, an older man that he recognized at once. What was his name? Korvik. The messenger that spoke with a whistle to his words.

Morianna's messenger.

Bloor sensed danger. "You have visitors, Lord Belsarus."

Korvik stood where he entered, content to watch.

"I'll see what he wants," Belsarus grunted, and moved away. He strutted across the sands, heedless of the mayhem about him.

"I know what he wants," Alwan said thoughtfully. The sun glared down on his face and made him squint.

Belsarus approached the man. They conversed. The messenger gave something to the trainer and then left. Belsarus made his way back across the field. He took note of a recruit and said something close to the ear of a watching taskmaster. Then he was back with the Cavaliers.

"For you, Lord Bloor," Belsarus mocked, holding out a resplendent scroll case with both hands. Bloor took it with a scowl. He opened it and read the message inside.

"You?" Alwan asked.

"Me." Bloor replied, grimness in his voice.

29

When she turned eighteen, several things changed for Morianna. She started to listen more to Alora. She would ask her teacher and friend for more guidance. She asked why her father barely saw her—why her father barely saw any of his children. She asked why she rarely saw any of her sisters. In truth, she didn't really mind this as much, because she thought her siblings' personalities were enough to turn one's stomach.

Her mother had died two years earlier, leaving them alone in this world. The queen suffered from poor health, it was said, but some believed it was brought on by a troubled environment. The queen isolated herself from everyone for reasons unknown. She ate and drank in excess and she brooded over her increasing size and age. When she died, Morianna attended the funeral with her sisters.

The day was bright and warm and not at all appropriate for the passing of a queen. Words were spoken by a priest as her mother's large form, trussed up in white silk like a spider's meal, was carried into the royal tomb. Morianna noticed then that not one person was crying. The king stifled a yawn, in fact. When the ceremony was over, Morianna barely spoke to anyone. She ignored the sloths that were her siblings and returned to her section of the palace.

A wonderful roast of meat and vegetables waited for her. There were fresh strawberries for dessert. Morianna ate alone that night while her servants waited and watched. The silence struck her so hard that when she opened her mouth to say something, a piece of food fell out.

No one said a word.

Once she retired to her chambers, Morianna summoned Alora. When her teacher arrived, she stood to the right of the princess and waited for her commands. Morianna looked up at the woman and said, "My mother died today, and here I am eating roast of lamb with strawberries for dessert. And I don't feel sad. Why is that, Alora?"

The teacher did not say anything, but there was pity in her eyes.

"Is that look for me?" Morianna asked her.

Alora nodded. "It is."

Morianna began to cry. She cried for her mother, and she cried for herself. Her sobs started small, but turned into great, frame-shaking sobs. Tears spilled down her face like ice thawing in the hot spring sun. Alora drew the princess into her arms. Morianna was eighteen years old, and it was the first time that she could remember, in a very long time, that someone had reached out and held her. Alora hugged the princess, smothering her grief as best as she could.

The two of them talked about a great many things after that. It was as if the chasm keeping them apart had been crossed. Morianna asked many questions of Alora, and the teacher answered them. Her questions were not in preparation to impress her father, but were about a subject she knew almost nothing about: people.

"When I die, will I have a funeral like my mother's?" Morianna asked one afternoon when spring rains drenched the city. They sat alone in Morianna's quarters. The window was open, and the hiss and spatter of rain could be heard outside. Morianna was now a young woman and Alora had grown older. The teacher's hair had turned grey, and the lines in her features were many and deep.

"You will," she told her princess.

"Will anyone cry for me?"

Alora did not think a lie would help anything at this moment. One of her roles to the princess was protector. Alora was charged with keeping Morianna away from any emotions that could affect her in the unlikely event that she ever came to the throne. Those were the words of the king. Alora wondered if the man ever thought about the existence he imposed on his children. In fact, she wondered if he ever thought of them at all. Probably not.

"No. No one will cry for you," Alora told her, sadness in her voice. Why tell her otherwise? Morianna was not dull-witted, and could sense a clumsy lie. She knew the truth, anyway. She had known the truth for a long time. Perhaps it was that knowledge that drove her to distance herself, even farther, from the people around her.

"No one will cry for you," Alora told her gently.

"Why?" she wanted to know.

Alora took a breath. "Because no one loves you," she informed her, while the rain continued to pour down.

"Not even you?"

"Not even me."

"Ever?" Morianna's breath hitched. She did not look at her teacher. "Even after all these years? You feel nothing towards me?"

"Only pity, my dear."

Morianna might have cried then, as the moment was tender enough. Instead, she looked into the eyes of her teacher and only true companion for so many years.

"I will change that," the princess said, decisively.

The transformation was a slow one, and at times, painfully embarrassing. The princess tried to be more genuinely pleasant towards her servants. Reactions were varied. The people who had waited on her hand and foot, who had endured her lashings and public scathing, did not trust her. After all, this was a woman who would have them eat her table scraps from the previous day. They saw only a ruse and refused to accept the new princess, thinking the moment they did, the trap would be sprung.

On the rare occasions when her sisters saw her, they tortured her mercilessly for her sudden display of weakness. She had lost her fangs, and they delighted in making fun of her smiles and blushes of anger held in by will alone. Her father remained indifferent, until she surprised him one day with a kiss to his cheek. The king sent her to her chambers for that indiscretion.

When she turned twenty, Morianna's stubborn will to change slowly began to succeed. Her servants, prompted by words from Alora, began to recognize the effort when they saw it and warmed to this new, improved Morianna. They began greeting her with genuine feeling. Morianna took the time to actually talk to them and show sincere interest in their lives. The cook had a husband, with only one eye, who worked at shoeing horses. Barlow had a wife until she passed away one winter from a terrible cold. His daughter married a cloth merchant and was expecting a child soon. Barlow retired and Korvik came into her employment. Morianna thought the whistle with his words was musical. She found out that the gardeners disliked the stable hands for letting the horses nibble on their immaculate flower patches and then leave steaming reminders. Morianna made it her hobby to remember whatever small details there were to know about the people in her employ, beginning with their names.

Next, she learned about staff personalities, likes, dislikes, and birthdays. Birthdays were the most surprising. Morianna held one for the elderly retired cook, Sera, first. The poor woman did not know what to make of the princess when Morianna hugged her and thanked the old woman for all of her years in the princess' service. She was even more shocked at Morianna's gift: a silk dress, bought directly from Barlow's son-in-law, the cloth merchant.

Sera's surprise and delight pleased Morianna more that she could have ever believed. She liked the feeling that came from making others happy. She wanted to experience those same feelings every waking moment. However, her attempts were not always successful.

Birthdays with her sisters were always a failure. Any effort at trying to brighten their day was looked upon with distrust and disdain. Gifts were scoffed at. One sister actually threw her gift back at Morianna. The princess came to realize that her siblings were not her favorite people. She thought she would teach them a lesson by not visiting them anymore. She eventually gave up on them when they made no attempt to contact her. Instead, she began to concentrate on those who were more thankful.

Not that the failure of her attempts to please her sisters was any real surprise to Morianna. Her sisters never did much like her to begin with. She pitied them, but did not want to stand in their hateful presence anymore. They reminded her of how she once was. She told Alora exactly how she felt about them and her father.

Now twenty-two, Morianna felt much better about herself and what she had done for people. Things were not perfect, and as Alora once told her, one could not hope to be rosy all the time. There are times when a person can't interact with people, for whatever reasons: a death of a friend; sickness; a broken heart. However, if a person could manage to give another a brief smile, even during the difficult times, she would find that there was always someone around who would help her get through, or so Alora believed.

Morianna listened and learned.

There was so much to do. She had limited herself to her pool of servants, making their existence much more pleasant, or so she hoped. Now that she felt more comfortable in interacting with people, she wanted to move out into the city. She wanted to get to know the people of Sunja. She wanted to show them that the royal family was not isolated and cold... or at least *she* wasn't like that. She wanted to prove herself different. She wanted to make a difference, or at least make an effort. When she sent word of her intentions to her father, he did not reply. She took that as permission to do what she liked.

Alora cautioned her not to be naive enough to believe all people would be receptive to her. Some would, of course, and some would be wary of the princess; there would be some who would try and take advantage of her. Alora suggested that, despite Morianna's noble intentions, precautions should be taken. She should bring along a protector, and not just a group of warriors. A royal Axeman would be preferable, as size was always a natural deterrent to trouble, and the Axemen were all giants. Alora would place the request with the king, if Morianna so desired. The princess thought about whether or not she wanted anything from her father ever again. She banished such foolish thoughts, for without her titles and wealth, how could she help people the way that she wanted to?

Then Bloor appeared. When Morianna learned of his return, she decided to ask him back. She remembered treating him as badly as she had all of her servants back then, and wanted to make amends. *If* he would come back. When he did see her, his presence so unnerved her that she could not ask him what she wanted to ask. All she could manage was a heartfelt apology. She was quite relieved when he accepted it. She decided to contact him again at a later time.

Morianna and Bloor met again, in the same study where Morianna did not want any part of the frightening man of war. Now she wanted him back so very much. "Thank you for coming again, Lord Bloor," Morianna said.

"My Princess."

"I hope I didn't trouble you by asking you back a second time?"

Bloor said nothing.

She waited a moment before realizing that he *wasn't* going to answer her. There was no fear of her anymore, if there ever was. If anything, Morianna feared *him*. "I have a request for you, Lord Bloor. And before I ask it, I would first ask you to give my request some thought before answering."

There was a knock at the door, distracting the princess. "Oh yes," she said. "I forgot about him."

The door opened and in walked Tarco. The Cavalier, clothed in the same manner as Bloor, stopped beside the other man and kept his eyes fixed ahead. He dipped his head in greeting, "My Princess."

Bloor kept his eyes forward.

"My thanks to you, Lord Tarco, for coming so soon after arriving home."

"Whenever and wherever I can be of service to you, my Princess," Tarco said, ignoring the man standing next to him. As far as he was concerned, Bloor had died sometime in the war. The years had made a hard man of Tarco. He considered himself above Bloor and any other Cavalier in status and ability, and he was willing to prove it to anyone who doubted him.

"Thank you again, Lord Tarco," Morianna said. She took a breath. "I've summoned you both here today to hear my request. I ask both of you to give it some thought, as it is extremely important to me. Consider my request, not as coming from your princess, but from a person." She paused for a moment, studying their faces in turn.

Both men appeared alert and distinctly aware of the other, as they waited for her to continue speaking.

"Both of you once served me, but were drawn off to war. Now, I have need of capable protectors again, and you have both returned, for a while at least. While you are here, I would like to have you both as my protectors again. My father will allow me anyone, but I would prefer to have you."

"As you command," Bloor said at once.

Morianna shook her head. "No, you have to choose for yourselves. I feel I owe you something for my poor behavior in the past, when you served me. You may choose this time, if you wish to continue what was once your duty, but would now be… a favor."

"I will serve you, my Princess," Bloor said in a heartbeat.

"As will I, my Princess," Tarco pledged immediately after.

A smile lit up Morianna's face. "Thank you both. I will leave whatever preparations or arrangements you feel are necessary up to you. I don't need both of you at once. Only one, as we did when I was younger. And there will be only one of you accompanying me around at all times, not like before. There will be no additional guards. We can't spare them. I'll let you leave then, and talk about the days ahead. I'll need one of you in the morning. And thank you again. I will arrange a place for both of you to stay in the palace. Goodbye until the next time."

Both Cavaliers bowed and left the study, leaving a princess beaming with relief.

Once outside, Tarco asked "Do you know where the armory is?"

"Yes."

"Let's go there now." Tarco started walking, shoving his way past the other. With a controlled breath, Bloor reluctantly followed.

Upon reaching the armory, Tarco dismissed both of the guards there. Tarco went into the room first, closing the door in Bloor's face. With formidable control, Bloor went in after him. He slid one locking bolt across, and then turned to face the other man. This was the main armory for the castle and palace. It was a small room, but neatly crammed with an assortment of swords, shields, and other weapons. Along one wall was a row of fine-looking chain-mail vests, hanging from pegs. Tarco stamped back and forth in front of the armor.

"What did you just do?" Tarco demanded.

Bloor faced the man. He tried not to be sarcastic. He was never any good at it. "I pledged to protect my princess," he replied calmly.

"Yes, you did, you righteous bastard."

This perplexed Bloor.

"Don't you understand, you *dolt*?" Tarco threw at him. "I can see that whatever ideas I had about your intelligence gave you too much credit."

"Why don't you explain it to me then," Bloor said in a dangerously quiet tone.

"Why didn't you say no?" Tarco demanded.

"I had no wish to," Bloor replied calmly.

"Yes, and so by accepting, you gave me no choice but to also accept. If I hadn't, it would have been an insult to that bitch," shouted Tarco.

Bloor gripped his sword, and in one swift movement, had it in the air, pointed at Tarco's chest. He stepped forward, the tip of the weapon unwavering. "You'll address her as a princess."

Tarco kept his hands at his sides. "It's you who brings out the evil side of me, Bloor, you and your damned, pious nature. Whatever senses you have locked me into servitude to the princess at a time when I want nothing more than to return to the front. If I didn't say yes to her, following your damned lead, I would bring dishonor to myself, my father, and my family. You blurted out your 'Yes' before I could lay down an excuse about having to return to war."

"It's an honor to serve the princess." Bloor repeated doggedly.

"I *know* it is," Tarco almost yelled. "But I'd rather cut out a name for myself on the front! That's where your true name will be made and remembered. That's where the game is afoot, not here, behind the skirt of a princess, walking in her shadow! That's not for *me*! But now you've locked me into this! *This!* I mean, why doesn't she just nag her father and get an Axeman? Why us?"

Bloor sheathed his blade.

Tarco stabbed a finger at him. "And if you raise your sword to me again, I'll fight. The years of war have done me well. I'll show you what I did to those Nordish bastards. To think *you* would even go so low."

Bloor had a fair idea what the years had done to Tarco, and he wished that he had said no to Morianna, if for no other reason than that he be spared of this man's company. He turned to leave.

"Where are you going?" Tarco demanded, as if he was addressing an insolent child.

"We are finished here."

"No, we are *not*."

Bloor paused at the door, his eyes downcast. "I have no desire to stand watch with you. I have no desire to share a duty with you. I'll watch her during the day, and you can take the night shift as before. With all of your fire, I doubt you could sleep, anyway."

"I'll be talking to my father about this," Tarco informed him.

Bloor opened the door to leave, not bothering to reply. The brief exchange felt like a knife in his flesh. Talking to Tarco was like talking to a child. It appeared his days of leisure were at an end. He hoped Tarco *would* talk to his father. He was not looking forward to sharing a guard duty with the young Cavalier. Anything Tarco said, did, or didn't do would reflect badly on Bloor, and Tarco would use any excuse to discredit him. Perhaps this was a good enough reason to get drunk on mead? He made a face. It was the best reason he had had since coming back to Sunja. He might even ask Alwan if he wanted to join him. Compared to Tarco, Alwan's company was bearable.

Alwan somehow anticipated Bloor's request. As the sun went down over Sunja, he and Belsarus stood waiting outside Bloor's quarters.

"Look who is fresh back from the strumpets," Alwan remarked. "Learn anything, Bloor?"

"Only that I still have no liking for your face."

"And you wonder why you have no friends," Alwan informed him.

"I wonder why *your* friends haven't killed you yet," Bloor replied in a dark tone.

"Mostly because I dispose of them before they can act against me. I usually poison their drinks."

"What do you want of me, he-bitch?"

"You best ask him then," Alwan said to Belsarus. "He doesn't seem to be taking to me just now."

"I can see that," the taskmaster said with a smile. He held out a hand. "Let's drink some ale tonight, Bloor."

The Cavalier regarded the two men, wondering if he could bear the company. The other choice was to fume and think about the day alone, and that would mean thinking about Tarco. He did not want to do that.

"Lead on," he relented.

Belsarus did just that. Bloor followed, glaring at an unoffended Alwan.

"You'll have to do the talking more often, Belsarus," Alwan commented, as he fell into step behind the man.

In the morning, Bloor showed up for his duty on time. He did not drink too much the night before, yet his spirits were in a dull mood. It was Tarco. He could not help thinking that, at the end of the day, he would have to see the man. The thought of enduring his presence for even a moment brought a frown to his face. He regarded the door to the inner chambers of the princess, trying to remember the names of the two guards who had stood with him so many years ago, and only vaguely remembering their faces. There was no sound coming from the room. Everyone was still sleeping, no doubt, as it was only an hour or so after dawn. He should have been feeling more tired. The previous night would have gone on later, if Bloor had not reminded Belsarus of their duties the next morning. Alwan had no duties at all, but he left when the others did. Breakfast had been light: bread, cheese, and water.

He had a craving for pork, and thought that perhaps at noon, something might be ready in the kitchen. He wondered if anyone from the kitchen would remember him. Once again, he remembered faces but could not put names to them. The door behind him opened.

"Good morning, Lord Bloor," Morianna said sleepily. Bloor was shocked. Morianna's hair was usually immaculate, at least to his memory. She would never step outside her door without looking like a princess. The present sight of her startled him. Her hair was a tangled clump. As she passed by, he caught a scent of foul morning breath. He kept his face neutral.

"My Princess," he addressed her.

"Have you eaten yet, Bloor?" she asked.

"I have, my Princess,"

"Oh," Morianna murmured, still half asleep. She didn't care to get dressed up for the morning anymore, and had pulled a simple dress over her sleeping garments when she heard Bloor at the door. It was comfortable and hid her hips quite nicely. She wiggled her feet into a pair of white slippers.

"What did you have?" she said in a raspy voice that needed something hot to drink.

The suddenness of the question caught Bloor off guard. "Bread and cheese, my Princess. And water."

"That doesn't sound like much of a breakfast,"

"It was fine, my Princess."

The sleep in Morianna's face disappeared for a moment and she appeared to think about something. With a shrug, she ignored whatever it was and began walking towards the kitchen. Dressed in leather armor and with his hands at his sides, Bloor followed her.

They moved along the stone-cut corridor in silence. Ahead, an old servant dressed in blue spotted the princess and moved out of her way.

"Good Morning, Brysus," Morianna greeted. "Did you sleep well?"

"I did. And yourself?"

"Very well, thank you. It's breakfast time now."

"Enjoy it then," Brysus said, smiling at Morianna. As she passed by, he bowed.

Bloor scowled at the man, erasing the old servant's smile in an instant. The Cavalier would have liked to have talked to the old man about addressing the princess as her title demanded. He memorized the servant's features for later discussion with him about this issue. However, Bloor realized that Morianna had actually greeted the old servant first. The man had answered and even seemed to enjoy speaking to her. Even more surprising, Morianna did not berate the servant.

Curious, Bloor thought, and glanced about to see if there were other servants nearby. It would be interesting if this scenario was repeated.

"When did you change guard?" Morianna asked him from ahead. She walked with care, as if her legs were still waking up.

"Only a moment before you opened the door," Bloor replied.

"I would've asked Tarco to eat with us."

Bloor had nothing to say to that.

Sensing something amiss, Morianna half turned to him, "You don't care for each other, do you?"

"We are Cavaliers, my Princess. What we think of each other is not important."

"But you don't like him, do you?" she persisted. Bloor did not answer, but was clearly uncomfortable.

"Well," Morianna said before things became truly awkward, "he certainly has changed. I know that much. He's not the Tarco I once knew. Did you know that he used to talk to me, when I was younger? He did sometimes. He tried to keep silent, but I suppose I teased him into conversing with me. He doesn't seem very talkative now, and I don't like to tease people any more." Morianna considered something. "He seems a lot more like you are now."

"I thought my Princess didn't tease anymore," Bloor replied.

A sleepy giggle left her. "Not like before, anyway. I hope we have some hot tea. Boiling hot. So I can sip on it. Tea is so very nice. It wakes me up."

"Yes, Princess."

"You don't *have* to call me princess all the time, you know. Not when we're alone, anyway. Morianna is just fine. Or just Anna. You'll get on my nerves if you keep calling me 'My Princess,'" she ended in a mock-offended voice.

"Yes, my Lady."

Morianna stopped in her tracks and regarded the Cavalier following her. Her eyes twinkled at him, and she exhaled wearily. With a shake of her head, she resumed walking toward the kitchen. "*You* certainly haven't changed," she muttered. He was still iron-stiff when it came to court courtesy, something that both amused and infuriated her. It would be fun to loosen him up, if such a thing were possible.

She saw how the seven-year war had changed men, but Bloor remained the same. Tarco had certainly changed, and for the worse. The young Cavalier who would once blurt out an answer and charm her with his inexperienced smile had disappeared in the war. Tarco disturbed her now, and she was glad he wasn't around. However, Bloor was still Bloor, and thank Seddon for that.

Her thoughts went to breakfast. "Good morning, Lindee," Morianna called out upon entering the kitchen. From around a corner, a bonnet-covered head poked out and lit up with a smile. This, again, surprised Bloor. Here was another servant who actually seemed happy to see Morianna. He did not bother to contain the puzzlement on his face. To his fortune, neither of the ladies noticed him.

"Good morning, Lady," Lindee replied, spotting Bloor. The slim, freckled young woman moved into sight towards the main table dominating the room. She carried a single pan of freshly-baked bread. The smell of it tempted Bloor.

"Oh, it's all right," Morianna waved a hand at the Cavalier. "He does as I command him. Isn't that right, Bloor?"

He did not hesitate. "That is correct, my Lady."

"Then you'll ignore titles and anything else that Lindee calls me. Understood?"

Lindee placed the bread on the table and wiped her hands on a white cloth about her waist. She eyed Bloor with sass. "He's a hard-looking one, Anna. Right scary, this one."

Bloor scowled without thinking and Morianna's finger came up. "You'll ignore all of it. Remember now, Lindee is the daughter of Sera. You remember Sera, don't you? She was the cook here. She retired from my service but left the kitchen in the capable hands of this sweet lady here, who also happens to be my dearest friend."

Morianna has friends? Bloor contained himself. It would be embarrassing to lose composure, standing before them both.

"And you'll watch over her, as well. Treat her like the royalty she is. Like the gold she's worth," Morianna ordered Bloor, running a hand down the braid at the back of Lindee's head. The woman broke into an embarrassed smile.

Bloor absorbed this. "Yes, my Lady."

"Oh, I like that idea. And you see how he swallowed it? You're going to have to make it more difficult for me to not tease you, Lord Bloor," said Lindee.

"Call him Bloor," Morianna whispered into her ear. "He likes that."

Lindee brightened even more. "Bloor. Almost like boar. Or bore, like boring. Neither, I hope. Are you hungry, Bloor?"

"No."

Morianna waved the answer away as if canceling out an irksome spell. "We both are. What have you got?"

"Apples," Lindee said, pleased with herself, "and fresh bread—which you are sniffing at. Please don't. And honey butter and jam and porridge. We'll have a fresh roast later this evening. I'm looking forward to that. Kall will finally take the axe to that bastard, Pig."

"That's the pig," Morianna explained to Bloor.

"Kall's favorite pig," Lindee added, "but a biter and a shite flinger at everyone except Kall. I can't figure it out. They say pigs are smart, but Pig isn't smart. Kall raised him to be butchered, and butchered he'll be this day. If Kall can do it, I suppose. Pig is like a lovable dog around him. It's disgusting to see."

"You're jealous," Morianna said.

"Of Pig?" Lindee said, incensed. "It's just so stupid. I mean, I'm the one who brings him all the table scraps and a treat or two and the only thank you I ever got was filth being flung at me. Kall waves a knife at the beast and I swear the animal smiles at him!"

"Pig's a good shot," Morianna confided to Bloor, as she sat down at the table.

"He'll be getting a good shot, today," Lindee said, eager for the kill. "I'll be there to see it, too. See how happy the little beast is then!"

"If he butchers Pig, I doubt we'll have a roast this evening. Doesn't cleaning a pig take time? And then there's the hair."

"Hmm," Lindee mused, moving off. "Well, maybe tomorrow then. I still want to see those round eyes pop when Kall cuts him. 'I told you so,' I'll say to him."

"Maybe Pig is smart, after all. Maybe Kall will make it really quick?"

"Maybe Kall will slip, too," Lindee said, steepling her hands together as if to pray.

"Badness," Morianna flung at her.

"Only towards Pig. He ruined a dress my mother gave me. Even after I gave him apples. Apples! The louse!"

"She'll miss him," Morianna told Bloor. He had positioned himself to her left. She twiddled her fingers at him to sit down. Bloor did not.

"Please sit," Morianna asked gently. "Please. And have something to eat. I hate it when there is someone in the room who isn't eating. Look at that bread. Doesn't it look good?"

It did. Bloor nodded.

"Do we have jam, Lindee?"

"Yes, just like I said."

"Sorry. What kind?"

"Partridge berry."

"Oh," Morianna said, eager to start slapping the jam on. "I'll get it," and she bounced out of her chair, leaving Bloor where he was to simply watch, agape. *Morianna was getting her own jam?*

Lindee was back with a wooden plate full with quartered apples. She placed it in the middle of the table. "Juice!" She noticed it was missing and went to get it. Morianna returned with a fancy dish of red jam. She began cutting the bread, sawing it into slices. She paused to take a piece of apple and began chewing on it as she finished cutting the bread.

"Don't you like jam?"

Bloor regarded her.

Morianna stopped chewing. "Haven't you ever tried jam?"

"No."

Her eyes widened. She shoved the first piece of bread onto a plate and placed it in front of him. A gob of jam was smeared over it completely, right up to the edges. Lindee returned and sat down next to the princess. To Bloor's amazement, Morianna served her first. In turn, Lindee poured them goblets of juice. She took a piece of apple, bit into it, and carried on talking about Kall. For the moment, both women ignored the stiffly-formal Cavalier.

Bloor regarded the slice of bread smothered in red berry jam. The answer he gave Morianna was true. He had never tried jam before, never. It was a luxury never afforded him.

The women were enjoying themselves and their food. They talked of plans and work for the day. Morianna said something about going to the public market. Bloor kept on staring at the morsel before him. The women talked about fashions and baubles, but the Cavalier heard only bits of it.

The bread filled his senses. He glanced up for a moment and studied the kitchen. There was no one else around.

His attention went back to the bread. It did look good. Gently tapping his teeth together, he took the slice with a wary glance at the others. They didn't notice him. Still trying to look everywhere at once, Bloor bit hesitantly into the bread and jam. It was sweet. He took a bigger bite, and then another.

"Is it good?" Morianna asked right away. Lindee sat across from him, watching.

Bloor stopped chewing and sat up straight with jam smears about his mouth.

The ladies waited.

"Yes," he reported. "Good."

Lindee put a finger to spots around her mouth and indicated that he should do the same. Bloor did so, his cheeks burning with embarrassment. Lindee smiled at Morianna.

"Take your time. Take your time. No need to rush, and there's more where that came from," Morianna encouraged him. However, with both ladies watching him eat, a self-conscious Bloor felt every need to bolt the food down his throat. In two bites, he gulped it down as would a starving gull. He ran a cupped hand over his face, hoping it was clean.

"He snapped that up fast enough," Lindee giggled.

"He did. I guess our Cavalier doesn't like to be watched while he's eating. You see how long it took him to take a bite?" Morianna asked her.

"I did. I felt myself growing old, I did. Didn't think he was going to do it, actually. He's a proper one," replied Lindee with a chuckle.

"He is," Morianna agreed with girlish mirth. "We'll have our hands full trying to change him. What do you say to that, Bloor? Want to be changed?"

If he did, he did not show it. "As you wish, my Lady."

"Proper," Lindee tsked.

"We have our hands full. You'll help me, won't you?"

"I'll try. But I make no promises," Lindee replied. "Are you taking him to market with you?"

"I suppose I have to. He is my protector. The other one doesn't come until night. So this one will have to do." She began drumming her fingers on the table and looked apologetically at Lindee. "What are we having for supper tonight? I forgot already."

"A roast," Lindee reminded her.

"Will you need anything for that?" Morianna asked.

"Mushrooms, if you can find any. I haven't made a list just yet, but that doesn't matter, as I'll go to market another day. Today is always busy and I hate the crowds."

"You need a Cavalier to protect you," Morianna told her. "They can be quite useful to part a crowd."

"I need to be a princess for that," Lindee countered.

"Lindee thinks I'm a prisoner," Morianna said to Bloor.

"She is, you know," Lindee added.

"I am," Morianna sighed, her shoulders heaving dramatically. She began twirling her fingers in her hair. "So tell me, Bloor, do you like long hair?"

Bloor blinked. The question caught him completely off guard and it showed on his face. Morianna smiled at him. "Short, then? You must have a preference. Tell me."

Lindee pitied the man. "I don't think he knows."

Bloor's voice fluttered in his throat and failed him. He had fought seven years of war, survived the Field of Skulls, foraged deep behind Nordish lines, and yet one simple question had caused his face to flush and his lips to tighten. Why had she asked such a thing?

Morianna saw his discomfort, and after a moment, decided to let him off the hook. For the moment.

"You think on that then, Bloor. But I expect an answer later. Perhaps when Tarco relives you. And that's a command."

"Yes, my Lady," he gulped uncomfortably.

Lindee let a whistle of amazement fly. "I'd want to be a princess just to see that again," she said, laughing at Bloor's obvious discomfort.

"You're badness, Lindee. Embarrassing the man all the more."

"I don't think he's been embarrassed enough," Lindee stated, folding her arms. The words fell across the table like a quiet snowfall, and both women exchanged looks. She was probably right on that assumption. However, to speak of it or question the man on the subject seemed rude, and so they spared him. There would be time enough to talk about him when he was not around.

"Well, then," Morianna said. "Time for the market."

"Yes, time for the market," Lindee agreed.

Thank Seddon, a glum-looking Bloor thought.

30

The day was overcast and grey, and the air had a scent of dried sweat, wishing for a breeze to blow it away. People lined the streets and meandered in and out of each other's way like blind insects. Bloor watched them all as he steered the open wagon.

"Stop glaring at them," Morianna ordered.

Bloor looked at his princess. The transformation still surprised him. They had gone back to her chambers where a waiting Alora took Morianna inside. Bloor stood at the door as usual, hearing only snippets of conversation from within. When the door opened, two different people emerged. Gone were the stately dresses. Morianna's long dark hair had become short and blond. Her clothes replaced by coarse grey and white wool. Alora was dressed in much the same way. Smiling at him, they presented him with his own disguise...

Then they were on their way to market. Morianna explained to him that most people really didn't know who she was, so a wig was perhaps not even needed. It was the clothes that really gave her away, that and the guard escort. However, once dressed as they were and with only one man watching over them, they could move throughout the streets without incident, just like the common folk. Bloor could tell that Morianna enjoyed the illusion, and she smiled at him from underneath her blond locks.

"Now you're glaring at me," she informed him with a frown.

"Perhaps he needs to glare at someone?" Alora said from behind. Bloor could sense the smile around her words.

"Well, stop it anyway."

"My Lady," Bloor said, the wagon hitting a bump in the cobblestone streets.

"And don't be calling me that out here," Morianna whispered out of the corner of her mouth. "Out here I'm Clea. Remember that."

"Clea."

"Yes."

Bloor nodded sullenly. "This is dangerous."

The princess just grinned. "That's what makes it so much fun. Right, mother?"

Bloor did not see the little nod Alora answered with. He was trying to convince himself that all would be fine. Nothing would befall them. They were only three people heading off to the market area, and nothing in their appearance suggested otherwise. His own clothes had been replaced by coarse woolen ones that made his skin itch. He still carried his shortsword. Morianna could not make him give that up. As he steered the two horse wagon along, he felt the weapon's pommel against his lower ribs. It was better to have it and be perceived as willing to use it, than having nothing at all.

Morianna wiggled on the wagon's seat beside him. "Your scabbard is poking me," she said, and shoved it back against him, gouging him in the side. The sudden dart made his scowl deepen.

"What now?" she asked.

"Sit still," Bloor told her.

"Sit still what?"

Bloor fumed. "Sit still...*Clea.*"

She beamed at him. Her hand suddenly waved at someone. "Oh stop here! There's Aymar! Aymar! Hello!"

Bloor halted the wagon. A fat merchant who looked like an abandoned pirate stood in front of a vast assortment of vegetables and fruit. His sable beard and hair made the man look all the more sly. When he recognized who was calling his name, his face lit up with a coyote smile.

"How are you this cloudy day, Clea?" he said.

"Very fine, thank you. Do you have any mushrooms?"

"I do indeed."

"Wonderful!"

"Ah, your face brightens up the day for me, my dear. If you give me that look once more, I shall leave my wife for you!"

Morianna feigned shock and held it for a moment before bouncing down into the crowds. She moved so fast that she was gone before Bloor could say otherwise. A stab of fear lanced through his core and he made to go after her.

A calm voice stopped him. "You cannot stop that one. Just keep an eye on her," Alora said soothingly. "You'll make yourself addled if you try every time she does something like this. Just stay close by, and really, it's all she wants. Remember, out here she is a different person, and that person runs errands for the Salish priesthood. And the Salish are always making efforts to help the less fortunate."

"The people believe that?" Bloor glanced back at her.

"Without question. Clea is quite convincing at times. As you'll soon see..."

That quieted him, and Bloor cast his attention back at Clea, now haggling with the one called Aymar. The man moved closed to her and was stroking her bare arm. Something made him look up, and he saw Bloor glaring at him. His smile drooped. Bloor leaned forward, deliberately shifting his arm so that his scabbard came into view. Aymar's smile vanished, and his hand dropped away from Clea's arm. He stepped back from the woman who flittered in and around baskets of vegetables, and clasped both of his hands behind his back under the driver's continued stare.

Morianna suddenly realized that Aymar's cheerful banter had disappeared. She saw the man's distressed face and she whipped around to face Bloor. The banishment in that one look obliterated the Cavalier's gaze. With a scalded face, Bloor blinked away and began scanning the people swarming about the wagon. Morianna quickly finished her business with Aymar and wished him well. She beckoned Bloor down from his perch.

"Load this up," she said frostily, hauling a sackful of carrots to the wagon. Bloor did as he was told, and within moments they were both back on a half-loaded wagon.

"Don't ever do that again," Morianna warned him. "He's a friend."

He certainly appeared to be friendly, and that's what bothered the Cavalier. He got the wagon moving with a snap.

"We aren't in any danger here, Bloor. The war is going on out there. Not here. These are the people that remain, and I won't have you making their lives harder with threatening looks. Try frightening the shite out of someone else."

At the one word, Alora's head snapped around. She taught Morianna never to use such crude language. Such were used by people with lesser qualities and education.

The one word surprised Bloor as well. "I understand," he said quietly, squinting at the road ahead. "I will try to... do better. My apologies."

It was Morianna's turn to be surprised. She did not expect an apology out of this man of war, but there it was. Perhaps she should swear more often. "Good then. That's good. Keep on straight and I'll tell you where to stop."

They said little after that, clearing the air of the little confrontation. Around them, merchants and Sunjans chattered away. All manner of goods were on display, and Bloor wondered if the people knew there was a war on Sunja's borders. Hides and leather, food and wine were all being bought and carried off home. The people appeared happy, for the most part, and again Bloor felt a twinge of disbelief. There were men-at-arms about and constables upholding the king's law. Bloor could discern no law breakers about or any suspicious behavior. However, he kept on looking, as all too often a man died on the front the moment he relaxed, especially when facing the Nords who sometimes managed to sneak behind Sunjan lines to create havoc. Bloor and others believed that those elusive groups of Jackals wanted nothing more that to cause further battle stress to the Klaws of Sunjan. The Nords' level of strategy was frequently underestimated, and Bloor wondered how many disasters it would take for their leaders to realize that their foe was more than capable enough to formulate and execute plans.

Bloor remembered once sitting around a campfire with a group of Cavaliers from the Fifth. They were eating, drinking, and talking with the ease of men thinking themselves safe. One Cavalier, a man called Rolus, was raising a cup when a Jackal's arrow killed him through the eye. The angle suggested a long, lucky shot, but one that stole Rolus' life easy enough. The Jackal escaped.

"What are you thinking about?" Morianna asked him suddenly.

"Nothing."

They made several more purchases, filling the wagon with a collection of foodstuffs, clothing, and even footwear. Bloor actually wondered what Morianna was going to do with it all, but rank forbade him to question her. She directed him to drive the wagon to a part of the city where the majority of the men were away fighting the war while the families remained behind to survive as best as they could. A soldier's monthly wages could be chosen to be delivered directly to one's family. Bloor only heard of one or two heartless bastards with families who did not send their wages home. The houses in this lower class area were old, but surprisingly well kept. Several husbands killed in battle left women with little idea of carpentry, and a good carpenter was expensive. The streets were clean, yet the folks here looked worn and none of the joviality of the merchants' square could be seen. Bloor smelled the faint odor of ripe sewage coming from somewhere, not yet strong enough for comment. These people knew there was a war on, and it was affecting their lives. When people spotted Morianna and recognized her as Clea from the Salish priesthood, old men, women, and even children began following the wagon. Morianna chatted with several, surprising Bloor again. She knew most of these people. She listened when a person needed an ear, and she showed empathy when required. These people were glad to see her.

This was the Morianna that he once guarded when she was a child? The same person that once delighted in calling him "Horseface?"

The driver's fearsome eyes unsettled many of the people, but Morianna's bell-like voice drew them nearer. Bloor gave up on the womenfolk and the old men, and settled in on some harder looking individuals skulking about alleyways. He knew ruffians when he spied them, and there were three or so that were paying attention to the crowd gathering around the wagon. He greeted each predator with a glare of terrible warning, and this time, neither Morianna nor Alora protested. Each gaze he met he stared down. For all their rough appearance, these men were not stupid, it seemed. Even wolves know when there are shepherds around the sheep. It was for this that the Cavalier was needed, and Bloor felt better about insisting on his weapon.

They stopped the wagon near a public fountain in the shape of a fish sprouting water. Morianna produced an inkwell and quill, and jumped down amongst the people. Alora stepped into the gathering crowds and both women began calling and checking names. The women turned to the wagon and began to pull out goods and distribute them. Bloor stayed where he was, a watchtower for trouble, and none would approach him. Not him. He had the look of one not to be crossed.

Beyond what was happening at the wagon, across the street and standing with his shoulder against the side of a house, Bloor saw the face of a human weasel. Dressed in light clothing, he was obviously not as bad off as the people meeting with Morianna and Alora. A bully, or an underling of one, the man lounged and played with something in his mouth. A lazy grin spread across his features, and Bloor felt an urge to smash it from his face. He wondered how often the constables made patrols of this area. He wondered how many of the people living in the area actually lived in fear of men such as these, how many of the women slept with a knife near their bed, their doors locked and barred from the inside.

Seddon above, this bastard was giving him the eye. Bloor wondered if the weasel would still be watching if he got up from his seat and approached him. Probably not, but Bloor did not get up. Whole campsites could be plundered and soiled by Nords when Sunjan Koors decided to split up their forces to investigate strange noises in the timberland. No, Bloor would not leave the wagon or the princess below, so he made himself content with warning the man off with murderous looks, though it became clear to him that this particular breed of smiling weasel did not scare easy.

A stupid man. Worse, a stupid man thinking himself to be smart.

The weasel gave Bloor an affable nod as if they were old friends and disappeared down the alley. Bloor got the message: *When you are gone, I'll be back.* He kept his eyes on the alley for a few moments before studying the ring of surrounding houses. The other grubby-looking individuals also had disappeared, but Bloor felt eyes upon him.

"What are you up to?" Morianna asked him from below.

"Watching."

"I can see that," she commented sarcastically. "What?"

"Nothing."

Morianna looked about but saw nothing. Bloor wanted to tell her that there was danger here. He wanted to ask her if there had been trouble here in the past. He studied the faces of the people around the wagon. They seemed pleased enough with Morianna and her gifts, but there was desperation there as well. Why was this part of Sunja home to so many desperate people? Would any of them speak of any trouble if it was watching them? The princess went back to handing out goods until the wagon was empty. She promised them they would be back in a week with more. Alora made notes of names and the amounts they took home. Morianna stood amongst them, talking to some of the children: little girls in dresses that might have been potato sacks at one time, and little boys without shoes.

"Thank you, Clea!" they sang. "Thank you!"

Morianna waved and pulled herself back up beside a watchful Bloor. She cast a glance back at Alora. The woman nodded that she was ready to leave. The princess was about to tell Bloor to move when a young woman came up to the wagon. A mop of dark hair fell about her long face, and her green eyes pierced those of Morianna.

"Thank you Clea, and thank the Salish for their generosity. If it were not for them, life would be much more difficult."

"I don't think it's enough," Morianna said. "I'll try to bring more next time."

The woman's eyes flicked down for a moment before asking, "Could you bring more shoes for the children? I teach in a small school with my father, the scholar Lute. The children need them. Winter will be here soon enough. Too soon for some of them."

"Certainly."

"You are too good," she handed a piece of parchment to Alora. "These are the measurements and number of pairs we need. Thank you so much."

"I haven't *asked* the priests yet," Morianna smiled at her.

"But the priesthood has already been so good to us. I have no doubt they will give us something for the children. And there are always other things we need."

The princess rocked back and forth for a moment, thinking. Bloor also heard the woman's words, and her face suggested something more. Perhaps something more than Clea and her priesthood were capable of providing.

"Just tell me what you need, and I'll ask the fathers," Morianna said.

"Thank you, Clea."

"You're welcome."

"Let's go," Morianna told Bloor, and he started the horses up with a flick of the reins.

"Are you going to bring them shoes next time?" Bloor asked her quietly as the houses went by. He kept an eye on the alleyways. As an afterthought, he glanced up at the rooftops.

"I will try. It all depends on the finances of the brothers and the sisters of the Salish."

"They have brothers and sisters there?"

Morianna brightened a little. "They do. And mothers and fathers. It's a grand church, I think. Though sooner or later there will be converts, and I'm not so certain how to deal with that. Even today some had question about the priesthood and I had no idea how to answer."

Now Bloor was interested. "How do the Salish feel about this?"

"They know and they don't mind. It works out for them as their image is polished quite nicely, and they do sometimes contribute to the pot. But mostly I just use their name so as to not draw attention to myself. My father gives a certain amount back to the people every season, after they are taxed of course. What he doesn't understand is that it isn't enough, so I help out anyway I can with my own allowances. He knows nothing about this. Not yet anyway. If he found out that I was spending money meant for me, he would be... annoyed, shall we say?"

"He may find out."

"Maybe," Morianna conceded. "But I'm not worried. There is not much he can do to me, Lord Bloor."

It occurred to him then that the princess might actually be mocking his title. *Brave little bitch.* He saw a pair of constables wandering the streets. He stopped talking, feeling he might already have said too much to the princess. Still, he was feeling something that he hadn't felt for a while. He was quite impressed with Morianna. She was helping these people with her own resources. How many of the royal family did that?However, something odd stuck in his mind.

"Those people, the menfolk are away to war?"

"I suppose," Morianna said.

"The Sujins are all paid, to my knowledge," Bloor muttered, in mild confusion.

"Not enough from what I see. These people barely have enough to get by on," the princess looked at him. "What were you looking at back there?" she asked him. The wagon went by the two officers. Bloor saw that they were going in the direction they just left and felt better for it.

"Trouble," he said finally.

"That's a troubled area of the city."

"So I saw."

They returned to the palace grounds, and Morianna directed Bloor to the stables. "Over there, please," she requested, as she removed her wig and shook free her hair. The motion drew Bloor's attention for a moment, but he looked away before she noticed him. He steered the wagon towards the stables, taking note of the high walls behind the building. Soldiers made their ways across the battlements, casually observing the wagon, and perhaps all too bored with the day. Morianna pointed again, past the stables, and Bloor complied. The wagon moved towards a fenced-in compound. It was the first time Bloor had visited the livestock area, and the smell of barnyard animals made his nose crinkle. There were a line of smaller buildings to the right, being consumed in the growing afternoon shadow of the palace.

"Why are we here, dear?" Alora asked Morianna from behind. She held her sleeve to her nose. "I'm not fond of this place, you know."

"I want to see Pig before Kall butchers him."

"I would think Pig has already passed on," Alora said, but as soon as she finished, a single figure emerged from the building next to the fence. The man wore high muddy boots, dark wool trousers, and a grey shirt. He scratched at his head as he peered into the pen. Bloor saw the knife in his hand. The blade looked well worn from repeated sharpening. At the approach of the wagon, the man turned. His young face, tanned by the sun, dissolved into shock.

"My Lady," he said immediately.

"Kall," Morianna said, looking past him. "Couldn't do the deed I see?"

Kall looked sheepish. "I'm afraid not, my Lady. Tis' harder than I figured it to be."

"Why?"

The man shrugged. "Pig keeps looking at me," he said with a little smile, showing yellow teeth. "I mean, I raised Pig from when he was little. Even let the little git run around my own kitchen at times. Fed him straight from the table."

"I'm sure he enjoyed that," Morianna said.

"Better than a dog," Kall added. "But…well, now…"

"You can't do it," Morianna finished for him, suddenly delighted. "You can't kill poor Pig!"

Kall shrugged again. Behind him, a huge form pressed itself up against the fence and pushed its mottled pink snout into view. Portal-sized nostrils sampled the new scents on the air.

Bloor took a breath. Pig was an impressive specimen. Pig was enormous.

"You cleaned him off?" Morianna asked.

"Oh yes, can't have a dirty D-I-D pig," Kall whispered. "Figured it would be easier this way. But, well… don't worry. I'll do it. It's just catching him unawares is all. He knows there's something up. He doesn't know what, but he knows there's *something*."

"He can't do it," cried out Lindee as she bounded down a walkway towards them. "I've given up on having a roast today because of him." She jabbed a finger at a blushing Kall. "We'll have chicken now. I figured he wouldn't be able to do the monster in."

Kall grimaced at the accusation. "First animal I've had to butcher, I'll have you know. I only raise them for the most part, not kill them."

"You eat them fast enough," Lindee countered. "You shouldn't have that big a problem."

"Yes, well…" Kall shook his head, unable to answer.

"Don't you chop the heads off chickens?" Morianna asked him, still smiling at Kall's inability to take a knife to his porky friend.

"That's different."

"Different, is it?" Lindee almost squealed. She gave a hard laugh, clearly enjoying Kall's discomfort.

"Pigs are smarter than chickens," Kall asserted. "If you were around animals as much as me, you'd know. Chickens are stupid. Even the name smacks of being stupid. Listen to it. *Chicken*. Why do you think you eat so many of them?"

"I don't know," Lindee said, stopping well before the pen. She remembered Pig's accuracy with flung dung.

"Because they're *stupid*," Kall said. "If they even have a thimble of a brain, then that's a waste. Mindless, they are."

"They run when they see a person," Morianna said. "That's smart."

"That's instinct. I tell you, pigs are far smarter. Chickens are like fish."

"Or scared," Morianna suggested further. "After all, they must know that we eat them."

"I doubt it," Kall said, looking fondly at Pig. The big animal's nostrils fluttered and withdrew inside the pen.

"Well then, are you planning on staying out here all night then?" Lindee asked them.

Kall shook his head. "I'll get to it, just give me time. I already cleaned him before separating him from the others."

"Why don't you just let Croaker kill him?" Lindee asked.

Kall shoulders sagged. "A fine point but... I couldn't. Croaker, well, I see how he does in the other pigs, you see. And the chickens, too. He's none too gentle about it."

"Kall," Morianna said, containing her amusement, "how can one be gentle in killing an animal?"

"You can do it. You can relax them. Sure you can. But not Croaker, he grabs and snaps. Takes and chops."

"I can see you'll never be a butcher," Morianna said.

"Never wanted to be a butcher," Kall said. "I like raising them. Just so happens Pig got the best of me, is all. I have good memories with that animal, dare I say it."

"Where is Croaker, anyway?" Lindee asked.

"Went home."

"Laughing too much, I wager?"

Kall didn't answer her. Behind him, Pig ambled about his confines, grunting little pig grunts every so often, and rubbing his face into the muddy earth as if trying to erase something. The noise silenced the onlookers, and they watched the mottled brown animal lumber about.

"It is a pretty pig," Morianna commented, her head lilting to one side.

Lindee rolled her eyes. "I'm sure he'll cook up nicely." The pig would rue the day it tossed filth in her direction.

"Well," Morianna began, "if Croaker went home, then there's no one about to do the job is there? I doubt Kall can do it."

The man looked even more miserable.

"I thought so," Morianna affirmed. "Then water Pig and feed him, and let him enjoy the night."

"I'm sorry, my Lady," Kall said weakly. "I'll...I'll let Croaker have him in the morning."

"Sensible," Lindee said. "So you'll have one more night with your friend. Enjoy it. You hear me?" she threw at the pen. "Tomorrow the *chop*!"

Pig looked up at Lindee's voice, but seeing nothing interesting, went back to gouging the ground.

"I'll be in the kitchen, then," Lindee said. She could wait another night for Pig's head.

"I have your mushrooms," Morianna informed her. "As well as a few other things."

"Wonderful. Bring them up, please."

"What will you do then, Kall?" Morianna asked the man. The animal raiser shrugged.

"As you said. Make his night comfortable. Have Croaker do him in the morning," he said unhappily.

"It's just a *pig!*" Lindee cried out as she made her way back to the kitchen.

"Follow Lindee, Bloor," the princess told him. He flicked the reins and got the wagon moving, steering it along the path. He thought about Pig and Kall. He believed he understood the man, as he had witnessed it more than a few times on the front and in the pitched tents of healers trying to save the dying: friends saying goodbye to the companions before they passed on. Friends delivering the killing blow themselves to spare hours or days of needless suffering.

"I was thinking," Morianna said beside him. "You could have done that."

"Kill Pig?"

"Yes. No trouble for you, right?"

Slowly, Bloor nodded. No trouble at all.

31

Happy with the day, Morianna had Bloor dine in the kitchen with Lindee, Alora, and herself. He learned that Morianna did not dine with any of her family, preferring the company of her small staff, a change from the times when he first guarded her. Lindee served them up roast chicken with barley and other herbs, with a steaming bowl of vegetables in gravy. Bloor ate easier than he did in the morning, He was famished, and the food was delicious. Conversation was light and he was spared from it. At the end, Alora returned home to her waiting family, and the meal dissolved into cleaning. Morianna got to her feet just as Tarco entered the room. The stony face of the man made Bloor's full stomach rumble.

"My Princess," Tarco greeted formally.

"Lord Tarco," she turned to Bloor. "You may leave when ready, Lord Bloor. And thank you for the day."

Taking the dismissal with a curt nod, Bloor got to his feet and left. In consideration of the ladies, he said nothing to Tarco, not having anything to say anyway. He did not even look at Tarco, not wanting to upset his stomach.

He immediately went to Toth's tavern and ordered two mugs of mead. He downed the first one as soon as he got it, and handed the empty mug back to a watching Jilly. She left Bloor to sit and enjoy his second mug. The Cavalier did so, studying the patrons and staring at no one in particular. The night air was warm, and Toth had opened a window. There was an aroma of chicken coming from the kitchen, but it failed to tempt a full Bloor. Given the evening was still young, he imagined that Toth would have a fairly good night of business.

He recalled the day, sipping on his drink. The face of the weasel filled his mind, hanging back from the crowd and just watching, grinning, and stinking of trouble. Perhaps he should have done more. A smaller version of the Field of Skulls went across Bloor's mind and he grimaced. He knew he could easily gut the man. The thought made him pause. He could bleed the weasel and it would not bother him in the least, much like the man Croaker, he suspected. Bloor remembered killing his first man, dark-faced and bearded, a brigand, young and fiery and attacking a line of wagons heading for Marrn. Back then, it was only guard duty and Nordun was still only a country. The juice was in Bloor's veins so strong that he struck down the brigand without a thought and struck at him again when the man was on his knees, giving him what the Sujins would call "a haircut." The first man he ever killed, and it didn't bother him in the least. He could put them down quickly and methodically and he never blinked an eye, never felt a twinge of guilt, never had the trembling that some men experienced when bringing themselves down from a battle high. He just never did. He worried about it for a while, wondering if there was something wrong with him. Then the war began, and he stopped worrying.

Sipping on his drink, he stared off into space.

Morianna.

Bloor played with his mug, turning it this way and that. How she had changed; it was startling. He could not believe how the little bitch he once protected had sprouted up into the young woman he accompanied today. Nature had a grand way of working at things, and he smiled just a little. She even got on with her servants now. The servants actually *talked* with her. Incredible.

Do you like long hair?

He never really thought of such a thing. She caught him unawares with the question, and she knew it. It was all there in her face, but she only embarrassed him just a little. She did not push him. Considerate. She had her fun and decided there was no need to go any further. He sipped again. He did not want to think of bad things this night. Thinking over Morianna's transformation would be enough. She would make some prince happy. A little smile crinkled the corners of his eyes and he raised his mug again.

There was a commotion outside, just beyond the main door. Sounds of a scuffle drew the attention of several of the patrons. A scream of pain shot through the air. There were sounds of boots scuffling on wooden planks, and Bloor caught a glimpse of someone having their head rammed into the wall of Toth's tavern. The man collapsed right there with his lower legs partially blocking the entranceway. Then the frame filled up with the form of Alwan. Bloor sighed.

There went his peaceful night.

Alwan entered, banging his shoulder against the doorframe. He turned on it and swore a line that made some of the older men in the place wince and bow their heads. Alwan sized up the wooden frame, as if considering ripping it out, and when no further assault came, he turned away from it and stepped inside. The people inside deliberately looked away and tried very hard to continue their discussions. Alwan made his way to the bar, the people clearing a path. He got a pitcher and surveyed the interior. Seeing Bloor, he lurched towards the Cavalier. Bloor was glad, in a way. It was obvious that Alwan had been drinking earlier, and was open to the idea of cracking some skulls if the invitation was there. Many of the patrons gave the Cavalier a wide berth as he made his way to Bloor's table. He stopped before him and placed the pitcher on the table.

"Bloor," Alwan greeted, thrusting out both of his hands as if wanting a hug.

Bloor nodded back. Alwan's eyes were swimming for dear life in their sockets. Toth's place wasn't Alwan's first stop, but Bloor wagered it would be his last.

"YOU!" Alwan suddenly directed at the tavern's occupants, "have NO idea who is amongst you. NEITHER did any of the Nordun shite piles HE put down in the dirt. Seddon above but this boy can gut—"

Bloor stood up. Alwan quieted immediately and blinked in puzzlement. "Wuzza speaking too loudly?"

Bloor nodded that he was.

"APOLOGIES to ALL!" Alwan announced and dipped his head. Sighing, Bloor sat down again.

"May I?" Alwan asked.

"Before you fall on it?"

"Yes."

"You better then."

"Thank you," Alwan collapsed on the bench. He landed with both elbows on the table, making the drink in Bloor's mug jump. "Didn't upsheet anyone, did I?" Alwan asked innocently, though he was gulping down air ominously.

"Only the one outside."

"Who?" Alwan craned to see. "Oh. Him." He thought for a moment. "I'll buy himma drink."

"That will make things better?" Bloor asked.

"Can't hurt."

Alwan peered into his pitcher and looked around slowly for his mug. Seeing none, he peered back into the pitcher and made a face. "Hate this stuff," and then a thought occurred to him. "I didn't pay for this."

"You can pay me," Bloor said.

"You," Alwan pointed. "You are a *good* man. A good man. I respect you. Him," a head toss at the man outside, "wassa punce. You, I respect."

And you make me nervous, Bloor thought, keeping his eyes on the man.

"You know why I respect you?" Alwan asked. Bloor shook his head.

"Because you could kill me," Alwan stated and grinned. He sipped at his pitcher. "Truly. You could. Easily. Well. Not *easily* maybe. I'd get in a cut or two. But I'd still be dead. *That's* why I respect you. And it's not fear I mean. Not fear. Respect, Bloor. None of these maggots though. None of these."

Mead dribbled out onto the table, and Alwan grimaced. "Too good to waste," he said, putting his sleeve down to soak the drink up. He suckled at it.

"Why are we here, Bloor?" Alwan suddenly asked.

"Alwan," Bloor asked after a moment. "Why are you like this?"

The Cavalier's features trembled for a second before deflating into disappointment. "They didn't thank me."

Puzzled, Bloor asked, "Who?"

"Those bastards outside."

"For what?"

"Fighting for them."

"They thanked you," Bloor lied, trying to sound calm. "I saw them. You were talking to me at the time."

"Then they thanked me to my back," Alwan said, looking contrite. "Low."

Bloor never suspected the man could drink himself into oblivion as he had done tonight. It was disturbing.

"They won't send me back, Bloor," Alwan abruptly said. "I went to see Lord Maullus this day and asked to be sent back to the front. He wouldn't do it. Lord *Maullus* would *not* do it."

"Why?" Bloor managed, stunned yet again. This was news.

Alwan shrugged as if trying to throw something off. "Don't know. Wait—he said," another ominous gulp of air, "he said... I would be needed later on. As an escort. An armed *escort!*"

"What's wrong with that?"

Alwan jerked back as if Bloor had just stabbed him. "An *escort*, Bloor? I belong out there, cracking heads with the worst of them. I..." he struggled to put out the words and gave up. "I'm a *killer!* A *butcher* of men! An animal! Not some...*escort*. I deserve to be on the *line*, not holding someone's hand! I'd be too damn tempted to hack the hand *off!* I was angry with Maullus, and he could see it. Ordered me to take it, and what by Seddon's pisspot are *you* looking at?"

The caught patron quickly averted his eyes.

Amazed, Alwan shook his head. "Thought so."

He gulped air again and puffed out his cheeks as if holding down his dinner. Controlling himself, he focused on Bloor again. "Been waiting here for word to go back. I don't need a respite. I need to be back on the front. I don't want to be the escort of some bloated dignitary tit who probably has a boy to clean his arse for him."

That wasn't an image Bloor wanted in his head at the moment.

"Not for me," Alwan lamented. "If I'm here for much longer, I'll...I'll do something...stupid. I can feel it. That one there. Just now? I wanted to SMASH HIS FACE INTO THE TABLE just for staring at me. There. Topper won't be looking this way anymore tonight. I wanted to feel to his skull crack open. Just like cheap pottery. Still do. That's not good, Bloor. Not goo...," he belched loudly, and forgot what it was he was talking about.

This time, Bloor nodded. Alwan lapsed into sullen silence and sipped at his pitcher. He glared at the knots and gouges in the table's surface, trying to make sense of things.

"I'm not sure of what to do," he said.

"Finish your drink and we'll go," Bloor said.

"Go?"

"Go. We'll get you back to the barracks. Sleep this off, and in the morning I'll give you something to do."

"Why not now?"

"Because you're too dangerous."

"Aw," Alwan sniffed loudly and waved a dismissing hand. "I'm only *threatening* now. Haven't gotten to *dangerous* yet. You know me."

Bloor knew the man spoke the truth. Then he had an idea and it showed on his face. Alwan saw it immediately.

"What is it?" Alwan asked, eagerness in his voice, his breath laced full of mead.

"What do you think about pigs…?"

32

Summer morning. The sky was gold and red, with ribbons of dark clouds being hauled back from the rising glow. It was a beautiful morning, and in between the pauses of bird song, Kall moved to the pen of Pig. He carried a small bucket of apples from Lindee's kitchen. She wouldn't approve, of course. To her, Pig was only a pig, but to him, the animal was a friend. That this would be his friend's final day, and Kall felt Pig should get to eat something special. He escaped his end yesterday, but he would not this day. Today, Croaker would have him, and that would be that. He rounded the corner, breathing in the ripe air of what only a fenced-in pig could summon up, and called out Pig's name. The great bulk of the animal lay up against the fence, sleeping.

Kall halted. His pail dropped and the apples spilled out.

Pig lay in a pool of his own blood. The pool buzzed alive with flies. The cut across his throat was spent, the ground lapping it up.

Kall's breath hitched in his throat and his eyes near exploded from his head. Croaker was nowhere in sight or anyone else for that matter. He entered the pen and walked up slowly to his friend. Flies buzzed around his head, but he ignored them. Holding onto the fence for support, Kall reached out and placed a hand on Pig's great head, and though his thoughts were sad, there was also a chord of relief inside him as well. He patted the animal between the ears, and with a sigh, sat down on Pig's cool carcass. From there, he turned his eyes towards the brilliance of the morning, and remembered better times.

"Did you eat this morning?" Morianna asked sleepily.

"I did," Bloor replied. "My Lady," he added, when she made a sleepy face at him over her shoulder. They walked down the corridor towards the kitchen. Bloor was feeling well with the start of the day. Morianna, having woken up early, sent Tarco away and so spared him having to see the man. Any morning where he did not have to meet Tarco was a good one.

"What did you have?"

"Bread and cheese," Bloor reported. Morianna groaned.

"Don't they pay you enough to afford better food?"

"What do you mean?"

"For food! There are other things to eat in the morning. Or can't you cook? I suppose not," Morianna answered for him. "Well, in any case, from now on you'll be eating with us in the morning. And lunch. Oh, and dinner as well. And not a word of protest, either. Bread and cheese, Sweet Seddon. You'd think you were in prison."

Bloor said nothing. He had eaten worse in fact, but she would not understand. He reminded himself of the men waking up to eat exactly what he had this morning, or porridge with a piece of dried apple if they were lucky. For *them*, he would do what she commanded. They would be wishing for what he would be eating in the days to come, and would never ever receive such an order from a princess. It was his duty to his sword brothers.

"No arguments," Morianna looked back at him as they walked along the cool stone corridor. Bloor shook his head.

"Good. And remember not to call me 'Lady.'"

"My apologies."

"Tarco can call me by my title; however, I don't like him. I'm thinking of sending him away."

"What if the king finds out?" Bloor asked.

"I don't care if he does."

"I do."

Morianna turned on her protector. "Very well then. I'm too groggy right now to argue with you. Maybe later though."

With that, she continued on down to the kitchen. Bloor realized that there weren't as many servants about now as there were years ago. Had she dismissed most of them? There were some men and women flittering about and doing cleaning of sorts, but nothing like the huge staff from before.

"Good morning, Anna," Lindee said brightly as they entered the kitchen. Her hands were busy with a basket of fresh eggs. "Good morning, *Boor*."

Bloor frowned at the woman.

"He'll be eating with us from now on," Morianna told Lindee.

"Figured as much," Lindee sang softly. "I know you too well."

"Do you mind?" the princess asked her.

No no no, Lindee mouthed silently with an annoyed face. She should not even be asking such a thing. "He doesn't bother me and he keeps his mouth *closed* when he eats. I like that. Someone taught him manners. We'll have to keep him clean when he gets into the jam though," she finished with a mischievous wink in Bloor's direction. The Cavalier winced at the memory. He would have to be careful around this Lindee—she liked to remember things he would rather forget. They sat down at the table.

"Where did you learn your manners, Bloor?" Morianna asked him, covering her mouth while she chewed on a piece of sliced apple. "And don't think I've forgotten about my question from yesterday. So what is it? Parents? Or are you an orphan?"

"You are…persistent," Bloor regarded the princess with a blank expression. "One thing you've carried over with you into adulthood."

That got him a smile. "Now there's a mouthful," Morianna said to Lindee. "I don't think I've heard him say quite so much in one breath. What brought that on, hmm? And yes, I am persistent, but in the sweetest of ways." She popped the last of the apple into her mouth. "So what of your upbringing?"

"I am an orphan."

Morianna's face drooped. "Oh dear. I'm sorry, Bloor. I thought you had parents for certain. I understand if you don't want to talk about it."

"It seems you wish me to talk," Bloor said.

"You can't blame me," Morianna countered. "Have you tried speaking with Tarco?"

"I have."

"And?"

His face darkened, and Morianna giggled. "You see? You know what I mean. And I really don't mean any badness asking about you being an orphan. Who raised you then?"

Bloor smiled easily. "You are persistent."

"I am."

"She is," Lindee added from behind them. The snap and sizzle of frying eggs filled the air. "I call her a *nag*, however."

"He won't call me that, though," Morianna said. "He's too well-mannered to do that."

Bloor chewed on his inner lip. He wanted to say something witty and sarcastic to put her in her place, but he couldn't. She was still a princess, and a woman. Both facts kept his mouth shut.

"See?" Morianna beamed.

Lindee did not look. She was too busy preparing breakfast.

"Don't worry, my Cavalier," Morianna pouted, "before too long, I'll—we'll—have you chirping like the birds outside a morning window."

Bloor didn't have any birds outside his bedroom window. They had all learned to stay away from the Cavalier.

"The Cavaliers and taskmasters took me in. Started my training when I was boy."

"Ah," Morianna said, chin in her hands. "None of the men tried to make a pet of you?"

"Pet?"

"Yes. In that way."

"What way?" Bloor asked, confused.

"She's asking if any of the men tried to bugger you?" Lindee clarified.

That brought back the familiar frown. "No. No one lifted a finger to me like that."

"So then, what of friends?" Morianna asked.

"None really. Except my peers. I did know Lord Winter and Maullus when they were Koors, but I would not call them friends. They were teachers."

"No friends then," Morianna said, in mild shock.

"I remember," Bloor bit at his lip for strength, "a certain young girl that had no friends whatsoever. Only sisters."

"Only bitches," Lindee spoke without fear. Morianna said nothing to reprimand her, and Bloor was not certain how to react.

"I suppose it's not so hard to believe then," the princess said, drawing his attention, "that of all the people in the world, there would be others who were as solitary as myself."

"Solitary?" Bloor questioned. That wasn't quite the word he would use.

"Yes. Alone." Her chin lifted. "Except for Alora, I suppose. But then my childhood was miserable."

"And has only improved by a little," Lindee said boldly. Bloor turned to see her, but Morianna touched his hand, drawing him back.

"It's alright, Bloor. I do have friends now, you see."

"She has me," Lindee said.

"I have her," Morianna agreed. "And Alora and a few others. Mostly servants, but friends nonetheless." Her fingers began tracing spirals in the surface of the table. "When you were young, did you ever do anything bad?"

"Bad?"

"Yes, bad."

He thought about it. "No. I wouldn't dare."

Lindee brought over breakfast: fried eggs, bread, and honey butter. "Proper, weren't you?" she said to him.

The serving of breakfast interrupted his line of thought. No, he had done nothing bad in his youth. However, in his adulthood, he had done wicked things aplenty. Morianna had been wicked in her youth, but he could see that she was making amends for that. There would be no making amends for what he had done in the war.

When they finished, conversation was light, and Morianna again helped Lindee clean up. She told him the princess would throw a fit if she didn't help out. Lindee simply wanted to avoid a fight with a princess. It was far easier and much more fun to let her help with the cleaning. Bloor stood back and watched how well they got along, like two sisters.

He watched, and at times his mind drifted.

Morianna announced it was time for a walk and gestured for Bloor to follow. Lindee watched them go with a pleasant smile. They exited the kitchen through a rounded portal and into a small room filled with cut wood for the cooking fires. The air was fragrant with the smell of split bark. There was a bolt locking the door, and Bloor tried to get around the princess to unlock it. Morianna would not let him pass. "I can do it," she said, and did so with some effort. Bloor liked that.

They stepped onto the palace grounds. He studied the far-off walls surrounding them before following the princess along a carefully kept white stone path. Guards in polished armor patrolled the inner grounds in pairs. Some servants performed gardening work around one copse of trees.

"We'll go to the gardens," Morianna smiled at him. "It smells better there. I get sick of all this stonework sometimes."

They made their way to the royal gardens, the pathway turning into clean swept white tiles with the edges marked with rounded beach rocks. A soft lawn stretched out either side, and in places, huge beds of brightly colored flowers were in bloom. Elm trees towered in places and offered shade from the sun.

"Smell that?" Morianna asked him. Bloor shook his head.

"The air!" Morianna exclaimed. "How nice it is. How clean! We're breathing in the breath of the gardens!"

He took a lungful in, savored it, considered the smell and taste, and exhaled.

"Well?"

"Nice," Bloor managed, causing Morianna to roll her eyes.

"Is that all you can say? You have been away for too long. Your sense of smell is gone. If I had a choice in the matter about any sense to lose, I'd give up sight. All the others are too dear. Then again, I suppose I could lose taste, but never hearing. Not ever to hear music again? Or laughter? Terrible."

Bloor's expression was blank again. He'd seen warriors with limbs lost as well as head wounds causing a loss of any number of the senses she mentioned.

"If you had to lose one, which one would you choose?" Morianna asked him.

"Sight."

"Strange for a Cavalier to say that. I would think sight to be fairly important."

"I'd be a Cavalier no more if I lost my sight. But if I had to lose one, sight would be the one."

"Why?"

Walking through such a wonderful landscape of sculpted greenery, Bloor did not want to explain years of seeing Nordun and Sunjan atrocities on the front. He didn't want to open that chest of battle horrors. "I've just seen things done that I wish I had not."

"Oh." Morianna sensed it was time to change the subject. "So, do you like long hair?"

"I've never though of that before," he said.

"I can see that."

"Then you should wear it however you like."

"We aren't talking about me," Morianna corrected him.

"Oh," his face was feeling hot again.

"We're talking about you. So now, what is it?" she asked again, seeing color bloom in his face. It wasn't everyday she got to make a Cavalier uncomfortable. And over such an innocent question!

"Yes," Bloor answered. "I like long hair."

The princess chose a pathway to the right and led him deeper into a small forest. To her right, bushes were bursting with rose petals. "Now that wasn't so bad, was it? Now, for the next question: How do you like my hair?"

Winged insects flittered by his face. "Your hair is fine, my Princess. Very fine."

"Oh," Morianna said, unconvinced by his tone. "Thank you."

"It really isn't my place to..."

"To answer my questions?" Morianna interrupted him. Bloor held his tongue, his embarrassment blazing now. "It's unfortunate that you are so easily embarrassed, Bloor. I mean how will you feel when I ask the next question?"

His eyes narrowed in trepidation. "What?"

"Do you think I'm pretty?"

Later that evening, in his quarters and lying on his cot, Bloor stared up at the ceiling. His hands were folded across his bare chest. A pitcher rested on the nearby table, full of water with two mugs beside it. A chuckling Alwan sat nearby, dressed in the Cavalier's traditional green and white. The light from an oil lamp threw shadows against the wall.

Outside the night was quiet, encouraging those not sleeping to keep their voices low.

The story made Alwan feel better, still recuperating from the previous night. The Cavalier eventually controlled himself. "So what did you say to her?"

"What could I say?" Bloor replied. "I felt quilled. Like a mark on the archery range. I tried to change the subject, but she wouldn't let me."

"Sounds to me like she's hunting for something," Alwan said in a lecherous tone. "In the garden too, no less. Amongst the roses, eh?"

Bloor shook his head. He should have known better than to confide in Alwan.

"A waste there," Alwan said, smiling. "You should have taken her while you had the chance. Remember the boys on the front. You owe it to them to bed down a princess. You *owe* it to them! She is a woman now, after all. Perhaps next time she'll drag you into the bushes."

"I doubt that."

"You doubt that," Alwan repeated, amazed at the man's denseness in these matters. "You are a priss, Bloor. Come to think of it, you always were a priss."

"Well, what would you have done then?"

Alwan's face brightened with evil thoughts. Annoyed, Bloor turned his attention back to the ceiling. "How did you get in here, anyway?"

"You let me in."

"Another mistake made this day," Bloor commented, making a long face.

"Ah," Alwan pounced. "So you *wanted* to bed her down. Tell me the thought at least crossed your mind. One good—" his fist pumped the air. "Eh? *Eh?*"

"Did the pig give you trouble?" Bloor asked him.

The fist dropped and Alwan looked insulted. "It was a *pig*. I had to make a challenge of it by slipping past the guardsmen. A big animal, but too friendly."

"The blood-letting didn't satisfy you?"

"No," Alwan said and became silent. "To take a life, Bloor is perhaps one of the greatest pleasures I know. I live for it. I feel best when I'm stabbing something. Is that wrong? I don't think so. That's what I am. It's my work. More than that, it's my purpose. Just as the cobbler knows it's his lot to fix boots, or the baker to make bread. Mine is to take lives. Lesser lives, if you will. Good or bad. I don't think of myself as an evil man, but I do know there are those that see me as such. But I am what I am. Perhaps when I finally die, there'll be a place on the other side for me. For now, I *crave* to do what I am meant to do."

Bloor's eyes regarded the Cavalier sitting by his table. "You should have made that speech to Lord Maullus. That might have convinced him to send you back."

"I get nervous around that one," Alwan admitted. It drew a chuckle form the other man.

"He does that to me, too," Bloor said.

"Well then," Alwan straightened. "Do you have any more pigs for me to butcher? Until the day I ride back to Nordun?"

"I'll think about it. I'll tell you if I do."

Alwan got to his feet and yawned, wiping his face. His teeth flashed in the orange light. "Don't wait too long. Killing pigs like that could never be a pastime for me. Maybe I should consider butchering animals as a full profession? Or small contrary children?"

Bloor half-smiled. He never could be certain if this one was joking or not. Alwan's self assessment could not have been more accurate. The man was indeed an ender of lives. Without a word of goodbye, he left Bloor and closed the door as he left. Bloor remained in the quietness of the room and the glow of the lamp. He lay there, smelling the fresh hay of his bed, thinking of when it would be changed again. He thought on some of the things Alwan had said. He thought about Pig and Kall. Before he drifted off to sleep, he thought about Morianna and gardens of bright flowers.

33

The next market day, a fresh cool breeze pushed its way through the people crowding the market square, lifting the summer heat. Morianna, Alora, and Bloor rode along on their wagon, enjoying the wind. It felt wonderful to Bloor. He imagined it would feel even better on the plains below the city rim. He was beginning to feel caged within Sunja's walls, and longed to have a horse underneath him, galloping across open swards of grassland. He wondered what would happen a month from now if that need wasn't filled. Would he be taking it out on civilians, like Alwan? Would he do worse? Steering the wagon, he cursed and stabbed warning looks at numb-minded people stepping directly into his path, not watching where they were going. Stupid people. If he were to run them down, it would be *his* fault. The only recourse then would be to kill someone.

Where did *that* come from? He scolded himself while watching a lady carrying a brown cloth sack step directly in front of his horses without a look or a care. Bloor checked the urge to step down and throttle the bitch. Perhaps he should have been the one to execute Pig.

"What are you thinking about?" Morianna asked him.

"Hmm?" Bloor glowered. "Oh. Pig."

"Ah, yes. I wanted to ask you about that. Did you kill him?"

"No. An acquaintance of mine."

"A butcher?"

"Yes, a butcher," Bloor answered without missing a beat. "A very good butcher."

"Is he a friend?"

Bloor considered it for a moment. "No."

"Don't you have any friends at all, Bloor?" Morianna asked him.

"No."

"Oh. Well, sorry then," Morianna said mildly enough. "Too bad. You seem pleasant enough."

The Cavalier looked at her as if he had just taken a bite of something unpleasant, and Morianna smiled. Pursing his lips, he kept on driving the wagon.

"My," the princess said to Alora, "he can be a frightening man, easy enough. I've heard that when men are fighting in a battle, they wear a different face. Not just any face mind you, but a truly terrifying one." She looked to Bloor. "Is that true? Do they make faces?"

"Some, yes," Bloor supposed.

"Do you have a face you make?"

Bloor squinted. How should *he* know? "I don't know."

"Really? I find that hard to believe. How long have you been a Cavalier?"

"Eight, nine years."

"And you don't know how you look when you're fighting?"

He wanted to ask if she thought there were mirrors on the front, but instead said, "No."

"The others do, though?"

He sighed. "I have seen others."

"Do they seem scary?"

"Yes."

"Do they scare you?" Morianna asked innocently, for she really had no experience with war and death.

"No."

"Why?"

"I've learned that appearances can be the opposite of what is in a person's heart."

"Really?" Morianna asked, liking his answer. Bloor only nodded. He never really gave it much thought, but he felt he should say something to her, and the words seemed true enough.

"Show me yours then? Before you fight someone."

His face lit up in surprise. He really should have seen the request coming. "No…and please do not ask me again."

This, in turn, surprised Morianna, and she decided it was best not to push him. She would wait for another time, perhaps when Alora was not around.

They did their business with the merchants. The way the princess handled them quietly amused Bloor. She was a challenge to refuse. To think that the woman was once a little girl that he considered to be the spawn of Saimon below. Her transformation was a wondrous one, recalling how much better she treated her servants. How she spoke with them and had them eat meals with her. He remembered a time when he once saw the girl standing before a bubbling black cauldron where the leftovers from her meals were dumped into and churned into a gruel, the same slop that would feed the servants for the next day or two. The same cauldron that was rarely emptied and never cleaned. At least, Bloor never saw anyone clean it.

In one particular memory, he saw a young Morianna spit into the vat.

However, not these days. A magical transformation had occurred over the years. Morianna had them eat together, especially at dinnertime, and if someone missed a meal, it was Lindee's task to see that it was kept for them. She had changed so much that he found himself wondering if it was possible for anyone to change their ways. Never once did he ever think of changing himself.

Morianna ran a hand through her hair and hooked it behind an ear. Bloor watched the merchant she haggled with drink it in like a fine mead. Yes, she was a charmer indeed, and damnation if she didn't strike a fine figure in the unflattering clothes she wore on these expeditions. Bloor then noticed who he suspected to be the son of the merchant. The young boy, perhaps fourteen, sneaked looks at the princess. Bloor stared at the boy, wondering just what it was that was so damn interesting about her. The boy felt the Cavalier's gaze and turned red in an instant, shamed at being caught. He rushed off to finish his chores. Finishing her buying and the wagon loaded, Morianna climbed up into the seat beside Bloor, pressing into him shoulder to shoulder, thigh to thigh, hip to hip. The sudden contact made him flinch.

"Sorry," she said, "but we have so much this time, and Alora has no place to sit but up here."

With that, Alora hauled herself aboard, accepting Morianna's hand for help.

So it seemed, Bloor figured, but it did nothing to ease his discomfort. Morianna continued pressing into him and he swore in his mind. How much room did two women *need*? It wasn't as if they were huge or anything.

"Comfortable?" Morianna giggled, pressing into him again and this time actually swinging an arm around his broad back. The action mortified the Cavalier, and he scrunched himself up even further.

"You aren't going to fall off are you?" she asked him.

"I'm fine, Clea."

"You said my name," she said, sounding pleased. In response, Bloor got the horses moving, and the sudden jolt of the wagon starting made Morianna squeeze up against him even more. With such a distraction, driving the wagon became a challenge for him.

They stopped twice more, once at a cobbler where Morianna and Alora fussed and haggled over shoes and boots. The cobbler, a man grey of beard and with only three teeth in his head, joked and carried on with them both. All the while, Bloor watched Morianna from the corner of his eye, ensuring no harm came to her. When the business concluded, they piled everything onto the wagon and made way.

"You're right, Alora," Morianna said to her friend. "A smile and a kind word can easily sway a man. Present company excluded, of course," she added, looking at Bloor. "After all, you *have* to do as I say."

The joke was lost on Bloor, who frowned ever so slightly as Morianna's laugh chimed pleasantly in his ear.

They arrived at the fountain of the spouting fish. The crowds, already alerted to their coming, gathered around and waited. A few old men standing like worn fence posts were scattered amongst the greater numbers of women and children. Bloor spotted the weasel as soon as he flicked a look towards the same alley. The man leaned against a wall and studied the wagon with scheming eyes. He'd dressed himself in black again, and Bloor suspected the man probably did not even change clothes at all. Sensing that he was being watched, the weasel dipped his head in brazen greeting and smiled.

A scowl came over the Cavalier's face. Why shouldn't the man smile? The people here had just been delivered a substantial amount of food and goods. The food wouldn't be easily made note of, and the cotton shirts and footwear they brought weren't of much value either, but Bloor knew that great value was not needed for predators such as these. There were only old men around to protect the womenfolk, and not one constable in sight. A Nord would think Seddon himself had blessed him, or whoever the Jackals prayed to.

"Stay here then," Morianna said to him with annoyance in her voice. She had been speaking to him while he was thinking, and thus ignoring her. She got down from the wagon and began distributing the wares. Bloor focused on the people about them, happy at a glance, especially the children, but weren't the womenfolk reserved just a little? Their smiles seemed forced to him, and masked something greater.

He spotted a second man walking around the edge of the crowd. He was as big as the weasel. A brother perhaps, with his thumbs hooked in a length of thick rope around his waist. He looked equally slippery, and he eyed Bloor with loathing. When the second man smiled evilly at him, the Cavalier knew that something was afoot and that someone would die. Both these men seemed to be healthy enough. Why were they not dressed for battle? Why were they away from the front? What were they doing in a public square intimidating the masses? Bloor contemplated these things while he sat, hunched over his reins. The second weasel threw back his head, flicking his hair back and dismissing Bloor with a look of contempt. Both weasels exchanged comfortable looks. There was no fear between them. The second man joined the first, and both lounged in the shadows.

Alora noticed where Bloor was staring while she was handing out provisions. The schoolmistress accepted thanks from a woman and quickly assessed the two watchers in the alley. What she saw made her turn cold. Morianna stood with her back to both men and did not see either of them. Alora looked to Bloor, grateful that he was with them and vigilant, and that he had his shortsword. Feeling her eyes, he met her gaze for only a second, before turning back to the two men. In that moment, Alora saw the calm assurance there. It was enough for her to resume her work. Despite him being there, she still stole looks in the direction of the watchers.

Towards the end, Morianna climbed up onto the wagon. She noticed the men in the alley immediately. "Who are they?"

"Friends," Bloor replied, keeping his eyes on the pair. They were still quite comfortable where they stood, patient that their time would begin once the wagon was gone. Bloor had no doubt of that. He intended that their time would indeed come.

"What do they want?" Morianna asked.

Bloor's mouth twisted. "What their kind always want. Trouble."

"What are you going to do?"

At her questions, he seemed to awaken. "Bring you back to the palace."

"What about these people?" Alora asked. Without answering, Bloor snapped the reins and got the wagon moving. The crowd parted for them, and Morianna saw then how unhappy the people were with their leaving, but she was not certain as to the true reason. Desperation could now be seen in some of the faces, and even the old men were grim looking. She felt a need to say something when Bloor cut her off.

"What would you have me do then?"

"Notify the constables," she said immediately.

The constables reminded Bloor of the front. "They will disappear as soon as the constables show themselves." He had seen it before, and he doubted anyone would speak to the authorities. He wondered if anyone had already tried and was punished for it.

Morianna became quiet then. She let Bloor drive on, and they left the people behind to whatever fate waited for them once they were out of sight. Shame swelled up inside her. Leaving the people to the mercy of those bandits made her sick. There was more at stake here than winter clothing, and yet she still said nothing, letting the wagon take her away to her guarded palace. She had once vowed to right all the wrongs she had ever done to the people around her. What was she doing at this moment if she wasn't deserting them? But this was beyond her, wasn't it?

"What could you do?" she asked him quietly.

"Do?" Bloor asked back without looking.

"Yes, do."

"If they are doing what I suspect them to be doing?"

"Yes."

"Kill them," Bloor said simply.

The words made the princess pale. She gripped her seat to steady herself, and she felt a hand touch her back as Alora sought to comfort her. The reaction was not lost on Bloor. He knew then, as much as she had changed in the years and as caring as she was towards her people, Morianna was not ready to give Bloor the permission he needed to explore and deal with a problem. She was not hard enough to unleash him. He did not think badly of her for it, but in the meanwhile, people would likely suffer.

"I can report it to Lord Maullus," he offered.

"No," Morianna said. "He would ask where you saw them. No one should know about my helping the people here."

"The Salish know."

"They swore to never tell."

"Lord Maullus is a Cavalier Commander," Bloor pointed out.

"And one loyal to my father. I don't want to chance it. I'm sure the people will be fine. We're just imaging things is all. Only our imaginations."

However, she did not sound convinced, and became quiet and concerned.

Nor did the thought rest well on the Cavalier's mind, remembering the faces of the happy children they left behind.

34

"And?" Alwan asked. He did not like unnecessary suspense. They were not on the front. They sat in Bloor's quarters. A scent of fresh straw soaked the air and Bloor sat close enough to a burning lamp to watch the flicker of the flame. He felt his room was safer than the confines of Toth's tavern, where anyone could be listening in. There was also the chance that someone would be watching Alwan, not that Alwan cared.

"And that was it," Bloor said finally. "She ate very little at dinner, and excused herself early. She didn't speak of it at all."

"But she was thinking of them?"

"I think so," Bloor acknowledged. "Not quite ready for the job though."

"She's still only a girl. Chances of her ever having to give an order like that will be slim, I wager. Why are you smiling?"

"Morianna," Bloor heaved out, "was a monster as a child. When I first met her, she would throw things at me. Spit on her table scraps that would be her servants' food. She would dump whatever she had left over into a great pot that I never saw emptied once or ever cleaned, only filled and filled again. The fire would be lit up later, and whatever was inside was heated up and served. We would eat better on the front. That was the extent she cared for the people working for her. I suspect those men are bandits. Brigands. And I told her what I would do to them if they were just that. But she actually looked ill when I did," Bloor chewed on the inside of his mouth. "If I pressed her into making a decision, she might have emptied her gullet right there. These past few weeks has shown me that the princess I once knew has disappeared. The person that is Morianna now wants nothing to do with her childhood and hates to hear of it. This Morianna is doing what she can to help the people around her."

"Like cleaning up after meals?" Alwan asked. He was shocked when he heard that. Royalty getting their hands dirty!

"That, and helping the people with these goods. She has a guilty soul that one, and she seems determined to do the right thing. But she was frightened at letting me investigate these dogs, and putting them down if need be..."

"Maybe that's too harsh for her?" Alwan suggested.

"Maybe it's too easy for us?" Bloor countered.

"Maybe."

They thought in silence for a while before Bloor said, "It's interesting to see how she turned out."

"She's weak when she needs to be strong," Alwan said.

"She doesn't want to bring it up to her father," Bloor explained, "because then she'd have to explain how she came to know of all of this. And somewhere the buying of food and other things for peasants will come out and that frightens her. She is brave behind her father's back, but if he did discover what she has been doing, well..." he trailed off.

"We could tell Maullus," Alwan said. "Or I could. I wander about enough to notice things like this. Perhaps I'll take a walk and see what I can see. Maybe the weasels will come sniffing around me."

"Do you want to do that?"

"After cutting up pigs, why not?" Alwan grinned.

"Tell me what you find out," Bloor said.

"Hmm," Alwan said, getting to his feet. "Might as well start now."

The man's decision did not surprise Bloor. Alwan had been inactive for too long now. "Good hunting then," he said.

"One can hope," Alwan growled, and departed.

Bloor laid back and stared up at the ceiling, wondering what the next few days would bring. The thought remained in his head that Sujins earned decent coin in the king's service, and yet, they were delivering food to the Sunjans that clearly needed it. What was happening? Did he truly want to find out?

Alwan would find out what was going on. Bloor slept easy knowing a Cavalier was asking questions.

By the third day, the comfort Bloor was feeling in having a Cavalier investigate the weasels began to diminish. Alwan did not return, nor did he send any word of his searching the shadows. Part of Bloor scoffed at the thought that a pair of thugs could have gotten the better of Alwan, but stranger things had happened in the past. By the fourth day, doubt began to gnaw on his mind. He could not speak of the situation to the princess, as he believed the less she knew was best, but Bloor became increasingly eager for the next market day.

Except Morianna did not speak of it.

Though he was becoming more comfortable in her presence and in the way she wanted things done, Bloor still did not feel quite at ease to approach her with his concerns. He still considered her a child in these matters, and she was not capable of making the decisions that he needed in order to act. He could go to Maullus, but he was uncertain as to how the commander would react. After all, Alwan felt he was already in disapproval with Lord Maullus. If the commander found out Alwan was doing something without getting permission first from him, things could become black for the Cavalier. Bloor was unhappy for not thinking things through a little more. He should not have let Alwan rush off into the night.

So Bloor did the only thing he could do: He waited.

By the fifth day, news came.

He was sitting and eating toast covered in sweet partridge berry jam. Lindee and Morianna sat nearby, prattling on as they usually did. Since the last market day, Morianna said little of heading out once again to the public square, appearing unsure of what to do there. Her silence on the subject made Bloor all the more eager to venture there during the day and perhaps even discover Alwan's whereabouts.

"Did you hear about the fire the night before last?" Lindee asked. Hearing the word "fire" made Bloor stop in mid-chew.

"No," Morianna exclaimed, "what of it?"

"A storehouse caught fire and burned down to the cellar," Lindee reported. "Some of the houses and buildings nearby got burned too, but they managed to save them. It rained as well, lucky enough, but not soon enough to save the storehouse. Or the poor buggers in there."

"People died?" Morianna asked.

"Died. They're picking through the remains even now, I imagine. Horrible thing to be cooked while still alive. I can't imagine the suffering."

Bloor sat, his back straight and his eyes fixed on a space between the pots hanging over the cooking fires. Morianna stopped eating. "Don't say any more, please. You'll make me sick for the day. And I imagine I'll be sick aplenty after I see my father."

"You have to see him today?" Lindee asked.

The princess nodded. "I received a summons last night. He wishes to see me this afternoon."

"What about?"

"I have no idea. But I hope it's only me, and I hope it's short. I don't want to spend all day in the presence of my father. You're coming too."

Being addressed snapped Bloor out of his wondering of Alwan's fate. "As you wish," he said, feeling less strange at not using her title. He would take care to use it in the presence of the king, however.

"He wants us for the afternoon lunch," Morianna played with the edge of her plate. "Which should be interesting, since I hardly remember the last time I ate with my father."

"You're an excited one now, aren't you?" Lindee said, seeing her friend's lack of interest.

"As excited as Karl was over killing and serving up Pig. My father does nothing without reason. Especially when it comes to his children. I can only guess at why he wants to see me. There isn't a birthday as far as I can remember. No ceremonies. No dignitaries visiting."

"You think there will be trouble?" Lindee was a little concerned now. She learned a while ago when to trust the princess' ability to detect trouble in the air. "What could it be?"

"I don't know. We'll find out this afternoon. If anything, my father will be brief. He always is. Especially when it comes to his children."

Lindee said nothing to defend the king. She knew, as did most everyone else on his household staff, that the importance of the children to the king was always an afterthought, an indifferent result from a winded coupling with his departed queen. He never concerned himself with raising them, except for appointing people who could. He had enough people on his staff and in his power to ensure his children received a quality upbringing. It was said that he preferred the company of younger women now, and took greater care in preventing a child than in his younger days. The whisper around the halls was that it was good to be the king, and that when he was too old to perform an act of coupling, he would appoint someone to do that as well and then simply watch, perhaps even give instructions. However, those were jests not even Lindee was brave enough to say in the presence of Morianna.

Morianna regarded Bloor. "Be ready when we get there."

Not knowing exactly what could happen, her Cavalier guardian nodded anyway.

The first thing Bloor noticed when he entered the king's hall was the white marble floor veined with lines of velvet green. The wealth needed to possess such a floor alone froze his mind, after seeing the rest of the palace being tiled in polished, fine-fitting stone. Bloor could not imagine how expensive it was or how long it took to construct such a floor, and that people actually walked upon it? *Extravagant and a waste*, he thought. No wonder there were so many Axemen about. He counted about two score of the feared giants, and those were clearly in sight. Armored giants in silver plate armor, standing with their formidable pole axes held high. There were five of the ogre-sized guards on either side of his majesty's blue cushioned throne.

The stories flew about the royal Axemen and their devotion to the king, and only the most skilled at arms were appointed to the position. It was said that if he released them to fight the Jackals, there would be enough dead meat to feed the kingdom for a dozen winters. Bloor did not doubt it. He had witnessed some of the Axemen train in between shifts in their secluded compound. The giants swung their eight-foot pole arms like they were scythes cutting through hay. Practice targets were often cut in half, or limbs shorn off like the stubble on one's chin. In between strokes, the men would sharpen their weapons to an infinite keenness. Against such monsters, if one had to face them, it was wise to just get out of their way, or take them down with an arrow. Trying to stop one of those swings would be just what the Axemen wanted.

The throne room shined from its marble floor up to its arched ceiling, but it was all outdone by Morianna.

Before leaving her chambers to see her father, the princess called her servants to assist in getting dressed. As much as Bloor suspected she loathed to do so, she had been told to dress befitting a princess. Positioned as he was outside of the chamber door, he could faintly hear the cackle and the fury of activity within, but he paid little attention to it. However, when Morianna emerged, she took his breath away. He did not realize just how dressed *down* the woman had been in his time with her. The sight of her in resplendent regal attire caused him to stare long enough for her to notice.

"See something, do you?" Morianna asked.

The warmth in Bloor's chest constricted his reply. He merely nodded, and cleared his throat. Upon Bloor's summons, a complement of six men at arms waited on the princess when she left her chambers, and he was grateful to have them. Never had he been so distracted in all of his life. Still, he kept his silence all the way to the requested meeting, and he was thankful that she was preoccupied with meeting her father. She didn't say a word to him.

Now, standing in the huge hall, it was clear that Morianna was indeed a princess. If she looked, she could easily see the effect she was having upon him. The Morianna he once knew and despised had grown into a woman, and dare he admit it, a stunningly beautiful one at that. Her cheeks were colored the barest shade of plum red, highlighting their diamond points. Her hair was bound upwards into a bejeweled cone that glittered with the light and accentuated her large dark eyes. The royal colors of gold, white, and threads of green clung to her generous curves. Bloor found his eyes wandering and he knew that he was paying too much attention to her. He willed himself to focus on the room, and cursed himself quietly when his eyes found her again.

At one point, while still waiting for the king, Morianna walked over to where her Cavalier stood and whispered, "What are you gawking at?"

The answering flush in Bloor's cheeks pleased her. He managed to say, truthfully, "Your dress, my Princess."

"Everything in place is it?" she asked with a little smile. "Seeing as how you've had time enough to appraise it."

"Yes, my Princess."

Morianna smiled again at him. "Walk with me. It's your place to be at my back when the King appears."

He nodded and followed her to stand a few paces away from the throne.

Behind Morianna's party, a new group entered the hall. They marched slowly, with an exaggerated purpose, which Bloor found annoying. If Belsarus were here, he would be bellowing at the lot of them to pick up the pace. The group of men were soldiers, except for the man in the lead. He was no doubt of royal blood, dressed in gleaming plate armor. They stopped beside the princess, and Morianna did not bother to mask her curiosity. The man at the head of the group was a tall man and in good physical shape. His black hair was shoulder length and straight, clean and shiny looking. He had pale features, as if he avoided the sun, and his skin was clean of any blemish. He was handsome enough, and he turned only slightly to acknowledge Morianna's presence. She curtsied. A brief look of disdain appeared and vanished on the man's features, but he dipped his head. The gesture was full of smugness. Bloor wanted to throttle him.

Then King Juhn entered the hall and awed silence fell. The man was tall and walked with a measured grace, as if he counted each step to his throne. His hair was unnaturally long and black, and his face was snow white with powder. An equally black beard, as if dipped in ink, hung like a broad spear tip from his chin. Twelve attendants, all dressed in angelic white and castle black, followed in his steps. At his heels, carrying the edges of his white gown, were two dwarves, bearded, and full of an overblown pageantry that made Bloor embarrassed to watch. He had never seen the king before, and never knew just how much of a *woman* he was. It bothered him. The king before him did not show any of the strain or worry of a land locked in a death struggle with Nordun. The king did not appear to have much of a care for anything. Standing behind her, Bloor could not see Morianna's expression. He wondered what Lindee would say about the king, and guessed that she would say an earful.

There was a moment's confusion with one dwarf who failed to properly fold the corner of King Juhn's robes when he sat down on the cushioned throne. There was a void of silence, deeper than the one upon the king's entrance, and Bloor strained to hear a sound, any sound. The dwarves made swift adjustments to the robes while the king's eyes looked onwards stoically, waiting. He acknowledged his daughter by fixing her with his own dark eyes, yet said nothing.

The dwarves finished their folding away of the robes and an older man detached himself from the king's followers. He seemed to be the masculine equivalent of Alora, and he began reciting the many titles and achievements of the king. The introduction went on for several moments, and Bloor felt puzzled over why a man would need to remind people of his accomplishments. All within the hall listened and endured, and even Morianna, who Bloor felt might have rebelled somehow, stood column straight and kept her head held high. Not accustomed to such lengthy introductions, Bloor wondered if the king went through the same ritual every time he had an audience.

"The Lord and Protector of grand Sunja greets his majesty, High Prince Lollar of glorious and esteemed Marrn!" announced an elderly man standing to the right of the king. Being formally addressed, Lollar bowed in the king's direction.

"His Majesty, great King Juhn, gives you his daughter to your left. The Princess Morianna!"

Lollar gave the barest of nods in her direction, not particularly impressed.

"His majesty," the elderly man continued, "in all of his regal generosity, would be honored if his highness, Prince Lollar of Marrn, would take the hand of his remaining daughter in marriage to further strengthen the ties between our two countries, to further strengthen the newly-established bonds of trust and support we have agreed upon earlier this day. Such a union will deliver only the finest children unto our lands. The wedding ceremony will happen at the end of the week if his highness Prince Lollar wishes it so."

A gasp escaped Morianna then, and if Lollar heard it, he chose to ignore it. Bloor heard his princess, and he struggled to control his own outward appearance. The abruptness of the words stole the breath from Cavalier's lungs as if they were hooked on barbs. *Marriage? At the end of the...*

"I do not," Lollar announced imperiously, cutting off his thoughts.

"The Prince wishes to speak?" the court official asked, uncertainty sagging his face.

"I do," Lollar boomed again. The man had a presence, but Bloor felt he merely liked to hear himself talk. "I will not marry her highness in Sunja. As she is my *third* wife, I will request that she be delivered to Marrn at the end of the month. The marriage will be on the eve of Outkawling, the seasonal holiday of well-wishing for the coming winter and spring. A marriage at that time would bring good fortune to both our countries in the struggle ahead, as well as making my mother, the queen, pleased at seeing Sunja honor our customs. It will greatly strengthen the bonds forged here this day."

If King Juhn heard the prince, he did not show it. The king did not stir, and Bloor wondered for a moment if he were deaf. After a long uncomfortable moment, his highness beckoned his court official to his side with two white fingers. The king bade him close and words poured into the official's ear. The man nodded his understanding. When he was finished, King Juhn sat back with a hint of exhaustion on his face, already tired with the proceedings. The court official straightened and cleared his throat.

"The King acknowledges Prince Lollar's request and blesses his wise considerations. As the Prince wishes it, so shall the marriage take place as he requests. In consideration of Marrn's tradition, one month from this day, the Princess Morianna, daughter of Sunja's magnificent Lord King Juhn, will be honored in the marriage to Prince Lollar. Arrangements will be made for Morianna's departure from glorious Sunja to equally glorious Marrn, and with her goes the King's dearest and deepest blessings for the union between you both and the hope she provides you with many children."

To this, Lollard did not bother with an answer. He merely nodded in the king's direction, who may or may not have noticed the prince. Lollar seemed to mull over something, but decided not to say whatever was on his mind. He turned to the princess and measured her up and down as if she were livestock. The prince lingered on her legs, her hips, her breasts, and finally her face. Morianna said nothing, still standing and facing her father's throne, but Bloor wanted nothing more than to thrash the head in of this ill-mannered prince.

With a barely-heard grunt of approval, Lollar bowed again to the king and turned to leave. He marched through his shining escort of warriors, and they fell into a march at his heels. They disappeared in moments, walking in the same slow aggravating manner that reeked of pompous ceremony. In the quiet of their leaving, Bloor thought he heard a long despairing sigh come from the princess. King Juhn remained seated as the prince departed. He showed no expression at all as the men went from his sight. Indifferent as he was, he sat upon his throne, simply breathing and contemplating. A hand rose up and stroked at the spearhead of a beard hanging from his chin. After a few moments, his head lilted to the side, while his bored eyes centered to the right of his daughter. He did not bother meeting her gaze.

"You like," he spoke in a dangerous tone, "helping the people, I've discovered. Well then, consider this marriage the greatest help you could possibly do for them."

Morianna looked to her father, sadness in her face, and wanted to say something to this man, but in the end she could not bring herself to do so. For so long, she had been raised to bend to the king's wishes, that she simply accepted whatever he said, no matter what her thoughts. At this moment, her thoughts were whirling in her head, and she could not grasp one of them long enough to force it into speech. She felt that if she protested at all, the well of emotion in her would break, and she did not want for her father to see her tears. What good would it do, anyway, on a man who only now told his remaining daughter that she was to be married to a stranger? As punishment for helping his subjects?

"You may leave," King Juhn's fingers whisked out, as if shooing away a fly.

Slowly, Morianna curtsied and left the room without looking at the king. Bloor and her escort followed. They walked back through the luxury of the main palace, out the main door, and towards the smaller palace of Morianna. All the while, the princess was silent about the summoning and the announcement of marriage. Bloor walked just behind her, looking everywhere at once to ensure her safety. They walked her back to the place Bloor saw more and more as a gilded prison for the princess. Morianna lived there all her life, barely venturing outside to see the world, and learning all there was to learn of it from her books. Now, within a month, she would leave this place for another without even the decency of a choice, and live the remainder of her days in a foreign land with a man she did not know.

"I won't be eating tonight," Morianna said to Bloor as they climbed the steps to her chambers. "I'll ask Lindee for something later. Please tell her."

A need rose up in Bloor to say something, but in the presence of the extra guards, he did not. He found it difficult to talk to Morianna about anything. How could he breach the subject of her newly-announced wedding? What could he say to her? He had no idea of how she felt. The princess closed the door behind her without wishing him a good evening. That alone tipped Bloor as to how much the day's events distressed the young woman. Perhaps Alora or Lindee would visit her later, and they, being women, would be better suited for any emotional outpouring. That thought made him feel better, but it was clouded over by the idea that things were often as cut and dried here as they were on the front, remembering more than a few officers who, on orders, went to their deaths, knowing it well in advance. Morianna had been given over to a Prince of Marrn. There was no discussion about it and no choice. Life was fine one moment for her, and then the next she was slated to seal the promise of a newly-forged alliance. She had her orders. He knew she wasn't going to her death, yet he was certain that her future would not be any better than a life in Sunja.

Bloor sighed. *No, there wasn't much difference between here and the front at all.*

He ignored Tarco's arrival and went to the kitchen. He relayed Morianna's request to Lindee while avoiding her questions as politely as he could manage. Sensing something wrong and deciding to go directly to the source, Lindee let the Cavalier off the hook and allowed him to leave. He returned to his quarters in a foul mood. He stopped at his door, realizing that someone had been there. The keyhole had been vigorously scratched at. A moment's surprise passed, and he gripped the door's handle in one hand while grasping his sword. Perhaps, if he was lucky, the person would still be inside. They would have a lot of explaining to do, if he decided to let them live.

He threw the door open, exposing a room of blackness. "Who is there? Come into the light and I'll let you live. If I have to come in, I'll drag you out by your guts."

The darkness in the room shifted, as if considering the threat, and then Alwan appeared.

"Where have you been?" Bloor demanded in a stern voice, disguising the relief he felt in seeing the man alive and with all of his limbs.

"Get inside and close the door," Alwan said in a low voice. "I took care so that no one followed me, and if anyone did, I'd have no worries now. Not with the two of us."

Bloor entered and closed the door behind him. "What are you talking about?" he asked, studying Alwan for a moment, as the man barred the door from within with a length of thick wood. "Never thought I'd see you doing that in Sunja."

"Well, times have changed, I've found out," Alwan replied.

"Oh?"

"Just a precaution."

"I'm sure it is. You did a fine job on the lock. Use an axe next time."

Alwan frowned. "That lock took me almost an hour."

"Couldn't use a window?"

The Cavalier looked uncomfortable. He pulled on his black beard. "Forget about that!" He whipped around one of the chairs in the room and sat down.

Bloor sat on his bed and leaned forward, spreading his hands out in a gesture of "So?"

"Been wondering where I've been, have you?" Alwan asked with a smile.

"Thought you might be dead. I heard a story about a fire in a storehouse and people dying in it."

That drew a smirk. "After all these years Bloor, and you still don't know me."

"I don't *want* to know you," Bloor declared, drawing a snort of dark amusement from the other man.

"Do you want to hear a story, then?"

"I do," Bloor said.

Alwan looked around and spotted a pitcher on the table. He poured himself a mug of water. "Get comfortable then,

Bloor. You're about to learn that the king's house is full of rats."

35

Alwan clothed himself in rags. He dirtied his face just a little, hunched himself over at the shoulders, and left his shortsword at the barracks. He found a cowl and draped it over his head and face. He spilled mead and beer onto himself, smiling at the waste and happy with the smell. The disguise complete, Alwan went hunting. He meandered into the public square on foot, shuffling along, and when he reached the fountain, plopped down in front of it, placing his back to its cool stonework. The smell of fresh water perked up his senses, but he kept his eyes downcast, looking as non-threatening as he possibly could. Then, comfortable that this was the place he was supposed to be, he began watching. Every so often, he would glance this way and that, scanning the crevices between the houses and buildings, looking for ruffians.

He did not have to wait long.

Two men came out of one alley and stood at its mouth, as if guarding it. They weren't big, but they carried themselves with the air of men that knew they could do as they pleased, and they did. Women walking by were leered at, or asked to step into the shadows when they got rid of their children. Old men were scorned as they shambled by, and twice the two sentries actually took a swing at passersby and laughed afterwards. They openly swung and swore at children if they wandered too close, enjoying themselves immensely. Power was as heady as strong drink, and it was plain that these two had consumed a fair share. They were both armed, openly displaying sheathed shortswords, and wore leather vests that gave them a look of hardened thugs. When there was no one about, they joked to one another, and Alwan guessed that one of the men was the weasel from his smile alone. The same man felt the Cavalier's eyes, not unusual from one with developed senses, and looked in Alwan's direction. Seeing only a drunk farmer slouched down in front of the fountain, he slung a few curses at the unmoving form. When there was no answer, the weasel went back to amusing himself in other ways.

Fool.

Whoever they were, they were not smart, or they were confident enough to be careless. This puzzled Alwan. There were constables in the area. He had seen pairs and groups of four walking their patrols in the city. Were they not afraid of the king's guardians? If not, why not? Alwan did not like the idea forming in his head.

An hour or so later, a pair of constables wandered into the area. They sauntered over to where the two men stood and were hailed as they drew close. Moments later, the constables and one of the pair went into the alleyway, out of sight. It caused Alwan alarm. He wanted to warn the officers, but only a little time later, all three men returned. All three wore contented looks; one even smiled. Alwan did not like what he was seeing. The scent of water relieved the odor of beer and mead, but he was beginning to catch whiff of something even more foul. He smelled bribery. The two officers strolled away from the weasel and his friend, ignoring the looks of the people in the area. The more Alwan thought about it, the more he disliked what he was seeing. There were more involved in this business than just these two. They alone, as rough as they appeared, could not establish the lines needed to conduct and arrange bribes. Judging by the ease of how the constables met with the men, Alwan suspected something had been happening here for a very long time.

A very long and *profitable* time.

Alwan took care not to draw the attention of the constables, and when they started to move, he got up and moved in the opposite direction. He went down a side street, and while no one was looking, sat down again in the shadows. If he leaned out, he could see the weasel and his friend.

As the day went on, Alwan watched the pair of men abuse just about anyone passing close to them. They left the alley twice and were out of sight for an hour or so both times, only to return. The constables came by once more, in the evening, and one actually nodded at the pair of men. By nightfall, it was too dark to make them out, although they still stood at the alley's mouth, making the most of any chance to intimidate the locals. Alwan watched as long as he could before retreating back to his own quarters, making efforts to ensure he was not followed. That night, leaving his clothes in a smelly heap on the floor, he thought about what he saw. He thought about it further the next day while he watched the same flow of events. The same men standing guard at the mouth of the alleyway, greeting the same constables as they made their patrols, the same smug confidence of men thinking themselves untouchable, and making the lives of those weaker around them miserable.

By late afternoon, something interesting happened. Sitting where he was in his own alley, Alwan watched as a woman, her silver hair tied at the back of her head, hobbled towards the pair of men. She greeted them and presented them with a small satchel. The weasel snatched it from her and tossed it to his grinning companion. He then shoved the old woman back, who stumbled and fell flat on her rump.

Alwan nodded to himself. It was exactly what he wanted to see; now he had no doubts. Other women came to them as the day went on, offering payments in sacks, cloth purses, or cupped hands. The two men took whatever was given them and laughed all the while at how easy it was. The constables were paid to ignore this, and it turned Alwan's guts.

The sun went down, drawing lines of orange and grey across the evening sky. The shadows became long and deep. When it was dark enough, Alwan stood up from his watching spot. He shambled towards the pair of men standing at the mouth of the alleyway. There was no moon overhead, and the street lamps had been lit for perhaps an hour. Alwan was too impatient to wait any longer. He had seen enough to justify what he was going to do. He got halfway to them when the weasel noticed him.

"Got lost, did you old topper?"

His companion snickered. The old man continued on his course.

"You must have had your share of ale tonight, old bastard. You're steering straight on course with trouble," the weasel warned, both of his arms hanging loose at his sides. If the toothless dog got close enough, the weasel was going to grab and toss him for fun, then maybe hit him, just hard enough to loosen a tooth or two and to give a lesson. That brought a smile to his face.

"You hear?"

The old man came closer. He obviously didn't. The weasel sighed theatrically at his friend. Some people's children never learn.

He stepped towards the walker, and grabbed the front of his beer-stinking robes. He hoisted him up by the chest.

Then he felt the stab of a knife.

His companion heard the sharp hiss of breath and thought the old man had some life in him after all. The two grappled in front of him for a brief second before falling into the alley with barely any noise. There was a low grunt of pain, which struck the second man as curious.

Then the old man stood up from the weasel's crumpled form. He pulled the shortsword from the weasel's scabbard and threw back his cowl. Dark eyes glared at the thug at the mouth of the alley, and then he was walking towards him.

The man pulled his blade free as Alwan reached him. The Cavalier stabbed the man through the chest and heart with one punch of his shortsword. Then he twisted it against the bone and muscle. The dead man slumped forward, and Alwan dragged him a few feet, out of the sight of passersby, before dropping him to the ground. He wrenched the sword free and regarded the weasel behind him. "Are there more of you?" he said.

The weasel drew himself up against the wall, both fists locked around the dagger sunk into his thigh. His pallid face twisted with a snarl. Alwan noted he was no longer so happy.

"You're *dead!*" he spat out.

Alwan walked over and half lopped off the weasel's hand with one slash of his shortsword. The man screamed only as long as it took Alwan to grab him by his hair and throw him to the ground. The Cavalier pressed one knee into the weasel's chest. He poised the tip of his blade at the soft spot at the base of the man's throat and leaned over, peering deep into the weasel's eyes.

"Are there others?"

"*Yes.*"

"Where?"

The weasel whimpered before giving Alwan the information he wanted.

"Who are you?"

"*Turr Ralt*," answered the weasel immediately, showing teeth. "*Sujin of the Third Klaw.*"

This narrowed Alwan's eyes. "Sujin?" he repeated, not believing the man.

"*Aye,*" Turr Ralt grated, thinking his attacker's voice to be suddenly fearful. "*And there are enough of us to make your...*"

Alwan shoved the blade through Turr's throat, turning his words into a spawny garble. Alwan didn't feel like being threatened, and he certainly wasn't going to be threatened by a Sujin with balls larger than his brains. He leaned over the hilt of his borrowed shortsword and peered into the man's eyes as the light hurried from them. Alwan noted the weasel wasn't smiling any more; he supposed he wouldn't be smiling either. Now the Cavalier knew where to find the rest of the pack. If they knew what was coming for them, no one would be smiling, just like this one.

He studied the man for a moment more. Then, with a sigh, he yanked the sword free and inspected it. It was a Sujin's shortsword. There was no mistaking the thick straightforward design. So there were Sujins gone astray? He would have to investigate more.

From the mouth of the alley, he heard a noise. Two looming forms stepped into the shadows. Turning to face them, Alwan recognized them at once: the constables.

They drew their weapons, expecting trouble.

And Alwan killed them both.

"Where are they?" a thick-necked Sujin called Bar Bar spoke, squinting out a window. "They should've been here by now. Tits."

"Tell that to Turr's face when you see him," challenged one of the four men sitting around a wooden table. The air was stale and stunk of garlic from their afternoon meal. At their backs and stacked around them were boxes and barrels of stored goods stolen from people under threats of pain and death. Sacks of coinage were also packed into several wooden boxes, the price of not being terrorized by the Sujins. Business was good for them these days, and the men guarding this storehouse filled with their retirement money all believed that their treasures should be moved out of the city. The question was where, and who would bring the subject up with Two Knife?

"Don't think I will?" Bar Bar growled. He always had his mouth open, and never breathed through his nose. Scars etched into his face and bare arms made him look truly formidable. "Don't think I will? I'm not `fraid of that punce. Smash his face from one side to the other, I would. I will, too, if he don't get here soon enough."

"Then I'll remind you when he gets here," the man threw out. They called him Kutlass, and he liked it. His real name was Kut Lasstur, and he liked to carve his name into the chests of captured Jackals when he had them handy. Sunjans were nosier and nowhere near as defiant. "I'll say just what you just said, and then I'll stand back and make bets."

"He won't say a word," a leopard of a man hissed, picking at his fingernails. His name was Rule, and he killed as often as one might eat fruit. "Bar Bar's all talk, s`all."

"Not a word," the last man said, sitting across from the speaker. His name was Sutoar. He was a Sujin, but in truth, the rank meant little to him. He wanted to squeeze as much wealth from the populace of Sunja as he could before leaving the city forever. He cared nothing for the king, even less for the populace, and wondered what it would be like to kill another Sujin. He had killed plenty of Jackals, as his companions had while on the front, but never had he been able to cut the throat of one trained and conditioned for war as he was. The Jackals' strength lay in their numbers and ferocity. The Sujins' strength lay in their order and skill at arms. In one way, he realized he was a lot like Rusk the Two Knife, who was forever searching for the next test, the next challenge, to prove to himself and others that he really was as good as he told everyone. Sutoar wondered if a Sujin would be as easy as a Jackal. He hoped he would find out one day.

"Oh, I'll tell him," Bar Bar said, breathing through his mouth. The others were used to the noise, and didn't make jests of the big man for his habit. As much as they threw jokes at Bar Bar, none, save perhaps Sutoar, would dare push him too far to anger him. Bar Bar liked to break bones in battle, with his boots. It had given him a fearsome reputation amongst the ranks of Sujins. Men around him were glad he was fighting on their side. "I'll tell him. See if I don't."

Sutoar scratched at his neck and the abundant stubble growing there. "I'll be seein' then."

"I'll forgive them if they bring us something to eat or drink," Rule said, as he studied one fingernail and then the other. "Getting hungry. And thirsty. Some mead would be good."

"I hate the shite," Kutlass said simply.

"Then you can give me yours," Rule told him, rooting at something underneath one nail.

"I'll sell you mine," Kutlass said, bored.

"Hmm," Rule grunted. "You will, eh?"

"Kutlass'd sell his children," Sutoar said with a sour grin, meaning it.

"Sold `em, already," Kutlass said. "Daughters, too. All fifteen."

"Been busy with the sheep, have you?" Rule asked with a straight face, making Sutoar snort in amusement.

"You keep leavin' your wives alone," Kutlass replied smoothly. This time Sutoar guffawed, making Rule look at him over the edge of his thumbnail. Sutoar quieted. Rule was unpredictable at best. Since being away from the front, he had picked up the odd amusement of luring in children with promises of sweet fruit before slapping them as hard as he could to frighten them off. Bar Bar sometimes joined in with this sport. Sutoar believed he could take one of the Sujins, but he would only then have to kill the other. Not that it bothered him, he just didn't want to clean up the mess of two dead men afterwards.

"Someone's comin," Bar Bar announced at the window. "Just the one," he wheezed, and went to the only door to the place.

"Probably Turr. He went for something to eat," Kutlass assumed. Turr had a hole in the back of his neck when it came to food.

Bar Bar placed his hard face to the surface of the wood and strained to hear. He intended to yank the door open when whoever was outside got close enough. He liked scaring people when he had the chance. He listened and slowly grinned when he heard boots on the landing outside. His grin became wider when he threw the door open and roared.

The roar died in his throat when he beheld a stranger holding a shortsword. Alwan stabbed him once, then twice. He grabbed the big man by the shoulder and pushed him to the side. The Cavalier stepped inside as if easing into a crowded room. Bar Bar's bleeding carcass crashed to the floor, stunning the three men sitting around their once pleasant table. In the stillness, Alwan closed the door behind him and marked them all with his black eyes.

"I'll let one live," he told them all, "to tell me what I want to know."

Rule's eyes nearly popped out of his head. Sutoar was already on his feet, his blade out. A stream of curses spewed from Kutlass. All three moved around the table and went for Bar Bar's killer.

Alwan rushed them.

Sutoar's sword came up and parried Alwan's first thrust, but the Cavalier stepped in close to the Sujin and rammed his fist into the man's nose. Sutoar's eyes squeezed shut in pain and he buckled backwards, throwing himself away from his attacker. Alwan let him go. He darted forwards and met Rule head on. The lean Sujin slashed at his head. Alwan jerked back and grinned at the man. Rule came on with a snarl, exposing a mouth of broken teeth. He swiped at the Cavalier's head again, and again, Alwan stepped back just out of reach. However, now he was wary of Kutlass approaching from his right. The Sujin poised his sword for a thrust from the shoulder.

"Stupid bugger," Kutlass purred. "Comin' in here all alone. You know who we are? We're Sujins! We're the king's own butchers! And by Saimon's blazing ass, you'll know it before the night's done."

Rule slashed again, forcing Alwan back to a wall of wooden boxes. The man grinned evilly. "Looks scared to me, Kut!"

"He does," Kutlass agreed, face full of dark intent. He crept closer like a hunting spider. "You just relax now. We won't bleed you dead right away."

Rule's sword flashed again. Alwan flicked it away with his own blade. Behind the two men, the third man was getting to his feet, holding his nose and giving his head a furious shake.

"What's yer name, after all?" Kutlass said in a sly voice, edging in closer. "You can tell—"

When Rule's sword snaked out once more, Alwan swatted it away from the man's body and stepped inside his guard. He spun on his heel and took Rule across the throat in one fountaining gasp. Blood fanned out across the dusty floor. Alwan kept spinning. He caught the thrust of Kutlass' sword and arched it into the floor. The man jumped back, sword coming up to guard, but Alwan beat it aside and cut the man's shoulder. The Sujin could not react fast enough to the Cavalier's fine movements. Kutlass got his blade up and watched his quarry with dangerous eyes. Scowling, Alwan wasted no more time on the brute. He slashed and twisted, cutting off two of the man's fingers. Kutlass cringed, his guard dropped, and the Sujin was suddenly as exposed as a naked baby boy to a winter storm. Alwan swooped in and cut the man's left arm. Then he cut the right shoulder. Then he nicked Kutlass' wrist of his sword arm and drew a fine bloody line up the left side of his face. Kutlass' eyes bulged with insult and agony. He sucked in air for a barrage of curses, but Alwan would have none of it. He stabbed him through the middle and pulled his sword free before the Sujin dropped to his knees. Baring his teeth, Kutlass struggled to speak. It began as a growl scraping from his contorted lips and it grew in volume.

Alwan took the man's head half off with one razor swipe. Whatever the maggot's final words were, he had no time to listen to them.

"You bastard!" Sutoar roared. He stomped after Alwan, meaning to gut the man where he stood. He threw a series of sword thrusts and slashes and feints at his companions' killer, swearing and hollering all the while. Alwan turned them all away. When Sutoar paused for wind to fuel his next barrage, Alwan dropped to a knee and sliced the man's right foot away at the ankle. Sutoar crashed to the floor, landing on his side. Alwan stomped down on the man's sword arm, feeling it break. Sutoar reached upwards with a hand hooked into a claw, going for his attacker's groin. Alwan backhanded the man, hitting him square in the nose once more, this time with the pommel of his sword. Sutoar dropped back, eyes open but unseeing and glazed.

A breath left him, and Alwan stood over the man, surveying his work. His eyes ran over the valuables hoarded around him, and he wondered just how long such a thing had been going on. These Sujins had established a lucrative trade in terror, it seemed, and he badly wanted to tell Bloor of it. However, first he needed a little more information, and then he wanted to do something that perhaps he had never done before in his life.

At his feet, Sutoar groaned. His smashed nose was a mess. His head moved just barely, but Alwan could see the man was regaining his senses. The Sujin was tough, which was unlucky for him. It had been a long, long time since Alwan got to ply pain to one that could handle it.

Alwan asked his questions, and before he died, Sutoar screamed out the answers.

36

When Alwan had finished, Bloor's first reaction was silence. He scratched at the back of his head, considering the tale, and then sighed with the new burden. "I wasn't expecting that."

Alwan grunted. Neither had he. It was like pulling on a tail in the dirt, thinking it was a worm, and discovering you really had a dragon. "What should we do then?"

"I don't know," Bloor admitted. "Never thought I'd hear of a group of Sujins terrorizing the very people they took an oath to protect. And you say the leader's name is Rusk?"

"Rusk the Two Knife," Alwan said. "Apparently he's a Koor."

This impressed Bloor. "A Koor?" he wanted to go out and start hunting for this man himself. The idea of Sunja's own violating their code and then profiting from it burned his guts. "Does it go any further than him?"

Alwan looked doubtful. "I don't know. I got no other name. The man died soon after and I busied myself with rounding up whoever I could find outside."

"Why?" Bloor asked, his brow creasing in puzzlement.

"They had a lot stashed away in that one house," Alwan said. "I wanted to get it back to the people before I burned it to the ground."

Burned it to the ground and instructed the Sunjans to distribute the wealth amongst the people, while keeping it as secret as possible.

"This Rusk maggot might just be the ringleader of the whole pack. Maybe a hundred or so Sujins, maybe more. Bastards wounded on the front and brought back to Sunja, then taken off the lists of active warriors and written up as dead. This Two Knife knows someone who can fix the lists."

"Bribes," Bloor supposed.

Alwan agreed. "And he's convinced enough of his fellows to join him."

"The front is a dangerous place."

"But these are Sujins," Alwan pointed out. Even though he disliked the killers, it did not mean he didn't have any respect for them. The Five Klaws were composed of Sujins, and to a man they were iron-hard, razor-trained, and thought of as utterly loyal to the crown. Alwan was glad that Sunja had them, at least up until this day. The thought of a group of Sujins feeding on Sunjan citizens made his stomach uneasy. "Lord Maullus and Lord Winter will be poisoned with this news," he predicted, knowing full well how much pride the old war hounds put into the ranks. "Even now, these bastards are hunting for the one that burned down their storehouse," Alwan tapped his chest. "Two Knife's got enough to make me think twice about going to Lord Maullus or Winter. Who knows who these bastards are? And if we find this Two Knife and kill him, who's to say he hasn't got someone to just step in and take his place? If memory serves me right, Sujins can be right vengeful bastards. We'd have to hunt down every man involved in this outfit."

Bloor shook his head. "Dangerous. And doubtful we'll get them all."

"Right, and then we and whoever else started rounding them up would forever be looking over our shoulders, and from our own Sujins, no less. As if the Jackals weren't bad enough." Alwan did not like the situation. He disliked the odds or the idea of a Sujin blade finally gutting him. The idea that any of them could be part of Rusk's band of killers made his paranoia rise like the fur on a cat's back. "So what should we do?"

"Sleep," Bloor said, glancing out his window before getting up and closing the shutter. He began massaging his temples. *First Morianna, and now this.* "Think on it more tomorrow. No one saw you?"

"Only the men in the city. And it was dark until I lit the storehouse up."

"Why did you do that?"

Alwan shrugged. "Seemed right at the time. I think I'll be leaving in the morning however. As quietly as possible."

"Where?" Bloor asked.

"Not sure. Maybe the forest. I'll feel more comfortable with the brush around me rather than brick and stone. Too many people in here. Too many directions for a strike to come from. Out there, if anyone comes looking for me, they'll find me when I want them to, on my terms."

"I doubt they'll live long enough to find out what your terms are," Bloor said.

"Probably not," Alwan said, "but better this way than trying to ferret out a nest of traitors man by man. You'd never be sure you got them all."

That thought rang of truth in Bloor's head. In dealing with rats, it wasn't always best to find the nest and burn it. Even then, chances were there would be some stragglers, and they might do nothing or they might seek revenge. Both Bloor and Alwan had lived long enough not to gamble on such odds. It would not be enough to destroy the nest. Something would be needed to draw out the entire pack. Something sweet enough to bring them all out into the open, where there would be no doubt as to their destruction. Bait of the most irresistible kind, but what?

Thoughts blurred through Bloor's head and he struggled to stem the flow. "You've given me enough to think on for a year," he said. Alwan was already spreading out a blanket on the floor. He lay down with his sheathed shortsword on his chest and closed his eyes. It looked as if the man had died, and Bloor figured that, for Alwan, it would be as close to a peaceful ending as he would ever get.

"In the morning then," the man said wearily, already halfway to sleep. "Seddon knows I could use a good sleep. These past few days I felt like I was back on the front with the Jackals."

Bloor lay down on his pallet and stared up at the shadows of the ceiling. He did not hear Alwan's comment, for he was already thinking hard on what would be needed to solve this trouble with the rogue Sujins. He heaved a sigh. *Morianna.* The feel of her name in his mind brought about a feeling of loss, and it confused him. She was not lost, she was only promised to be married. So why did he feel as if he had lost her? Even more worrisome was why he even cared. Another sigh, and with this one, he began falling into that comfortable pool of sleep, a last thought whispering against the cozy darkness.

Things had become very interesting in a very short time.

Morning lit the little room up with grey half-light and long shadows. Bloor woke and summoned a servant, instructing him to fetch some food. The boy, a young lad with a mop of the straightest hair hanging over a round face, returned shortly with a platter. Bloor took the food and placed it on the table. When Alwan woke, he immediately helped himself to the bread, cheese, and fruit, gulping it down as if he were a starving gull. Watching him, Bloor lost his appetite. He rubbed at the dark rings underneath his eyes, stretched, feeling his back crack, and wondered why he didn't feel more rested.

"You aren't eating?" Alwan asked him through a full mouth.

"No."

Alwan went back to eating. They kept the conversation to a minimum, agreeing that Alwan would continue his search for information on the Sujin called Rusk the Two Knife. They agreed that Alwan would delay his departure from the city for a little while. He would continue to gather information, although he would listen only, with no action being taken. They did not want these Sujins scurrying for cover from the hunters, they wanted them to be relaxed and unaware of them Let them think the attack on the storeroom was only a one-time occurrence. Allow the vermin to go back to being lazy until it was time to draw out the entire pack of them.

Alwan believed his identity was unknown and that he should be safe from being discovered. Even if he was, he would make certain that he died before being taken as a prisoner by a traitorous lot of Sujins. Sunja was becoming a front of a different kind, a kind where forces moved in the shadows, without sound, and stabbed as quick and as final as a knife across a throat. Sujins could smell blood, but Bloor believed that because they were Sujins, and believing their own vicious reputation, they would be thinking that their attackers would be long gone from the city, rather than foolishly staying. They would search anyway, and when they did, Alwan would obtain the information he needed and get word to Bloor.

They parted ways without wishing luck to each other. They were veterans of so many missions that luck no longer was needed to be called upon. Luck was as indifferent as a cat, and neither Bloor nor Alwan had anything to attract its attention. Bloor hurried to his post, mulling over what Alwan would find and how it came to be that a core of Sujins no longer had Sunja's interests at heart. It was unbelievable. Sujins were trained to die in battle for Sunja, but not before taking a fair share of her foes with them. They looked forward to perishing on the field for their country, or so the stories surrounding the hellpups went, and yet this Two Knife had managed to gather around him a group of Sujins not so inclined. In one way, Bloor could almost respect that independence, but when it fed and grew upon the suffering of Sunjan's common folk, he could not allow it to live.

They would not be brought to justice. They would have to be killed to a man, and Rusk the Two Knife's head would have to be hung in a public place. Curiously enough, Bloor found himself not liking that image, and he struggled to reason out why.

He made his way through the palace, dipping his head in morning greetings to servants that he once ignored. Though his heart was not into it, Morianna had taught him that some degree of respect to these people was not a bad thing. That notion alone struck him as ironic when he remembered her as a child and the terror she caused the people around her. Now, it pleased the older Morianna when he did so, and because it pleased her, he continued doing it. He liked pleasing her. He liked seeing her smile. There was a childlike quality in it that was not there when she was a girl.

A surprise waited for him when he arrived. Two large royal Axemen stood with pole arms almost touching the arched ceiling. Bloor slowed to a stop and inspected the two warriors, wondering why no one had bothered informing him of this little change.

"Why are you here?" he asked, though he already knew the answer.

"By the command of his majesty, we are to ensure the safety of the princess up until her marriage to the prince of Marrn," one of the Axemen answered promptly.

"Am I replaced then?" Bloor asked. The man who had spoken looked at the Cavalier.

"No, Lord Bloor. We are only an addition, and are under your command."

Bloor somehow doubted that, but he said nothing. The words were spoken to smooth over any ruffled feathers Bloor might have over not being notified of the change in guard. He wondered how many more surprises were waiting for him in the days to come, and once again, Tarco was no where nearby. No doubt he crept off when the sun began to peek into the windows. The man's behavior burned Bloor, and he wished he could be free of him. Tarco placed too much faith in having his father's high position protect him.

The replacements for the night Axemen arrived a beat after Bloor. He nodded at the two hulking warriors. They relieved the night watch with only the barest of acknowledgement of the Cavalier. The two impassive Axemen assigned to the night left to find their quarters. Bloor waited until they were out of sight before addressing the newcomers.

"Who is in command here?" Bloor asked them quietly.

There was a silence from the two new Axemen. Bloor was already missing the nightwatch. One of the Axemen finally spoke. "You are, Lord Bloor."

"Then you will salute me as soon as you set your pig eyes on me. Do you understand?"

The eyes of the one that had spoken widened. He did not like this Cavalier's tone at all.

Bloor could care less. He stepped up to the Axemen, coming up to the big warrior's chin and glaring at the man.

The axeman exhaled and set his gaze on the wall ahead. "My apologies, Lord Bloor. It will not happen again."

Bloor could not discern if the man disliked saying the words, but he backed away from him in acceptance of the apology. There was no need to further chew him out for the slight, not now, but he would give that and more if the man repeated the mistake ever again in his presence.

"Is that you out there, Bloor?"

Morianna's muffled voice coming from behind the thick door drew his attention. He stepped up to it. "It is, my Princess."

"Go on down to breakfast without me. I've no appetite this morning. I might eat something a little later."

Bloor's face drew tight in concern. "You didn't eat anything last night, my Princess."

"Lindee brought me something last night. I ate in here with her. It's alright. I have a little chicken left with me if I change my mind."

Bloor glanced at the stony features of the axeman on his right.

"Just tell Lindee for me, please," Morianna spoke again, and then nothing more.

Bloor stared at the arched doorway as if he could see her crouched behind it. He did not like her decision, but he would not insist on anything in front of the elite guardsmen of her father. No doubt anything he said here would be heard by the king later in the day. "As you wish," he relented.

The door did not speak back. Even more worrying, Morianna did not thank him. In the short time they had been reunited, her incessant thanking of everyone for even the most basic of gestures, services, or items almost made him snap an oath off in her presence. He did not, of course, and held his annoyance. She was a princess after all, and again he reminded himself of how she used to be when she was a child.

"Watch everything," he instructed the two Axemen. They dipped their helms upon hearing the command, satisfying Bloor. He left for the kitchen. As he neared, the smells and sound of sizzling bacon reached him. He regretted eating such a skimpy breakfast with Alwan.

"Good morning," he said to Lindee as he entered.

"Good morning," Lindee chimed, waiting to hear Morianna's voice. When she didn't, she popped into view from around a corner and looked at Bloor. "Where is she?"

"In her room. Good morning, Karl," he greeted the man sitting at the table. He was devouring a bacon strip sandwich, and Bloor caught him with both cheeks dangerously puffed out. Showing manners Bloor would not have thought a pig handler would have, Karl covered his mouth before nodding a good morning in return. Bloor liked Karl better than the Axemen he left behind, and he sat down at the table directly across from the man.

"What's that?" Bloor asked with mild interest, indicating the sandwich. His shyness around the kitchen had disappeared.

"That is Karl's own creation," Lindee spoke for him. "Seems bacon and eggs just isn't good enough for him anymore. No, he wanted the bacon to be on two pieces of buttered bread."

Karl muttered something from behind his hand that Bloor could not make out.

"Oh, be quiet," Lindee snapped at him without any anger. "Just eat. The faster you eat, the faster you can return to your new pigs."

Karl nodded that he would do just that. He nodded excitedly at Bloor.

"Oh, shut up about them new pigs," Lindee's voice cracked again. "All I heard from you yesterday. Today better not be the same. And then the news of Anna getting married. Oh, sweet Seddon above," the little cook moaned.

She placed a plate full of eggs, bacon, and bread before Bloor. "Here. Eat. Before he takes it to his damn precious pigs. You'd think he forgot where bacon comes from."

"I didn't forget," Karl was finally able to say after he swallowed. "But *these* pigs—"

Lindee held up a hand. She had heard enough of pigs. She sat down heavily at the table, and placing both elbows on the surface, resting her face in her hands. She gave Karl a hard look, but it softened when she turned to Bloor as he poured apple cider from a pitcher. He was going to stretch his stomach in eating the food before him, and it bothered him not in the least.

"How is she?" Lindee asked him as he was about to take the first bite. Bloor clamped his mouth shut and lowered his fork.

"Who?" he asked.

"Who?" she said, exasperated. "*Who* do you think? Have you forgotten about her already? She's not dead, you know. You're the one who's been guarding her with your life for the past few months. Remember now? Yes, so I see. That's *who!* Really Bloor! Who! When I want an answer like that, I'll ask this one right here," and she jabbed a finger in Karl's surprised direction. Karl didn't think he gave answers like that and would have said something, except his mouth was again full of bacon, and he was raised not to speak while eating. His chewing slowed, and he kept his eyes downcast, lest Lindee turn her considerable wrath upon him.

"Now I'll ask the question again, and forget about what just happened," Lindee said. How men could be so stupid at times was beyond her. "And you should be embarrassed. What do you think she would say if I went to her and told her of what you just said? I wonder what *who* would say to that? She'd be pretty damned hurt if you ask me. Pretty damned hurt. Now, *how* is *Morianna?* You know, the princess that you are sworn to protect with your life? I suppose I had you wrong all along. You really don't care one wick about her, do you? Well, now's certainly the time to discover this. No wonder she isn't down here with you this morning. I wouldn't want to be down here either with you. I don't want to be around you now!"

Bloor no longer had an appetite. He set his fork down and waited for Lindee's wind to abate. It was a violent storm, to be sure, but something told the Cavalier that he had seen nothing yet. He studied her for a moment, his cheeks feeling a pinch of chagrin, but he did not say a word back at her. She was right, after all.

He cleared his throat. "I don't know how she is," he said quietly. "I haven't seen her since yesterday."

Lindee watched him. "Some color in your face after all. Good. It's good to see you aren't a complete rock. You don't know what she's about. No surprise really. Just thought I'd ask. I can tell you one thing though, this isn't easy for her. Not easy in the least. If roles were reversed, well…" she fumed for a moment, and let the thought go unfinished. She almost made a very large mistake that Morianna would have disowned her for making, but it was obvious that this Cavalier did not know anything at all when it was right there before his eyes. Her face swished to the side, and she chastised herself in a furious silence. Bloor watched her with interest for only a moment. He did not want to draw her attention for a second time, so he kept his mouth shut. It was a sound tactic, and he was good at it. He was not good at emotions, especially the emotions of a woman. He felt that Lindee knew that, and if he told her such a thing, it would seem only a cheap and flimsy excuse. Whatever else was bothering her, he decided that it was more than just Morianna's arranged marriage, but he did not know how to approach the subject with Lindee, so he continued keeping his mouth shut.

"Not easy for any of us," Lindee finished, gazing hard enough at the worn surface of the table's wood to make it burn. "Damn that man! Damn him to Saimon's hell! If there is a place for kings there, I hope Juhn gets some very special attention."

Karl stopped chewing entirely. He paled fish-belly white when Lindee snarled her curse. She could not have picked a worse time to curse than in the company of a Cavalier. He had heard stories of Cavaliers and Axemen beating commoners senseless for such actions, and that was if they were lucky. If they weren't lucky, the offenders would be dragged off to face a month in the king's dungeons. If someone wanted to curse the king, then by all means, they should be given *reason* enough to do so. While this Cavalier had softened in their company, becoming almost a shade of being a companion, he was still a Cavalier, and sworn to defend the king.

Karl swallowed what he had in his mouth without tasting it, "She did not mean it, Lord Bloor!" he spat out as the ball of bacon and bread painfully stretched his throat.

"Oh, yes I did. Every damned word. Every damn word, you hear? I meant it all. As a matter of fact..." not one for holding her peace, the woman let out a barrage of unlady-like curses the likes of which neither Bloor nor Karl had heard in a very long time. Her string of oaths was powerful enough that Karl slumped back in his chair, figuring her to be dead. The Cavalier would take her head, and then he would no doubt follow her, as he secretly loved Lindee and would strike out at Bloor for killing her. Life without her would simply not be life.

However, Bloor did nothing. The man had stopped eating and waited until Lindee spent her wrath to the point where she simply had no energy left to continue. She sat with her back straight, looking at Bloor with two very red eyes that brimmed with tears but did not fall, waiting for his justice. He remained seated quietly, unmoving. Lindee glared at him, daring him now to do something, and her red cheeks quivered ever so slightly. Karl held his breath, wondering if he could get to a frying pan if a fight broke out.

Bloor thought about Morianna. He looked down at his now unwanted breakfast, knowing full well that there were men on the front that would pay dearly for such a feast. He then looked into Lindee's waiting face.

"I'm sorry," he said quietly.

"I'm sorry too," she said back, wiping at her eyes with an open palm, realizing now that the man was not going to do anything to her for her words against the king. For that, she felt she owed him something. She cleared her throat. "That woman is my friend if ever I had one. I know that there were times in the beginning when I doubted it, when I had other friends telling me to be mindful around her. You didn't need to tell me to be careful around her. I heard the stories from my mother. The Morianna of younger years drove my poor mother Sera to an early grave, you know. A very early grave. When I got the request to—and this was a request mind you—to appear before her, I was going to spit in her eye and curse her to Saimon's hell as well. Revenge for my dear mother who slaved for her and neglected her own children and husband because she was told to. The coin that she earned wasn't near enough for that, and she should've earned a fortune for the torture and abuse she suffered under Morianna the girl. You know as I do what she was like in the early years. Seddon only knows how my mother did it, but she did and she died for it in the end. I wasn't going to end up like my mother, and I was going to tell that to our bitch of a princess.

"When I met Morianna, we were in her study and she dismissed the guards around her. Only Alora was there with her. Well, let me tell you the surprise I felt when she asked me about my mother and when I told her she died because of her. She cried hard enough that I thought that she was going to shrivel up and die herself. And then came the begging for forgiveness. I'll never hear a princess beg for forgiveness ever again in my life, let alone *my* forgiveness. She threw herself at my feet, and I told her I couldn't give it, that the only person that could was no longer living. She told me then she would earn my forgiveness at least, starting with offering me my mother's job in the kitchen. Pay much higher than five of us put together, and freedoms that would never see me away from my family like my mother. She swore to me that she would earn my forgiveness, that she had changed, and you know something? She did. She got it. It didn't happen all at once, but as I came to know her, I saw how much she had changed and wanted to change, to put all the misery she caused in the past behind her, and to make it up to the people that she felt suffered because of her. She changed, and over time, so did I."

Lindee sniffed. "It's hard to be angry at a person when that person is trying so hard to help you. We became friends. I have a princess for a friend. I dare say I even have a sister in her. Yes, I would, Karl," she directed at him, when he rubbed at his forehead in embarrassment. "A sister to me, and I think my mother would have forgiven her five times over for all the things she has done for me and the other people around her, even the people in Sunja itself. And she still goes on, trying to convince everyone that she has changed, feeling so much guilt for how she was when she was younger. In my opinion, Morianna's paid her debts and she's running up a good size of credit with a lot of people. But now she has to repay her father for her efforts, which, when it came to the Sunjans, he didn't know about. They said this was a wedding to bond Marrn to Sunja? Well, that may be, but it's also Juhn's punishment for her spending his money and making people's lives so much better without telling him. He found out about her handouts to the poor and he didn't like it one bit. That's what he's like. He cares nothing for the likes of us or anyone around him. Even you."

Bloor wanted to challenge her on that, but he couldn't. He had seen the king firsthand. He had to admit that the man did not look like a person to easily bestow comfort where it was needed. He looked more like a man that had forgotten what it was like to show kindness to his people, or even his family.

With that, Lindee pushed herself away from the table. A terrible sadness flowed through her, and though she struggled to stop it, she succeeded in only making her shoulders shudder. She wanted to be away from these men, not wanting them to see her cry. She left the kitchen to find a place much more private so that she could wail in peace.

Left in Bloor's presence, Karl felt grossly out of place. He fidgeted, like a child brought indoors and forced to listen to adult talk when he really wanted to be outside in the sun. He tried to think of a valid excuse to give the Cavalier before the man decided that it was best to haul them both off to the dungeons for insulting the king.

"I, um..." his hands did a soft cadence on the table, "I have to..." unaccustomed to fabricating lies, he failed miserably. "The stables. You know. Well. Then. Goodbye."

He got up and left. Bloor did not notice him go. He continued sitting and staring, and thinking.

37

Morning melted away into an early afternoon. Lindee returned and ignored Bloor, who still sat the table pondering many different things. The food before him was untouched and cold. She removed his plate and eating utensils and did not bother making any attempt at conversing with the man. Bloor did the same. He had his elbows on the table and his fingers, laced together, touched his lips at solemn intervals. He did not notice Lindee moving about the kitchen. He thought of things he never thought of before. He thought of feelings and how a good many of them never entered his mind until today. He couldn't really describe some of them, as he really wasn't sure what they were. Some concerned the harsh memories of being at war with Nordun. Some were directed at the indifference of the king. Many more thoughts swirled, drew, and colored images of Morianna. They slipped in and around the little girl he once despised and transformed them into the woman he saw in a most wondrous gown; a woman now given up to a stranger from a strange land in the name of duty.

"I said…"

His eyes flickered in Lindee's direction. She was grateful he heard her the second time. She was ready to hit him with a pot. Seddon above, the man could think deep! "When did Morianna say she would be coming down?"

Bloor gazed upon the table. "Later."

"Well, it's getting on to lunch now."

He studied the woman as if she suffered from dementia. Then he realized she was right. He had been sitting in the same spot all morning, and Morianna had not appeared. Had she implied that he was waiting for Morianna to come down? Was he waiting for her?

"I'll go get her," he said, rising.

Thoughts now churning out ghosts and smoke, he made his way back to Morianna's chambers. When he turned the final corner, his throat seized up and his heart froze. The two Axemen he left at her door were nowhere in sight. Slowing down, he approached the unguarded door, his hand finding the hilt of his shortsword, There was no sound coming from within or without, and Bloor's uneasiness grew with each heartbeat. He paused at the door and wondered if he should knock or not.

Then it opened.

A lady servant stepped out of it, small and young and with a shock of blonde hair falling loosely about her shoulders. She looked up and jumped, seeing the balled fist of the Cavalier just above her head. She was familiar to Bloor, but he could not remember her name. "My Lord," she said.

"Where is the princess?" Bloor demanded, not having the patience for anything else.

The servant before him quivered as if she were barefoot on barbs. "She and the Axemen left," she blurted out.

"Where?"

"She said to the kitchen."

"She didn't *come* to the kitchen."

"Oh," the woman's face drooped, while her eyes only stared up at Bloor.

"When did you get here?" he asked in a hard voice.

"An hour ago. I was cleaning."

Bloor's lips pursed and he whirled away to storm off down the corridor, leaving the woman behind and relieved that she was still alive. He went through the palace in spurts of running and double stride, looking everywhere as he went along and interrogating anyone crossing his path. Another worry sparked in the back of his head while he searched, that being the rumors the servants might start. After all, wasn't he supposed to be at Morianna's side at all times? He could defend himself with the truth, that she ordered him to leave her and to eat breakfast, but the thought turned his mood sour. He should have been right there the moment she opened the doors, right beside the Axemen. His stomach knotted. The Axemen! The king would know! Bloor loosed a mental growl of anguish. He focused on tracking down the missing princess and her bodyguards. *An hour. Missing for an hour. She could be anywhere!* His features becoming pensive, he moved with undisguised urgency until he exited the palace and found himself on the royal grounds.

Scents of green lured him towards the secluded gardens and he went down the immaculate white stone paths. Moving quietly, he spied one of the two Axemen in the path just ahead, his silvery hide draped in a dark cloak. The man took note of the Cavalier approaching him and nodded behind his great pole axe. Bloor forced his heart to stop racing as he neared the man.

"Where is the princess?" he said, not hearing the note of concern in his voice, the same note the Axeman picked up on. The great warrior stood silent for a moment.

"She is there," he told Bloor, flicking his head in the direction further down the path. Bloor looked and immediately moved past the axeman, who moved in turn like some great elephant of war, wondering, with interest, where the little man was heading.

Bloor found her in a grove, alone. She sat on a pearly white bench, surrounded by leaves of color and blooms. A wind blew softly, shooing away the dead foliage. Morianna sat looking ahead, her hands in her lap, her head tilting to the side. Her brown eyes were filled with thoughts of mystery, and as Bloor neared her, he could see that they were not happy ones. She was drawn and pale and as fixed as any of the white marble statues decorating the garden, and she looked so very much alone. Bloor had seen the same expression on the faces of dying men waiting for the breath that would be their last, wondering what it would feel like when their body refused to draw another, wondering if they would know when it did.

Morianna looked defeated. It was a stark contrast to how he usually saw her: smiling, *glowing*. He suddenly felt empty inside. She looked lost, vulnerable, and despite all of his experience and skills as a Cavalier, Bloor felt just as helpless realizing that there was not one thing he could to comfort her or—dare he think it—*save* her. He caught himself then. Of course he could save her, but that would mean that her life was in peril, which it clearly was not. She was only to marry a complete stranger for the greater purpose of securing the new alliance between the two kingdoms, and thus saving her people. This was the way of kings and queens and princes and princesses. She had no need of being saved or rescued. However, even as the words formed in his head, his lip curled up and said otherwise. Why was he even thinking this way? She was lost to him, yet why was he thinking of her as being *lost* to him? She was never *his* to begin with. She was her own person, her own wonderful person who could not seem to do enough for those around her.

Until now. Until her father married her off.

There was nothing Bloor could do to prevent that. Seeing the desolation on her face, he wished he could do something for her. To whisk her away from Marrn and the wrath of her father, if either King Juhn or the Prince of Marrn would care at all. Would they care? Didn't he hear that the prince already had wives?

He stepped closer to her and snapped a thin branch that the groundskeepers had failed to remove. The sound made Morianna look up; Bloor winced. Of all the wounds he ever carried with him from the front, or any of the battlefields he ever traveled, this was the only time he openly showed his discomfort. However, Morianna smiled warmly at him and swept the hair from her cheek with one hand. "How long have you been there?"

"Not long," Bloor answered her, stepping closer. "Lindee sent me to find you," he lied.

"Oh, I see. Breakfast is it?"

"Breakfast," he confirmed. "Although it could be called lunch soon enough."

"Yes," Morianna said. "Perhaps it's best I wait for lunch then. I'm still not hungry. And," she sighed, "I suppose I should be losing some weight. At least make the attempt. My wedding dress will be here soon, I imagine. I'll have to try and fit into it, and this," she patted her tummy, "won't help."

Bloor straightened and looked about. He didn't like the sound of that. It kept him quiet.

"What would you do, Bloor?"

He blinked at her in confusion. The question, once again, caught him off guard. "I'm sorry?"

Morianna stood up. "What would you do if you were told by your father to marry someone you don't know? I mean, I don't even think he was personally introduced to me or not! I can't remember his name beyond his title! And yet, I'm to marry this person in a land I've never visited to become part of his harem, it seems. What would you do if you were placed in my position? I would like to know."

Later, he would replay the entire conversation in his mind, seeing again her round face, her dark eyes, and hearing the question posed on the air. He would be much more insightful, more understanding, and supply a far superior answer to the original one.

"I'd obey," the Cavalier said, clenching his jaw even as he said it. Saying the words he knew she did not want to hear.

Morianna's face wavered for a moment and then fell. Her gaze fell to the ground.

"Yes," she said eventually, but not sounding convinced in the least. "I suppose so. I will obey, of course."

This made Bloor's back stiffen.

"It's for the people," she went on. "For the ones I couldn't do anything for. It'll help the ones back in the public square as well. I didn't help them there, did I Bloor? I thought I was by giving them things, giving them food, but I was also helping those men. I ignored those men. I ignored those people. They needed more help than I was prepared to give, and I ignored them. But, I suppose if I get married, I'll perhaps save them all from the Jackals. Marrn will support us in the war, and our people will be saved. Isn't that right? Won't they benefit from it the most?"

Bloor chose to remain silent at the worse possible time and he cursed himself for it. He drew a breath to speak, but Morianna froze him when she looked into his face, waiting for him to say something. For the life of him, there was nothing that could he could think of to ease her mind, or so he thought.

She began to look away again.

"I," he lurched, and her eyes fixed on him in an instant. The need in those eyes startled him, and he lost his tongue once more. "I...think we should be getting back."

Morianna's face became as stone then. She glanced past her guardian. "I suppose so. What's Lindee having for lunch, then?" she asked without any real interest.

"Breakfast," Bloor said.

"Oh, still breakfast is it?"

He cringed. "Lunch. My apologies."

Morianna smiled at him. "Confused over what meal it is, Bloor?" she said and smiled, almost coyly. "You must have just as much on your mind as I do. But I'm really not interested in eating right now. I think I'll just stay here. You may stay as well, if you like."

The wind was crisp, but Bloor suddenly did not feel it. It might have been the lick of a blizzard. "Alright," he said. All at once, he felt very protective of this woman he had known for what seemed a very short time.

"I don't think anyone will harm me here," Morianna said. "Do you?"

Bloor thought of Alwan and a man called Rusk the Two Knife. There was rot at Sunja's heart. "No," he said. "Not while I draw breath."

"You'll protect me then?" Morianna's eyes were suddenly very wet.

Bloor did not hesitate. "I will."

Morianna blinked then, as if she had gone somewhere very dangerous and was only just now realizing it.

She lowered her eyes. "Yes. I know."

They returned to the kitchen area with the Axemen at their heels. Bloor and the Axemen waited outside, placing their backs to the wall while waiting for the princess to summon them. She sat at the table with Lindee, who was trying her best to coax some food into her. They became quiet for several moments, and Bloor again thought of goodbyes on the battlefield. The warm spirits once flowing from the kitchen were shut out this day. If he heard them crying, he would understand. He expected friends such as these to spill a few tears.

He was mildly surprised when they did not. Morianna emerged from the kitchen and walked back to her chambers with Bloor and the Axemen walking behind her. He only followed her for a short distance when she stopped and looked him in the eye.

"Walk beside me for once, won't you?"

Bloor did as she asked of him. They walked along in silence, the Cavalier's eyes scanning each nook and corner of the palace corridors, only vaguely aware of Morianna slipping in closer to him.

When she hooked an arm around his, he froze.

She looked up at him for a moment, uncertain of what to say. The rigidness in his face told her she had overstepped herself. "I'm sorry," issued from her lips. She continued on in a hurry, trying to reclaim the lost steps. Bloor followed her without a word, wondering what it was that had just happened. He dared not look back at the Axemen. What must they be thinking? He was both elated by her touch and crushed by his own awkward silence. It was another lost opportunity. He said not a word for the rest of the journey, and when they arrived at her door, Morianna went in alone, leaving her guardians outside.

The Axemen took up positions on either side of the door. Neither of them said a word about the incident in the corridor. Bloor waited a moment longer, wondering if they would so that he might exercise his command and bite a head off, but they kept their tongues. That suited him. He watched them both, unaware that he was glaring.

The sound of footsteps perked their ears, breaking Bloor's concentration. Alora appeared with servants at her sides and behind her. Two women carried a small ornate chest between them; dark wood and polished locks gleamed in the sparse light of the corridor. Alora gave a nod to Morianna's guards. Bloor moved as they came near, his hand already on the chamber's door.

"Thank you," Alora said as she and her servants went by. Bloor dipped his head and closed the portal behind them. He gave no further thought to the woman visiting the princess, knowing the reason why they were here. He did not want to think about what was inside the chest they carried, and so he concentrated on memories of the Nordun front.

At some point later in the day, the door opened behind him, and Bloor stepped alertly to the side.

"My Lord Bloor," Alora asked him, "would you come inside for a moment? We need your thoughts on something."

He bowed stiffly and went inside, closing the door behind. He would give as honest an opinion as possible, not suspecting in the least what it was he was about to comment on. The room was bright and smelled of rosemary. He once heard Alora say she preferred it as it promoted clear thinking. The walls and bed were draped in curtains of silk, a gossamer frosting that made Bloor think of white shores. Servants fluttered about the room as if the Cavalier were a hunter. They parted for him like wind blown reeds. Bloor did not notice anything else in the room at that moment, for standing in the center, on a raised platform sculpted from white, where a seamstress now backed away, stood Morianna, in a wedding gown that shined.

She stayed still, like something wild ready to bolt. Her dark eyes set upon Bloor nervously, wondering at what his reaction would be. Her hair had been tied back in a simple braid, exposing the whiteness of her flesh. Against the gown, it was cream on snow, begging to be touched, yet destined to melt if one did so. A faint dab of rose pink colored her high cheeks, and she struggled to keep her hands, clenching in and out of fists, at her sides.

Bloor had seen much horror in his life. His profession bathed in it. He had seen enough that even the most terrible of scenes, and he had witnessed a life's worth in the war with Nordun, failed to make him flinch anymore. However, seeing Morianna stand before him as she did now undid his stoic composure and made his mouth drop open ever so slightly, as if pausing for a breath. It was not the first time he had seen her dressed in such a manner, but the gown she wore to King Juhn's hall was a coarse sack compared to what she wore this moment.

I would marry her, his mind spoke then. *I would marry her this very instant if she would have me.* With that single thought, Bloor stood paralyzed in the radiance of the princess. He did not feel that by name what he thought was impossible, he only felt the explosion of warmth in his chest where the ice of his heart once chilled him day and night. It started from the center and burned outwards. He once heard of Cavaliers talking of riding the pleasures of smoked white lotus petals, and he thought maybe this would be as close to that forbidden sensation that he would ever get, except that this was so much better.

The silence of Bloor answered many questions in Alora's mind, as she gazed upon both the stunned figure of the Cavalier and the frozen princess on a pedestal. A scene from a fable, it occurred to her, and she read the look on both of their faces as clearly as anyone present in the room. One didn't have to have eyes to feel the flood of feeling coming from the warrior and the princess. Though she had only a plain face, attractive in its own way, it could be radiant at times. It was an attraction that Bloor felt for some time, but was unaware as to the hammer force it would smite him with, and how the weight of the blow would render him senseless.

A lock of hair fell across Morianna's face, and the picture was forever framed in Bloor's mind. It was in that moment, that precise *beat* of time, that he fell completely.

"You see," Alora spoke softly to Morianna, hiding her pleasure at Bloor's reaction. "He thinks the same."

Neither or them gave any inkling of hearing her.

Somewhere in his world, through the veils of silk in the room, Alora's voice reached him like an important echo. His eyes sharpened then, and his mouth clenched shut. The women about him watched with interest as whatever was gushing through the Cavalier was stemmed and relentlessly controlled. Alora felt she had just witnessed something incredibly rare.

"Don't you?" she directed at the man. Bloor looked at her uncertainly. "What do you think of her, Lord Bloor?" Alora asked with a hint of coyness to her voice. "Isn't she pretty?"

Bloor faltered and his eyes dropped to Morianna's feet. He shoved it from his mind. He thought of *pretty*. How could one tiny word describe the princess at this moment? No word spoken by the most seductive of voices could ever come close.

"Yes," he replied quietly, as if anything louder would bring the formidable Axemen charging in. As if anything more would shatter the spell weaving about both him and Morianna.

Then, the warmth once coursing through him like the most wondrous of music turned to acid, scalding enough for him to set his jaw as if he were gnawing through iron. A pretty *bride*. The prince of Marrn's bride. A man whom she did not even know the name of, let alone his character. Yet, his bride nonetheless. That one word, in a moment so powerfully pure, twisted into him like a poisoned dagger.

Bloor wanted to say she was a pretty bride, that she was far more than that to him, but for the life of him, his mouth would not open. He doubted if it would ever again.

Morianna gazed upon him and sensed the draw of him to her dissipate like steam in a rainstorm. She wanted to run to him. She wanted to throw her arms around his neck and cling to him. She wanted to bury her face in that space at the base of his neck.

She stayed right where she stood.

"That's all, Lord Bloor, thank you," Alora said, releasing him. When he did not immediately move, Alora knew right then that she had gone too far, but it was needed. Long had she spied Bloor watch the princess under the guise of being protective and indeed he was, but she could see that it was only a thin coating of ice on the deepest, saddest well of longing. She had seen the change in him now. Seddon above, a score of the blind could have seen it, before he sealed it up like uneven stitches in an ugly wound.

Composed now, Bloor bowed at the waist, not even looking at the bare feet of the princess peeking out from underneath the edges of her wedding gown. Morianna wanted to say something, but she did not know what. Instead, she watched him turn on his heel and march from the room, closing the door behind.

"Thank you, Bloor," she whispered to herself, feeling his name on her breath, knowing that the moment Alora and her servants left her, she would be saying the name over and over again, as she cried herself to sleep.

Alora, her back straight, looked upon the surface of the door for a time after it had been shut. Ever thoughtful, the lady turned to the woman she secretly loved as her own daughter.

"I believe he approves of you," she said.

The unhappiness in Morianna's eyes was all the princess could manage, and she regarded the gown she wore with a sad line of a mouth.

38

A day later, a pensive Bloor escorted his princess through the royal gardens once more. They walked along the white path, alone, having left the Axemen at the palace entrance. They were ordered to follow the princess' every move outside of the palace, but the king was not present this day when Morianna commanded them to stay where they were. She did not threaten them. She only looked at both of them as one whose time was very short. The princess and Bloor walked in silence until they came to a white marble bench. She sat down while he stood. With her legs slightly to one side and her hands in her lap, she looked into Bloor's face, her dark eyes searching for the same glow that was there only a day earlier, but Bloor looked away.

He still felt the acid burn of exposed feelings that should have remained secret to them both. He felt Morianna's gaze resting on his profile as though she were reaching out and touching him.

"Bloor," she said, breaking the silence. "You are my protector, correct?"

He never thought of it before, never realized it before, of how wonderful her voice sounded to him, like a light bell in a shade of summer.

He turned his face to hers. "I am that."

"You would kill for me?"

The words surprised him, and it showed on his face. Morianna had a gift of saying the most unexpected things. "Anyone," he began cautiously, "that sought to harm you. I would stop them."

"So you would kill for me?"

"Yes."

"Die for me?"

He was silent only for the briefest flicker of time. They had started this conversation before, it seemed to him, but it was never finished. "And die for you," he said. "It would be my honor."

"Oh please," she suddenly scoffed. "I've had enough of honor these past few days. Enough to make me sick to my stomach for a year. If you say something like that once more, I'll vomit right here."

That made Bloor's brow furrow. Vomit was a word that did not seem right coming from a princess. Then again, Morianna was unique that way.

"My apologies, my Lady," he offered.

"And what did I tell you about calling me that when no one is around? Didn't I tell you that it was perfectly fine to use my name when no one was around? Didn't I? You can, you know. I won't let anything happen to you if someone overheard. I can protect you just as well. No one would speak behind your back with me about."

A smile crept across his face. "So we'll watch out for each other, is that it?"

"Yes," she said. "For a time, at least," a sigh left her then. "You would give your life for me. If my life were threatened, you would?"

"I said I would…" he replied, but he suddenly wanted to tell he would die for her because she was Morianna and the person she had become, not for her title. However, something prevented him from doing so. "Willingly," he finished gently, and felt a strange mixture of discomfort and ease because of it.

The light in Morianna's eyes dimmed. "He would not. The Prince of Marrn. I know he would not. Not at all."

"That might change in time."

"Will it? You're showing more faith than I. Far more than I might have thought possible. But no, he wouldn't, Bloor. Yet, I have to marry him. Marry a man who doesn't love me. A marriage that is only a symbol. A stamp on an alliance my father might have need of in the future. And for that, my life is forfeit to a complete stranger that will be my husband after the winter. A man that does not care for me in the least. Can anything be more terrible, Bloor? For a princess?"

Bloor dare not answer. In truth, he did not know what to say.

"Lindee says that I'm helping the people more than I'll ever know, and I suppose that's true. I owe them that. After what I've done when I was a child. All the misery I've caused people. I know I don't love the Prince of Marrn, nor do I expect him to perish for me. I can see both of us faltering in this marriage. Yet I must, for the people of Sunja. Do you think that, by doing this, I can make up for leaving those people in the public square? Will this set things right for the people there?"

"The people," Bloor muttered, as if it were a dirty word. He wanted to tell her that the situation would be corrected, but to do that would admit doing things without her consent. Even if she supported his decisions, could she be counted on to keep a secret? He decided to keep that to himself for the time being.

"The people," Morianna repeated. "I have to do this for them. I owe them."

Then she smiled with a brightness that sucked Bloor in. "Well, we do what we can with what we have, I suppose.

And I suppose I won't be bored in Marrn. I imagine I'll have plenty of time to myself. Perhaps even a baby or two. Or I'll find a group of needy people I can secretly help disguised as a sister of a church. It won't be so bad. I only wish I could bring Lindee along. She won't, you know. She won't leave Sunja. She said that if she stays, it'll be reason for me to come back."

Morianna looked across the garden at a curtain of trees. "You would protect me at all costs, but something like this is beyond even you."

Bloor remained silent, and though the smile on her face wilted, he kept his gaze fixed on her face.

"Bloor," she said, still looking at the trees. "I feel so alone."

He took her wherever she wanted that day, watching both her and everything around her person. She strayed all over the palace grounds, not paying any particular attention to where she went, and sometimes mildly surprised at where she wound up. She had the air of someone deep in thought and heedless of where her feet took her, as long as her mind was uninterrupted. She barely spoke at all, and so Bloor, who only said anything when asked directly, was quiet throughout. If she did say something, he answered promptly. All the while, he watched her from the corner of his eye, studying her movements. She seemed full of despair, and Bloor wondered what he could do to help her. But do what? He would certainly protect her to the death, but dying for her now would not help her situation. If only he could steal her away from all of this.

Something like this is beyond even you.

But was it?

Lord Maullus would argue otherwise.

As the princess meandered through the royal grounds, looking at nothing in particular and keeping a depressed silence, Bloor's thoughts came to a crossroads, and easily turned to the extreme.

If only you could steal her away from all of this, a voice in his head repeated.

At the end of the day, Bloor returned the princess to her quarters and retired for the evening. He returned to his own room, and upon closing the door, he hung his scabbard off of the chair and collapsed on his bed. His fingers hung over the edge and caressed the smooth stone of the floor. Thoughts churned in his head, as thick as butter, and the light in his room became inky black. Where should he take himself? His rational mind told him to leave Morianna to her fate. Observe his duty and his code of morals and deliver the princess to a faraway prince. Another thought was to leave his duty entirely, to press Lord Maullus into sending him back to the front and then work out his frustrations on the hordes of Nordish Jackals. If he was lucky and he took enough risks, one of the Nords just might be able to kill him. However, the notion of leaving Morianna seemed so very hard to do. What if she wanted him to stay with her in Marrn? To stand guard outside the doors of the prince and princess on their wedding night? Unpleasant images of what would transpire behind those closed doors and the sounds of passion sawing through the night silence set his jaw clenching. No, he could not endure that. He would rather be captured and tortured by the Nords than to endure that.

So what could he do, he asked himself for the hundredth time.

Again, a voice in his mind corrected him: *What are you prepared to do?*

Morianna's face appeared behind his closed eyelids. He saw her laughing, saw her talking with Lindee and Karl, saw her helping the people of Sunja. All the while, he felt his heart starburst with a feeling he dared not think possible in him. He dared not think that there was one person in the world capable of infusing him with such a feeling, but Morianna had done just that.

He loved her.

There, in his darkened room, where the silence was thick enough to chew on, the words simply came to him. He opened his eyes to blackness and felt the moisture seeping into them. The words were not near as bad as he would have believed, and there was a delayed rush of excitement that filled him once again, as if he were seeing her in the wedding gown all over. This time, he let it flow its dangerous course.

He could tell no one, not even Morianna. His appearance of being utterly loyal until the end would be critical. His record was unblemished, so no one would suspect a thing.

A shiver went through him now. Was he really considering…

The setting of his jaw crushed the thought. He considered nothing. He would stop *at nothing*. Never in his life had he wanted anything, and now there was someone. He would do what he must do until the moment that Morianna was his. Damn her father and the prince of Marrn; they would never miss her. Bloor searched the black ceiling. He would need help. He would summon Alwan. A scheme began to form in his mind then, a plan that would steal Morianna away from the prince of Marrn, and solve the problem of the renegade Sujins preying on the people of Sunja. He would take care of Rusk the Two Knife before he left. It was the least he could do for Lord Maullus and Lord Winter, and the people of Sunja.

He sighed; there was much to do.

THE TROLL HUNTER

Jace ran.

He ran because his life depended on it. Sweat abandoned him in sheets, wanting no part of him or the thing pursuing him.

Especially the thing pursuing him.

He cursed himself with each step. He should have known better. He had hunted enough of the monsters to *know* he should have known better, and yet, once again, he underestimated the rage the creature was capable of, and the single-minded nature of the beast. He darted in between trees and ducked under thick limbs, he sprang over dips in the land, and his feet stung where he landed. Branches whipped at his face and one even lashed him proper just under his good eye; he did not check to see if it bled. Enough sweat was falling from him now to give up his scent to the beast behind. Blood would make little difference. As long as he could still see all was good, but if he slowed, if he looked behind, Seddon above, if he *stopped*...

Somewhere close behind him, the troll tore up the forest in its chase of the hunter. Where Jace weaved in between trees, the troll shoved them aside. Where the man ducked under branches, the troll burst through them with a roar to shake the hills. Where the man jumped, the troll stomped. The heat from its rage was almost hot enough to set the forest aflame. Its breathing sounded like the rattling of a fast moving koch, and its roar spiked a rush of frightful energy in Jace that he used to sprint.

The troll saw the man-thing bolt. The little one had hurt it. It would catch the little one and hold it in its great claws and break it like a pane of autumn ice.

Then it would eat it.

This simple thought of feeding and revenge was more than enough burning fuel for the troll to haul its monstrous bulk through the forest, gripping trees and using them to pull itself along to compensate for its weakened leg. It would heal later, but the troll wanted the man-thing now. It wanted the little one in its gullet. It would sleep and heal better with it there.

Jace cursed himself again. A memory of another time flashed through his head, when a pack of the biggest, most vicious men he could muster up had turned a full-grown troll into a pin cushion with their long spears. They thought it was dead, but when they approached the monster, it suddenly became very alive, alive enough to lash out and tear one man's arm out at the shoulder. The troll possessed life enough to kill two other hunters before it was finally slain.

Then they burned it.

From a distance.

With spears at the ready, just in case, until the thing was ashes.

Jace ran on, having no idea where he was going, yet anywhere away from the beast was good. He ran until the fire in his own lungs threatened to consume him, and then he ran some more, pushing on and on, trying to cheat the monster of his life. At one point, he dodged behind a sizeable boulder almost a third of his height, and more than enough to hide behind. He gulped down buckets of air, his single eye wide as he struggled to fill his lungs and calm his heart. He pressed up against the rock, feeling the sword in its scabbard twist at his side. A needle would have just as much effect on the troll, *if* he ever got in close enough to use it without having his head ripped off. He might have thrown it away, but a weapon was a weapon, and maybe if the thing swallowed him whole he could cut it open on the way down.

The thought made him smile.

He then realized how quiet it had become. The stillness worried him, and it quickly burst into fear. It seized his lower legs and quickened his heart. Had the thing given up? Did his cut to the thing's leg finally slow it down? It might have. Should he look?

He glanced up at the rock's jagged edge, expecting the thing's ugly head to rear up from behind it at any moment, for the claws that could crush a man's skull like a plum to dig into the boulder's flesh and send rock shards flying. He might get a stride or two away before the thing lunged for him, and if he were lucky, it would crush him in its pounce.

Where was it?

He wanted to peek, but did not want to expose his hiding place. He strained to hear over the blood pumping in his ears. He sent his hearing outwards, feeling behind the boulder, spreading out like a net seeking the smallest, most fluid fish. He held his breath and his heart ached because of it. He sought to shut down his body and squeeze out those few precious seconds of heightened hearing.

Silence!

It rewarded him.

He heard the flare of nostrils, a mighty expulsion of wind that made his eye flutter and go wide. It was out there. He could envision the thing trying to scry where he was. The scent had been lost for the moment, and the beast was going on best guess now that he was out of sight. If he ran, the thing would see him. If he waited, however...

Perhaps it would go by.

Jace would believe it when it happened.

His body gradually became used to his controlled intake of air. His strength returned. It was still out there, still smelling for him.

He heard the heavy crack of underbrush, so much akin to a man's spine being stepped on, followed by a ballooning silence. There was another rude snap of dead needles and branches underfoot. Followed by another, and another, and the noise grew.

Jace's blood quickened. The thing was charging in his direction. It had picked up his scent again. Or maybe it was guessing?

A roar shot by the boulder loud enough and strong enough to flatten the man's sweat-saturated hair to his skull.

Jace sprung out from behind the boulder just as two massive claws imprinted themselves into its surface in a cloud of rocky dust and chips right where his head had been. The roar whipping past his ears rose in pitch. The troll hauled itself around the boulder and after its quarry. It screamed and howled loud enough that if the sounds could kill then the air itself was charged with death.

Jace ran straight on, not caring where he ran just as long as the monster was behind him. Then he saw a faint light as he pushed through a wall of brush that sought to tangle him with its barbs. He found himself crashing into ground that sucked at his feet inside their boots. Yellow grass, tall and coarse, grew wildly and here, and pools of black water shone like obsidian in the fading sunlight. Small islands of crusty trees rose up in small lumps, ugly and bent over like sulking old men.

A marsh. A great bog land, as far as Jace could see. Open ground.

He flung himself back into the depths of the forest. He could keep ahead of the monster in here, for as strong as the thing was, it could only brush aside the smaller trees. It had to go around the bigger ones. As did Jace, but he still hoped to lose it somewhere in the tangles. In open ground, in a quagmire, the troll would have the advantage and Jace's chances of survival would plummet.

He raced back and away from the rampaging troll, hearing the harsh sounds of pursuit. Was it lessening? He pressed on, believing that he was not circling back. The forest was immense and unfamiliar to him, but he hoped his nose for direction would once again save his hide. He wondered fleetingly if he might run into some of the Sujins left to pick up the fallen treasure. There might be a chance of killing the troll if there were enough of them, if he found them.

He ran on.

In a few minutes he got his answer, for standing directly before him were five Sujins braced for a welcome. Their eyes almost exploded from their heads in surprise upon seeing the scout.

"Stop!" one of the five commanded.

Jace came to a halt, breathing as if he possessed three lungs and all burning oxygen like fire lighting up a lake of oil. He bent over and placed his hands on his knees, grimacing and fighting to regain his wind.

"That's one of the scouts," declared a voice behind a shield.

"So it is," another agreed. "Recognized his hair and the necklace of teeth."

The men spread out, surrounding Jace. He had nothing left to stop them even if he wanted to fight. He had spent himself by running.

Then came the roar, startling the forest gloom like a blast of thunder. It was not as distant as Jace believed, and he was suddenly *glad* to be around the five Sujins. He suspected these men to be part of Two Knife's force, but he didn't care. There was a greater danger in the forest than these men. The Sujins themselves froze in their places when they heard the sound.

"Saimon's love sack," one Sujin blurted out, "what in his blue hell was that?"

"Listen," another Sujin said uneasily. "It's coming this way, Hylan."

The Sujin called Hylan blinked. Two Knife had chosen several of them and sent them out to fleece the woods for the loyalists. Toffer himself had chosen Hylan and told him to circle about and to catch anyone crossing his path. Interrogate prisoners, sack their valuables, and put them to the sword, quickly. Hylan was a brutish man that looked forward to all of Toffer's instructions, especially the last one. Now that he and his dogs had actually found one, it would seem it would not be without some difficulty.

"What…" another Sujin began. Hylan told him to shut up. He squinted at the forest curtain, hoping to see something. The tip of his sword flashed just short of Jace's chin, and as he raised it, a grimacing Jace rose with it. "What is that?"

Jace didn't have the energy to be dramatic. "A troll," he said simply. "A big one."

Hylan's face soured. He would cut the truth out of the maggot before him if he had the time. There were no trolls in these parts.

Another earth shaking roll of a roar, much closer now. Irregular drumming came into earshot. Then the brazen sound of flesh slapping bark and the groan of resisting wood. Troll or no troll, something was coming towards their position, and Hylan would make certain guts would be on the ground.

"Seddon above," one man said, and pointed past them all, past Jace. The troll hunter turned himself, even though he knew what he would see.

Out of the forest depths, pushing and smashing its way past the trees before it, came something bent over and huge. It charged the Sujins with a howl of rage that went through their helmets like a hail of fire arrows and snapped Jace out of his daze. He darted away from the group, knowing he would never get the opportunity again.

The Sujins ignored him. It wasn't every day one saw a charging troll.

"Dog balls," a man named Muncan swore, eyeing the beast coming at them. He did not like what he was seeing in the least.

"Shields up! Double line!" Hylan barked at them. Professional to the last, the traitorous Sujins placed three men in front with their shields butted into the soil. Hylan positioned himself behind Muncan, placing his shield over both his and Muncan's head to complete the wall and to protect them from possible attack from above. Swords bristled out from the gaps. The troll would break upon the wall like a wave and they would skewer the animal and that would be that. They had done the same and worse to countless Jackal rushes. Hylan himself thought the thing's tusks would make a fetching helmet once they were through gutting the monster.

"Steady!" Hylan shouted. A stench of sweat and filth smacked into their senses, making him wished they had long spears.

The troll loomed up. It gripped and ripped the first shield up and out, yanking the man beside Hyman over the shield wall and flinging him high into the trees with a scream. The troll's other claw, balled into a fist, came crashing down on the suddenly exposed helmet of another Sujin. Both the line and the man's skull split like a flattened egg. In the scattering of men, a troll claw clamped down on the head of a third Sujin and jerked him up with such force that the man was dead before his feet left the ground. In a single expulsion of breath, three experienced Sujins, feared killers of Sunja, died.

The last two fought purely out of drilled reflexes. Hylan stabbed at the thing's boulder-sized belly and split fat and filthy hair as easily as honey butter. For his effort, the troll brought its fist down onto his upraised shield like a maul, slamming the leader to the ground, breaking both the shield and the arm bound to it. Muncan, swearing "dog balls, dog balls," over and over like a protective prayer, chopped and embedded his blade in the forearm of the beast. Red-rimmed eyes flashed on him and the bellow of pain and fury exploding from the troll's maw blew Muncan's helmet off his head. Both of his arms were gripped, and the troll pulled him apart. Hylan saw the Sujin being killed, the blood bursting from Muncan's person in a torrential spray. The spectacle froze the leader where he fell. The troll, realizing one little one still lived, stepped and stood over him in an unfair moment. Hylan glimpsed the blue sky above just before red claws enveloped his helmeted head.

Jace heard the shrieks behind him. He heard flesh smacking against the hollow wall of shields. He heard the rage of the troll. He even heard the wet shredding of flesh and the popping of chain mail links, reminding him of a fish having its spine removed. Then there was silence. None of it bothered him; those fools were dead once the creature struck. One did not stand behind a wall of shields and wait for a troll. A wall of spears perhaps, but not shields, but he thanked the fools all the same. They gave him the diversion he needed to escape the troll.

Or so he hoped.

It was so difficult to tell with those things.

39

Alwan peered down the forested slope, watching for movement. He placed his Sujins in a line to the right of himself. Only a handful of them now, and there would be fewer still by nightfall. It could not be helped. The scent of the forest calmed him, like it always did, and he breathed in deep of its smell. The Sujins had asked him questions, and he commanded them to be quiet. He told them to watch for their hunters. They would be along soon enough, and when they did, the loyalists could scream their heads off.

He glanced back at his horse. Unlike Bloor, he cherished his animal. The horse possessed the most wicked personality of any beast Alwan ever had encountered. It liked mischief and it liked to keep those around it on their guard. Alwan bought the animal from a trader in the market square of Sunja, and no sooner had the last coin plunked into the hand of the selling merchant, than the horse bit his forearm and tore a hunk of meat from it. The merchant howled loud enough to frighten those around him and loud enough for Saimon's hellions to sit up and applaud the horse. It was an impressive last bite the animal had given its former owner, and the first thing Alwan did to the creature was smile at it.

The second thing Alwan did was show it his sword, bringing it up close to the animal's eye. Not surprisingly to Alwan, as he suspected the beast to be highly intelligent, the hell horse understood the message and never once tried to bite or throw the Cavalier. Ignoring the curses of the horse merchant, Alwan and his new steed sauntered away from the stables. The horse was a hellion, and understood that only a hellion would ride it.

Alwan was that hellion, and he called his horse Saimon.

If the master of the abyss had anything to say about it, he could take it up with Alwan when they finally met. That put a garrote smile on the Cavalier and he took another glance at Saimon. Saimon looked back, ears twitching. Alwan paid close attention to the horse's suggestions. Saimon heard things where most men did not.

He looked back to the slope, hoping to see something amiss. He did not see anything, as much as he wanted to. Alwan wanted action. He preferred it and he was known to go looking for it if it were slow coming to him. He strained to spy anything moving out in the forest, and after a long lingering moment, he heard movement. The snap of brush carried long and far, and Alwan knew someone was cursing themselves out there. He pressed his face against the tree he hid behind. A short moment later, he saw figures moving towards the slope.

He counted five, all carrying packs.

His hand rose up at the wondering looks of his Sujins. When the approaching five got close enough, he stepped out from his hiding place.

"Where is Primo?" he asked.

The five drew up in surprise. Balto exhaled a sigh of obvious relief where the others tensed to fight. He recognized the black-bearded Cavalier as the one accompanying Bloor. "Behind us somewhere."

"Did you get it all?" Alwan asked, eyeing their packs.

"We did," Balto told him, not liking this man in the least.

"Hurry on then."

The five Sujins trudged towards them.

"Any sign of the maggots?" Alwan asked them as they passed by.

"Behind us," Balto answered. "Primo stayed behind and sent us on."

Alwan nodded in understanding, and Balto had another flare of unease about this character. He possessed a disinterest to make one wonder if he heard you at all. When he looked at you, an aura of unease followed, as if the man were debating right there whether or not you were expendable.

"You four will go on," Alwan informed them. "You," he stabbed a finger at the one Sujin unknown to them all, "will stay here. Go on then. We'll be along shortly."

The Sujins carried on, lugging away the packs full of wealth. Gatesin took the extra pack of the Sujin chosen to stay behind. He followed the three men ahead of him, casting a lingering gaze back on the thin line of men guarding their retreat. He did not agree with the plan, but he obeyed. He turned his attention to those ahead of him. Tungang and Balto both carried two packs each. Hatch carried the remaining pack, and appeared content with the arrangement; it was less to carry if he had to run. There was so much wealth amongst them all, Gatesin thought as he shouldered one of his two packs. The extra weight pulled at him, but he carried on, not wanting to be anywhere near the Sujins behind him. Something terrible was going to happen here. They were going to die.

Alwan went back to studying the foliage for signs of pursuers. "Go on," he said, as if he were a schoolmaster shooing children off to their homes. "We'll be along shortly." Or at least he would; the Sujins standing with him would not.

The four Sujins marched off into the forest.

In a small quiet glade, far from the troll and the hunter Jace, Bloor stopped so that Morianna could drink from a stream. He watched her figure as it bent over and cupped water to her mouth. Slurping the water from her hand wasn't fast enough for her, so she gave up and laid flat against the ground and sipped directly from the source. Gaps of bare back could be seen through the tears in her dress. Bloor realized it was the first time he'd ever seen her back, and her bare legs, for that matter. It was a pleasant sight.

"Are you looking at my legs?" Morianna asked him in between gulps.

However, his eyes were on the forest the moment he heard her.

"No," he answered, feeling it was the truth. *Half a truth, anyway.*

Morianna went back to drinking.

They'd been moving at a breakneck pace, wanting to place as much distance between the troll and the Sujins as quickly as possible. Bloor wanted to be clear of the forest before night, and if that wasn't possible, just being clear of their pursuers would suffice. He had a meeting place where he would find the Visigar to conclude their business. As soon as Morianna slaked her thirst, he meant for them to be on their way again.

However, Morianna had other ideas. It wasn't everyday one so narrowly escaped a fate worse than death, and being in the forest gave her a growing appreciation for the things around her. When she finished drinking, she rolled over and collapsed on the mossy bed surrounding the stream. She stared up at the faraway sky, and the dark tree tops reaching for it. Seeing her as she was, and trying hard not to look at her bare feet and legs, Bloor stepped closer, but not to crowd her view.

"How much farther, Bloor?" she asked him in a calm voice.

The Cavalier took in her disheveled hair, her ruined dress, the smudges of dirt across her red cheeks. She was exhausted and ungodly beautiful in his eyes. All he wanted was to lie down beside her and hold her, but he could not. Not at the moment. "Much. Sorry."

"Will it come looking for us?"

"Maybe."

She sighed. "Will you fight it if it does?"

"Yes."

"I should've known the answer to *that*," Morianna teased him, and it made him feel better. She was exhausted and terrified at one point, but she was recovering. The woman was tougher than she appeared.

She looked at him. Content that it was indeed Bloor watching over her, she closed her eyes. Bloor did not want her to sleep, yet he did not have the heart to deny it to her. Weariness sucked the life from him as well, but it was an old feeling that he was well acquainted with, and he needed to speak with her. He needed badly to talk with her. There was so much to be discussed, and now that they were away from Sunja, her decision meant everything to him. He struggled with the fear of saying anything, of putting off what he had to ask for fear of being rejected.

"Bloor," Morianna said softly.

"Yes?"

Her eyes came open, "What is happening?"

She had been thinking the same thing. With a sigh, he sunk down to sit beside her, driving his sword into the earth before him. He took a breath. "There are Sujins that want your dowry. They killed most of the Sujins loyal to your father to get it. The Axemen as well."

"They want the dowry?"

Bloor nodded somberly.

"Where is it now?"

"I have some Sujins getting it. They'll bring it to us."

The princess became quiet for a moment and continued staring up at the trees and their spires. The perfumed stream gurgled in the background. Birds darted across her vision without a sound, and the blue of the sky lay beyond it all.

"Bloor?"

"Yes?"

"Why did you kiss me?"

Fear lanced through him then. Fear of exposing his feelings for her, but when she held his gaze, that fear melted away. "Morianna..." he began, wanting to call her princess, even though she disliked it when he did.

He told her everything.

He told her of his plan to abduct her, to steal her away with the aid of a group of Visigar. The Visigar would kill all of her escort in exchange for her dowry. In return, Bloor and Morianna would be led to a land far away from her uncaring father, the masses, and the wars of Sunja. Her father the king had appointed Bloor as commander of her security and placed all aspects of the journey in his charge. He told her he was responsible for everything, including the recruitment of a hellion named Rusk the Two Knife. The same Sujin who was the leader of the rogue Sujins, and they were Sujins, not just ruffians, preying on the innocents of Sunja. He told her of his gamble in informing Rusk of the transporting of the dowry, but not of Morianna herself, and how he placed Rusk in charge of handpicking the four hundred Sujin escort, believing that the man would bring every cutthroat he commanded on the journey with the sole intention of robbing the dowry for himself. It was a huge gamble, and so many things could have gone afoul. The assumption that Rusk would be brave enough to actually rob the koch was one. The other was that Bloor really had no way of knowing just how many had fallen in with Rusk and how many were with loyal Sujins. Then there was the problem of surviving Sujins, what to do with the survivors if there were any, if Rusk's killers did not manage to slay them all. He hoped that any survivors would run back to Sunja with news of Rusk's treachery and the death of Morianna, for in truth, it was the safest way to be free of the king's wrath: to have him believe that all were killed in the robbery. Bloor told her of Alwan helping him, for reasons still unknown to him, and he told her of how he wanted no part of a king that would give up so precious a daughter as he had her.

"You think I'm…precious?" Morianna asked him, her face coming very close to his.

How someone could smell so wondrous was beyond him. A feeling so strong welled up within his breast. "You are to me," he whispered.

Morianna stared at him for a moment and smiled her dazzling smile.

There, underneath the greenest of canopies, in the vibrant stillness of a forest, the lips of a princess and a warrior met for the very first time.

Alwan felt them before he heard them. The war against Nordun had elevated his senses to a height almost magical. Some men smelled the approach of rain; Alwan smelled the coming of bloodletting. Most men distrusted him because of his ability to discern danger, but none would dare openly say anything to his face. Of the Cavaliers, only Bloor had the grit to do a round of duty with the man. Not only could Alwan predict when things were about to become dangerous, he had the talent of placing himself right in the thick of the action. He sneered at the ranks of Cavaliers who shunned that which they were born to do. Only Bloor stood at his side during the grimmest periods of time, and only Bloor had proven that he was as hard as the steel he wielded. If Alwan was darkness, Bloor was light.

The most dangerous kind of light.

The snap of a branch reached his ears and Alwan's face became stern. He inched his head out from behind the tree. Nothing. He withdrew and placed his shoulder to the wood. He glanced back at Saimon. Saimon stared back. Alwan winked. Saimon wiggled his ears indifferently, and found some wildflowers that were more interesting.

Alwan frowned. "I'll cut steaks from you one of these days," he muttered, and meant it.

The air became as tense as drawn bowstrings, and Alwan found himself wishing that he had a few archers with him. *If wishes were fishes, then the world would never be hungry again.* He remembered the old saying from somewhere and thought it to be the truth. The men with him carried only swords and shields. Loyal to the last, they would hold the line with their lives if needed. Such devotion to an uncaring king. It made the bile rise in Alwan's throat.

Delay. Alwan wanted to delay them.

"YA!" he suddenly roared out, shattering the stillness and causing his Sujins to jump as if stabbed with sticks. Curses stitched the air.

"YA!" Alwan cried out again. "You maggots that once called yourselves Sujins! Is the pus-sucker called Rusk amongst you?"

Silence.

From where they hid, the loyalists froze, straining to hear what the answer, if any, would be.

"No?" Alwan barked. "Or does he go by another name now? I once heard a name tossed throughout Sunja's Five Klaws. I'd say it now. I could use the laugh for sure. Are you there? Or, by Saimon's blessing, did someone manage to stick you, Two Knife? There! I said it without pissing myself! Are you there, TWO KNIFE!"

At the absolute edge of the forest gloom, just barely seen through the brush, a man stepped into view. His swords were sheathed and his hands were at his hips. In a flash, they were flung wide in defiance.

"I am Two Knife!" the figure announced without fear. "And I'll gut the man who just spoke from ball sack to chin if he has the guts to show his face to me."

This brought a grin to Alwan's face. "I'm Alwan. And I have guts to spare!"

"I don't know that name."

"You'll hear it plenty in Saimon's hell," Alwan told him. "Show yourself!"

"To the likes of you? One that would kill his swordbrothers like fish on a beach? I think not."

"You're a brave one, aren't you?" Two Knife mocked, throwing the insult across the forest. "Here I stand in full view while you are hugging a tree. Show me you have balls and step out. I'll make it a quick Sujin haircut."

Alwan grinned again. Just like the man he heard talk of; he was a scrapper, to say the least. It was a shame that he went bad. "No. I like where I am just fine."

"Coward!" Two Knife flung at him.

"You should know, I suppose. Cutting down Sujins when they least expect it. I should just stick you full of arrows now and be done with it."

If Two Knife was nervous, he did not show it. "Arrows? I thought I killed all the archers you had?"

News there. "Not all."

"So loose them. I promise I won't move," and with his words he slapped his armored chest twice. A brave bastard indeed, Alwan thought. It was a shame that he went bad. He could have liked this Two Knife in a different life.

"What are you waiting for then? Strike me down! Maybe you'll frighten off the dogs following me if you kill the leader? Isn't that reason enough to shoot?"

A pause.

"Because you can't," came the sneer. Two Knife shook his head. "I hope you have the coin with you. I might forget what you said earlier and kill you quick if you do."

"We do. What do you say to splitting it?" Alwan shouted.

"What?"

"Are you deaf? Let me talk to a punce that can hear then!"

The mention of the treasure caught Two Knife's attention. "You have it?"

Alwan did not answer. Let the cur stew for awhile. He idly felt the hilt of his sword and rubbed his chin. He could talk horseshit all day with this idiot if he wanted to. Alwan once enraged a Jackal to screaming obscenities at him from the top of a hill. The more filth the Nordish warrior flung at the Cavalier, who listened atop his own hill, the more livid the Jackal became. It was an amusing day. However, the Jackal had to ruin it when finally, blinded by fury, he actually ran down his hill and up Alwan's to reach him. Alwan let Saimon kick his head in when he reached the top. It was a disappointing way to end an otherwise hilarious conversation. The Jackal swore at him with the most amusing accent.

However, Two Knife had no such accent, and Alwan was already getting bored.

"You have it?" Two Knife repeated.

"What did I just say, topper?"

The renegade Sujin paused again. It impressed Alwan the way this one thought. Interesting. He could almost feel something akin to respect for the man, but it was only for a moment and gone on the next breath.

Two Knife glanced to his right where Toffer and a gathered force of Sujins crouched, waiting for orders. Toffer bandages were so bloody and filthy looking, he looked as if a bear had devoured him. The man shook his head, and Two Knife looked ahead. They couldn't see anyone ahead, either. Either it was one man, or only a handful. Either way, it was all a bluff. He understood now why this fool was talking to him. Did he have the treasure? Something made Two Knife doubt it. It suddenly occurred to him that the treasure was on its way *away* from him.

Far away and making good time while he was wasting time talking nonsense. The revelation ignited a poisonous glow in his innards.

"You," he stated in a loud voice, "are wasting my time."

The accusation made Alwan's brow crinkle up in consideration. That was fast thinking. He gave a slow appreciative nod. The man wasn't so dim-witted after all. Alwan glanced over his shoulder at Saimon. The horse was scuffing at the ground with a hoof, letting him know in his own way that they should both be on their way; smart horse.

Alwan straightened. He could hear men approaching their position now, a lot of men.

Two Knife started walking forward, motioning for his Sujins to follow. They fell into a black gleaming mass behind their leader, bristling with bared weapons. The march impressed the onlooking loyalists, for Two Knife was indeed a bold one.

"Wasting my time," Two Knife went on, his swords flashing out and cutting the air about him. "I'll show you what happens to men that waste my time, Alwan. I'll show any bastard standing with you. I'll give you the same I gave Tarco and the Axemen and you can greet *them* when you wake up in Saimon's hell."

"Stand fast, lads," Alwan said in a calm voice, despite the growing numbers coming towards them, materializing out of the forest like murderous wraiths. They came on with their swords swishing and their shields at the ready. They came with hatred on their faces and not a drop of mercy in their eyes. Alwan reminded himself that these weren't Jackals he faced now. These were Sujins. Sunjan men of the hardest steel. He gave them no further thought. These bastards had chosen wrong to face them, and they would all die,

However, not just yet.

Two Knife scanned the wilderness before him. He spotted men here and there, restless and fighting the urge to turn and run. "Face me now, Alwan! Face me, and if you manage to kill me, you have my word your maggots will get a quick death!"

A dark glance back at Toffer informed the henchman differently. Toffer grinned. He so liked the way Two Knife thought.

However, Alwan did not answer. Alwan drew back on Saimon's reins, having quietly retreated and mounted while his men were fixed on the tide of Sujins. With a tug, he steered the horse away. One loyalist turned his head upon hearing the dull thud of hooves on earth and spotted the

Cavalier leaving. The man's eyes narrowed to slits and he cursed his fate.

The advancing Sujins saw the lone horseman, and Two Knife's breath caught in his throat. "Alwan!" he shouted with both swords rising into the air. His Sujins charged when his blades fell. He cried out Alwan's name again and again, but the sound was lost in the battle cries of the loyalists. True to their pledges and king, the few loyal Sujins held the line as long as they could before falling. Their death cries echoed through the halls of the forest.

Alwan rode on.

He let Saimon have his reign, and the mighty warhorse drove though the wilderness. Greenery whipped by, and he hunched down close to Saimon's head. The battle sounds behind him died quickly, and he focused on catching up with the last remaining Sujins. They would be easy enough to find. Then it was Bloor and the princess and leaving Sunja for good. They rode on.

With his attention elsewhere, he did not see the shape loom up from the long shadows of the forest to cut Saimon's legs out from under him. The horse rattled off a shocked scream, and Alwan flew from the saddle and rolled to a jarring stop against the base of a tree. He spat out blood from where his teeth almost bit his tongue in half. With a groan, he got to his feet, still reeling from the shock of being thrown. He shook the black starbursts from his vision, seeing a vast timberland before him. He turned his head back the way he had come, and the land dipped and wobbled in the frame that was allowed. Then he saw Saimon, hell-born Saimon, laying still on the ground in a growing pool of blood. His right foreleg had been sheared off just above his knee, and a bright puncture hole oozed where the horse's ribs were. The dead animal slowly turned the forest floor into a sticky soup of yellow, brown, and the deepest berry red. Alwan sucked in air, willing his head clear with each lungful. As he gained his senses, the loss of Saimon began to sting like an unknown wound being realized.

Then he spied the other figure, just in the corner of his eyesight, previously hidden by the flickering blackness plaguing his vision. It was standing still, and while Alwan's mind dealt with Saimon's death, Saimon's killer almost escaped attention.

If escaping was his intention, but Klytus had other ideas.

The Sujin watched the dazed Cavalier struggle to his feet and put his back to a tree to steady himself. He watched the man tense up when he saw his animal.

"You," Alwan finally spoke. "You killed my horse."

The mountain that was Klytus took a single step towards the Cavalier.

"You killed Saimon," Alwan said, his voice still groggy. A line of blood fell from his lips, sparkling in the remaining light. He pulled out his shortsword, knowing that the longer blade was on Saimon's carcass. Klytus paused for a moment, considering the weapon. He did not fear this man. It was the Cavalier that should fear him. Then his own shortsword came up, thick with the life blood of the horse. It appeared to Alwan that the man must have stabbed Saimon after he had brought him down.

Alwan readied himself. The Sujin had a shield as well as a blade, a shortsword that should not have taken the animal. He thought on how he believed Saimon was invincible. Undying.

Klytus stepped closer. The smell of the animal's death hung off him like a butcher. The smell reached Alwan, and his anger began to rise. He looked into the big Sujin's eyes and the killer stared back. He stopped not three steps away from the Cavalier.

Then he lunged.

The Sujin moved to stick Alwan straight through the pelvis, seeking to punch his sword through him like he was a thin wooden plank. The blow would have taken Alwan off his feet and lifted him into the air, but the Cavalier darted backwards, not near as dazed as he appeared. Klytus held his shield before him and slashed as his target nimbly stepped to one side, splitting the air before the Cavalier's face. He moved ahead with the cut, and Alwan stepped back. Blood from the Sujin's blade dappled his face. He held his own sword at arm's length, studying the Sujin from behind his extended guard.

The Sujin advanced, stabbing as if he were trying to take down another warhorse. Again, Alwan weaved about the thrust and stepped to the man's side. He flicked out with his own blade and split the leather bracer covering the man's heavy foreman. Klytus yanked back his swordarm with a fright, thinking for a moment he had lost his arm. He stared at the Cavalier from over the edge of his shield, eyeing his opponenas they circled each other. The man looked to Klyus' legs and struck out at them. Klyus deflected the attack with ease. The Cavalier's eyes fixed on his right shoulder, and when he slashed for it, Klytus pivoted his hips, turning the sword aside with his shield while smiling behind it. This was a Cavalier? Leading each of his blows with his eyes? Perhaps the man was still addled from the fall. Regardless, on the dog's next attack, Klytus would stop it again on his shield and run him through with one quick thrust. He watched the man's eyes.

As before, the man's eyes told Klytus where he was about to strike: his shoulder, again. Klytus would take the man's arm off at the elbow.

Alwan started to stab outwards and Klytus unleashed his own sword, hacking downwards and cutting nothing but air, realizing in an instant that he allowed himself to be taken in by a simple feint. The Cavalier lopped off his sword arm as if it were a block of stiff butter, right at the elbow joint. When Klyus roared out in pain, Alwan swept his sword low and took off a leg above the knee. The big Sujin crashed to the ground, swinging his stump at a shadow as he went down. His teeth rattled in his head when he hit and he felt his shield being kicked away. Then his world exploded when Alwan's boot smashed into his exposed jaw, shattering teeth and bone.

Slipping in and out of consciousness, Klytus struggled in vain to understand what was happening. His vision swam with trees and darkness. Then, out of the shadows smelling of blood, a silver figure came into sight and stood above him, sword poised. Klytus heard a voice.

"Killed my horse," it spoke to him, echoing in his brain like a soupy dream. The pain that came after the voice granted him the briefest flare of clarity, and with it, Klytus tried his best to scream.

When Alwan finished with the Sujin on the ground, he snorted out his breath and regarded the sightless eyes at his feet. He spat on the face. Then he looked back at the still form of Saimon, its cooling blood now a dark pool against the forest floor. A lump of regret worked its way through the Cavalier's chest and throat. He hated leaving the beast in the middle of nowhere, but he supposed he was a fool for believing it might have been otherwise for a horse of war. At least this way, no one would be cutting him up for the evening's meal, and he smiled at the countless jokes he himself made of doing just that. Saimon's steaks would have choked someone to death anyway.

With a deep breath, Alwan turned and left his dead friend where he lay. He went after the last of the loyalist Sujins. He still had a lead over Two Knife.

He left the corpse at his feet, but not before delivering one final kick into its head.

40

It sat on its haunches, the knuckles of one great fist down on the soft ground. The other fist fed its mouth the remains of one of the little ones, and it cracked and suckled on the bones as if it were candy. Sweet the meat was, so very sweet. The little ones certainly did taste better when they fought, though it did not think of why this was so. It didn't need a reason, really. The troll only knew, and remembered. Something else it knew: Its chase of the quick man-thing had taken it far into the forest, for it saw the great marsh. The stretch of quagmire was not unknown to the mountain, the legend that was this troll. It had traveled across it before, and preferred its cold, soft wetness about its ankles to the hard earth of the woods. The forest was far too confining and bothersome to the troll, but the marsh was freedom. It could lair there, and the lair would mark the great marsh as its own. No other of its ilk would come there unless they were females and wanted to lair with it. The males could be tolerable, but only after the mountain beat them into their submissive places.

The troll snapped off the bone it was sucking on like a weathered branch. It spat out one white meatless end, and derisively tossed the other into the bush. It gazed around, grading the remaining corpses and grunting its opinion of them. The troll had consumed the meatier parts of its victims and the scraps that remained weren't worth the effort of carrying all the way to and across the great marsh. It wanted fresh meat, *whole* meat, for its lair.

A light of memory sparkled deep within his massive skull: little ones. There were *more* left in the forest. There was even the rabbit that had brought it to this place. It smelled the air and inhaled its sweet coppery flavor. The aroma was heady, but it did nothing to help it locate the other man-things. As if it were suddenly repulsed, the beast stood up and drew back from the Sujin corpses. The rabbit it had chased was gone. Perhaps it was nearby somewhere? Slowly, the beast arched its sight back towards the way it had come. That would be the easiest way to travel. There would be little ones at the end of the trail as well. Perhaps if it hurried, it could catch them. It vaguely remembered two of them somewhere back in the forest. A deep rumble of contentment issued from its throat; it was a good thought.

It began the long walk towards Bloor and Morianna.

"Morianna," Bloor began, peering deep into her wondrous eyes and almost losing himself in them. He paused again, and in the passing of seconds she searched his face with neither fear or uncertainty; this from a woman who only a short time ago was in the grip of a monster. Bloor smiled gently in spite of the thoughts and emotions churning in his head. His smile calmed her even more.

"Yes?" Morianna asked in a voice that suggested that she already guessed what it was he wanted to ask. It wasn't hard to fathom after he told her his plans. The corners of her mouth played with a smile. She knew that her Cavalier had indeed rescued her. All he had to do was to put his intentions into words.

"Your escort is practically gone," he told her in a controlled voice. "If no one returns to your father, or if only those that survived Rusk's attack, the whereabouts of you would perhaps never be found. You would be thought dead with the rest. We would all be thought dead." The thought occurred to him that the appearance of the troll was a good thing, albeit a dangerous one. It had almost killed her, but the belly of the beast would be her final resting place. The tracks and the wreck of the koch would be found and all would assume the princess had been killed and eaten by the troll. There would be no attempt to find the body. They could slip unnoticed into a neighboring realm and become anyone they wanted. She could even summon Lindee and Karl if she so desired. She would be forever free of her father's dangerous indifference.

His face close to hers, he explained all of this. When he finished, Morianna looked as if she were about to cry.

"You would have me do this?" she asked him in a whisper. "Leave my people and my family? And drift away where no one would know me? Alone?"

"Not alone, Anna," he said to her, taking her hands in his. "With me, of course. If you say the word, you'd never be alone again. I've taken you away from one prince, and if you will have me, I offer myself in his place."

"Say what word, Bloor? Can't you say it for me? You've taken commands for so long it seems, until now. Just this once, I'd like to hear you make a decision for yourself, so I know no one has put the idea in your head. Please."

Then she smiled that smile of hers that stole his heart perhaps as early as the first time he saw her as a woman, and he wondered if this wasn't the purest form of love—the kind that you don't realize until it bursts within and leaves a person giddy. He never thought it would be possible for him to love anyone, but he loved this woman.

"I cannot list the things I've done in this life, both good and bad, all done in the name of a king that doesn't care if I live or die. But today, I had to do all of this because if I didn't, it meant living the rest of my days without you. If you say yes, we'll be together until the end of our days, Anna. I will be with you if you will have me. I will forever stay by your side and keep harm from you. I love you, Anna."

His words shattered whatever control she had left and she began to tremble. Not wanting him to see her cry, she threw her arms around his neck and buried her face in the hollow bellow his chin. Bloor clasped his arms around her as if he were a bear. And there, in the space of the forest, on a carpet of wild white flowers, the princess of Sunja took his face and kissed him full on the mouth. They held it for moments, her hands touching and tracing the lines of his face. For so long, she wondered how it would feel. She meant to take her time, without any shyness and only the wonderment of why she had not done so earlier. This Cavalier was not so hard to read, as Alora once mentioned. It was only bringing life to his pages that was the problem. Morianna kissed him, and he responded with a tenderness that surprised her enough that at one point she opened her eyes and giggled.

He had opened his.

"I heard that to have one's eyes open during a kiss is bad luck," Morianna said, caressing his cheek.

"Foolishness."

"I think so too," she agreed. They kissed again and broke away after a short time, the taste of each other fresh and mesmerizing. His fingers came up and touched her cheek.

"I've loved you for a long time, Anna," his words spilled from him now that the ice of his fear had melted away. He wanted to tell her so many things, now that there was no need for any secrets between them. Morianna did not give him the chance, for no sooner had he uttered the word "time," she was kissing him again.

Toffer pointed out the head on the ground. One visible eye was cringing as its face was half mashed into the earth. A lull fell upon the onlooking Sujins as Two Knife stepped in for a closer look. There was no mistaking Klytus. It looked as if someone had given his face the boot and Two Knife briefly thought back to the axeman he killed not so long ago. The memory twisted his mouth up. Klytus had been his enforcer for as long as Two Knife could remember, and he did not believe that there was a man alive, besides himself, that could have killed the giant. He doubted that he would ever come across an individual that performed his duties with such grim enthusiasm.

"Alwan," Two Knife growled to himself, "has a lot to answer for."

"Never thought I'd see anyone kill Klytus," a Sujin nearby muttered. Two Knife flashed a lethal look that silenced the man.

"He could not have gotten far," Toffer said, coming to the man's rescue. He pointed to the dead horse. "Klytus got his horse. And if I knew Klytus, it won't surprise me if we don't find someone dead up ahead."

That thought appealed to Two Knife. If there was justice in the world, this Alwan would be still alive when they found him. Then he would feel Two Knife's boots, and oh, how he would dance on his skull. No one spoke while Two Knife fumed and plotted. Toffer took the opportunity to check on his bandages. His wounds still bled, though slowly. He marveled at how he was still able to stand. Greed was a powerful motivator.

"Alright then," Two Knife said, wrenching his eyes off the frightful head at his feet. "Maggots, listen here. Yours and mine is being carried off in that direction. We are only behind it. They are tired. They are carrying heavy coin. And they know we will gut them the moment we catch them. The princess is ahead as well, and I'm guessing if we find fortune, we find the other. Toffer!"

Hearing his name snapped the man to attention.

"Think you can stop bleeding long enough to find the Sunjan bitch?"

"I'll do what I can," the hurting man said.

"Get help then," Two Knife snarled at him. He pointed his swords at the trail before them. His gaze was intense enough to start a brush fire. The hunt had gone on long enough, and the loss of Klytus clawed at his nerves. There were too many of them dying out here. He would find whoever was left of the loyalists and kill them on the spot. If they prolonged the hunt any longer, he promised himself again that their deaths would linger. He sucked in hot breath and cleared his head.

"Let's get our coin."

They smelled the blood before they found the carcass of the horse stewing in the drying puddle. A cloud of black flies rose up when the Sujins came near, disturbing their feast. Balto's nose screwed up and he stretched his neck with disgust. "Seddon above," he said sourly. "It's not a good day for horses. That's a damn sight for certain."

"We'll have something to eat at least," Tungang said, easily bearing the pair of backpacks full of treasure. He dropped both packs onto a dry patch of earth. "Damn fine eating at that. Horse is a good meal."

"You'd eat Bloor's horse?" Gatesin asked him in a doubtful voice. He dropped his pack as well. A short rest would do them all good.

"Right in front of him," Tungang replied.

"You," Gatesin said as he sank to the ground beside his packs, "are a very stupid man."

"From what I hear, the man doesn't care for his animals in the least," Hatch said, leaning against a tree, his packs hanging from his hands.

"Where'd you hear that?" Balto asked him. He moved beyond the dead horse, not liking the flies in the least.

"From some of them Lancers. They all know about Bloor. That one's got a reputation. And all of it bad, I can tell you."

Balto exchanged looks with Gatesin. Both men knew of Bloor's reputation firsthand. Or at least, they thought they knew how ruthless and hard the Cavalier could be. Neither knew about his indifference to horses.

"Well, then," Tungang said. "He won't mind at all then."

"I'd still ask him for permission first," Gatesin warned. "You never know with that one."

"What do you know of it?" Tungang growled at him. Gatesin rolled his eyes. There was no telling Tuns anything; they had to find out the hard way. Tungang took the silence as an invitation to inspect the horse. He waved away the flies whirling about his face.

"Only an hour or so dead. Not bad at all. If I had the time, I'd gut the thing now and cut out some fair steaks."

"You are a *stupid* man," Gatesin muttered, shaking his head.

"I agree," Hatch threw in. Balto chuckled. There *was* no telling a Tun anything.

"Take a look here," Hatch said and pointed. Trees had their bark split while smaller ones were broken. A pathway of destruction went off in one direction, out of sight. Gatesin screwed up his face and Balto merely sighed in appreciation of the power needed to cause such destruction.

"Big bastard," Hatch said for them all.

"Yes," Balto agreed. "Big bastard."

They became quiet then, and watched Tungang sit on the ground, doing nothing to the dead animal. He had no intention to cut anything off the horse. Traveling as they were, he would have no real time to enjoy it, and horse was one of those meals that one should take time to prepare, and savor with better company. He didn't want to share anything with the other three men. The lot of them rested their aching limbs and felt their lungs settle down. Air went down their gullets just as refreshing as water. Balto glanced about the area, appreciating the unspoiled timberland and trying to forget the troll's path. He wanted to build a cabin in a place something like this, overlooking his brothel, of course.

However, then the thought of what followed them seeped into his mind. He'd faced dangerous times before. He made it his life facing down dangerous times and comparing every one to the Field of Skulls. This one wasn't as near as disastrous as that black night in history, and knowing that he survived it made his mind rest a little easier.

Gatesin concentrated on the path they would be taking and what Bloor's reaction would be when they delivered the dowry to him. Life would be so much simpler without Bloor knowing he was alive, as Bloor was a reminder of that night when a Klaw of Sunja was destroyed almost to a man. It was Bloor who believed Gatesin to be a spy of the Jackals, though he later proved himself loyal to Sunja. He still believed that the Cavalier suspected him to be a spy of the Nords, even though he publicly conceded the Sujin was innocent. It was enough for him to want to disappear and he had for a while, thankful to forget about Bloor and that evil night in Sunja's history. He exhaled, feeling lost, and realized that in the packs at his feet was a small fortune, money enough to disappear to some other friendly realm and start a new life, enough to even convince dear old Balto to join him if he wanted. Open up a brothel of a quality unheard of. Perhaps even find a pretty wife. It would be so easy to do with what he had picked up.

As his breathing steadied and his thoughts deepened, his attention drifted from Balto to Hatch until finally coming to rest on Tungang. Balto continued inspecting the timberland about him, while Hatch had closed his eyes and looked asleep. Nothing beyond that constant itch in his crotch seemed to trouble the man.

Tungang felt he was being watched and scowled back.

Gatesin's eyes went to his packs.

The big Tun also felt the tug of temptation. He was a mercenary in the eyes of many, having joined the Sujins with the promise of being able to freely loot Nordun. The looting never came, and every day it seemed the front was being shoved back and away from the looting he was promised. It made him sick to think he joined the wrong side, but the Nords were barbarians even by his people's standards. In the land of Tun, a dominion of Sunja, there was little to look forward to in life. One was born, grew, took a trade, and got old. Some of the men signed up with the regular Klaws for excitement, but his father never was a warrior. His father was a blacksmith, and a fine one at that. His parents were good to him and afforded him whatever they could. For that alone, he wanted to return and take care of them. He would marry, have children of his own, and raise them in much the same way his parents raised him, to be a monster on any battlefield. It surprised even him how he turned out sometimes. Yet, if he was lucky enough, he would be honored to live out his years with his mother and father, and ensure they would be comfortable until their passing.

He had never revealed his plans to any of the Sujins around him. They would never understand his people's loyalty to those that sired them, and he despised them for it. He never met a more bitter group of men in his life than these Sujins. It seemed that in their spare time they relished flinging scorn at anything and everyone outside and particularly inside their ranks. Men willing to die for each other delighted in making each other's lives miserable. The irony smacked Tungang as brazenly as the smell of the dead horse before him. In any case, it was them that turned him into the hardest and most callous of them all, just so they would shun his company and he would not reveal his plans to them while in some drunken state of mind. These few men that were with him now were actually fine by him, though he would never admit it to any of them. He secretly liked both Balto and Gatesin, both of whom reminded him of old uncles back in his village. This Hatch was a Sujin straight through. Tungang did not know the man beyond that.

His hands clenched the straps of the packs. They were brimming with riches. Tungang would never know such wealth again, or so he believed. It would be so easy to leave these men and lose himself in the forest. They would have no time to pursue, if they wanted to get the remainder of the dowry to Bloor. He could be back in the land of the Tuns in a week, and return a rich man at that. He could take care of his parents as they deserved, and all he had to do was leave these men. He doubted the killers of Two Knife really knew how much they carried, and two missing packs would not be missed if these three were caught and killed. If they were not, if the Sujins returned to Sunja with the packs, they would inform the commanders there of his treachery, and his homeland would very well be ripped apart while they searched for him. The thought made hims frown.

If these three got back to Sunja.

Tungang sighed then, a loud noise in the quiet forest, and smiled to himself. Quite the day it was turning out to be.

Nearby, Hatch's thoughts were floating behind his closed eyes just as the others, and they were far more personal. His nether regions burned as if something was building a hive down there, and he badly wanted to bring a torch to the afflicted area. However, this would not do, so he simply scratched at his parts with vigor. Mites, he heard from some other Sujins, either from infected bedding or whores. It was just his luck that they began biting the day this entire fracas began. It was just his luck. He had not the time to see a healer, and in truth, he thought it was a passing thing and taken care of with water. That was not the case. Washings did not solve his problem. The weight of the packs kept his hands from scratching, torturing him. He wondered how he was going to get through the rest of the day. If he did, he meant to splash burning oil on his topper and berries the first chance he got. The thought lingered while his hand strayed to his crotch yet again. Then the noise of something coming through the forest roused them all and their eyes flew to each other in turn. Their weariness was forgotten. Balto raised a hand for silence and carefully got to his feet. He held his sword at his side and slowly peeked around a tree, looking off into the growing shadows. The other men climbed to their feet and placed trees at their backs, trying hard to stay hidden.

When Balto saw the running figure of Alwan approaching them, he did not feel a wave of relief. "It's that one called Alwan."

The lot of them were silent with the news. If it was only the Cavalier, then the others were gone. They were all that remained of the troop destined for Marrn. Gatesin cursed the day he was chosen to be a part of it. Moments later, the Cavalier stood amongst them and regarded them all with a menacing eye, his chest heaving. "What's this about then, old man?" he directed at Balto. "Feeling an ache in your bones? You'll get plenty of sleep if the maggots behind me catch up."

"Who says they'll catch us?" Gatesin answered for his friend, who looked back the way Alwan had just come.

"They caught your sword brothers back there," Alwan told him. "Put them down with nary a blink."

"You seemed to have got away fine enough," Gatesin pointed out with his sword. Alwan regarded the bare blade for a moment, and an unnatural gleam flared up in his eye, almost welcoming Gatesin to use his weapon. The Cavalier turned his shoulders in his direction and his hand found the pommel of his sheathed blade. Gatesin hardened his features in reply, not afraid in the least. After enduring the likes of Bloor, the Cavalier would have to try much harder than dirty looks if he sought to intimidate the Sujin.

However, Balto spoke, diffusing the situation. "Where's your horse, Lord?"

The dangerous eyes blinked and fell away from Gatesin. "Killed," he answered, letting the word fall from his lips like a single raindrop from a black cloud. "Right out from under me as I rode away from the line. One of them managed to get up behind me."

"You left the others to die?" Tungang found his voice and laced it with a dangerous tone.

"You're questioning *my* decision, Sujin?"

Tungang ground his jaw and kept his tongue.

"No one is questioning you here, Lord," Balto said, stepping in again. He saw the Cavalier's fingers flex on his weapon's hilt. "We're just tired, is all."

"I'm not," Gatesin declared. He did not like the posture of this Alwan. He was too much on edge.

"Nor I," Tungang growled.

"I'm getting there myself," Hatch said. He did not like the looks of the Cavalier either.

"Don't get the idea you're worth more than you are, Sujins," Alwan warned. "I'd strike you all down right here if I thought it would save the princess."

"I'd say," Gatesin said and nodded at the packs behind him, "that we're worth something to someone right about now. That is, if you think you can carry these packs all by yourself."

Alwan did not like the insolence in this one's voice. Balto thought that the man would lash out at his friend. Gatesin was challenging the Cavalier, and the man stewed where he stood, not liking it in the least. Then, just as Balto thought something terrible would happen, the corners of Alwan's black eyes crinkled and his face lightened just a bit.

"That you are, Sujin," he admitted. "That you are."

His fingers dropped away from his sword. "There are still many of the dogs left behind me. I could do nothing more than sacrifice the Sujins to buy some time so that I could get the message to Bloor. I was the only one with the horse, and I just barely got away. But, if we keep talking about this, I'll get the chance to make a last stand with you when those maggots catch us."

His gaze went to each man surrounding him. "And they are coming."

This time, Balto kept his mouth shut. He didn't like the sound of that in the least.

"Feel like making a fight of it then?" Alwan smiled evilly. None of the Sujins answered. "Thought so. In that case, pick up those packs and let's be off. Bloor can't be too far ahead." He indicated the dead horse. "I'm not the only one having trouble this day."

41

The forest was unkind to Morianna's bare feet. Moments after their rest in the glade, Bloor hauled her up, and only then noticed that she had no shoes.

"I didn't wear them in the koch," she told him. "And I didn't have my slippers on when the monster took me."

"Can you walk at all?"

"Certainly out of here!" she exclaimed.

She had gotten only a few steps when a sharp stick speared the soft arch of her right foot. With a yelp, Morianna jerked it back, falling against Bloor. He gave the cut a quick inspection and frowned at the bleeding wound. He did the only thing he could with it, ripping a length of cloth from the bottom of her gown and tying it around her foot.

Then he carried her.

Hoisted up onto his back with her bare legs sticking out, they headed for what Bloor believed to be north. Morianna held on to his shoulders like a child on the back of its father. Despite the sting of her foot, she could not contain the smile on her face. Bloor needed only to look over his shoulder to see its brightness. It was enough to urge him onwards.

"We should have done this long ago," she whispered into his ear, her breath warm and pleasant.

"If you wished it," he said.

"You would have let me ride you?"

Though the question was completely innocent, the startled look on Bloor's face made Morianna giggle.

"That's a question for another day, I think," he said, focusing on the woods ahead.

"I hope so," she said in a coy voice.

"You weigh as much as a horse," Bloor told her. She scoffed and he felt her breath again in his ear. It made him smile. If he could keep her mind off of their plight, it was all the better. He was worrying enough for both of them. Were they still being pursued by Sujins? He wondered as he marched through the thinning brush. Then again, he didn't really care, as he had the woman he wanted on his back, and he was getting her to safety. Suddenly the threat of the Sujins seemed far away. Even the memory of the troll left him. All the dangers were behind them and all the time of the world lay ahead. The feeling made him move a little faster.

"You're strong," she said to his ear. "I had no idea how strong. Well, I had some idea, but never this. Am I really that heavy?" she asked sweetly.

"Yes."

The shake she tried to give him tore a brief laugh from his lips.

"You have a wonderful laugh," she told him and caught the sideways look he gave her. "Really. You should laugh more."

"If we get out of here, I'll laugh enough for my arse to fall off."

"That would be something to see."

"Morianna," Bloor panted. "I *really* can't talk now."

"That's fine," she said and laid her head against her shoulders. "Just listen. That's a command."

"Yes, my Lady."

"I told you not to call me that."

"Yes," Bloor grunted. Then he panted out, "My love."

Though he could not see it, Morianna's eyes widened ever so slightly at his words. A warmth spread through her. She clutched him tighter. Whatever was behind them was behind them. She was with Bloor now, and she could not be in a safer place.

"That's better," she said in a little voice.

Jace stopped running. He listened.

Nothing.

He strained to hear anything, as it would be difficult to hear the troll if it was hunting him. When he still heard nothing, he felt unabashed relief at escaping the thing. The Sujins managed to distract the monster long enough so that he could escape. He sucked in a great lungful of air and smiled for perhaps the first time this long grim day.

However, the troll was still back there.

As were the Sujins of Two Knife, and the girl, and Bloor. Jace frowned. He owed them nothing. His task was only to scout, and that ended when the Sujins started cutting each other to pieces. He thought of returning to Sunja to report on the Sujins' fate, but if he did so, without knowing the fate of the princess, the king might not take kindly to his mercenary hide. He needed that about as much as he needed three trolls clawing the hinterland apart for him. Something told him the wisest course of action was to simply slip away. He would be given up as lost, just like the rest of them. He ran a hand over his dirty hair. His one eye narrowed in concentration. Then there was the troll, a big troll, and it was in these woods. Who would have known? The thing was as ferocious as any other monster he had encountered and killed. He kicked loose underbrush as memories of the beast spiraled through his head. Was he actually thinking about letting the thing escape? He remembered why he sought to gut every last one of the mindless brutes. If anyone had asked him, he would have said that his hate for the monsters knew no limit.

A hatred spawned from a troll killing his entire family.

So long ago, it had happened, and yet he still had to take a breath to steady himself. The first troll he had ever hunted down and killed was a young one, smaller than the creature somewhere behind him, and it had ripped apart his family. He had been away when the thing struck their home in the forest. He convinced five other men to accompany him on the hunt that followed. The troll was a young monster with the destructiveness of a wild child. Its first and last mistake was taking Jace's family. The thing only sought to feed for the winter. They tracked and cornered the beast in a shallow cave where they burned it alive.

That troll was enough to set Jace on a life of hunting down each and every troll he could find, for as long as there was strength in him. For thirteen years, he sought out and killed the monsters, and with each slaughter he felt a grim satisfaction. Some folks would say that killing every troll in sight would not bring his family back. Jace would slap such utterly stupid people across the face. Bringing back his family was not the point. Exterminating every last troll on the face of the world would put fear back into the monsters and keep them out of the affairs of simple folk. That was the point.

By Seddon's hairy arse and Saimon's ballsack, each troll he strung up made him feel better for not being with his family when they were killed.

Killing a troll was the only bit of happiness he found these days, and here he was contemplating running from one. He looked back the way he had come. Back that way was perhaps the biggest troll he had ever encountered. He could tell by the length of the tusks and the color of its hide. The size as well, as Jace believed that the creatures never stopped growing.

He decided to help Bloor and his princess. He decided that killing this troll, this giant among giants, would certainly make an otherwise grim day better. He felt the hilt of his shortsword and sighed.

He only wished he had better tools for the job.

Alwan took the lead and brought the four Sujins through the brush. He looked for signs that Bloor and Morianna were ahead. He was experienced in tracking, and yet in this undergrowth, even he found himself pausing more than usual. He might have lost their trail, if he ever had it, back at Bloor's dead horse. He knew Bloor would head north, to meet with the Visigar just at the edge of the forest. There was a place there where they had all agreed to regroup if the plan had somehow gone wrong. The idea brought a ghost of a smile to Alwan's lips. Things could not have gotten any worse, and the forest was a huge place. Who knew how long it would take to follow the treeline back to the meeting place? Two Knife's cutthroats weren't making things any easier.

Alwan looked back twice at the remaining Sujins. Suffering from a lack of sleep, carrying heavy packs, and no doubt tortured by the memories of being betrayed by their own comrades, it all had begun to take its toll. Whatever energy fear or anger had given them, it was damn near spent. As much as he didn't want to admit it, he needed these dogs. He could not carry the entire dowry by himself, and they needed that treasure to pay the Visigar mercenaries. He bared his teeth in memory of how things were supposed to have gone. Most of the Sujins were to die, that was expected, but some were supposed to live to return to Sunja and tell the story of Two Knife's treachery. How were they to deal with these Sujins once they were ordered to hand over the princess' dowry to the Visigar?

His thoughts clouded his alertness, and he missed the bright berry drop of Morianna's blood on the stick that had stabbed her. Still wondering how the day ahead would finally play out, he moved past it. With their eyes on the back of the Cavalier, none of the Sujins saw the little sign.

They moved deeper into the forest.

The troll abruptly stopped in its tracks and peered at the trail it had created, leading it deeper into the forest. With its belly full, and a longing to be back in the freedom of the bog, its mind rumbled with indecision. There was a marshland to the north, so why lumber through the halls of the forest? Like a contrary old man, it forgot the initial reason why it started out, and looked back the way it had come. Its small brain heated up with thought and blood-rimmed black eyes narrowed in consideration.

Then it chose, and began wandering back towards the marshland.

The princess and her protector slowly traveled north, noting how the forest thinned out until they were on the edge of a great bog. Yellow grass smothered the land, and dark hills could be seen across its great berth. Bloor strained to see, looking left and right. There were no horsemen in sight. Satisfied for the moment that they were at least headed in the right direction, he exhaled and felt the weariness in his arms and legs catch up with him.

"I have to put you down," he said to her.

"Alright," Morianna replied close to his ear. He laid her down gently on a rim of hard earth. Morianna immediately inspected her foot. Sitting down next to her, Bloor watched her feat of flexibility and felt a twinge of regret.

"Wish I could do that," he muttered.

"This?" Morianna said, her foot practically lying on her opposite thigh. "Can't you?"

"No."

"Old man," she said, with a grin that Bloor could bask in all day.

"Yes, I am."

"But that doesn't bother me."

"Oh. Good."

She tore a length of dirty cloth from her gown and replaced her old bandage. "I can't keep cutting myself, though. I won't have any clothes left."

Morianna did not see the pleasant look falling over Bloor's features.

Finding a second dead horse, Two Knife paused briefly. Some animal had ripped it to shreds much like the horses back at the koch. Toffer drew in close and made a face. He felt uneasy about being in these woods. It was clear to him that were things about that they were better off not crossing paths with.

"It might be still about," Toffer said, holding onto his sword as if it would ward off a greater evil.

"Aren't you dead yet?" Two Knife asked him harshly. Though he had spoken little of it, he still felt the shock of Klytus' death. Anger coursed through him and gave him a terrible energy. He snarled. "Pass the word on. No one makes a sound from here on, and everyone stays in sight of the man at their sides, two lines deep."

Toffer did as he was told.

Two Knife pushed forward with both of his blades at the ready. His eyes were on the ground, searching for signs of fleeing Sujins and Cavaliers. Perhaps a horseless Lancer as well, but Two Knife was betting there were only Cavaliers. The revelry and armor adorning the dead horse smacked of Cavalier.

His force of renegades moved through the forest, eager to find their swordbrothers and to finish what they started.

When Two Knife raised his hand to stop, the pack of them had passed over a large tract of land untouched by man until now. Tracks were still evident before him, but he spied something even more interesting. He spotted a single crooked finger of pointed wood, its tip dabbed in dark blood. He signaled the Sujins behind him to halt while he crouched low, and with a single finger, reached out and rubbed at the drop of crimson. He brought it up to his face and studied it. Then, finishing his thoughts, he lapped it up with one lick of his tongue. It was leading off the trail. What did it mean? Was his prey trying to misdirect him?

His instinct said it was, but first he wanted to see something.

He took a step, then two steps more, and then broke into a jog. He waved for his cutthroats to follow at his heels. Two Knife's twin blades flashed in the forest light and his teeth were bared. He forced himself to move on. This would be finished soon, and he meant to be victorious.

There, in the middle of the woods, discarded in a ragged ring, lay a small pile of Sujin backpacks.

His senses buzzing now, Two Knife froze in his tracks and surveyed the forest, searching for signs of a trap. The Sujins behind him tensed up, ready for a fight. Their quarry was nearby. They would not simply drop the treasure-laden packs and run. Two Knife spun about in a slow circle. Not a sound was made by any of the men. If any of them did, Two Knife just might take the offender's head and bounce it off the forest floor.

Toffer's eyes darted from the abandoned packs before him to Two Knife's profile. The warlord peered off into the shadows cast by trees. He looked away in another direction, attempting to detect the barest flicker of an ambush. In the end, Two Knife stepped forward, shaking in his head in disdain. He scanned the heights of the trees and saw no one aiming an arrow at his chest. In truth, they should have been struck down by now if the Sujins had bows, or they were long gone.

Two Knife did not think they were long gone. No, he suspected them to be close by, and his jaw clenched with the thought.

"Sujins!" he suddenly yelled out. "I know you can hear me. So listen. You have spared your lives in dropping the treasure here. You're wise. If you go now, if you leave this place, you'll live. But I swear, once my back is turned, if you choose to strike out at it, I will hunt you down and gut you. If you hear me, then you are wasting your time. You should be off. Go!"

Two Knife waited for a moment. He then swung back towards his men.

"Do you think they're gone?" Toffer looked at him slyly.

Two Knife did not answer right away. "If they're smart, they will be. If they aren't, we kill them. Gather that up," he ordered, indicating the treasure packs.

Six men sheathed their blades and slung their shields. They fell on the booty and gathered the packs up and over their shoulders. Their breathless sounds of wonder made Two Knife's spine tingle.

"Is it all there?"

"I don't know if it is or not, Two Knife," one man said, flipping open the canvas flap so that others standing nearby could see the gleaming wealth. "But I'm happy with what's here!"

"That's good enough for me then," Toffer said with a greedy smile.

"One thing though," Two Knife said as he watched his men work. "We're going back that way."

"Alright," Toffer shrugged. "But why?"

"There is still the matter of a missing princess," Two Knife hissed, "and if you think this is good, wait for what we can get for her pretty hide."

From beneath the red bandages covering his head, Toffer's eyes narrowed. "How do you know?"

"This is a lure," Two Knife sneered at the obvious bait. "Left to draw us away from her. Remember the wagon? Her shoes were there. She didn't have time to put on her shoes for whatever reason, and she cut her foot back there on the trail because of it. I'm gambling here, but I can see them drawing us here to this, to this point, and giving all this up to save their own hides and the princess. She went in one direction while we followed this. Marrn is to the north of here, and the signs were leading in that direction. We go back there now, and I'll wager on finding more. That's my guess. What say you?"

"So you think they split up?" Toffer asked, scratching at his chin.

"I think they split up."

The smile spreading across Toffer's bloody features were genuine. He knew for certain now that, for the second time this day, he was not wasting his time with this man.

"Lead on," he said.

It wasn't until Two Knife and his dogs had taken the packs and left the area that Alwan started breathing again. He lay on his back, hidden well enough by the undergrowth to avoid being seen, and yet close enough to hear Two Knife's words. Sighing, he folded his hands and gazed upwards at the dark green canopy overhead.

"Now what do we do?" Balto asked from nearby. The Sujin remained on his stomach with his head pressed down into the damp earth. He kept it there the instant he thought Two Knife had spotted him.

"Let them carry it for a while," Alwan sighed again and closed his eyes. He wished that the day was done and that he could take the rest that his body so badly wanted. Balto fixed the man with an annoyed glare. At first he though the Cavalier merely looked evil, but now he added another characteristic he didn't care for. The man spoke a little too carefree for Balto's taste.

"We're going to let them make off with all of that?"

"No," Alwan said with his eyes closed. The other Sujins lay close by and listened to the exchange. Gatesin could sense that his dear old Balto was becoming annoyed with the horseman. The Cavalier had the same condescending arrogance about him as Bloor did. Did all the Cavaliers act the same way?

"I'm waiting," Balto informed the quiet Cavalier. He could feel his temper rising. He was quick to chastise laziness in other Sujins, and damn him to Saimon's hell if he was about to allow this Cavalier to let his rank protect him.

Perhaps reading his thoughts, Alwan opened his eyes and studied the hard face of the Sujin questioning him. He recognized experience when he saw it, and with experience came impatience to half answers. Balto would never know it, but at that moment, Alwan marked him as a man who obviously was a hair above the common Sujin.

"We'll wait here," he said, believing that telling the Sujin of his plans should inform the Sujin that he was privileged, at least at the moment anyway. "We'll follow them in a bit. They'll be going after the princess and Bloor now. I missed them back there. He didn't." Alwan had to give it to the renegade Two Knife. The man was quicker at finding trails than he was. "Maybe we can catch them unawares somehow."

"You think he's going to let the five of us kill him in his sleep?" Balto scoffed. "You'd better come up with something better than that."

Alwan thought Balto had a resemblance to Lord Maullus, in attitude at least. Lord Maullus was not a forgiving man. He took in the dark treetops. "We'll follow them at least. And if you have any better ideas, make them be known before we strike."

"You mean to attack them?" Balto asked.

Alwan did not blink. "I mean to gut every last one of the bastards."

Tungang smirked. He liked the way the man thought.

42

The sun began sinking into the horizon and the shadows deepened. The clouds lumbered across the sky, hiding the darkening blue. Soundless birds darted across, rising and falling like something hunted them. Bloor watched them soar up and then down again as they went across his vision and out of sight. Then he was captivated by Morianna's face.

"Are you ready?" he asked her.

"Are you?" she asked back.

"I am."

"Then I am too," she said with a smile. "Where do we go from here?"

"There is a place, but we have to follow along the edge of this marsh, I think."

"You're not sure?"

The question made Bloor frown with a hint of doubt. "We are a long way from where I wanted to be, but I think I know where we are."

"You probably wouldn't tell me anyway, even if we were lost," Morianna accused him. She was right. "Will you still carry me?"

"I will."

"Then," she exclaimed with a twinkle in her eye, "we should be off at once."

A smile leaked into Bloor's face. He should have known. Then he froze.

Morianna saw it immediately, but before she could speak, Bloor hushed her with a look. His eyes set on something over her shoulder. Following his stare, she looked before he had the chance to stop her.

The troll emerged from the forest as if it were coming through a doorframe that was too confining. Its huge arms swung wide and cavernous nostrils flared with the freshness of the marsh air. Such empty territory begged to be lived in, and the troll felt immensely better to see it. It snorted and looked from side to side, a massive fist reaching out for the support of a nearby tree. It considered which way to go and since it had no conception of left or right, it heaved its bulk into one direction and began to take long strides, the land sucking at its every step. It moved at leisure, deciding that there was no need to hurry, and enjoyed the wetness squeezing in between its toes. Its stomach was full and had ceased demanding attention. Looking to the darkening sky, it would be a fine night, and night was an excellent time to hunt.

Then, a scent drifted across its nose and its great nostrils leeched it from the air. The troll's head perked up as if hooked. It stopped and gazed in the direction of the treeline, nostrils flaring and straining to catch another hint of something perhaps good to eat. It caught the scent again, and the beast's red-rimmed eyes furrowed. It wasn't hungry, but blood was blood, and something had bled recently.

With a grunt, it moved along the treeline with no fear of the forest or anything in it. Each great stride made loud sucking sounds as the land sought to swallow the troll down. It slowed when it came closer to the marked spot, sucking in air and savoring the scent of fresh blood. It searched the ground and found the source of the smell within seconds. The creature moved forward and drew in closer to a place that now had its full attention. There, amongst the yellow grass, lay a shred of bloody cloth. Too small to pick up, but in the area another scent lingered, fainter than the blood. A memory sparkled in its head. The morsel it had planned to devour at a later time, the little one that had somehow escaped. It was near.

Hunching over, its death promising eyes stabbed at the depths of the forest. It flexed its claws and moved over the bloody bandage on the ground, easing its bulk back into the woods as quietly as cloth soaking up water. The smell of prey lured it back, and the great monster slipped into the familiar role of hunter.

As the forest raced by him, Bloor noticed Morianna's bare foot sticking out before him with its fresh bandage. Where was the old one? In that instant he knew the troll would be hunting them. The old bandage would draw it to them, and he wondered how quick the creature would take up the hunt. What was it that Jace said about the trolls and being drawn to blood? He could not remember, but he knew it to be bad. Where was the old man now? If he was smart, he would have left this entire situation behind.

"Is it coming?" Morianna breathed into his ear. When she saw the beast emerging from the forest, her breathing quickened. She saw the horror that she thought to be behind her, and if she were lucky, would only encounter again in the deepest, most terrible dreams. However, there the thing was, standing like a deer might before venturing out into the open. Then Bloor was hauling her back into the veil of pine-smelling boughs, his hand over her mouth. He gathered her up onto his back and began moving as quickly as his legs could carry him while trying to be quiet. It was difficult for him, yet she wanted him to move faster and willed the message to him to flee at best possible speed.

However, Bloor knew better. Making noise in the snapping underbrush would only bring the thing on faster.

Right now, the troll only had its nose. Once it saw them, there would be no need for stealth.

"Is it coming?" Morianna asked again, making Bloor wish she would not.

"Yes," he told her. The barest of moans went into his ear then, making him want to do whatever he could to protect her. A thought of how sheltered her life had been went through his head. What was the most danger that she had ever know? Perhaps nothing beyond being forced to marry a complete stranger, and even that could not compare to the troll. For really, what was more terrifying than the ages' old fear of being eaten by a monster?

Bloor forced the question from his mind. With the Nords, he could expect torture and then death. With the troll, he could expect being consumed just as if one were tearing into a fresh loaf of bread straight out of Lindee's oven. The image made him move faster. He weaved in and out of the trees, and clutching their limbs as a frightened snake might. He did not look behind to see if they were being followed. He did not want to know.

"I can't see it," Morianna exclaimed.

"Don't do that," Bloor told her.

"Do what?"

"Lean back to look." The drag she created not only slowed him but sapped his strength. He would need every last drop of it before this day played itself out. Seddon above, night began to look sleepless as well. He swore again at gods that he had no patience for. Of all the challenges and hard spots Bloor had found himself in, now was perhaps the first time he had even thought of praying. He hoped the entities didn't think of him as being desperate.

Morianna straightened herself, and then it happened. Bloor slipped and felt his weight go to the right, her legs splayed out on either side. Morianna's right foot smacked into a solid trunk of old wood whose bark flesh had been gnawed bare. The connection drove her leg back, and she fell from Bloor's hold. The Cavalier tried to right his balance, maintain his hold on the princess, and cushion his own fall, all at once. With an expulsion of breath, he landed across Morianna's leg. He expected the sound of snapping bone in a split second of dread.

The bone did not break however, nor did Morianna cry out. She clenched her jaw, fought back the pain, and Bloor loved her for it. He sprang up from her like a cat repelling from water, and cupped her grimacing face. Her eyes opened at his touch and he was grateful for the alertness he saw there. "You're fine, you're fine. Nothing is broken. Is anything broken? Can you move?"

Red cheeked, she nodded, and the tension slowly began to seep from her face. Bloor wished he could afford her the time to better ride out the pain but he dare not. Knowing his thoughts, she reached out and together they stumbled to their feet and she mounted his back once more.

Then Bloor saw the bandage on the ground. A blossom of red dotted the cloth. His teeth snapped together in annoyance.

"What are you doing?" Morianna asked, even as he started to bend. Dressed as he was in heavy armor and carrying a full-grown woman on his back, the Cavalier ignored the pain and stress in his joints and body, and bent to one knee to pick up the bandage.

With a heavy breath, he regained his feet and felt the barest spin of dizziness. He shook it away and saw the dead tree that had stopped Morianna's foot. He saw the stain of blood on its bare wooden flesh, and he watched as a single drop of blood dripped from Morianna's foot before him.

"Oh," Morianna hissed in horror, "my!" She felt the trickle of blood drop from the puncture wound in the arch of her foot. She felt the torturing dribble of it down her soft heel. She saw the blood drop away. Fear, like a cold block of midwinter ice, pushed into her stomach. She clamped onto Bloor's back and fought it, and pressed her head into his broad back.

Bloor stood there, stupidly allowing two drops of her blood to dapple the ground. He did not think he had the time to bandage it but he could not run through the forest with her bleeding each step. Without a sound, he dumped her on her back. The sudden movement startled the princess, and a little grunt escaped her as she hit the ground. The jarring impact sent needles of pain through her rump and lower back. Kneeling down next to her, he grabbed at her ruined gown. He yanked a long strip from its shortening base, and gnashed it free with his teeth. He bound the foot with an energy borne of desperation and the unfairness of it all, and Morianna could see from the expression on his face that things weren't going as he wanted. Neither of them looked back the way they had come. They would not need to if the troll was close by. Morianna waited, expecting to hear the monster come crashing down on them any second. Bloor looked into her eyes when he finished tying the knot. The determination there was frightening. He hoisted her up onto his back. She pressed her head against the nape of his neck and held on tight.

This time, she said nothing at all.

The troll caught the scent of fresh blood, as perhaps a drunkard would catch the whiff of wasted wine. The smell drew it up in its tracks and it smelled the air, gently sniffing at it as if it were coaxing a flame into life. Certain it was heading in the right direction, it crept further along. Then there was the dead tree before it with it tempting mark. The troll's red-rimmed eyes narrowed on a stain. Drawing in closer, it smelled the blood there. Its jaws parted, and a tongue licked at the surface. The flavor teased it and summoned up the pangs of its appetite. It straightened up and moved past the wood, focusing on the yellow and brown and green of the forest: more blood, drops of it. A single great claw flexed out and circled the spot where the drops spattered. The troll snorted. Its meal was just ahead.

However, like any great hunter, the thing would not charge after it just yet. Not until it had its prey in sight.

Then a cry of pain cut though the forest, perking its head up in surprise. It peered ahead, but the droves of timber hid where the sound came from. Then sounds of fighting: metal on metal, little ones fighting little ones. A scream of pain.

Cautiously, the troll hunched over and edged forward, claws at the ready.

In the course of his lifetime, Bloor could count on one hand the number of times he had actually been surprised. The Field of Skulls was perhaps the greatest of them all, and the most dangerous, as he barely escaped the Nordish Jackals and their slaughtering of the Sunjan Klaw. Even then, he shared the surprise with a group of battle-hardened Sujins. Their survival depended on hard choices, harder fights, and the knowledge that they were not alone, that they were there to watch each other's backs while breath flowed into their lungs.

However, what he suddenly saw surprised Saimon's hell out of him.

Bloor saw the line of Sujins through the wild growth of the forest and he realized with an exploding sense of danger who they were. He was alone to face a pack of cut-throat mercenaries. Worse still, he carried the woman he loved on his back. There were more Sujins than he could count, and more than he could possibly fight. All that was needed was for one of them to grab her and place a blade to her throat, and they were finished. He could not outrun them, and he felt her grip on him tighten when she saw the men.

"Are they ours?" she panted in his ear.

A weary sigh left him. "No."

He eased her down against a tree. She stood with her hurt foot hitched up and her hands holding the trunk for support.

"Keep your back against the wood," he instructed her.

"What are you going to do?" she asked.

The hard look he gave her was answer enough.

43

The Sujins drew within twenty strides of the pair and fanned out, spreading around them. Bloor's heart sunk. There were too many, and they were too careful. One Sujin from the middle of the line stepped in close to Bloor with a sword and shield held at guard. The man recognized the Cavalier, and with a face full of contempt, drew up mucus from the very depths of his lungs and sent it flying at the ground before the man. Bloor glared back. That was enough for the Sujin.

The traitor broke ranks and charged, coming in fast with his shield raised to his eyes, seeking to stab upwards with his shortsword. Bloor spun around the shield, avoiding the sword underneath it, his own blade whipping around to chop at the back of the Sujin's neck. The blow snapped the man's head forward and he dropped to the ground. Another Sujin broke ranks with a scream and flung himself at the Cavalier. He thrust his sword and yelled out when Bloor slapped it aside. The Cavalier stepped in close and stomped down on the man's toes, crushing them into the ground. The Sujin's face froze in a rictus of pain, and Bloor stabbed him through the chest. Chain mail links popped as his blade slipped between them.

Stepping away from the two dead men and placing his back to Morianna, Bloor regarded the remaining Sujins with hard eyes.

No one else dared to approach.

"You can have those two," Two Knife said. "If they were stupid enough to forget my orders and break ranks, I don't want any part of them," he shook his head.

Then Two Knife's blades came up and pointed at Bloor. "You, however."

Bloor caught the renegade's meaning and his brow furrowed.

"That's right, *Lord*. Just you and I and no one else," he threw a look at the Sujins gathered around. Toffer said nothing. It was fine by him. In his condition, he had no intention of fighting the Cavalier single-handedly.

Two Knife felt the rush of excitement build up inside him just like before, when he put down Tarco and the Axemen. The same surge of power he felt just before he squared off against any opponent he felt would be a challenge to kill. Here was the Cavalier commander, a man whose skill at arms was almost as legendary throughout the Klaws as his own, the very one that Two Knife felt an instant dislike the moment he met him. For all of the quiet disdain Bloor flung at him while he was in command, Two Knife meant to make his end as painful as possible. He was the better man, and he knew it. Today he had proven it twice over. No one was better than he, and Bloor's death would solidify that like the mortar sticking Sunja's walls together. Sizing up the gleaming Cavalier before him with one sword, Two Knife knew the man's head would split apart as easy as any other.

He gestured with his blades, waving Bloor to come forward. "We'll fight in the middle," he declared.

Bloor shook his head slowly, as if a child were talking to him. Two Knife waited for the man to speak, but no words came. Rather than let anger affect his control, Two Knife grinned. "Then I'll come to you. After this day's walking, a few more feet won't make a difference to me."

There was a nudging at Bloor's foot. He looked down to see Morianna's bare leg outstretched, her eyes catching his, pleading for him to be careful. Begged him as much a look would allow.

Bloor smiled back.

Then the Cavalier faced the Sujin.

"We have the coin, Bloor," Two Knife informed his adversary as he stepped towards him. He saw the look the princess and her protector exchanged. "Now all I want… is her."

Bloor's hooded eyes became downcast for a moment, then centered on the challenge of the man before him. He made it clear that he was looking at a corpse. Bloor held the gaze of Two Knife as he took another wary step towards him, his twin swords flashing in the dimming forest light. Then, over Two Knife's shoulder, a bear of a man standing at least two heads above the Sujin he stood behind stepped into view. The axe he held came up in a swing.

The widening of Bloor's eyes made Two Knife hesitate, and he turned halfway just as Tungang's axe came down to cleave the helmeted head of the Sujin he stood behind. In that crash of metal on metal, the four other men that had quietly stalked the traitorous force struck out with all of their fury from the day. Their plan was simple: kill as many of the Sujins as they could as they made their way to the princess, surround her, and then protect her to the last.

When Tungang killed the first man, the savage reaving began. The loyalists struck down seven Sujins where they stood in a fury of sound and iron. Then Two Knife's Sujins jumped back from the avenging loyalists, trying to assess this new force, while four more of their numbers died screaming. With sword and shield and axe, the four loyalists, joined by the killer Alwan, tore into the traitors with the determination of making right the day's shameful betrayal.

Two Knife looked back to Bloor and got a blade up to parry the Cavalier's first stroke. The Cavalier had taken advantage of the Sujin's distraction. Two Knife smiled evilly at the sly move, and gave Bloor an approving nod. It was something he would have done himself. Perhaps Bloor was worthy after all.

Bloor did not like the smirk on the man's face and sought to remove it.

At the neckline.

They crashed together and the whirling blades of Two Knife were stalled and deflected by the single lightning sword held by Bloor. They fought toe-to-toe for a moment, seeking to kill each other quickly, but when it became obvious that it would not be settled in such a way, they began circling, and the strikes became slower.

It was at that moment that Balto slashed out a Sujin's midsection once, twice, sending the dead man flying backwards from the force of the blows and separating the Cavalier and the renegade leader.

Two Knife screamed out at the interruption. Bloor spun to the side and punched his sword through a nearby traitor's ribs. The man hissed a shocked death cry, impaled as he was. Then Bloor turned to make his way to Morianna; Two Knife was secondary to him.

Three Sujins came between him and the princess.

Three Sujins died.

Gatesin killed a man where he stood and drove his sword into the throat of another whom he recognized. He did not think on it, for something else caught his attention and his jaw dropped in astonishment. He drew breath to shout a warning as Bloor moved, unobstructed, for the princess.

The Cavalier's free hand stretched out to her.

Morianna reached up for him, her dark eyes wide with fright.

Then a roar engulfed them all.

The troll stepped out from the shadows of the forest and grabbed a startled Sujin by his head. It yanked the man off of his feet and swung him like a doll at Bloor, striking the Cavalier full in the chest and flinging him up and over the other combatants. Bloor's breath left him, and his legs clipped the head and shoulders of two men as he flew by, spinning them off their feet. A tree stopped the Cavalier's flight, and all hearing the awful crack of flesh and armor on wood knew that Bloor was dead. The battling men cringed back from one another, fighting the urge to get away from the monster among them. Morianna screamed out. The troll roared again, drowning her out. Two Knife froze where he stood, seeing the absolute might of the troll for the first time, and knowing now what had wrecked the wagon. He moved back from the creature, his eyes never leaving the thing, his blades at guard.

Balto and Hatch stopped, staring in equal awe at the beast in their midst. Alwan looked up from the Sujin he had just killed. One look at the troll left him wishing he still had Saimon with him, and a very long lance.

The troll swung at one of Two Knife's Sujins nearby and missed. The man flung himself backwards and the mighty claw aimed for his chest raked the tough bark of a tree in a flurry of splinters. Another roar sent the Sujins scurrying back. The troll moved around the tree and glared at the little ones about it. There were many, but they were terrified. Then it saw the one it wanted, the one it had fixated on.

It reached down and grabbed at Morianna's kicking legs. Screaming as if she were being pulled apart, the troll jerked her up off of the ground and swung her over its broad shoulder. Two Knife's mouth opened as if he were about to protest, realizing that it would do no good at all. Barking a warning at the men in the woods, the troll whirled on them all and retreated back the way it had come. Its wounded leg pained it, but the troll ignored it and gathered speed. Tungang was in perfect position to see the creature rush deeper into the forest and to catch a glimpse of a still screaming Morianna flopping about helplessly upon the monster's grey-green back.

Alwan looked to the fallen form of Bloor and then to the path of the troll. He gave no further thought to the issue, and baring his teeth, set off after the beast, killing two Sujins as he went.

Seeing the Cavalier bolting after the troll while screams echoed throughout the woods, Two Knife's paralysis ended. He firmed his grip on his weapons. Bloor was dead and forgotten. The troll was running and it had the princess. Toffer looked to his leader and was about to shout that they still had the dowry and didn't need the princess. The ransom wasn't worth following after that monster. However, Two Knife cut him off before he could say anything.

"AFTER THEM!" he shouted at his Sujins, and gave chase. His Sujins hesitated for only a split-second before following their leader.

With the Sujins breaking away from them, Gatesin looked across the forest ground and met the eyes of Balto. The old warrior shrugged and broke into a run. grinding his jaw, Gatesin followed. Tungang was only a second behind. He was not about to let those two face the monster alone.

Looking about the clearing, Hatch saw that the Sujins had left the packs of treasure on the forest ground covered in brown needles and yellow leaves. It was all there for him to take. Then he saw the motionless form of Bloor. He paused for a second, and, shaking his head, made after the others. He feared that if he did take the packs full of booty, an undead Bloor would somehow come back and find him for his crime.

The thought of it made him run faster.

44

The troll plunged back through the forest at its best speed, one arm shoving aside smaller trees seeking to slow it, and pushing away the limbs of the larger ones. It could hear the sounds of pursuit behind it. A snort flared from it, and the monster gnashed its tusked jaws. It would crush any of them trying to stop it from getting to the great open of the swamp. Its wounded leg still bothered it, but the marshland called to it and lent it energy. Anger would armor it against the little ones following. The mountain that it was, would not let them have its prize. The little one it carried belonged to it from the beginning. They would not have this little one.

Two of the faster Sujins caught up with the troll and closed in upon its flanks, seeking to stab at the creature's legs. Its great red-rimmed black eyes, peering though the shock of sewage-colored hair, caught movement on either side of it. Snarling, the troll lashed out with its free claw and snapped the neck of one Sujin, dropping the man in his tracks. The other Sujin dropped back and let the monster run on.

Two Knife was at his heels a moment later. "What are you waiting for?" he stopped and stared at the Sujin, who appeared uncertain. The man indicated the fallen Sujin with his broken neck. Other Sujins flashed by them, intent on pursuit.

"That thing did that."

"So you don't want to be a part of this any longer, do you?" Two Knife stepped in close to the man, who retreated, wary of his leader. He shook his head.

"Then *get going!*" Two Knife barked at him. The reluctant Sujin did just that, remembering how Two Knife danced on a fallen axeman. Two Knife watched the man go and knew he would have to keep an eye on him. He might even have to make an example of him. They were no longer part of Sunjan's Klaws, but they were still Sujins. He started after the troll once more, casting a glance back the way they had come.

Trying to keep up as best as he could, Toffer chugged towards him. The man was a mess of cuts and bloody bandages. It was a wonder he was still on his feet. However, Toffer wasn't a problem. The troll was.

He ran after it.

Toffer watched Two Knife bound off into the wilderness. He set his jaw and tried to get more speed out of his legs, fighting off the lightheaded feeling gathering behind his eyes. He felt sick from blood loss. He continued on, chugging away and slowing down despite his best efforts. The sounds of the chase grew fainter in the distance, but Toffer had no doubt as to its conclusion: They would have the princess.

His ears began to ring then, and he thought about stopping for a bit, just to catch his wind. Just a quick rest would perk him right up. He slowed to a walk just as a figure flashed by him.

Toffer's eyes went wide.

It was Bloor.

The Sujin opened his mouth to scream, but the Cavalier was already swinging his sword. The backhand cut fanned underneath Toffer's chin and a second lipless mouth zipped open and gurgled red. The Sujin dropped his weapon and clutched at his fatal wound, knowing his time had come. His legs failed him. He collapsed onto his side, feeling his life gush from him, and watched the figure of the Cavalier run on.

Bloor!

Then blackness.

The troll pressed on, unstoppable. A Sujin tried to smash the edge of his shield into its foot but missed. The troll stopped long enough to rip the man's face off in a savage downward slash of its talons. The corpse's legs began kicking as if the whole head had been removed. Another Sujin flung himself at the troll's face, screaming and stabbing as he sailed through the air. The troll swatted the warrior down with a backhanded slap, bouncing the man off a thick tree. It screamed out and started running again. If the little ones running about it at the edges of its vision wanted to fight, they would have to come closer. The troll disliked having the forest around it. Once it was in the great marshland, then it would deal with these little ones. He heard them scream at one another in their voices, and it hurt its head. It saw a group of them forming up, as if preparing to strike. The mountain drew itself up. It would show these little ones what it meant to hunt one of its kind. Its huge claws came up and flexed.

In doing so, it dropped the princess.

One Sujin saw the troll drop the princess just before the beast lunged at a knot of his swordbrothers. The air became charged with the sounds of flesh on metal, skin that ripped like wet cloth, and the screams of men. The Sujin knew he would not have another chance. He moved in on the woman, dropping his shield as he reached for her lying on the ground.

"Get up!" he shouted at her.

The princess looked into the man's eyes and did not recognize him.

She's lost her senses! The Sujin's mind blared. He grabbed at her arm and dug his feet in to pull her to her feet. With a scream, she shook him off.

The body, still wrapped in chainmail but missing both of its arms, slammed into the Sujin's upper body and knocked him flat on his back. The wind left his lungs in a gush and his helmet flew from his skull. His vision blackened for a moment, yet he felt his sword still in his hand.

Then the troll stepped on his head.

Barely feeling the vase like shattering of the bone, the troll yanked the little one up again by both of her legs and slapped her over its shoulder. It smashed another Sujin rushing at it from its side, ramming the man into the ground and stomping on him before he could rise. A roar left the troll then. It did not like the feel of little ones between its toes. Whirling about, it put its great tusked head down and aimed for open marshland.

Two Knife's Sujins kept pursuit, doggedly keeping at the beast's heels, but well enough away from any sudden attacks. The thing had killed seven of their number without pausing and then continued on its way. Those that remained wondered how they would ever bring such a beast down without harming the princess.

Some others were realizing that the troll wasn't the only thing in the forest.

Seizing opportunity where it presented itself, Gatesin, Balto, Hatch, and Tungang kept up with the running figure of Alwan, ducking and weaving in and out of the tall trees like a snake born to water. As they ran, the four men felt a growing appreciation for having the Cavalier on their side. Alwan steamed through the wilderness like a metal bull, running down any stray Sujin clearly not part of the four behind him. He moved like a ghost, and the men he came upon and killed did not know he was there until he was past them and they were dying in his wake. He had no qualms about striking a man down from behind, and he left behind at least three Sujins wondering what had killed them.

Though he had not the breath to express his feelings, Balto was indeed grateful to have the man on his side. He watched as the Cavalier bounced up behind another of Two Knife's Sujins and took the man's leg half off with one powerful slash. Tungang bounded over the fallen Sujin, cursing in disbelief. The Cavalier impressed even him.

A group of traitors loomed up from out of the brush and Alwan skirted around them. "Kill them!" he yelled back at the loyalists, running around the Sujins poised for an attack. Gatesin bared his teeth. Tungang screamed. Two Knife's Sujins screamed back and the loyalists smashed into the knot of traitors. The fight was short and without mercy. There were five traitors against four loyalists, and those that were responsible for the ambush so long ago did not stand a chance. They were hacked down where they stood in the space of seconds. In the aftermath, as the chase continued on without them, the four men faced each other and scanned the area for other prey, still high off the rush of battle.

"No more," Gatesin panted, gazing around.

"All gone ahead," Balto added.

"Bloodsobitches," Hatch growled and then he gawked in surprise. He pointed. The other followed his pointed arm and tensed up, but only for a moment.

There was no mistaking Bloor emerging from the timberland.

45

Two Knife kept his eyes on the retreating form of the troll. He looked about him and realized with dismay that there were only a handful of Sujins remaining. Where were all the others? He saw what the troll did to the maggots that flung themselves at its legs. The monster smashed and crushed and tore the life from them, and the images in Two Knife's mind lent him a terrible surge of energy as well as respect. He feared no man, but this thing…?

His swords swished at his side as he kept up with the beast. He could see that the thing had sustained wounds. At least some of his dogs managed to cut the thing. However, the troll surged ahead like a monstrous wave destined to crash against some faraway wall and willing to roll over everything in its path. It was a thing of incredible strength, and therein was the problem. While it could not outrun anything here in the tangles of underbrush, in a drawn-out chase, the thing would leave them all behind. The legs…The legs had to be crippled.

The trouble was, everyone that had tried to cripple it was dead.

With boughs snapping in his face, Two Knife did not like the idea of letting the beast simply get away. Something like that would be hungry soon enough, and it was clear what it had in mind for the princess. Though he had no love for the woman, he did not want her *eaten* by a troll. She was worth a fortune to him, and the only way to keep the thing from devouring her was to keep it running.

Which brought him back to the monster's legs.

He heard and saw figures racing in the same direction as the troll. Then he saw one of his Sujins fall. An armored man darted through the brush, running parallel to him.

A man of silver.

Two Knife smiled grimly. Alwan, or Bloor, but Bloor was dead. Or was he? It would not surprise Two Knife if the man lived and at this point in his day, to kill either or both of the men would be a prize. However, he did not deviate from following the troll.

The troll's lead increased as the footrace went on, as the men pursuing it could not keep up wearing the armor they did. They eventually fell back into the distance. The troll's wounds began to ache now, and its blood spattered the branches and ground in black gobs. Bloor saw this as he ran along, leaving behind the Sujins following. He was driven by something greater than mere duty to save Morianna. He found the wreckage of the troll's trail and the blood marking it. A coldness surged through Bloor then. The thing was going back to the marsh. Why that stretch of land held terror for him, he did not want to find out. He knew he had to stop the troll before it reached the marshlands. He had to get Morianna away from the thing. It gave him the energy he needed to run faster, past the broken boughs and footprints left in the earthy mat of the forest. Bloor saw Alwan jogging behind a fence of trees and he waved, indicating to the Cavalier that he should fan out further. Alwan nodded, panting as he went.

Then a great scream shook the forest, and the sound halted Bloor in his tracks.

The troll was close now to the marsh, it could smell the freshness of the bog and it filled its lungs with the air. It pushed away the irksome trees seeking to slow it down. It hated the trees. It hated the forest. Now it was almost home.

It passed by one large tree and a new scent wafted across its nose, strange enough to make the creature slow down.

It was then that Jace struck.

Peeling himself away from the cover of a tree, the troll hunter struck with his sword and plunged it into one of the monster's legs with all his strength. The beast jumped forward, yanking the weapon from Jace's grasp and dropping Morianna in a heap. The troll screeched and howled as it twisted its bulk to get at the thorn sticking out of its leg. Blood-rimmed black eyes narrowed to slits. It recognized the sword of the little ones. It saw the little one scoop up the other little one and run back down the trail it had left behind. Rage swelled up inside the thing's primitive mind. It grasped the weapon in one claw, ignoring the bite, and ripped it free. The howl of pain made the forest tremble.

Bloor stopped in his tracks and wondered what the sound meant. Was the thing dead? If so, who could have killed it? He thought briefly of Jace and how the hunter moved through the forest. If there was one man that could possibly take the beast down, it would be him, but Bloor did not dwell on it any further.

For six Sujins sought to surround him.

"Kill him!" Two Knife shouted. He heard the troll's howl as well. He would investigate as soon as the Cavalier was put down.

A Sujin stepped into the Cavalier, stabbing for his gut. Bloor parried, and his backhand cut split the man's face in two, whipping his head back. A second Sujin tried to attack Bloor from behind, aiming for the Cavalier's lower back. Bloor darted away from him, jabbing his blade at a pair of

Sujins as he went. The three converged on the man, seeking to overwhelm him with swords and shields.

Bloor killed them all.

Two Knife stood with both of his blades ready. The last remaining Sujin standing with him moved for the Cavalier. He only took two steps before the form of Alwan came crashing out from the trees, stabbing the man cleanly though the middle.

Faced now with two Cavaliers, Two Knife retreated with a curse, disappearing quickly into the cover of the forest. He gritted his teeth as he did so, meaning to avenge his men at first opportunity, preferably when the Cavaliers weren't standing shoulder-to-shoulder.

He only got so far.

Both Bloor and Alwan were about to chase the Sujin when something filled the troll trail and caught their attention.

"Hey!" Jace's screamed at the two standing Cavaliers. Both Bloor and Alwan turned to see the troll hunter floundering towards them both, carrying the unconscious princess in his arms.

"Give her here," Bloor told him. Jace dropped her into the man's outstretched arms.

"I got it in the leg."

"You didn't kill it?" Alwan demanded.

Jace gave him a disgusted look.

Almost as if she were aware of her childhood protector, Morianna gave a little moan when Bloor gathered her up. "Where is it?" he asked Jace.

The forest shook again, and all three men turned to see the hunched form of the troll clawing its way towards them, over the same path it had pounded down only minutes ago. The sight of the men infuriated the monster, and it welcomed the power the rage lent it. The sight of the huge troll hauling itself along by its arms paralyzed the three men. Tree limbs cracked and snapped with the weight of the monster and the troll's terrible voice filled their ears. Jace had seen this many times before.

The troll had gone berserk.

"Run! Anywhere! But not together! It'll go after only one of us!" Jace yelled at the Cavaliers.

However, the troll thought differently. Aware of the little ones' proclivity to bolt, it yanked a sizeable limb off a tree and threw it. The missile scissored through the air, a piece of wood the length of a full-grown man. Bloor turned a second before the jagged end clipped his head, dropping him to the ground with the princess. Jace and Alwan flung themselves to either side of the fallen Cavalier, rolling as they went and hoping that nothing landed on them. The constant screaming of the troll echoed throughout. Bloor cracked open his eyes to peer into an angry set of black ones. The troll pulled Morianna away from him, and he was powerless to stop it. Black stars flared before his vision and blood ran down the side of his head from an ugly gash. Once again, Morianna was slung over the monster's back. It looked down at the motionless Cavalier. It remembered this one. This one had stolen from it before. With a growl, it raised its fist to smash in the little one's skull. There would be no taking from the troll ever again.

Then Alwan was there, slashing his sword across the broad back of the monster, faster than the eye could follow, and drawing terrible lines of black blood beside the limp form of the princess. The troll straightened up and the fist poised for Bloor lashed out at this new pain. The little one ducked away, slipping behind more trees. The troll screamed out its frustration. Trees! Oh how it wanted nothing more to do with such a place! It threw its shoulder into the tree the little one darted behind and heaved with all its might. The ground protested and roots snapped and the air suddenly smelled of dirt as the monster began pushing the tree over onto its attacker. It roared again, seeking to blow the needles from the boughs covering the tree. However, the intertwining limbs of other nearby trees preventede the troll from uprooting it victim. In a matter of seconds, coupled with its wounds, the troll had exhausted itself. With a deflated growl and a gnashing of tusks, it regarded the half-usurped tree and rolled its massive shoulders.

It would let this one live.

Wanting nothing more than to get back to its marsh, the troll turned about and made its way back the way it had come, with Morianna, once again, slung over its shoulder. It forgot Bloor, and sought only to make best speed to the marshland, towards freedom.

Back on the forest ground, Bloor propped himself up on one elbow and watched the troll disappear. His squeezed his eyes shut, willing his sight back, and realizing how lucky he was to still have his senses. The chunk of tree the thing had thrown at him would have crushed his head if it had fully connected. He dabbed at the wound in his scalp and looked at the blood covering his fingers. Raw determination hauled him up to his feet and the forest spun. Hands found him and his eyes met those of Gatesin.

"It's got her," the dour-faced Sujin informed him.

Grunting, Bloor turned and picked up his sword. Alwan and Jace came into view. The remaining Sujins fell in behind him. Taking a deep breath and weary to the bone, Bloor went after the troll.

Slowly, the distance between the two began to shrink.

46

The troll burst through the veil of the forest and took two steps before it realized where it was. The marshland! It was finally home! A roar left its lungs and it snapped its jaws at fresh air. Then it felt something. It spun to its right, and the blood-rimmed black eyes went wide in anger. Little ones! Was there no end to them?

On their way to meeting the Sunjan Cavalier, the score of Visigar horsemen halted in their tracks. War horses trained not to flinch rose up in fright before the bleeding mass of the troll. Some riders fell from their mounts, dropping weapons as they crashed into both ground and trees. The Visigar that did not fall fought to steady their horses. The leader named Prong forced his horse to his will, keeping his eyes on the troll only a short distance away. The beast was a terrible sight for even him, and he wanted nothing more than to clutch at the blade in the scabbard on his back. The smell of excrement and filth screwed up his nose, pushing his fear and revulsion of the thing even higher. The smell was terrible, and the big Visigar felt his pale features drain even whiter in contrast to his black hair and beard.

Shaking its fist at them in warning, the troll stomped across the open bog it considered home, showing these little ones its back. It did not fear them. It did not fear the four-legged ones, either. It had devoured them all in its time, and it would do so again if they chose to follow it. It was weak, it knew, but it had strength enough to deal with anything getting too close.

None of the Visigar thought of pursuing the monster. The beast was traveling on ground that was treacherous to their horses. One corner of Prong's mouth hooked upwards in distaste. They saw the figure on its bare back: someone dead. Not one of them carried any bows. One Visigar warrior tried to throw a spear while trying to calm his horse at the same time. The weapon fell well short of it mark, splashing down into the swamp. Rising from where he had fallen, another Visigar warrior grasped his spear and set his feet. The thing was moving fast, but he might still have a chance to hit it. Hoisting it to his shoulder, he aimed and threw it.

"NO!" Bloor screamed as he burst onto the marshland.

The spear flew true, arching high in the air, gaining punching power as it came down... Straight into the troll's shoulder, opposite Morianna.

Bloor's wind caught in his throat and his legs felt weak. He stumbled in the wetness of the grass, shortsword in hand.

The troll straightened up without a sound. It half-turned, dropping Morianna as it did. The Visigar witnessed the limp human form falling from the monster's body. Terrible pain burned in its shoulder, but the troll bared its teeth and reached around. It gripped the shaft of the thing, hurting it, and pulled with too much force. The wooden shaft snapped off, leaving the iron head in its flesh and bone. It roared then, a mixture of pain and frustration. The right arm was barely usable now, sending agony to its brain when it tried to lift it. It had never known pain like this before. Never had it seen so much of its own black blood flowing down its frame. Even as it watched the blood run down its body, it felt itself growing weaker. It turned about to the little ones behind it, black eyes bearing down on where they stood. So many now, and all of them ready to fight. It roared at them again, making most of them stop where they were.

Except for one.

The shining one.

The Troll's great frame heaved with breath. This one was like itself somehow, it believed. Twice now it had the little one at its feet, and twice the troll had taken its prize back. However, now here was the shining one again, still wanting to fight for the prize, and it had something in its hands. The troll flashed its frightening tusks at it, but the shining one came on.

Then, the troll knew what it would do.

If this shining form was indeed like troll kin, then it would recognize the offering and it would give up. With a low growl full of pain, it reached down and grabbed one of Morianna's arms. It hauled her to her feet like a doll.

Not thirty paces from the creature, Bloor froze in place, not wanting to make any movements that might infuriate the troll into harming Morianna. He had hoped the thing might move away from where she fell, and just as he thought Seddon above might actually exist, the troll reached down and grabbed her again.

Then, the troll did something more frightening. It grabbed Morianna's other arm, and with both talons latched on and pulling outwards, it held her up into the air with the setting sun at her back. Blood ran down the troll's form, turning the water at its feet into ink, and the agony of forcing its wounded arm to work clawed at its senses, but it forced its brain to be clear. This shining one meant to fight, and the troll knew that its own hurts were too serious to risk a fight. Its wounds were too many and too deep. It had no desire to fight anymore; it only wanted to be on its way. Howeer, it had to satisfy those that hounded it. It would give the shining one what it wanted. The troll decided to be generous.

Then it reconsidered.

It would need food for its recovery, and the troll might not be able to hunt for a long time after this day. Still, it knew the shining one would come after it if it did not give up the prize.

It reconsidered again.

It would not give the shining one *all* of the little one.

It would give him *half*.

Pain flooding her mind and her body, Morianna felt the sudden ferocious pull on her limbs and the sudden increase in pressure snapped her head up just as the troll tore her apart.

Bloor's jaw dropped as if a lance had been run through his heart, as Morianna's shriek, just as her right arm came free of her body, cut his soul in two.

The troll sized up Morianna's arm, torn out at the shoulder. She had come apart like a flimsy wishbone, a bright red stream fountaining across the chest of the troll. Morianna's short scream died abruptly in the stillness of the marsh. The troll considered the arm in one talon, and then the greater part of her in the other.

Then it threw her.

At Bloor.

Morianna splashed down in a heap not five paces from Bloor, and he rushed to her side, dropping to his knees. He saw the blood pumping from her horrible wound. He gathered her head up into his lap. His eyes welled up, and tears he never knew he possessed streamed down his filthy cheeks. He had seen enough wounds in battle to know what his chances were of saving her. A choked sound escaped his throat, meaning to be Morianna's name, but sounding like a wounded grunt. Slowly, Bloor bent over her, placing his forehead to hers.

The troll watched the shining one for a moment. Then the shining one screamed out, and the troll felt relief. It was good: The shining one had accepted the peace offering.

Turning now, the troll kept the lesser half of the prize, glad that the shining one had accepted its generosity. It would need more food to heal, but this would do for the moment. Growling as it walked, it made its way to someplace where it could recover in peace.

Bloor cradled Morianna's head in his lap. His hands stroked her pale face. Her eyes half opened, weakly, and she saw him. She struggled to say something, as her life spilled out into the marsh and her flesh cooled to the touch. Her breath took longer to come up, as if her lungs had sunk fathoms. Her lips lost their color. It was in that moment that Bloor gazed down and saw not the woman that he had come to love, but the little spoiled girl that he had first met so very long ago. A child who on the rarest of days would show a glimmer of the kindness that lay so deep inside her, and would only emerge in later years. Morianna struggled to shed those years and to prove to people that she was a different person as an adult. She struggled to right each and every wrong she inflicted upon those around her when she was a child, wanting only to make amends, but this was too much, far too much to pay for a past life. She was the most precious thing to him now, of all the lives he had ever encountered in his travels. To lose her now was too much. He stroked her hair from her face and tried not to notice the blackness flowing from her. Another breath, fainter than the last, hit his mouth. He waited. Another breath, further from the last, caressed his chin like the rarest silk. Bloor kissed her nose, her cheeks, and finally her mouth.

As if recognizing his touch, Morianna focused and found his red eyes. She struggled to say something and gave up. Her eyes blinked as if incredibly drowsy, and she beheld her wonderful Cavalier. She wanted to touch his face. Why was her man, her beautiful man, crying? His tears touched her core. Her man was crying, and she did not understand why. She tried to ask him, but couldn't summon the strength. She gazed up at his face, feeling his fingers on her cheek and remembered his kisses. Bloor actually *kissed* her.

Kisses full of love. The thought warmed her.

She smiled then, breaking Bloor's heart as she did so.

And died.

Tears rolling down, Bloor smothered his face over hers, and kissed her even as she stopped breathing and her eyes closed forever. All heard the great sucking hitchings in his chest as he grieved. From the treeline, the survivors of the long march from Sunja gazed onwards, too stunned to move.

They were good only to witness what would follow.

"BLOOR!" Two Knife roared out, emerging from the forest with a splash. His swords caught a glint of the day's dying light.

The Cavalier did not appear to hear. Like the Sujins and Visigar alike, Two Knife could not believe how the day had finally played out. A fine plan executed perfectly and yet here he was, the last of his pack, without the dowry he wanted, and without the ransom that Morianna would have brought him. He had lost everything this day, and the rage of it all took him by this throat. "BLOOR!" he yelled, frothing. In another time or place he might have given anyone else a moment to grieve. Might have, except this anyone was Bloor, and the corpse he held in his arms was the one thing Two Knife had gambled everything on and lost. Now, with the sun dropping and the land becoming dark, a mist rose up. Two Knife had evaded the gathered men along the treeline. He ignored them. They might kill him later, but that was after.

Both blades swishing in the air at arm's length, Two Knife heated himself up to kill the Cavalier still on his knees.

"BLOOR!"

This time the man's head rose, if only a little.

"I've lost everything, Bloor! But there's one thing left for me to take and that is you!"

Hearing him now, the Cavalier placed the head of his princess down and got to his feet. He turned towards the sound of Two Knife's voice. He picked up his sword from where he had dropped it, glancing in the direction of the retreating troll.

It was almost swallowed up by the descending night.

It was almost gone.

"BLOOR! Only you and I now. And soon it's only going to be me!"

Bloor turned back from the shadowy shape of the troll. He focused on Two Knife.

And charged.

With a scream, Two Knife charged as well, and both men hazarded the unsure footing of the marsh, splashing towards each other, the sound of feet smacking into the wetness. This was what Two Knife wanted, the final trophy. The Sujins he had killed, Tarco, and even the Axemen were all nothing compared to Bloor's head. It would be here that he would kill a legend and create a new one. Two Knife's blades whirled about him like a flashing machine as he came on. The distance between them shrank in a heartbeat. Bloor's face was filled with hatred; Two Knife's was full of insane glee. They were mere feet from each other and the watchers from afar could only guess where the swordsmen were aiming their first strokes.

Then Bloor did the unexpected.

He threw his sword.

The weapon flashed through the air and struck Two Knife square in the chest, embedding half of its length in his chest bone and cutting one lung in two. The force of the impact blew the renegade Sujin backwards, both swords flying from his hands. The Cavalier's sword stuck straight up into the air like a grave marker. Gazing upwards at the deepening night sky and the winking of stars, Two Knife struggled to breathe, trying for air that was akin to drawing up mud from a well. There were no thoughts of trophy kills now; there was only the shock of death.

Then Bloor towered over him.

Without a word, he yanked his sword free. He paid no heed to the dead man at his feet as he sheathed his weapon. He stumbled back to Morianna and crouched at her side, never wanting to leave her.

Watching the shadows on the dark stage before him, Jace saw the man loom over the woman and he remembered another time from long ago, when it was he that mourned for lost loved ones. He remembered finding his own dead wife and children in the wake of a troll, and the memory tightened his own throat.

"What's he doing?" Tungang rumbled from nearby.

Like some vengeful specter, Bloor stood up. In his hands was a long spear; the spear thrown by the Visigar horseman trying to calm his startled horse.

Get one on a spear and you'll know it, the troll hunter once said.

Bloor's eyes streamed tears.

He wished to know. *Seddon above*, he wished to *know*.

He began to walk into in the growing darkness, following the same path as the troll.

To his surprise, Gatesin moved to follow the man. He was stopped with one warning hand from Alwan, who shook his head. Not another man called out to the Cavalier on the trail of the troll. Not one made a move to help him. They stood and watched as he marched deeper into the night, the mist rising up and turning him into a silvery ghost.

Bloor kept on walking. He would not let the beast disappear into the mist like some bad dream with the dawn. A fearsome hatred welled up within his frame, burning away the fatigue of the day, burning away the ache of his hurts, veiling the loss of Morianna in a haze.

He began to run.

The silvery ghost winked out of existence. They could no longer see him run, but across the stillness of the marsh they heard each soppy footstep Bloor took. Then they heard his pace quickening, just as their own pulses began to race and their vision failed.

Then a scream, a frightful scream that made all that stood staring jump at the sound, a scream of raw hate.

And the swamp exploded with the most terrible roar any of the gathered men had ever heard.

THE TROLL HUNTER

A sound they would hear again in their deepest dreams.

47

They buried the princess at dawn.

Bloor returned from the marsh after killing the monstrous troll. No one doubted what he had done. They had all witnessed the power of the troll. If Bloor did not kill it, he would not have returned. However, return he did, early in the night, to where the Sujins and Visigar waited. In the Cavalier's absence, Alwan had them all make a campfire. It was to this glowing beacon along the edge of the marsh that Bloor returned, simply appearing at the edge of the light, carrying the body of Morianna and her detached arm. The two groups of men watched quietly as the Cavalier bore the princess into their camp, and went into the forest to be alone with her. The unfolded events of the day had taken whatever past differences there were between the two parties and postponed them for another day. The Sujins were too tired to do anything but sit and eventually sleep.

They buried her in a glade, surrounded by a carpet of white wildflowers growing freely amongst the trees. The Visigar left Bloor to his mourning, much to the obvious distaste on some of their faces. It was only a woman! However, Alwan was there to keep order, and he ensured the horsemen kept a respectful tone. He doubted he would ever feel the same way for a woman as Bloor did, but he had seen this many a time before. It was best to let the man take his time now that Two Knife had been removed.

He appeared amongst them early in the afternoon, much to the relief of the Visigar. He summoned them all around and together they made their way back through the forest where the Sunjan dowry lay on the ground. Bloor gave three of the packs to the Visigar as payment, giving it as thanks for aiding in the removal of the traitorous Sujins. None of the four remaining Sujins dared question the Cavalier's actions. Then the big Visigar known as Prong offered the Cavaliers two of their horses.

"May these get you to where you are going," the pale-faced leader said, gently smiling at Bloor.

Bloor silently accepted the parting gift.

With that, the Visigar left the Sunjans in the forest.

When they were out of sight, Bloor turned to the remaining Sujins.

"These are for you," he told them, indicating two of the three packs still on the ground. "Do with them what you will. Return them to King Juhn if you want. I don't care. But as far as I am concerned, you all died here this day. Alwan and I will return to the king and report what happened here, and tell him of the death of his daughter."

"Will he believe you?" Balto asked.

The Cavalier regarded him with icy eyes. That one glance told Balto that the king would do well to believe him. Then Bloor looked at Gatesin, and the Sujin frowned. He wondered when it would come down to him. He wondered now if Bloor would blame this entire unfortunate event on him or just kill him outright.

Instead, the Cavalier looked away and walked over to inspect the horse the Visigar had left him.

Alwan regarded the Sujins. "You're all dead," he told them, going from face-to-face. "So have a good life."

Then he turned his back on them and moved to the other horse. He mounted it easily and considered Bloor standing nearby. He was fitting the final pack of dowry treasure onto the back of his horse. The man looked as if he had aged twenty years this morning, and Alwan felt something he rarely ever felt: pity.

"What of me?" Jace asked from nearby.

"What of you?" Alwan said to the man, answering for Bloor.

"I'm free to go?" Jace asked, his one eye crunching up in confusion.

Bloor turned to the man. "No. Come with us, if you will."

"Back to Sunja?" he asked.

Bloor did not answer. Jace frowned for a moment, and decided to hold his tongue. He could wait for a little longer he supposed, at least until he was away from these Sujins. Bloor mounted his horse and did not look back at the men. He pointed his horse towards Sunja, and urged it into a slow walk. Alwan did the same.

Shrugging his shoulders, Jace nodded at the Sujins and followed the Cavaliers on foot, wondering why he couldn't have gotten a horse.

The four Sujins watched them depart, and in moments, they were alone with the two packs of riches on the ground.

"We're dead," Balto said, staring off, becoming thoughtful.

"We are," Gatesin echoed, liking the sound of it.

Then Hatch hoarked and spat into the ground. He squatted down next to the packs and opened one. He fished out a priceless brooch made of gold and whistled at the way it sparkled in the light.

"I'm liking being dead just fine," he said to the standing men.

Tungang glanced over at Balto and Gatesin. Gatesin began to smile.

"Still need a man for that brothel of yours?" he asked Balto.

"Be needing more than just one, I think," the old man answered, a grin lighting up his face. Hatch was now marveling at a fine necklace. Whistling, Tungang got down next to him and held out a hand, which a grinning Hatch filled with the necklace. The Tun gnawed on one pearl of the piece and nodded with approval.

"Be needing more than just one," Balto repeated, and sat down next to the pair. Gatesin did the same, thinking the man was probably right.

In the distance, three men marched on towards the Sunjan capitol. Alwan gave a dire look in Jace's direction, indicating that the man hold his tongue for the time being. However, after a while, Alwan's curiosity got the best of him and he drew up next to the Cavalier. He cleared his throat.

"Are we really going back to Sunja?" he asked Bloor's profile.

"No," Bloor answered after a moment, and that was all.

It was enough for Alwan. He wondered what the man had in mind for them if they weren't going back to Sunja. It was no great sorrow to Alwan. His home was always the open ground of the plains, the hollows of the forest, and whatever battlefield that lay in between. Bloor would tell him what was on his mind when he was ready. He let the man take the lead, comfortable in following for the moment.

Bloor thought for a long time. Feeling the movement of the horse beneath him, he swayed in the saddle as his thoughts drifted to images of Morianna, and all of the lost opportunities. He wished he could hear her voice in his ears and feel her breath on his neck. He wished he was back in Lindee's kitchen, with the kitchen table full of breakfast, a smell of bacon lingering on the air, listening to the two women prattle on. His throat constricted and his eyes welled up. He wished he could have said Morianna's name again, without any titles, just to see her reaction.

Just once.

Then he remembered Morianna kissing him for the first time in the forest, and the blessed delight in that first touch.

Taking a heavy, shaking breath, Bloor looked ahead.

The three men moved on through a forest alive with afternoon sounds and light.

TWO YEARS LATER…

Thunderheads rolled in from the east and wrestled with one another in the sky, rumbling their amusement and spitting light. Villagers in the small town of Pritch cast worried looks to the black clouds. The coming storm would hit with all the power of a mace and the rains could flood. In another moment, the heavens opened up and pissed on the land, emptying themselves in an unending gush. One traveler, tired with his long journey, frantically steered his spent horse to the village stables and got himself inside only after being soaked to the skin in a matter of seconds. Cursing, he paid the hand taking his horse, and asked for directions. The ostler gave him the information he wanted, speaking loud to be heard over the growing howl of the winds outside and the hiss of rain.

    Casting a wary look back outside, the traveler gave a thanks devoid of any real gratitude. He readied himself to enter the storm again. In this downpour, any walk in the rain would be a long walk one. He thought about running, but seeing how muddy the roads had become, he decided a slow careful walk was best. He did not want to slip and fall into any of the filth covering the road.

He made his way through the throat of the storm, feeling its breath becoming stronger with each step he took. He was drenched to the bones by the time he entered the tavern he sought, but he was thankful to be finally out of the rain. He would get a room this night, and one with a bath, but first he had business to attend to.

The newcomer looked around the interior of the tavern, seeing the warm glowing fireplace set in one wall. Across the room and behind his counter, the barkeep studied him with a reproachful eye for tracking in so much water. Tables illuminated with candles dotted the room, and a skeleton gathering of patrons hunched over wooden mugs. He shook off his traveling cloak and hung it from a collection of pegs near the door. He hoped it would still be there. The way the thing stank of a week's travel, he guessed it probably would.

Then he saw the one-eyed man standing at the bar. A necklace of long teeth adorned his neck, making him appear all the more intimidating. His long hair was tied into a neat knot at the back of his head. Veins of silver ran through it. The one-eyed man felt the traveler's gaze and regarded him.

The traveler went to him.

"My name's Critch," the traveler introduced himself. "Are you Jace?"

Jace fingered the black eye patch he now wore over his empty socket. He nodded at the man. "I am."

"Good," Critch smiled. "Lucky for me to find you this easily."

Jace nodded. "You came through the storm out there?"

"I did."

"Brave," Jace whistled. "I think you want to speak to that man over there."

Critch's brow crinkled in puzzlement. He looked towards the dark corner where two men sat in the shadows. "Was I not to talk to you?"

Jace's one eye either winked or blinked at him, Critch could not tell which, but he felt it was a wink. "You'll be talking to the one on the right. Go on now. Quicker you do, the quicker you can get out of those wet clothes and sleep out the night."

That was true. "My thanks," Critch said without really meaning it, and moved past the one-eyed man. He bought a mug of ale from the barkeep and approached the pair of men in the corner. He slowed as he drew closer, feeling as if he was standing before two very dangerous individuals. Critch nodded his head and smiled nervously. The shadows did not respond.

"I'm Critch," he tried again, no longer wearing a smile he did not feel.

"Sit down," the man on the left said. Critch did as he was told.

"Nasty night out there," the man said. He had a black beard and his eyes were lit with flicks of silver. "That rain looks wet."

"It is," Critch said, feeling and despising how his saturated clothes squished against him when he sat down. He kept his arms off the table, knowing if he put them there, water would run onto the wooden surface. Over the low mumblings of conversation in the smoke smelling tavern, a deep grumble of thunder rang out, making most pause and look to the ceiling.

Critch looked to the men. "That one-eyed man told me to sit here."

"That one-eyed man is with us," the man on the left said. "We heard from him you're having some trouble in your village?"

The memories of bodies, half-eaten and dead, flared up in his mind's eye. He saw graveyards being violated and monstrous things stalking them both day and night, feeding off of them as if they were stuttering chickens. Critch fought the images down. This was why he had come so far to this place; to get help from these men when their own efforts did little more than enrage their monsters.

"Yes," he said, placing his now cold hands between his thighs and keeping them there. "We've...had some trouble."

"We like trouble," the man on the left said, his smile like a curved sickle. There was no warmth there.

"Who are you exactly?" Critch asked them. He was only told to seek out a one-eyed man. Who were these men? He needed to know before he proceeded with anything else.

"My name's Alwan," the man on the left said, "and this is Bloor."

Critch believed he heard the names before in some other tavern, perhaps while in drunken bliss. Some small piece of information came to his mind. "I think I might have heard of you. Weren't you once Cavaliers with one of the Sunjan Klaws?"

The smile never left Alwan's face, but it seemed to become colder, and Critch felt a terrible feeling of dread come over him. Once again, he said something he perhaps should not have brought up. The man's dark eyes drew Critch in.

However, before Alwan could speak, the other man, Bloor, cut him off. He spoke in a low tone that could only just be heard over the heavy pattering of rain outside.

"You're mistaken," the man said quietly, ominous thunder rumbling at the end of his words.

"We hunt trolls."

About the Author

Keith C. Blackmore is the author of the Mountain Man, 131 Days, and Breeds series, among other horror, heroic fantasy, and crime novels. He lives on the island of Newfoundland in Canada. Visit his website at www.keithcblackmore.com.

DISCOVER
STORIES UNBOUND

PodiumAudio.com

www.ingramcontent.com/pod-product-compliance
Ingram Content Group UK Ltd.
Pitfield, Milton Keynes, MK11 3LW, UK
UKHW041300180426